THE SERPENT CALLED MERCY

ROANNE LAU

DAW BOOKS
New York

Jacket illustration by Rowynn Ellis

Jacket design by Katie Anderson

DAW Book Collectors No. 1977

DAW Books
An imprint of Astra Publishing House
dawbooks.com
DAW Books and its logo are registered trademarks of Astra Publishing House.

Printed in the United States of America

Library of Congress Cataloging-in-Publication Data

Names: Lau, Roanne, author.
Title: The serpent called mercy / Roanne Lau.
Description: First edition. | New York : DAW Books, 2025.
Identifiers: LCCN 2024054779 (print) | LCCN 2024054780 (ebook) |
ISBN 9780756419448 (hardcover) | ISBN 9780756419455 (ebook)
Subjects: LCGFT: Fantasy fiction. | Novels.
Classification: LCC PR9619.4.L379 S47 2025 (print) | LCC PR9619.4.L379
(ebook) | DDC 823/.92--dc23/eng/20241125
LC record available at https://lccn.loc.gov/2024054779
LC ebook record available at https://lccn.loc.gov/2024054780

First edition: March 2025
10 9 8 7 6 5 4 3 2 1

To Vern
for lighting the first spark back in those halcyon days
and telling me I had what it took to be an author when we grew up

CHAPTER ONE

A SLUMDOG'S LONG-AWAITED REVENGE IN THREE ACTS

LYTHLET TAIREL WAS ordinarily fond of lightning-bees, but on this rainy winter's night, she wished they would silence their incessant buzzing.

She stood beneath a streetlight, shivering in the cold. A hive hovered overhead, the colony whirring as its thumb-sized citizens illuminated the street. Two were squabbling, their droning dissonance heightening her agitation.

The loan shark would come at dawn to collect on Desil's debt, and they would not escape unscathed if Lythlet didn't scrounge up enough coin by then. If past experience was anything to go by, they'd end the day with bruised ribs and threats painted over their walls.

A sly thought nudged her toward a downhill road: thievery would stitch together her purse strings.

But Lythlet hesitated. It had been many years since she had last turned to thievery, and it weighed heavily on both her conscience and her pride that she had to resort to it again.

She pulled her last copper out of her pocket, deferring the decision to fate.

"Tell me where my story leads tonight, Sunsmith and

Moonmachinist." Clapping her hands together thrice, she stared at the heavens. Rain splattered over her cold cheeks, but she remained unblinking. "Heads, I listen to my good conscience, return home, and wait for the loan shark's punishment. Ship, I go thieving in the night and make what I can from the squalor of Setgad."

With a flick of her thumb, she sent the coin soaring overhead and caught it in her palm.

The Fated Ship stared back at her.

"Thy will be done," she murmured, pocketing the coin and taking a deep breath. She pulled her hood up and began the hunt.

She could not risk making a single mistake, and the fires of her wit were being stoked to full flame tonight. Dewa Road, Mandol Lane, Westiri Alley, she regarded each with a prompt judgment, a calculation of all the variables present, and their potential outcomes. Too brightly lit—she would be seen far too easily. Too sparsely crowded—she needed a blur of people to disappear into. Too many potholes and rubbish heaps lining this road—it was risky having such terrain if she had to run away.

She turned away from one man, his impressive build too risky for her to challenge. A lithe woman smoking a pipe under a streethive was less so, but her coat was so thin she would immediately notice a stray hand entering her pockets. That slope-shouldered man was the best so far, seeing how distracted he was by the woman at his side. But Lythlet had seen him two streets earlier, emptying his entire purse at a hawker's stall on a serving of fried mashed Jhosper berries mixed with makrut lime leaves, which he now split with his lady friend. She'd be wasting her time on a man with nothing left in his pocket, and even if he had the coin to spare, she couldn't quite muster the energy to ruin what was possibly a rare romantic night for him.

Then the perfect victim emerged on the bustling road of Fithan Avenue, the heavens serving her a careless lackwit on a silver platter as her eyes fell upon the pocket of a thick winter coat scuttling across the street. Dangling out of it was a long black string, no doubt a coin purse attached to the other end. It took a shocking naivety to not mind one's pockets in Southeast Setgad.

She slinked through the crowd, strides lengthening as her heartbeat crescendoed.

But her steps slowed a stride away from her prey, bravado vanishing.

No. No, not him.

The winter coat hung off a frail, old Oraanu man tottering along the litter-strewn street, pushing a one-wheeled cart filled with stacks of bamboo charcoal. He was likely returning from a long day hawking his wares at the Midnas Street market.

He looked old enough to be someone's grandfather, judging from the wispy strands of white hair he kept in a limp ponytail. Lythlet had never known her grandparents on either side—they had passed long before she was born, may the white wind guide their souls—but she could imagine the grief that robbing an old man would cause.

So she remained still, bitterly watching him leave. But as he journeyed on, she couldn't ignore the loose string hanging out of his pocket like bait hooked for hungry fish. Even if she had some mercy to spare tonight, other thieves would not.

"S-sir?" she called, rubbing her freezing hands nervously behind her back.

The man hobbled to a stop, his cart creaking until its one wheel stilled. Wrinkled face wary, frown lines heavy, he regarded her silently. Strangers did not talk to each other in Southeast, not unless they wanted trouble.

She nodded toward his hip with a jerk of her head. "P-pockets," she said, annoyed that her childhood stutter was rearing its head now of all times. "Mind your—mind them."

He patted them, finding the purse string, and tucked it in hastily. He gave a nod of gratitude in her direction before picking up his handcart once more, dragging it over cracked pavements and poorly laid cobblestones until he joined the tail-end of a queue leading to a rattan-and-bamboo trishaw selling *muna-muna*— parcels of lemongrass-seasoned fish wrapped in banana leaves, an imported recipe from the southern islands of the Ora Empire. Though the city-state of Setgad existed independently from the Empire, it was a patchwork tapestry that borrowed from both the Oraanu, the pale-skinned, dark-eyed moon-worshippers whose first home remained in the Ora Empire to the west, and the Ederi, the manifold-colored descendants of exiles from the far east.

Ederi as she was, Lythlet had loved Oraanu food since she was young, and the fragrance of *muna-muna* sent her stomach growling; the briny tang of mackerel, lemongrass, mint, coriander, makrut lime—all together they reminded her she hadn't eaten since the morning.

Taking no comfort in her good deed, Lythlet made ready to leave the street behind and hunt for another target. She would only be rewarded for her mercy with the loan shark Tucoras's wrath tomorrow. She glanced back at the old man in the distance and froze in her step.

A pale hand was escaping the man's pocket, a coin purse with a long black string clutched between slender fingers vanishing entirely into another pocket—a thief pulling a sleight of hand, leaving without looking back.

Lythlet blinked. It had happened so quickly, she almost mistrusted her eyes. The old man himself hadn't an inkling he'd just been robbed, still waiting tiredly for his turn at the trishaw. No one else on the street had noticed, everyone minding their own business.

All none the wiser, except her.

Seizing the moment, Lythlet sprang into action, eeling through the crowd. She passed the unsuspecting old man and gained on the cutpurse, trailing him carefully.

He turned the corner onto Junda Road and strolled past the late-night eateries without a second glance, passing the local pig-farmer making his rounds through the neighborhood kitchens for slop to feed his herd.

Curious. If the thief hadn't come here to eat—and she highly doubted he had come to play with the stray dogs as she did—then there was only one place left worth visiting by this route at this time of night: the ginhouse at the far end of the road. That meant she had about ten minutes to empty his pockets before he sat down and did it himself on a night of drinking.

He was an experienced pickpocket, she could tell as much, so she didn't want to risk robbing him too brazenly without tilting the odds in her favor first. But she had to move fast. She scanned her surroundings and smiled for the first time that day at a familiar sight resting under the awning of a closed eatery.

"Good to see you again, old boy," she said, bending down to pet a mangy mutt missing an eye. The stray wagged its tail and pressed its whitening muzzle into her palm tiredly. She was glad to know it had survived the winter; they'd met a year ago, and she'd come to feed it when she had something to spare. She had even taught it a handful of simple commands over the months. "Have you time to assist me? I'll reward you with food."

At the last word, the mutt stood up, waiting expectantly. It followed her as she crossed the street to one of the neighboring eateries, nearing the pig-farmer and his nasty-smelling pail of slop, the stench of day-old food waste making her stomach roil.

"Filthy strays," the farmer muttered at the sight of them, turning down the other end of the street. Choosing to ignore how the pluralization indicated his opinion of her, Lythlet leaped forth and silently snatched a half-eaten turkey wing from his pail.

The mutt wagged its tail.

"Not yet," she apologized, holding one finger up. It obeyed her gesture, waiting patiently.

She dashed down the street, making short work of the distance between her and the thief, the dog scampering only a few paces behind her. She quietened her footsteps as she approached him, letting her presence fade into the unceasing noise of Setgad at night.

The thief sauntered along, relishing his success too much to take note of a scrawny young woman and a hungry mutt trailing him.

His coin-laden pocket was within reach, but she ignored the distended patch of cloth. Her eyes homed in on the pocket on the other side instead, flat and unremarkable.

Drawing closer, Lythlet hooked the wing bone into that empty pocket and stepped aside into the shadows, flashing an open palm at the mutt behind her.

The mongrel sprang into action, bouncing forward and tugging at one end of the wing, eager to fetch its reward.

The pickpocket stumbled and shouted in alarm, turning to barely make sense of a stray dog trying to rip a turkey wing from his coat. He wrestled with the mutt, retracting his hands with a frightened yelp whenever the dog growled.

Lythlet slipped in then, hand dipping into the unguarded pocket. Retrieving the pilfered coin purse, she darted away, completely unnoticed, sprinting to the end of the road and turning the corner.

Streets away, certain she had been neither noticed nor followed, she checked the old man's coin purse, eyeing the coins wistfully. Then she looked up and saw the mutt trotting toward her with a wagging tail and a muzzle full of bone and half-chewed turkey.

"Good boy," she cheered softly with her second smile of the day.

BIDDING FAREWELL TO the stray, Lythlet returned to Fithan Avenue, but the old man was nowhere to be found. The queue had completely vanished, the *muna-muna* trishaw closed up for the night.

Loath as she was to admit it, she felt relieved the purse would stay with her. She needed all the coin she could get, and those four extra coins in the old man's purse were practically a fortune at the moment.

But I still need more, Lythlet thought glumly. *Tucoras expects three white valirs tomorrow, and I haven't even a quarter of that.*

It irked her how a sum of three coins—just three!—was causing her so much grief. As a bookkeeper, she had handled accounts worth a thousand times that, accounts belonging to those unlikely to even notice the absence of three white valirs. If she could only pay a brief visit to one of the mansions in Central Setgad, she'd have all the coin she'd need without anyone noticing. Just grazing the pocket change of someone like Governor Matheranos would likely end all her problems.

But even stepping foot into the governor's precinct would be the death of her; the bulk of the city's watchmen were posted there, protecting the rich from slumdogs like her. No—if she were to turn to thievery tonight, it would have to be amongst her people, the underclass toiling away in Southeast Setgad. The watchmen did not care to catch petty thieves so long as they stole only from petty lives.

Petty lives like yours truly, lives easily cast aside by those whose fingers tighten the purse strings. She paused. *Those like Master Winaro.*

Now that was a man who deserved a reckoning and a half. It was his temper that had put her in this desperate position, after all.

Seven months in all, she had worked under Hive-Master Valanti Winaro at his hive maintenance workshop. Both government and civilian markets commissioned him to tend to the lightning-bees, to clean the rot out of their hives and prolong the lives of the colonies. After years of working for crooks and fraudsters, Lythlet had been overjoyed to work as the money-minder for someone who ran a clean business, no numbers in his books needing alteration.

To all beyond his little workshop on Destaro Street, he was renowned for being reliable, working hard from dawn till midnight. Yet she alone within the walls of his workshop knew his temper and bore the brunt of it. It would rear its head at the end of a long day, when there remained shelves and shelves of hives to tend to after he'd taken on too many in too little time.

It had begun with him cursing her, but curses she could survive. She knew how to swallow her pride for coin, and she and Desil were desperate for it. But as a crisp autumn had paled to a gray-skied winter, bruises began to pockmark her bony brown body.

It happened once, and he apologized. It happened twice, and he apologized. Thrice and a third apology, and she could no longer convince herself these were aberrations.

Yesterday evening had been the last time, and it had begun with—of all things—a visit from Governor Matheranos.

Lythlet had been sterilizing a tray of scalpels Master Winaro used to scrape away the white rot that accumulated on the bioluminescent hives when the bell by the door tinkled.

She'd raised her head, half-covered by a thick protective shroud so she wouldn't breathe in the poisonous rot residue, to bob politely at the customer—and was stunned to see none other than Governor Matheranos entering, a swath of cloaked guards escorting him. They stood in formation behind him, the ship-within-a-diamond emblem representing the United Setgad Party stitched onto their cloaks, nightsticks and short swords hanging on their belts.

The hive maintenance workshop was frequently commissioned by the governor, but she had never expected the twice-elected leader of Setgad, second in power only to the twelve judges of the Einveldi Court, to actually deign to visit their premises himself.

Master Winaro's eyes widened, and he yanked down his own protective shroud as he bowed.

"Bow," he snapped at Lythlet, even as she made her torso parallel to the floor.

He slapped her back, pushing her even lower, as if he wanted her to prostrate herself on the ground the way she would before the divine or to her parents. A needless gesture, transforming an act of respect into one of subjugation—but with that one unsubtle gesture, Master Winaro had signaled two things to the governor: that according to the hierarchy of Setgad, Lythlet was the lowest person in that room, and could thus safely be ignored, and more importantly, that Master Winaro was respectful enough of the governor's ranking above him that he was willing to debase his subordinate as such.

"Please, hive-master, none of that," Governor Matheranos said with a laugh, waving them up. His famed mane of wild white hair shook as he gave a brief, pitying smile in Lythlet's direction. Lythlet demurely lowered her gaze; the governor would consider her ill-bred if she met his eyes directly for too long.

"To what do we owe the honor of your presence, Governor?" Master Winaro said, an oily smile greasing his face.

"I've come to make a special request. I'm entertaining a gaggle of ministers from the Party later this week, and I intend on taking them on a brief tour through some Southeastern streets."

"Here in the slums?" Earnest concern laced the hive-master's words.

"Oh, not to worry, Valanti. We'll have enough watchmen to protect us from cutpurses and whatnot. My friends are simply curious about the way life is led down here, and I deemed it my duty to educate them. Which brings me to my request: these streets must be lit as brightly as possible to make their tour more hospitable. Unfortunately, their hives haven't been serviced in a year, and rot is dimming the lights. Here's the list prepared by my advisors on the streets to be serviced by the end of this week."

Lythlet peeked up from the scalpels to the parchment in Master Winaro's hand. Her gut sank at the length of the list—yet even more long sleepless nights were waiting for her.

"Will there be any issues, Valanti?" the governor said.

"None at all," said Master Winaro, bowing graciously.

"Excellent," returned the governor jovially. "Your work in keeping the hives of the southern sectors clean has not gone unappreciated."

"I would, of course, be very happy to take on the business of servicing the northern hives," Master Winaro said hopefully.

Governor Matheranos laughed. "All in good time, Valanti. The hive-master we commission up north does good work, but if he ever retires, we'll come to you."

Forcing a polite smile out of his tightened jaw, Master Winaro bowed once more. "It is an honor beyond words that you would come to me personally with this request," he said, manners cloaking his chagrin. "I know your governorship has been harangued by much trouble lately."

Governor Matheranos barked a harsh laugh. "You mean that rabble-rouser Corio Brandolas? Pah, he's nothing but a bloviating popinjay trying to oust me so he can be governor instead. Honestly, he wouldn't even be given the time of day by anyone if it weren't for the family he married into." He leaned in. "Just between the two of us, the Einveldi Court has decided today to ban the sale of his book. Almost a unanimous decision—eleven to one! News will be released soon."

"Oh, certainly a most wise decision," said Master Winaro, nodding obsequiously.

Lythlet cast a brief side-eye at him—Master Winaro's dog-eared copy of *The Setgad Dilemma*, an incendiary polemic advocating for the removal of Governor Matheranos written by Corio Brandolas, the leader of the Coalition of Hope party, was sitting just beneath the counter, no more than a foot away from Governor Matheranos.

Master Winaro and Lythlet bowed once more as Governor Matheranos took his leave, the bell tinkling overhead.

A groan left the hive-master the moment the door swung shut, and he shook the list the governor had given him. "Ten streets to be serviced in two days," he muttered. "Madness. Does he think a hive takes only five minutes to clean?"

Lythlet grimaced. That was at least a hundred hives. She'd be sleeping in the administration quarters again, this commission making returning home a wistful daydream.

Master Winaro looked sharply at her. "This is your fault," he snapped.

"Yes, Master Winaro," she said, knowing better than to argue.

"If you weren't so slow, we'd be able to clean dozens of hives a day. But now we've this backlog to deal with, and more to come." He waved a hand over the apiary shelves housing scores of hives awaiting his maintenance.

"Yes, Master Winaro." *Just keep working.*

"Honestly, how hard is it to obey my instructions? Even a child could work quicker than you. It says much about your father and mother that they never taught you an ounce of diligence."

At the invocation of her parents, something inside Lythlet snapped. "It says much about you that you would insult my parents when they have nothing to do with this," she spat, flinging a scalpel into the tray with a ringing clatter.

Master Winaro stared, stunned at her outburst.

"You hired me as your bookkeeper, not your assistant," Lythlet continued, enraged. "It is not my duty to tend to the hives, and never has been. The only reason I'm doing this is because you've scared off every single hive-tender you've ever hired with your foul temper, and I'm the only one desperate enough to stay on."

He turned crimson, his gaze lighting up with rage. "You dare speak to me this way?"

She flinched, already knowing what was coming next.

He balled up the list of streets and lobbed it at her face. Then came the dog-eared copy of *The Setgad Dilemma*, the hardcover slapping her cheek. Corio Brandolas's book fell just in time for her to catch sight of Master Winaro's hand wrapping around the neck of a bottle of rot-softening solution.

She ducked just in time to miss the bottle cracking her skull. It grazed the top of her head and shattered against the wall instead, and her heart thumped at the near-death sensation. A rain of glass shards descended upon her, one flicking across her forehead. Pain spiked, and blood dripped over her eyes.

She sprang to her feet, furious, too outraged to retreat into feeble silence for once, but he fetched an unsterilized scalpel from his tool-roll. Its sharp edge glittered as he held it before her.

"Get out," he spat, backing her toward the door. "If you ever come back here, I'll shank your disrespectful throat myself."

And with that threat came the splinter in her foundation that sent her spiraling down to this moment, out in the streets as a common thief hoping to scrape together enough coins for a debt-collector.

As her memories unspooled, her boots took on the cobblestones with compounding fury, storming through the streets.

Lythlet was still a distance away from the hive-master's workshop when she halted by a road, spotting a piece to add to her burgeoning revenge plot. The street was dimly lit, the hives emitting a soft, milky light that indicated neglected colonies. She dusted her fingers, then latched onto the nearest hive-post. She climbed the length of it, hands and feet moving gracefully, her childhood pastime of scaling bamboo poles reducing a difficult task into pure muscle memory.

At the top, she fiddled with the latch, making short work of the lock with a pick she'd owned from childhood. Then she reached inside the glass case and pulled out the hive.

A gentle, nutty smell filled her nose. As pleasant as it was, hinting of hazels, she had worked long enough at the hive-master's workshop to know intimately the smell of hive rot. Although not instantaneously perilous to breathe in, prolonged exposure was decidedly unwise.

"Come along, little bumbles," she sang softly to the bees, landing on the ground with a soft thud.

The lightning-bees buzzed peacefully around the hive she held captive, trailing her as she resumed her route. Some came to rest on her fingers, illuminating her knuckles, and she stroked their fuzzy, luminous bodies, marveling at how small they were. So small, yet together their light breathed life into the city even in the darkest night.

She came to a small plot of undeveloped land, weeds overgrown, rubbish scattered in heaps. Children of the slums rarely went to bed early—if they had one at all—and there were a handful playing there, occupying their last hours of the dying night, and she sought to hire one.

One caught her eye.

The boy was young, ten at most, and his short hair stood up in messy tufts, reminiscent of leafy vegetables. He sat by himself, blowing hard against a leaf, trying to make music from it and halfway succeeding.

"Boy, come here," she said stiffly.

The boy jerked in fright, the leaf fluttering to the ground.

She realized belatedly the error of greeting a child the way she would a dog. "I'm not going to hurt you," she said.

The boy wheeled around on his heels to retreat.

She frantically dug into her pockets and plucked out a coin. "Listen, lad. I have a business proposal. I'll give you this spira if you hold this hive and ask a man some questions about it. That's all."

The boy paused, then looked over his shoulder, a mischievous glint in his eye. "I want a black valir."

"Don't be absurd," she scoffed. "A spira is all a boy your age needs. I'll give you *two* spiras and you'll be grateful. If not, I'm sure one of these other tykes would be happy to accept in your stead."

After a moment's thought, the boy relented. "Fine. What must I do?"

She guided the boy to the workshop streets away, sending him in with the stolen hive and instructions to ask as many questions as he could about his family's hive-lantern. *Do these bees look sick to you, Master? How long would it take to have the rot cleaned out? How much would it cost? Goodness, that's an awful lot of money. Couldn't you make it a bit cheaper, sir?*

Meanwhile, Lythlet went around the back to the side entrance.

Slipping her lockpick into the door and making quick work of it, she found the cramped administrative quarters empty as expected.

Somehow, in a single day without her, the quarters had become overwhelmingly messy, reams of ledgers and contracts spread over the tables, glinting tools tossed haphazardly around. She fetched the coin jar Master Winaro kept for change from a drawer.

Cascading clinks rang throughout the small room as she cleared it out with a vengeance, pouring it into her coin pouch.

She tightened the purse strings, but froze, ears pricking up. Steps were clicking close, light and faint but very much there on the other side of the door. Her chest seized with terror, and she bolted into the nearby closet, squeezing into the coat-stuffed nook and shutting the door after her.

Who is it? From murmurs in the distance, she knew the boy was still dutifully unleashing a barrage of questions at Master Winaro, so it couldn't be them.

The door opened, and footsteps drew closer.

Lythlet pinched her lips tight and gripped the nearest coat. She'd be skinned alive if whoever it was came to collect their coat. Fear sank its claws into her bones, but her mind refused to quieten, curious as to who it might be.

She hunted for any patterns to draw conclusions from. The footsteps—they had been light, almost dainty. Then Lythlet noticed the fabric of the coat she clung to—Master Winaro wore a rough woolen coat, but this was a fine-threaded paletot. It belonged to a lady, small and tailored so.

His wife must have come to help him with the books in my stead.

Outside the closet, drawers were pulled open and slammed shut.

"Nothing ever kept in order around here," Madame Winaro muttered. "He wasn't hitting the girl hard enough if she never had the sense to clean up once in a while."

Lythlet stilled, those words choking her in one single timespun breath.

A minute later, Madame Winaro retrieved what she had come

for, and the door shut once more, her footsteps vanishing into the distance.

Lythlet lingered, clutching the paletot tightly, fingertips white from pressure. She pressed her bandaged forehead against it, the soft fabric caressing her skin, her spirit sapped of all strength. It grieved her to think of how meaningless her pain was to these people.

Let me grant you as much mercy as you've ever shown me, she swore, rage resurfacing.

She rammed her hands south into the pockets of Madame Winaro's coat, ripping out the contents by the fistful and shoving them into her own pockets. She tore out of the closet, out of the hive-master's workshop, to the end of the street, where stood a small shrine dedicated to Ezrinara, the warden of wisdom and justice.

The effigy of Ezrinara stood forebodingly tall, a stern woman wielding the Fire of Retribution between her palms. Behind her, at the back of the shrine, was the altar to the Sunsmith and the Moonmachinist, cordoned off by a golden chain. It was considered inappropriate to make prayers directly to the creators of mortalkind, the immortal voyagers of the universe known and unknown, without guidance from a monk learned in the Poetic scriptures, their intricately tattooed backs proclaiming their liturgical mastery. Unguided prayers could be made to the twelve tutelary wardens instead, each governing specific domains.

There, alone but for Ezrinara's vigilance, Lythlet pored through everything she'd stolen. Coins, plenty of them—at last, there would be enough to pay the loan shark tomorrow.

But buried under a fistful of coins was a thin silver chain. She had plucked it from Madame Winaro's coat without noticing what it was. Two ornate silver rings clung to the chain, as did a thin star-shaped pendant with a sapphire center. It was a wedding pendant, clear as daylight.

This is too much, spoke a quiet voice within her. Coins were one thing, but this would have precious sentimental value. The vindictive rage was gone now, and she was alone with the remains of her soul, a feeble, wilted thing.

She turned and stared warily at the manifestation of Ezrinara. The gaze of her cold stone eyes bade Lythlet be still. Unbidden, the opening prayer recited before the divine controlling their fate ran through her mind: *umera venturi, asigo venturi*. We live according to your whims, we die according to your whims.

She ought to return it. The coins alone would be enough to keep the loan shark happy for the month. Of course, the wedding pendant would pay off an even greater portion of Desil's debt— but returning it would be the right thing to do.

So spoke Ezrinara, She of Good Counsel, but Lythlet turned her heart away. Madame Winaro may have never raised a hand against her, but neither had she ever lowered her husband's.

Staring up at the effigy, Lythlet made her case: *You cannot condemn me for doing what I must to survive. You cannot render my life a tragedy, then damn me for fighting to overcome it. I owe the Winaros nothing. Not a single iota of mercy, not a single iota of guilt. May they reap thricefold every bit of pain they have ever sown in me*, she cursed the workshop, grip tightening over the chain.

Wouldn't it be poetic justice if she ended her night on three victims, anyway? First the pickpocket, now the two Winaros. A proper Ederi story concluded with three, Lythlet had learned that much from all the storybooks she'd stolen in her youth.

Moments later, the boy caught up with her, hive still in hand.

"Did what you asked, ma'am," he announced cheerfully. "My fee, if you'd please."

"Very well, little loan shark. Two spiras, as promised. Run along now. It's late."

"What shall I do with the hive?"

"Keep it, if you like."

"What for? A dying hive's not worth much," he said, scrutinizing it. "Buying a hive's never the expensive part, maintaining it is. I doubt I'll get more than five pennies for it. Look at all this rot here! I'll probably get sick if I hold on to this any longer. These bees are worthless. The sooner they die, the luckier they are."

She bristled at him. "How did you wind up such a miser at your age?"

"I was born this way," said the boy with pride.

"Careful with that now, or come ten years' time, you'll wind up like me."

"You can't be only ten years older than me," said the boy, staring in astonishment at her.

She shooed him away with a snarl, but not before snatching the hive.

"Don't listen to that nasty turnip," she whispered to the lightning-bees as she stalked away. One flew up and landed on her knuckle, limning her skin red with its soft moonlight glow, then buzzing happily as she stroked it. "None of you are worthless. You're all good, hardworking little bumbles. If it weren't for you lot, this city would be wreathed in darkness."

But the boy had been right about one thing: white rot was gathering at the base of the hive, the nutty smell faint. The bees would die soon if the hive wasn't tended to.

All it would take was Governor Matheranos signing a directive to have the lamps of that street serviced, but he was a man sitting in the safety of his well-lit chancery, blissfully unaware of the quiet suffering beyond his walls, signing edict after edict that seemed to benefit only people of his ilk and never hers. Rare was such a man who cared for small lives.

She returned to the street she'd stolen the colony from, lowering it back into the glass cage of the hive-post.

"I hope you all live a long time," she whispered as the bees swirled around in lumbering circles. She clung to the hive-post longer than she intended, watching the bees, feeling a strange sort of sorrow, a strange sort of camaraderie. It was in the days of her deep-buried bittersweet childhood when she had come to the conclusion that slumdogs like her had more in common with the lives of insects than the rich.

As thrilling as the night had been, taking revenge on the Winaros and getting enough money to pay off Tucoras at dawn, a deep melancholia filled Lythlet then. *My little adventure as a protagonist has come to an end now*, she thought as the bees flitted over her fingers, *and it's time to return to the margins where I belong.*

CHAPTER TWO

THE FINANCIAL STATE OF TWO SLUMDOGS

MIDNIGHT WAS UPON the city of Setgad.

Lythlet dragged herself toward home, her feet sore as they pressed over and over into uneven cobblestones. The triumph of the night had faded; she was now simply tired, her pockets heavy from her hard work. Her last stop had been a seedy pawnshop in Rendathos Ward, where she had exchanged the wedding pendant set for a handsome sum to hand over to Tucoras at dawn.

"Oi, is that you, Lythlet? Haven't seen you in a while!" A man waved at her from the other side of the street, his grimy hair framing a cheerful smile.

It took her a moment to place him: it was Finneas, an attendant at the local brawlers' square. They'd met a handful of times before, when Desil used to come for his matches. Though Lythlet had never had the time to watch a match—if she wasn't rushing off to work, she'd have errands to run for home or for her employers—there had always been time to briefly greet this fellow.

Finneas grinned knowingly at her. "Yet another successful heist, eh?"

She froze, fear striking her, the coins in her pocket growing heavier. "Pardon?"

He patted a rolled-up gazette sticking out of his coat pocket. "You know, that burglary at the Athernara last night by the Phantom. Between that and *The Setgad Dilemma* being banned for good, today's edition of the *Daily Diamond* was a ripper to read."

Lythlet heaved a relieved sigh. "Yes, the city has scarcely been talking about anything else. All done with work?"

"Just got some notices the bosses want me to nail up. Take one, will you? One less for me to deal with." He waved a handbill at her, and she took it gingerly.

CALLING FOR CONQUESSORS! announced the handbill in crisp baltascar-block print. **MASTER RENVELD DOTHILOS PRESENTS AN OPPORTUNITY TO RELIVE THE GLORY OF OUR ANCESTORS!**

"Conquessing? Some sort of bloodsport, is it?" she asked, vaguely recalling the name from somewhere.

"Right you are, Lytha. The match-master's hunting for fresh faces to pad out next season's roster, seems like."

"Is it similar to brawling?"

"Brawling?" he guffawed. "Not in the least. Haven't you heard your friends talk about it? The arena runs nearly all year round, matches held once a fortnight and recruitment for new contestants running every quarter like clockwork. The games may be outlawed on paper, but they're hardly the best kept secret these days."

"I don't recall Desil mentioning it before."

"Your other friends?"

"I have no other friends."

The attendant chuckled, misguidedly assuming she grasped the mechanics of making a joke. "Desil mentioned you've little knowledge of the world beyond your nose."

Stricken by self-consciousness, she remained silent. Desil wouldn't have meant that maliciously—it was fact, plain and simple. But it wounded her to think of just how much her world had shrunk in the last few years, of how isolated her life had become, rendering her foreign in her own home, ignorant of the latest whims of society.

With nearly all her hours slaving away for whatever ill-tempered boss she was employed by at the moment and the scant remainder spent sleeping and eating at home, if it wasn't something mentioned by either Desil or her employer, odds were she simply knew nothing of it. Desil was not the sort to willingly discuss tawdry matters like bloodsports, and Master Winaro in his better moods would much rather rant about how the latest motion passed by Governor Matheranos was only going to relocate even more resources away from the slums to the wealthier sectors. Even this extended interaction with Finneas was a rare moment for her, and likely would not have happened were she still under the employ of Master Winaro, bound to the administration quarters until the wee hours to appease his demands.

Finneas went on, "It's another bloodsport, except you're not fighting any regular bloke off the street the way Desil did. Killing sun-cursed monsters, that's what the game's all about!"

His choice of words was odd; the archaic turn of phrase *sun-cursed monsters* sounded like something Desil would recite from a passage of the Poetics. "You mean beasts from the wildlands?"

He grinned. "That's right. Sun-cursed monsters is what the match-master calls all them exotic animals—a most dramatic fellow, that one. Every conquessor pairing gets twelve rounds in total, one a month and each round dedicated to a warden. But getting someone to last that long's nigh impossible even in a good year, and I hear this year's been even worse. Contestants have been dropping out like flies, seems like. In for a round, out the next, and so the match-master's hunt for his next great contestants continues!"

"I suppose the prize is too meager for them to persist?"

"Oh, no, you're off the mark on that. Conquessors—especially the famous ones—reeled in some legendary jackpots back in the day. Brawlers don't make as much, truth be told. But it's one thing to slug a man in the face, and another to get chased around by some beastie with fangs and spooky bits. Gives me the shivers just thinking about it. Our city's built on proper holy land here, sacred and all that, and bringing in those ungodly beasties ain't right at all. Sacrilege! At any rate, they're recruiting conquessors to begin in spring. Have a look if you want. Desil might be good at it, you know. How's the two of you been doing?"

"Fine, very good," she lied, tightlipped. "And you?"

"I'm better than ever, meself! There's a gorgeous lass I've been talking to, and fingers crossed it won't be long before I'm plucked clean off the market again. Might pop by a shrine to ask for eight minutes of divine luck right before I propose courtship to her, hah! Say, I've been meaning to visit Desil at that teahouse he serves at. The, ah, what's it called now—"

"The Steam Dragon."

"That's the one! Love me a good brew, and they've some fine leaves indeed. But y'know, the square's been having a hard time of it since Desil left us. The bosses've been searching high and low for new talent to replace him, but damn if they've had any luck. Hard to find someone who can replicate the Desil Demothi streak. An undefeated champion for a whole bloody year! I still have to deal with spectators coming in and asking if he'll be returning to the square." Finneas looked at her hopefully, flashing a yellow-toothed grin. "I don't suppose he's been thinking of coming back?"

She returned a mirthless smile. "I fear not."

"It'd be a pity to waste his talent, don't you think? I know you never got to see him in action, but he was just magic at drawing a crowd. We'd get more coin in a single night with him than a whole month of everyone else on our roster. He might've left because the violence and all that didn't sit right in his belly, but he always trusted your advice, he said. If you talked to him—"

She shook her head. "He's much happier now that he can keep

his vow of peacekeeping to Tazkar. I won't ask him to return to brawling."

"Pity," said the attendant, lips pursed. Then he shrugged, carefree as ever. "Well, as long as you two are doing well. I thought you might be missing the money, that's why I brought it up. But I guess you don't need it! Good on you, Lytha."

She gave him a polite, pinched smile, his words stirring something tangled and prickly in her. "Well, I'm heading back home now," she said briefly.

"So am I, once I'm done with all this," he said, gesturing at the handbills.

She looked back down at her own. **RICHES BEYOND ALL MEASURE!** announced the brazen handbill. A brash promise she knew better than to trust. She folded it and tucked it into her pocket to dispose of later.

For tonight, there would be no more thought of fighting and brutality; she would return home to Desil and count their coins.

They had a future to budget for.

HOME, AND WHAT a bitter thought that was.

She had reached the copse of kataka trees, mammoth growths resembling an eerie huddle of giants. Seeds of light burst from the leafy cluster, hinting at residents within, still awake at the midnight hour.

The very tree she called home stood before her, swallowing her entire view with its height. Fifteen men abreast could fit across the trunk. Rope ladders dangled to the ground, wobbly old things leading to dimly lit homes, for built into the kataka's thick branches were small houses, each a rectangle no larger than a few arm-spans across.

Each home was a construction of the cheapest wooden boards to be found in the slums, nailed together with barely a care for what gaps remained. Deathly cold during winters, sweltering in the summers, and wickedly tremulous during the thunderstorms that roared midyear, a kataka treehouse was only worsened by the requirement to climb that damnable rope ladder all the way up and down every time, a feat that would quickly leave one wheezing for air.

In the distance stood the Tower of Setgad, the moonlit guilloche of the city's emblem gleaming on its glassy surface—a diamond, its boundaries breached by flames. The highborn peers who frequented the heights of the tower would never know the ache Lythlet's limbs felt, not with those winch lifts assisting their journey. It stole a sigh of envy from her.

She squeezed the bag of coins in her pocket, then began her ascent up the rope ladder with a groan.

Halfway through her journey, she heard something—a muffled cry, then a man saying something she could not make out. But she knew that voice, that sniveling tenor.

Tucoras? But he's not to come until dawn!

She scrambled up the ladder, hands and feet working in a panic.

"But our contract states we have until sunrise!" she could now hear Desil saying through gritted teeth.

"If you don't have the coin already, what difference will a few hours make?" Tucoras replied. "I thought you learned your lesson the last time, but it seems a reminder of what happens when you neglect a payment is due."

"Wait!" Lythlet shouted, burning her fingers on the rope ladder as she scrambled up the last few rungs. She pulled herself over the wooden ledge of her flat and held out her hands, pleading for time as she caught her breath.

The loan shark turned and bared a toothy smile. "Miss Tairel, what a pleasure to have you join us tonight."

Tucoras was a wisp of a man, tall, but hopelessly skinny. He wasn't much of a threat alone, but behind him were three of his lackeys, ridiculously oversized men with thick barrel chests, each pinning Desil down with a boot—one crushing Desil's brown curls to his cheek, another foisting its weight on his broad back, the last restraining his wrists to his bottom, the rosary Desil wore on his right arm peeping out beneath the muddy sole.

Beneath the first boot, Desil's face was half-hidden. He was as still as stone, and Lythlet feared he'd been harmed. She glanced at his fingers; they remained unbroken for the time being, at least. But his eyes flashed open then, meeting hers in grim humiliation.

"Let him go, Master Tucoras. I have this month's payment." She rifled through her pocket and held out a fistful of coins.

Tucoras grabbed them.

"That's not all," she said, digging deeper into her pockets. She remained crouched on the ground, knowing from experience the loan shark didn't like it when she stood eye-level with him. "We can pay off more of our debt this time."

The loan shark gave an impressed look as he took the extra coins from her. "Look what we have here. A few years of this and you just might repay your debt in full."

Relieved, she started to crawl over to Desil.

Tucoras tut-tutted and slammed his boot down on her fingers.

"I didn't say you could move yet," he said coldly as she shrieked in pain. "Have some manners and wait until I've finished counting, little bookkeeper." He took his time to thumb through the coins, humming under his breath.

Lythlet remained crouched on the ledge, staring at the flecks of dirt Tucoras's boot had left imprinted on her fingers, simmering in humiliation.

At last, Tucoras nodded. With a flick of his hand, his lackeys pulled their boots off Desil, who groaned as he sat up and rubbed his wrists.

"I always admire those who try to pay off their debts faster," said Tucoras, smiling noxiously in Lythlet's direction. "I shouldn't expect less from someone trained in matters of the coin. You know what it means to let the interest compound, after all. How fortunate for Desil to have a friend like you."

She did not respond, afraid of encouraging him. She rubbed her sore fingers instead, brushing away the dirt he'd left.

He frowned. "You needn't be so frightened, Miss Tairel. I'm nothing but a plain and simple merchant trying to recoup his investment. Haven't I been very generous with my payback schedule? Other usurers would demand the sum and interest back all at once, but I've allowed Desil to drag out his payments for so long."

"And we're grateful for it, Master Tucoras," said Desil quickly. "Very grateful for your generosity."

Tucoras nodded, appeased. "I'll be off now. I look forward to seeing you again next month."

He left their ledge, his bulky lackeys trailing after him like obedient hounds.

Once alone, Lythlet crawled to Desil. "Did they hurt you?"

"I'm fine," he said, grimacing as he swiped away the mud from his cheek. "I'd just returned from the teahouse when they ambushed me. How's your hand?"

"Fine," she assured him, flexing her fingers. "I'll count my blessings he chose not to kick me in the head like the last time. Shall we continue this inside before we give our neighbors more fodder for this week's gossip?"

Denizens of the kataka copse were staring at them from their flats, one drinking from a steaming teacup silently. At least this time, Lythlet and Desil wouldn't have to spend hours cleaning off threats painted over their walls.

With the door swinging shut behind them, Desil pulled a tiffin carrier and a bound teapot out from his satchel, checking them over. "Lucky for us, those brutes didn't damage our supper. I brought back some leftovers from The Steam Dragon. You haven't eaten, have you?"

She shook her head. Her stomach had given up growling hours ago, resigning itself to emptiness. "Not since morning."

He gave her a look of concern as he fetched their hive-lantern and two wooden cups from a corner. They had little by way of furniture, save for a rice-paper partition that split their flat into two rooms, one for him and one for her, two sleeping pallets, and a singular jumbled pile of their possessions from which Desil had fetched the goods. Lythlet slid down by his side on the floor, unbinding the teapot's spout and pouring out the tea. The smell of lukewarm lavender *vinigri* tea filled the air.

A smile stretched across her tired face as she watched him unlock the tiffin carrier and spread out the small tin canisters on the floor. "Did you bring back any—"

"Roast duck skins? Of course. One can hardly offer you a meal without their presence." He grinned at her, relishing this chance at normalcy. Pretending nothing had happened was always the best way to forget abject humiliation.

"What about—"

"The pickled vegetables? Brought back a serving and extra. The kitchens had plenty to spare."

"And—"

"There were no rice cakes left but look at what I have here." He lifted a shining lid with a dramatic flourish.

"*Muna-muna*!" She lowered her head to breathe in the aroma of the lemongrass-seasoned fish, then unwrapped the banana leaves tied around it.

"We so happened to have two parcels left, and Madame Millidin said I could bring both back. What luck!" He passed her a fork, and they dug into their meal. Although meager in portion and completely cold by now, she shoveled everything into her mouth with the fervor of a prisoner savoring their last meal.

"So, what happened tonight?" Desil asked after a moment, the tines of his fork ringing against a tin canister as he meticulously scraped it clean, pushing the remaining droplets of spicy, sour red pepper sauce into his mouth before swapping for another tin.

She knew what he was actually asking: *how did you get the*

money? But she didn't want to answer that, not yet. "I met Finneas just now," she said instead.

For a second, Desil looked uncomfortable, and she regretted bringing it up. It had been a year since he left the brawlers' square, yet even the slightest mention of it now would unsettle him.

But he brushed his discomfort away glibly. "I haven't seen him in ages. How is he?"

"Chatty as ever, that fellow. Look at what he gave me." She retrieved the handbill from her pocket and unfolded it for him.

"Conquessors," Desil read aloud with surprise. He leaned in to get a better look at the text. "Haven't thought about them in a long time."

He was midway through the handbill when her stomach interrupted him with a nasty growl.

"Sorry," she said, blushing. She set down her now empty tin, every inch of it licked and scraped clean, her gnawing hunger only half sated.

"Here," he said, holding out his own tin of *muna-muna*. "You can finish mine."

She shook her head, but smiled weakly, pushing it back toward him. "Eat your share."

"Nonsense. You haven't eaten all day. I snacked some at the teahouse, so don't worry about me. Besides, you took care of the debt, so the least I could do is take care of your belly. How did you get so much coin, anyway? Did you convince Valanti to pay you your fortnight's wages?"

There was no escaping the matter now. "No," she answered heavily, eyes astray.

"Have you found new employment already? Did they give you an advance on your pay?"

"No."

His smile slipped. "Did you borrow it?" he asked, a tinge of nerves to his query.

"You know I'm not foolish enough to pay off debt by going into even more debt."

He didn't persist, but his gaze was pinned to her face, and she flushed with the burning flame of Ezrinara.

"I don't like keeping secrets from you, Desil," she said at last. "But I know you won't be pleased to hear that I stole it."

Wordlessly, he set down the tin.

"I did not steal from anyone who did not deserve it," she continued, a harshness to her words.

"Who?"

"The first, a pickpocket I caught red-handed on the streets. The second, a man who had beaten and broken me until yesterday. And the last, his wife."

Judgment crossed Desil's eyes. "You stole from Valanti's wife, a woman who has never wronged you?"

"A woman whose silence cut deep, who I heard with my own ears tonight saying I ought to have been beaten harder."

Her voice choked, and she looked away to blink back sudden tears. Immediately, Desil embraced her. He stroked her arm, and she brushed at his calloused fingers.

"I am fine," she lied, a colorlessness shielding her words.

He was wise enough to ignore it, continuing to embrace her. "Tell me everything that happened tonight."

Reluctantly, she recounted her night, which had begun with a coin flip and ended with a hive of lightning-bees. Throughout the telling, her gaze would dip uneasily to the rosaries of the Twelve Prayers he wore on his wrist, thinking of all the virtues she must have offended. Indeed, there was conflict scrawled across his mien, and she ended her account in tense apprehension of what he'd say.

"In a way, it's my fault," he said at length, surprising her. "The debt is mine, after all."

"It's debt you took on for my sake," she reminded him.

He stared tiredly at his rosary. "But if I were still brawling, we wouldn't be struggling as much, would we? Look at you resorting to thievery because I couldn't handle a brawl once a fortnight."

"No," she began, but she could not find a way to deny the truth. Desil was a hard worker—his days were split at both the teahouse and the metalworks—but his meager salaries combined had never matched Lythlet's as a bookkeeper. The hive-master had been cruel, but bookkeepers could nonetheless count on a more dependable salary by Southeast standards. The only time Desil had been able to match her was when he'd joined the brawlers' square to supplement his earnings. At length, she said, "You needn't hold yourself responsible. You weren't made for the brawling square. I never minded providing for the both of us, and I still don't."

"And to provide for us, you've become a thief."

"Enough of that—thievery it was, but if I stole from those who deserved a little pain, from those whose crimes would never be punished by the Court, why must we sit here in guilt for that?"

"What's done is done, and I won't press on it further," he said. "I only fear what happens after this. Are we going to find ourselves here again, turning to crime to make ends meet?"

She stared at him wearily. "We're slumdogs living deep in debt. We most certainly will find ourselves here once again. In a desert, all roads lead to despair. But what's wrong if I turn to the streets to pinch a few pockets? I brought justice tonight and lined my pockets in the doing. A little bit of greed will not hurt the world."

His olive-flecked eyes turned sharp. For all he had grown, shedding behind his youth as his flesh became a man's, she could always find something boyish in his gaze. But not then.

"There's no such thing as a little bit when it comes to greed. You drew the line tonight at three, and at those who've done wrong— but a compass can be pulled permanently askew when surrounded by enough coins. You're brilliant, Lythlet, and you always have been. And there's nothing more dangerous than a clever mind set loose to its own designs with no morals to guide it." He heaved a deep breath, stroking the bracelet of rosary beads on his wrist. "I'll return to brawling."

She shook her head. "I won't have you do that to yourself again."

He brushed her hair fondly. "You worry for me to the point you no longer care about yourself. All these months, you lied to me, telling me Valanti was treating you well. You would've kept lying to me if it weren't for your bleeding brow yesterday. And all because you wanted to help me pay off my debt. If it's for you, I can forsake my prayers to Tazkar once a fortnight. Better I break my vow of peacekeeping than you get yourself in danger."

"I haven't forgotten what your brawling days were like. You came home miserable every time. If there are other ways for us to make ends meet, we can look for them, but returning to brawling is not one of them."

"There's nothing else we can—" He broke off, struck by a thought.

"What?"

He retrieved the discarded conquessor handbill from his side. "*Riches beyond all measure.*"

"You can't be serious. Put that away. Do you think it wise to trust such a shameless promise?"

"The matches are real, and they do pay," insisted Desil. "I've friends who are acquainted with conquessors from previous seasons. They dropped out after only a match or two, but they always received their fee fairly and immediately after a match. Each match requires two conquessors, so you and I could join together. I'm not imagining we'll last the whole twelve rounds, of course. But even a single match's jackpot would make a dent in my debt to Tucoras."

Her brows knitted together. "And now you're comfortable with fighting?"

He sat still, deep in thought, and she knew he was poring through all the verses he'd memorized. Eventually, he spoke, "The teachings of Tazkar say we must live in peace with our brethren.

But nowhere in the Poetics does it say the wild beasts are to be spared, and there is no bloodguilt in the slaying of a sun-cursed beast. If I'm by your side, I could protect you as well."

Lythlet was surprised by the eager determination in his eyes, lit by a wild flame. "I never thought you'd consider this." She stared at the grotesquely flamboyant words on the handbill: **RICHES BEYOND ALL MEASURE!**

Rallying her nerves around that promise, she dragged a coin out of the purse, one of the few she'd kept from Tucoras. She would rely on fate once more tonight to determine where her story would go. "Heads, we listen to our better senses and stay away from these games. Ship, we go in search of this match-master to find out more."

Desil nodded, rising on a knee to get a better look at the coin in her hand.

With a sharp flick of her thumb, she sent it soaring skyward, catching it before it dropped onto the wooden floorboards.

Centuries ago, their exiled ancestors must have felt a great, keen, anxious hope as they left behind their sinking island for a new life aboard a Fated Ship. And now once more, a Fated Ship was glimmering with promise at Ederi souls, the coin face gleaming back at the two of them in the low light of their hive-lantern.

"Thy will be done," Desil murmured, a quiet smile tilting his lips.

Lythlet took a deep breath. "And thus twice tonight is fate dragging me forth from the margins."

CHAPTER THREE

THE MATCH-MASTER

No. 221 Travent Street of Cantereve South Ward was a small, snow-dusted abode with high green gables that reminded Lythlet of the Demothis' home in Southwest. A pang of misplaced nostalgia hit her as she held up the handbill to confirm it was indeed the address of the match-master.

Taking a deep breath, they stepped up to the house and knocked on the green door.

A statuesque woman with dark brown skin answered, her kinked hair pulled tight over her scalp and gathered into a neat bun. A pair of glasses rested low on her nose, and she stared down at them with a severe expression. "How may I help you?"

Desil cleared his throat. "We're conquessing hopefuls, and we've come for an audience with Master Renveld Dothilos."

She nodded and let them in. "Excellent timing. The match-master is finishing up another interview." She shut the door behind them and led them down a long corridor dimly lit by the winter sun.

Every step Lythlet took rattled her nerves more and more. She was not optimistic about her chances of being accepted as a contestant;

she made a less than impressive first impression, more so now with her bandaged brow. Her dark hair framed a skeletal face, her bony brown cheeks jutting out beneath her asymmetrical eyes. She had the same gaunt, hungry look she had been born with, and standing next to Desil's broad, muscular build made her look even more pitiful than usual.

The door at the end of the corridor opened, and two shabbily dressed men ambled out of the room and away into the street.

In a clarion-clear voice, the woman said, "In you go," pushing them forth.

Lythlet tried to control her breathing as she entered the room. *Steady, steady.*

It was a pleasantly spacious office, the walls covered in dark lacquered wood panels. A massive cherry oak table stood as the centerpiece of the room, and behind it was a well-groomed Ederi man who tipped his head briskly in their direction. "Take your seats, you two."

It was difficult to guess the match-master's age—from some angles, it seemed he couldn't be beyond his thirtieth year, yet he would turn another way, and as the light upon his face shifted, he would age decades in a second. Every single one of his features was remarkably angular, as if he were a wooden statue crafted by a particularly harsh carver. He had thick blond hair and shrewd pale eyes that bore deep into her.

His gaze lingered on her face, a slight frown forming the longer he looked. After a moment, he turned away with a subtle shake of his head and reached out to a row of individual pen holders engraved into his desk.

Lythlet watched with a sinking heart as his hand gently brushed over an ornate lapis-lazuli-ribbed dip pen before shifting to a plain bamboo one.

Not good enough for the good pen, are we?

"As you may have already guessed, I am Match-Master Dothilos. Introduce yourselves." His voice was a smooth baritone that lingered in the ear longer than usual, a voice that could lull a cat to sleep at one turn, then rouse a soldier to march at another.

Tap, tap, tap, drummed his bamboo pen against the desk, rankling her nerves even more.

Suddenly very afraid her stutter might return, Lythlet discreetly tapped her boot against Desil's.

Understanding her signal, he spoke first, "I'm Desil Demothi, and this is Lythlet Tairel. We've come today hoping to become conquessors."

"Desil Demothi?" The match-master lifted his head from his palm, blasé attitude vanishing. "*The* Desil Demothi? The brawler of Chuol Ward?"

Desil's smile slipped. He shifted nervously in his seat, but regathered himself, nodding.

"You made quite a name for yourself in the local leaderboards, my boy," Master Dothilos said with an incredulous smile. "I watched a round of yours once upon a time and came away a little richer thanks to you. But then you left! At your peak, with an unbroken record, right when there was talk of you entering the bigger squares. I rarely dabble in the brawling world, but my friends in the bidding circle rant to this day of your departure. Is it *really* you?"

"Yes," Desil said tensely.

The match-master drew closer, pale eyes sparkling with curiosity. "So what took you out of the game? Found a better way of earning your keep, did you? You certainly had your share of adoring fanatics happy to pay for your company. Ah, handsome lads always do well in this world. Had I been born with your sun-blest face, I wouldn't have struggled half as much in life." He wagged his finger at Desil with a chuckle.

"No, of course not," Desil spluttered, appalled at the suggestion. He shifted nervously in his seat. "I left the square because I chose to reaffirm my vow of peacekeeping to Tazkar."

The match-master paused to reflect on this, sipping from his teacup. "Thus endeth the career of the undefeated darling of the square. Always a shame when so much potential winds up wasted on a fool pliant to religious superstition."

Desil was too stunned to respond.

"You're being rather rude," Lythlet broke in, pitying him enough to muster the courage to speak.

Master Dothilos held his hands out placatingly. "Settle down, little miss. This is no more than friendly banter. I'm simply trying to learn what I can. You understand how conquessing works, don't you? I pay a standard participation fee, but the good coin lies in getting spectators to bid on you. Should you survive a round, I'll give you a cut of the vigorish—that is, the profit I make from the spectators' wagers—but only the vigorish of the bids made in your favor. Hence, you don't earn much unless you rally the spectators to bet on you winning.

"Now, the odds are always against you, more so at the beginning, when few know who you are and why they ought to risk their coin on the chances of you making it out alive. But if I sell them the tale of an undefeated brawling champion, the bets will tilt in your favor. I can already see it: *come one, come all! Witness the return of Desil Demothi, darling of the brawlers' square!* His name alone may reel in a decent audience, so long as I craft a good story—and that's exactly what I'm doing research for. Come, tell me about yourself, Miss Tairel. You don't look much of a brawler."

"I am"—*currently unemployed* was too painful to say, *a three-time pickpocket* too glib—"a bookkeeper."

The match-master sat there, waiting for her to continue.

The currently unemployed three-time pickpocket sat there, waiting for him to respond.

A brief, painfully silent moment passed.

He blinked. "Is that all?"

"That is all," she said, blinking back.

"Have you a past in brawling or anything else to demonstrate your potential in the arena?"

A list of supplemental facts whirled through her mind, but she found herself instinctively resisting the urge to answer him. There was something about the match-master she couldn't ignore: he had the manic aura of a viper oil peddler, and Lythlet had worked under enough swindlers to know the most efficient strategy to avoid falling prey to one of their scams. One had to avoid giving much personal information, for these swindlers would gleefully leech onto even the most innocuous of statements to exploit another.

"Oh, she's very clever," Desil interrupted after giving a brief concerned glance at her. He seemed under the impression that her nerves had gotten the better of her. "Has the cleverest mind I've ever seen. She learns things quick as a whip, she's brilliant with numbers, and she even used to build trigger traps when we were young. She gave my family some complicated contraption to catch sewer rats, and it caught them all right. Nearly blew my ear off, too, but that's another matter."

"Charming," said the match-master in a tone that strongly implied he thought otherwise, "but these matches are fought purely with weapons I supply. You're not permitted to bring in any cheeky devices you've built."

"Well, besides that, she's very handy with a spear. She used to train with—"

"How about we let her speak for herself?" Master Dothilos proposed with a wry smile.

Desil fell silent, looking sheepish.

Master Dothilos turned to her. "As Desil was saying, you've had prior training with a spear?"

Lythlet stared back at him, this viper oil peddler in gentleman's clothing. "None, other than what was mandatory in schooldays," she lied.

Truth was, she'd been inadvertently trained by some of the best spear-wielders in the city. Her father worked at a local smithy, and when he'd discovered she'd taken to stealing in her free time after catching her stuffing her latest stolen tome beneath the ripped-apart floorboards of their home, he'd decided to take her to the smithy after school every day for her to spend the rest of daylight with him.

To keep her busy, he'd given her a spear: a small, short thing he'd crafted quickly for her, suitable for her height. His smithy made the weapons for the watchmen, so quality was to be expected of his craft.

The forge-master was a large, bull-faced fellow, but he was soft-hearted and never minded her father bringing Lythlet along so often. The other blacksmiths would come out and watch her when they grew tired of the heat and the noise of the forge. They'd shout at her what to do, to try, sparring with her. Some had mercy on the child; some didn't and taught her what it meant to fall over and over again.

Two of her father's smithmates were former mercenaries who'd left the beast-ridden wildlands for a peaceful life behind city walls. They were the meanest: they had tripped her until she learned to watch her feet, they had ripped the spear from her hands until she learned to tighten her grip, they had come at her with wooden planks to clap her around the ears until she learned to parry their blows. They were the meanest—but they had been the best masters to learn from. Few would ever deem Lythlet the deftest spearmaiden, especially compared to those who had pursued further mastery of the military arts, but she was not without a degree of proficiency uncommon for a penniless slumdog.

Desil shot her a confused look but said nothing.

The match-master leaned back into his seat, arms crossed. "Have you spectated a match before?"

They shook their heads.

"Like little lambs being led to the slaughter." He glanced uncertainly in Lythlet's direction. "You do understand what you're interviewing for, don't you? I'll be bringing in a beast from beyond the walls, and you're to survive a fight against it. Not some docile mule, but an actual beast, with fangs and claws and other nasty bits like that. Have you the stomach for that, little miss?"

"So long as you pay us at the end of it, I do."

Master Dothilos remained unimpressed and swung back to Desil. "You, my boy, I shall whole-heartedly add to the next round of contestants—I can rouse the audience with talk of your brawling days. Miss Tairel, however, I am not so keen on. Painful to look at and painful to listen to. I'm not quite sure what to do with you."

Lythlet almost nodded in agreement.

A flicker of hope crossed Master Dothilos's face. "Will you two be entering jointly or separately?"

"What do you mean?" she asked.

Master Dothilos sighed. "Little lambs, little lambs. Should you register as a sole conquessor, you sign in your name alone, and I'll pair you with another conquessor. I've a good eye for this, so you can trust me to find you a partner that will appeal best to spectators. What you earn, you split, exactly as it would be even if you were a joint duo.

"The main difference is that if you sign up *jointly*, you two are, in the eyes of the arena, essentially making a vow of fellowship together. Not *the* sacred vow of fellowship, of course—I am no shrine-master, and you need not recite the hallowed words to one another. But the arena is nonetheless a manifestation of the divine curse we mortals have been plagued with, that we must toil to survive in a land riddled with dangers such as the wild beasts. To bind yourself to another is a noble act in this world, that you would pledge to share in not only your joys but your sorrows and hardships. So we have our own version of the vow of fellowship that you may partake in by signing up jointly. If you do so, you must act on the approval of one another. If one forfeits a match, you must gain the approval of the other before your forfeit counts, and without that approval, you will be forced into continuing the fight. But should you sign up as a sole conquessor, when you forfeit, you forfeit on your own and are free to abstain from the fight. If your partner ends up continuing the match on his own and winning, you've lost your share to him."

Lythlet had made her mind up already, but she noticed Desil's bafflement, so she waited for the match-master to resume his explanation.

"This distinction is an important one to make, as it can affect your approach to the games. It's led to a bit of in-fighting with some previous duos I paired together, with one trying to chase the other out mid-game to hog the whole prize to himself. We don't officially sanction solo matches, as the odds of surviving aren't very good when you're alone, but some are confident enough. If you're willing to take that risk, signing up separately can be very profitable to you. The only benefit of registering as a joint duo is your partner being confirmed forthright, with no intervention on my part."

"Then we shall be joint conquessors," Desil said, confusion clearing.

Lythlet nodded.

Master Dothilos pursed his lips. "Demothi, I refrain from interfering unnecessarily, but for someone of your caliber, I must make an exception: I cannot recommend choosing this girl as your partner, not when you have a much better chance of winning. Allow me to pair you with someone who would sell much better to spectators. I have a couple of applicants in mind who might suit you."

Desil met the match-master's eyes unwaveringly. "I have more faith in her than any stranger you could match me with. I will partner with her or no one at all."

Chin resting on his palm, Master Dothilos drummed his fingertips against his cheek. "My, my. I'm beginning to believe you really are as naïve as you present yourself to be."

Expecting him to quarrel further, Lythlet was surprised when the match-master shrugged and turned to her.

"Very well. Let's try this again, shall we?" the match-master said, dipping his pen into the inkpot, then holding it poised over paper. "What's your story, Miss Tairel? You may try to win me over. I seek a compelling character the crowd can root for, someone worth spectating a match for." He sounded more like a man casting actors for his next stage play than a bloodsport's match-master.

Her gut still cautioned against revealing too much, but she knew she had to say something. Perhaps a little information wouldn't hurt, not when it was a common story for the southern slums. "We have debt—"

Master Dothilos looked up from the paper with an impatient glare. "Dull. Trite. I've heard this a dozen times before, and I'm talking about today alone." He set down his pen and looked her squarely in the eye. "Let me wrangle it out of you. You've a little brother back home and you need money to feed him because Papa's a drunkard and Mama's out gallivanting with strange men every night."

Bewildered, she responded, "No—"

"Then perhaps Papa's lost every single thing your family had in a bad bet, and you need a fortune to buy it back. There's a weepy little tale inside you, come give it to me."

Lythlet's temper flared, oiling her tongue. Hearing her mother and father invoked felt obscene somehow, profane. "If you have the temerity to insult my father and mother in your quest to craft a bullshit story to peddle to the masses, I refuse to sit around any longer for that. I've already told you we have debt—"

"Dull, trite! What do you really want?"

She spluttered, perplexed, "To pay off the loan shar—"

"Dull, trite! What do you really want?"

"I just want to be happier!" she exploded. "I want what my parents never had, nor my ancestors—to survive and prosper. I want coin, and I want a mountain of it. Must I have your pity first to justify my hopes? Must I forge for you some traumatic past before you'll grant me the same opportunity easily offered others?" Then she shrank into silence, split between embarrassment and surprise at her own outburst.

His questions ceased at last. "Happier? What an odd reason

to sign up to fight beasts on a monthly basis," he mused as he scribbled down some notes. He sat back, staring at his own writing for a moment, then looked back up at her. "But there's a streak of hungry greed in you that's quite alluring. The greedy are always ambitious, the ambitious always desperate, and the desperate never forfeit a match until they're on the verge of death. I do love those who cling on to the very end. Now what story lies between the two of you? How long have you known each other?"

"We've been friends since we were six," Desil answered, and to Lythlet's relief, he sounded just as bewildered as she felt.

Master Dothilos nodded as he scribbled away. "How charming. I can work with this. And would you say he's like a brother to you, Miss Tairel?"

"Sworn, not blood," said Lythlet.

His bamboo pen paused its flitting. "Meaning?"

"Blood brothers and sisters betray each other day and night, lying to and cheating one another. But Desil would never do that to me. If you wish to say he is like a brother to me, say he is a sworn brother, one bound by the virtue of oath over blood."

Master Dothilos snorted. "How quaint."

She leaned forward and read upside-down fragments of the match-master's notes:

dead behind the eyes—very strange face (looks like a battered wooden bucket)
not very bright, doesn't speak much, has an utterly bizarre cadence when she does
does not know how to pronounce temerity
strange word choices at times
will be a difficult sell to the crowd

She sat back, reeling at her flaws being so frankly ascribed to her. The match-master looked back and forth between the two of them, saying nothing for a while. At last, he threw up his hands in delighted exasperation. "A brawling champion and his greedy little friend pretending she has no story. This could either be very interesting or not at all! But if having you attached is the price I must pay to have Desil Demothi on my spring roster, then it is a cost I shall count. Let's see how long you last. These are your contracts."

It was a surprisingly terse and simple waiver absolving him of any liability; she'd signed denser contracts before. Curled at the bottom of the page was a familiar signature and the stamp of a red serpent swallowing the little finger of an outstretched hand.

"The Eza backs the matches?" Lythlet asked, eyes glued to the stamp.

For as long as the underworld had existed, there had always been its self-proclaimed master, the Eza, governing the hidden markets of the city beyond the purview of the Einveldi Court, arbitrating the law of the underworld and meting out punishments as they saw fit. It was said the gaol of the Court law was a far more pleasant way of spending one's time than the wrong side of the Eza.

"Who else but the Eza would be willing to? You don't think I could ever get an officer of the Court to condone this little business of mine, do you? It'd be the downfall of anyone beholden to the Twelve Judges. Imagine the scandal! The outrage! They might even get a public caning!" A shrill cackle whistled out of him, and not for the first time did Lythlet wonder if there was something ticking in the wrong direction inside his head.

But he resumed, "These contracts certify you know what you're signing up for. In the event you're torn to shreds, no one—not your darling parents nor your dearest friends—may hassle me for compensation, lest the Eza's servants come rooting you out of your homes."

Desil's lips were pinched. "How many conquessors have died?"

"Died? None! I was only teasing, dear boy."

Horseshit of the highest order. The glint in the match-master's eye hadn't escaped Lythlet's notice. But an early death did not bother her, not someone who had so little to look forward to beyond debt and strife.

Desil tugged on her little finger, looking concerned. "Are you sure you're all right with this?"

"Many do worse things for less," she said quietly. "And we need the coin."

Desil seemed comforted at that, to her surprise—she thought he'd waver a moment longer, but he signed then without further hesitation.

The match-master watched them with a smile, and as he rolled up their signed contracts for safe-keeping, there was a light in his eyes like the spark of a newborn star.

CHAPTER FOUR

THE ARENA OF INEJIO SETGAD

THE CITY OF Setgad was on the cusp of a golden spring when Lythlet and Desil received their invitations from the match-master:

Your match has been arranged for 10:00 a.m. on Hildenvind, the 5th of Fethaya. Meet me at Travent Street three hours prior for your briefing.

"Madame Millidin's already agreed to give me that day off," Desil said. "I'll have to rise before dawn if I want time to pray at the shrine."

Lythlet took a sip of her monkfruit tea, complimentary of The Steam Dragon and its proprietress Madame Millidin, who had grown accustomed to her visiting Desil as he worked.

A well-known establishment which Madame Millidin had worked on tirelessly for decades, The Steam Dragon with its authentic Oraanu tea menu was the pride of the otherwise dismal sector of Southeast Setgad. Even highborn peers from Central occasionally graced the teahouse with their presence, though hardly ever without a guard or two.

It was a sleepy, chilly afternoon with intermittent storms, and that kept the usual bustling hive of customers away. Only two middle-aged patrons were dining at present, while Desil and Lythlet occupied another table. Schwala, the teahouse dog, was lying by the moon-shaped entrance, staring at the rainy street with dour eyes, legs sprawled out froglike from behind. It was customary for Oraanu teahouses to keep a dog, for well-fed canines were seen as harbingers of prosperity.

Lythlet read the invitation over, absorbing the words in a relentless loop. "I'm nervous," she admitted to Desil.

"As am I," he said, but she could tell he was lying to make her feel better. There was a steely, determined gleam in his eyes. *Confidence borne from his brawling days. He knows full well how to perform for the entertainment of a massive crowd.*

She fidgeted in her seat at the thought of hundreds of strangers staring at her, judging her. Every single one of Master Dothilos's petty nitpicks flooded her mind. "Desil," she started hesitantly, "is the way I speak strange sometimes?"

"I think it's very uniquely charming," he assured her, which was quite possibly the kindest way of saying 'yes'.

Not cheered up in the slightest, she went on, "Do I mispronounce temerity?"

"I don't know that word, Lytha," he said, blissfully unbothered. "Does this have anything to do with conquessing?"

"No, I suppose not," she admitted.

He patted her arm. "Let's just focus on getting through the first match, shall we?"

One match. Depending on how many spectators bid on them, the jackpot could knock off a decent percentage of their debt to Tucoras. Perhaps it would even cover their rent, food, census tax, and other necessities for some time. *And the spectators may welcome us back to the next round with more bids—and a bigger jackpot.*

She exhaled, rooting herself back to the ground. She was getting carried away.

There is nothing more dangerous than hope, she warned herself.

* * *

COMPLETELY UNCONCERNED WITH Lythlet, Master Dothilos patted Desil on the back in greeting when they showed up on his doorstep for their briefing. "My dear boy, your name alone on the roster was enough to stir the spectators into a frenzy. I've been getting more bids than usual for a first round! Come now, follow me inside. The other first-rounders have gone ahead of us. Their match is scheduled before yours, so they're being briefed earlier."

"We're sharing our match day with other first-rounders?" Lythlet said.

"Of course," Master Dothilos said amusedly, as if the idea of doing it any other way were absurd. "First-rounders rarely amount to anything, and spectators willing to watch them are scarce. The only way I can make it palatable is by bundling you lot up so there's value in your match's ticket. Only by surviving your first match will you be granted solo match dates onwards."

Lythlet cast a glance in Desil's direction. "I thought given Desil's reputation, we'd be given some preferential treatment."

"You have. I usually have *three* pairs of first-rounders on one ticket. Count your blessings that the name Desil Demothi still carries some weight. Hurry now, come in."

"Surely we ought to have the briefing in the arena?" said Desil, stepping into the carpeted corridor alongside Lythlet.

"We are, my dear boy. Just follow me down to the basement and I'll show you something very interesting." That bright little twinkle had returned to his pale eyes.

Lythlet eyed him, not humored in the least. Few things were more suspicious than a shady fellow saying he had something interesting hidden in his basement. *It's a coin toss between a skeleton collection or a caged woman.*

Amidst the chaos of broken bowls and locked chests in the basement, the match-master prised apart the floorboards, revealing a hole in the ground. A ladder, reaffirmed with wooden slats, was etched into a side, leading down as far as Lythlet could see in the dim light.

"Mind your step, the two of you. We go all the way down, then the road twists and turns before we reach the arena." The match-master pulled at a chain around his neck, from which hung an oddly shaped piece of glass. She heard a tap, barely audible, and then a startlingly bright light glowed from it, brighter than any hive-lantern.

Could that be baltascar? Lythlet wondered, intrigued. But an even larger question seized her attention as she examined the revealed passageway: "We're going to Inejio, aren't we?"

Master Dothilos glanced at her. "The one and only. I don't suppose you two have ever been there before?"

Desil and Lythlet exchanged brief looks at each other, unbridled curiosity growing on their faces. Where their ancestors had first settled the sacred land was now called Inejio by Setgadians, an ancient ruin completely walled up and over, anyone outside the United Setgad Party strictly prohibited from entering.

By the time the then government had decided it was time to transform Setgad from a humble safe haven into a city-state with proper walls, Inejio—once the nexus of a burgeoning populace— had deteriorated into nothing more than a dismal slum, tatters of humanity trying to scrape by. With the aim of giving Setgad a fresh beginning with the newer sectors, everything was built over and around Inejio, segregating the shame of its poverty from its flourishing neighbors. Central Setgad had been constructed directly over it, the apex of modern civilization resting upon the dilapidated shoulders of its forefather.

Of course, there was plenty of hearsay of how Inejio was still very much accessible for those desperate enough to seek it, of how both miscreants and misfortunes had found a refuge for themselves in those sprawling ruins, of how you'd find yourself there if you took a path by so-and-so—but Lythlet and Desil had never had the opportunity nor the excuse to test the veracity of those rumors.

With a small, knowing smile at their silence, Master Dothilos went down the hole, beckoning them to follow.

It was a long ladder plunging deep into the depths of the earth, and trepidation filled Lythlet as she latched onto the rungs. She felt like an earthworm burrowing her way down the claustrophobically narrow tunnel. Relief flooded her when she could put two feet on flat ground again, but they had a long way yet to go. They followed an earthen road that snaked around in sharp turns, always going uphill at a slight incline, until at last they emerged through a wall into a blast of cool open air.

"This is it, conquessors," Master Dothilos said, spreading his hands around. "Inejio—the ancient heart of the city buried beneath Central."

Lythlet turned around in a circle, eyes wide at the long-abandoned world unveiled around her.

The home of their ancestors lay before them, a desolate ruin overrun with untamed green. Tall pillars, larger than any kataka tree, dotted the landscape at regular intervals, stretching like monstrous stone giants holding up the darkness above. Unwavering lights gleamed from them so that the entire ground was lit in an eerie pale glare.

Deserted streets stretched far beyond sight, made up of dilapidated buildings featuring broken windows and exposed rafters. A shrine stood near them, its majesty humbled by the passage of centuries, nearly all of its warden statues beheaded and delimbed by time and pillagers foraging for lucky charms.

Yet where there was ruin, there remained life. Tangles of flowering weeds sprang from the ground, and trees that had grown monstrously huge entwined themselves with abandoned buildings, roots and vines wrapping themselves over stone and brick. Flowers bloomed lush and vibrant in the aftermath of their ancestors, and fruit hung overhead, ripe and fresh.

There's no sun down here—how can anything grow?

Master Dothilos rushed them forth, and as they passed a row of old townhouses, their once colorful shutters now faded into demure shades, Lythlet peeped through the windows. Remnants of ancient households lay under dusty veneers, a quick-fire montage of life long evacuated embedded in the memory-saturated interiors. A rocking chair an elderly man might have played with his grandchildren in; a sweet-faced rag doll a child must've hugged to sleep every night now lying forgotten on a nightstand; a crudely carved eight-stringed izitana, a traditional Ederi instrument, that doubtless some youngsters had spent summers of their lives plucking away on with rapidly callousing fingers.

To think that a very long time ago, her ancestors had trawled through these very streets, living lives of which the memories were now lost to time. Slowing momentarily, Lythlet dragged her fingers across her collarbones and looped them over her heart, performing the ritual of remembrance. Bowing with hands steepled together, she muttered under her breath, "May the white wind guide your souls. Please watch over my match today and lend me your good favor."

"The filial sort, aren't you?" remarked Master Dothilos, glancing over his shoulder, his brisk march not faltering for even a heartbeat.

Lythlet dropped her hands, embarrassed, and picked up the pace. "I didn't think anything of Inejio still stood."

"There had been government plans to rejuvenate the area eventually, actually. Tear down the slums and turn it into an opulent, exclusive haven for certain dignitaries—and of course, all that's been forgotten. But I've heard word of that changing soon. Fascinating, isn't it? This whole place is like walking through a time capsule."

"Yes, much better than a skeleton collection."

"Pardon?"

"Nothing." A question pricked her thoughts as they turned a corner onto a street of old terraced shophouses with cantilevered walkways, wooden doors hanging on their hinges, berry-laden vines twisting around arched doorframes. "Is it true the unregistered live here?"

"Where else could they? Census scribes don't bother coming, of course. Too tedious, not worth checking on. So the unregistered sleep here, and if they ever need anything, they run up using one of the many paths and come back down if they spot any wandering scribes."

Those who could not afford to pay their city taxes escaped the repercussions by failing to assign themselves to any address— and in doing so, they snapped loose all ties to society, rendering themselves unable to partake in any services the Court checked upon. Schoolhouses, health wards, moneyhouses, the usurers, Faravind Post, landlords and landladies—anyone who wished to survive an audit by the Court turned away the unregistered.

Lythlet kept quiet. If they ever failed to pay Tucoras again, their only choice would be to run away and become unregistered themselves. The debt may have been in Desil's name, but she was so entwined with his life, the loan shark would inevitably chase her into vagabondage. She stared at the ruins surrounding her, a sense of foreboding rising as she contemplated how much her future rested upon her upcoming match. As scenic as it was, a verdant microcosmic glimpse at a bygone era, she prayed desperately this level of segregation would never become her fate.

"Here we are," said the match-master jovially, slowing for the first time. Looming before them was a tall, roofless, circular structure. Many glassless windows ringed it, its formidable height supported by flying buttresses rooted into the earth around it, like a falcon's talons sinking into the flesh of its prey.

"It was built hundreds of years ago—a proper symbol of mankind's hubris," said the match-master with a glimmer of pride, as if he had been the one painstakingly laying stone upon stone. "Our ancestors found a sacred safe haven, and what did they do? Decide to bring in monsters and kill them for jollies! We are a wonderful, sensible bunch, aren't we? I restored the arena when I took over the matches, and it looks as good as new, if I do say so myself."

Boastful though he may have been, credit had to be given to him. The arena stood tall and proud, the pale walls gleaming under the Inejio light like a well-preserved relic.

"Right this way." Master Dothilos ushered them around and through a small gate, one appearing more functional than extravagant; no doubt the main entrance was somewhere else, a cavernous mouth permitting throngs of spectators through.

After a series of long, narrow corridors, they reached a small room lit by a few hive-lanterns.

It was an armory, all but one wall furnished with nearly any weapon one could think of. Rows of swords of various shapes and sizes, including traditional Oraanu blades; all varieties of polearms, bladed or otherwise; axes and hatchets; knives and daggers; rope darts; massive maces; bulky clubs; slings accompanied with heavy stones—

"No bow and arrow?" Lythlet noticed.

The match-master scoffed. "Never. No crossbows, either. Too easy for conquessors to climb up the scaffolding and pick off the beasties one by one. Too cheap a shot means no risk, and no risk means dissatisfied spectators. I save them for my servants to use on beasts after conquessors forfeit."

Before she could examine the selection of polearms further, Master Dothilos had them follow him into another long hallway with a lifted gate at the far end. "You'll come through here and wait for my summons before going through that gate. There will be an oath to swear on before you fight. You know the words to say, Desil, the same as brawling."

He didn't bother explaining what they were to Lythlet, she noted with slight offense.

"After that, my men will bring in the beast and the fight will commence. No holding back, please. There was an unfortunate incident a year ago when a couple of conquessors panicked at first sight of the beast. Didn't even remember to forfeit! Thoroughly entertaining, but it took my men days to clean up the gruesome aftermath."

Desil's glare turned sharp. "I thought you said none have died."

"Did I now?" the match-master returned absent-mindedly. "I don't recall."

Horseshit of the highest order.

They crossed the gate and entered the arena proper. It was much larger than Lythlet had expected from the outside. The only time she had seen such a huge circle of land, unfettered by buildings or taken up by shanties, was when she had worked on a farm, going through the wide fields for the harvest. But the ground here was different, not covered by soft grass but with hard-packed dirt, dust, and sand. The other pair of first-rounders was standing at the diametrically opposite side of the arena, two young Oraanus being briefed by one of Master Dothilos's men.

Empty spectator seats stretched in a full circle above. Beneath them were protruding bamboo scaffolds ascending in random patterns along the walls. In the center of the arena, eight enormously tall and thick bamboo poles erupted out of the ground, jutting into the heights, taller than even the topmost seats.

A vivid childhood memory swelled up in her, of swaying atop thin minstra bamboos and feeling the breeze on her face as funeral drums beat around her.

But these can't be minstra. These are ginormous in comparison.

Lythlet pointed at the bamboo ring sprouting from the center of the arena. "What type of bamboo are those?"

"The platforms along the walls are made of common minstra bamboo, but those huge freestanding stalks in the center are yutrela poles. Lacks the fire resistance of the minstra, but they're ten times thicker, as you can see, and a thousand times stronger."

Lythlet paused, startling at the name. She had read about it in the legend of Atena in her youth, recalling how Atena had cunningly used a single yutrela leaf to calm one of the Heavenly Dragons, before learning of greater gifts awarded by scaling the heights of the bamboo. "Yutrela? Isn't that a divine touchstone?"

Divine blessings were scant in their part of the world—while their Anvari brethren to the far east were still blessed with bloodrights that gave them the power to manipulate the world around them, the Ederi in the west had nothing more than the common ability to interface with divine touchstones, the few vestiges of the heavenly left behind in the mortal world: bits of nature that bestowed a temporary reward should you show respect to it by fulfilling its requirements.

Master Dothilos nodded. "Divine, indeed, if you believe the legends. Sadly, it's been decades since we've seen anyone actually climb it all the way to the top, let alone manipulate the cosmoscape with it. Used to be a requisite skill for any conquessor when the games first began—it was nigh an art in those days. But none have the skill nor the daring nowadays. Pity."

Lythlet circled the base where the yutrela cluster was planted. She examined the length of one: natural notches ran along it, spaced far apart. It was indeed a great deal taller and thicker than the minstra poles of her youth. She ran her fingers along the rough texture of the bamboo, memories of joining mourning companies stirring in her. Bells ringing, drums beating, all to chase away evil spirits and usher along the soul of the dead. Herself, high upon a minstra bamboo pole, waving a white-and-gray pennant from the top, letting the breeze send the tangles of her hair askew.

Her thoughts progressed from the past to the folkloric, the legend of Atena gripping her mind. If there were any truth to it, whosoever had the persistence to reach the very top of one of these poles and issue the right prayer to the divine would be blessed with no more than eight seconds to understand and alter the pattern of gravity written on the map of the cosmoscape, one of the most powerful meridian networks of the universe.

All things were governed by the thousand-layered cosmic

landscapes of the universe mapped out by the Sunsmith and the Moonmachinist—as the flash and burn of fire belonged to the solarscape, so did the ebb and flow of water to the hydroscape; as the cycle of blooming greens and curling vines belonged to the florascape, so did the wild ways and whims of beasts to the faunascape. The canon of the Poetics did not divulge a comprehensive inventory of all the cosmic landscapes, and mortalkind maintained an imperfect understanding of these elemental meridian networks, but two were understood to be the most powerful of them all: the cosmoscape, which governed the warp and weft of the unseen laws and forces of three-dimensional space, and the chronoscape, which governed the concept and flow of time.

A shrill whistle from the match-master pulled Lythlet from the abstract to the present.

"Are you done daydreaming?" he asked impatiently as he checked his pendant watch.

Still entrenched in thoughts, she nodded and feigned a polite smile in his direction, teeth bared, eyes glassy.

Master Dothilos grimaced. "May the Maker unmake you, you ugly beast. Refrain from showing that smile to the spectators. Anyway, come back here, I've something important to discuss."

He procured from his pocket two glass pendants hanging from clasped straps, much like what he himself wore on his neck. One of the pendants had a thin red line running through its core, the other green. Yet the glass itself seemed otherworldly, a mother-of-pearl sheen tinging the pendant.

"This is how you forfeit. You each have one. Put it around your neck. If you wish to end the match—and keep in mind, you will be surrendering all prizes if you do so—smash this glass on the ground and announce your decision. When the glass breaks, smoke will pour out into the sky. Then my men will come in and handle the beast—and hopefully it's not too late for you to escape unscathed."

She pointed at the two forfeit pendants. "That's baltascar, isn't it? You carry something similar around your neck, the thing that glowed with light during our descent into Inejio."

"Exile-glass?" said Desil excitedly.

Master Dothilos smiled. "Never seen one up close before, have you? Not often you southern underclassfolk get to see one, although they're becoming common in other sectors. Hive-lanterns may still have their foothold in Setgad, but baltascar bulbs are popping up one by one in the northern sectors as the scarblowers improve their manufactory processes." This, Lythlet knew—Master Winaro had groused about the potential impact this would have on his hive-workshop in the future. "If you were wondering why greenery still thrives in Inejio despite being trapped deep beneath stone, the answer is that all the pillars are laden with solar-augmented baltascar, tempered into imitating the sun. Meanwhile these forfeit pendants are aero-augmented so that they can contain and release colored smoke at a high pressure. Very clever, all of it. But enough of that—back to forfeiting. My only advice is that you time your forfeit well. You must remain in the game for at least ten minutes if you want to receive your participation fee. Neither bull nor bear will be happy to see you forfeit too early, not if they want to have their gamble pay off."

Desil frowned. "Pardon? What's this about bulls and bears?"

"Bulls are spectators bidding in support of us. Bears are spectators bidding on us losing or forfeiting," Lythlet answered.

"Very good," Master Dothilos said, nodding approvingly. "A bit of jargon we borrowed from the speculative equity markets."

"The stock market," Lythlet whispered helpfully at Desil's lost expression.

"Correct," said Master Dothilos. "Can either of you guess why the rule of ten minutes was instated in the first place?"

Desil had clearly checked out of the conversation that was rapidly detouring beyond his realm of knowledge, but Lythlet attempted it: "Without that rule, it'd be easy for bearish spectators to collude with conquessors to start a game and immediately forfeit, thereby making bears win their gamble quickly. A ten-minute rule would ensure that conquessors have some skin in the game at least."

"Three for three, Miss Tairel," said Master Dothilos with a genuinely impressed tilt of his head. "Now, do you recall the special rule for joint conquessors?"

"Decisions must be made in tandem," she answered.

"Precisely. Forfeiting is not an individual decision, but one both conquessors must agree upon."

"And if they remain in disagreement, one wishing to fight and the other to forfeit?"

"The forfeiting conquessor will be deemed to be in violation of the so-called vow of fellowship and held in contempt of the arena until they agree to uphold their vows and resume the fight." Master Dothilos jabbed his finger at alcoves dotting the walls of the arena, high above the grounds. "My crossbowmen posted around will ensure the conquessor held in contempt remembers the legitimacy of the arena, and that no vows made within it are to be mocked."

Ah, Lythlet understood, grimly imagining herself riddled with bolts all over.

Master Dothilos paused, then said thoughtfully, "But beware that even if the forfeiting conquessor changes their mind and is no longer held in contempt of the arena, there will nonetheless be a repercussion for their misguided forfeit attempt."

"How so?" asked Desil.

"Despite rescinding your forfeit and continuing the fight, history has shown that spectator bids for your next round are likely to plummet."

"Even if we win?"

"Indeed. It shakes their confidence in you and turns them bearish. Spectators will look upon you as forfeit-keeners, so they'll either bid against you or bid a lesser amount in your favor—and that means your cut of future vigorishes becomes even smaller. It's a dangerous thing, testing the spectators—do not ever be held in contempt by them."

"I see," said Desil, still looking baffled.

"Spectators are investing in us, so to speak," said Lythlet, always capable of boiling things down to the nitty-gritty of financials. "And when it comes to investments, what markets hate the most is uncertainty. Introduce only a pinch of doubt and most will pull their coins away faster than you can blink."

Her explanation was met with brisk applause. "Your tongue loosens when it comes to matters of the coin, doesn't it?" said Master Dothilos, amused. "Bravo. I don't often meet conquessors with even basic financial literacy—it's not exactly a skillset that translates well to fighting. Any further questions?"

"What beast will we be fighting?" she asked.

"That's a surprise, of course. We never reveal that beforehand. Would the spectators trust me with their bids if they thought I was rigging the matches in your favor? Speaking of spectators, I can see our first audience members being ushered to their seats," he said with a growing smile. "Head back to the armory and await your turn, little lambs."

The match was about to begin.

CHAPTER FIVE

FIERNARA, OF THE WILD AND PURE

FOOTSTEPS ECHOED OVERHEAD in a steady pitter-patter, audible even through the stone walls of the armory.

Lythlet sat with a spear on her lap, hands kneading the wooden haft. Desil was beside her, resting his wrists on the crossguard of his sheathed sword. They were not alone; the other pair of first-rounders were pacing the floor, waiting to be called by the match-master. They were Oraanu, their pale skin offset by night-black hair, and they bore the same sharp chins and high nose bridges. Judging from their shared features, they were brother and sister.

The man paused his pacing to glance in Desil's direction. "You're Desil Demothi, aren't you?"

Desil looked up. "Yes," he answered, offering his hand for a shake.

The man grabbed it, heaving it up and down. "I heard we'd be fighting before some famous bloke, but I had no idea who. I was there during your final brawl last year—bloody brutal, from the first blow to the last."

Desil paled, casting an uncomfortable side glance in Lythlet's direction. "And you are?" he deflected quickly.

"Taovi." He jabbed a finger in his partner's direction. "And that's my sister, Una."

Una waved shyly in Desil's direction, cheeks flushed red. Her handsomely dark eyes seemed unable to peel themselves off his face.

Desil, oblivious as ever to the effect he had on most young women, politely tilted his head toward Lythlet. "This here's Lythlet. We're hoping to pay off my debt with conquessing."

"Much the same here, mate," Taovi said, seating himself beside Desil. "We're in a bad spot at the moment with our father's gambling habits, so we've come hoping to nab a jackpot."

"You wouldn't happen to know what we're fighting today, would you?" Una said hopefully. "We tried prying it out of the man briefing us, but he was as tightlipped as a clamshell."

"We had no better luck with the match-master," Desil answered ruefully. "Seems it's a well-kept secret in the arena."

At that moment, echoes of Master Dothilos's absurdly clear baritone penetrated the walls of the armory: "*Taovi and Una Sesona!*"

"That's us." Taovi rose, reaching out for his sister.

"All the best," Desil said. Lythlet bowed her head at them, hands steepled by her chest to express her hopes for their safe return.

Taovi grinned. "Thanks, mate. Listen, when all this is done, how about we head out for lunch?"

"Keen," Desil replied, slapping Taovi's offered hand playfully, yet again impressing Lythlet with his ability to make new friends wherever he went.

Taovi and Una left, his axe and her sword glinting as they disappeared down the corridor. The sound of the audience chanting and stamping their feet came muffled through the stone walls.

Lythlet shut her eyes, cutting her vision into black. Perhaps the aural experience of Taovi and Una's match could educate her in time for her own, guiding the brushstrokes of her imagination over the tabula rasa of her knowledge.

The incoherent rabble of the unseen audience reached her ears, the air shaking with their anticipation. Perhaps there were a hundred spectators today, faceless folk cheering with coins clinking in their hands. Then Master Dothilos's ringing baritone came through the stone walls, loud and clear and unforgiving.

"Today's match is dedicated to none other than fair Fiernara, she of the untamed wilderness and the pure of heart!" he bellowed, voice amplified by a speaking-trumpet. "We begin, as always, with a prayer to bless today's matches."

"*Hoo-rah!*" the spectators cheered.

Lythlet imagined him spreading his arms wide, bowing his head and inviting the rest to follow, playing the role of a shrine-master. Perhaps there was one of the twenty-four texts of the religious canon before him, the pages flipped to the prayer he'd selected for the day.

Solemn gravity inflected in his baritone, Master Dothilos read the Prayer of the Pure-Hearted aloud:

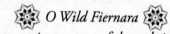
O Wild Fiernara
Make me an instrument of thy unbridled spirit
To live ever-seeking the immaculate light hidden within the darkness of every soul

His recitation come to an end, he maintained silence for the requisite twenty-four seconds of meditation.

Lythlet lifted one eyelid to confirm a hunch: Desil had shut his eyes to join the prayer, tapping a bead on his rosary, the one for faith which Fiernara represented.

The silent prayers ended, and Master Dothilos's voice, sonorous as it echoed, reclaimed her attention: "Today, we shall witness these two conquessors gain their honor and pay tribute to our ancestors by battling a sun-cursed beast in a showcase of strength that only the unbroken youth have. First—an oath! By the blood of your ancestors, do you proud Oraanu children vow to salt the earth with the blood of the demons that once gave death upon your ancestors?"

Taovi and Una's responses were inaudible, but from the audience's cheers, they had said the right thing.

Lythlet was about to ask Desil what to say for the oath, but Master Dothilos's next words cut her thoughts in half: "Bring out the beast!"

She braced herself, straining her ears for anything else. A hush had come over the audience. Metal squealed from somewhere. An unearthly snarl sounded, faint in the armory, but enough to make goose pimples rise on her arms.

Then a cacophony ensued, one that jarred her imagination's brushwork into frenzied, indecipherable streaks. She could not reconstruct the right visuals to match the hysterical screams, the garbled shouts, the collective gasps from the audience. Even the match-master's frenetic commentary made little sense without a view of the ongoings. Then one definitive shriek rose to the forefront.

"*Forfeit!*" A woman's voice, deeply distressed. Una.

There was no response from Taovi.

Lythlet paled, opening her eyes. She exchanged an uncomfortable glance with Desil.

More sounds—the audience jeering, the match-master calling his servants to rein in the beast. A clatter of noise approaching the armory from both sides: from the left, a physic emerged, already unwinding a roll of linen from his medicine bag; from the right, two of the match-master's servants carrying Taovi in on a stretcher, Una sobbing hysterically as she trailed after them, hair in disarray, clothes torn.

Where Taovi's arm once was, now a trail of blood leaked from a ruptured socket. His chest heaved with ragged breaths, whispering of hope yet for him, but his eyes had an eerie, lifeless look to them, of one's soul teetering over the edge of death's canyon.

Desil clutched Lythlet's arm tightly, the sight unnerving them.

"Head on," a servant snapped at them. "Master Dothilos will be calling you any minute now."

What in Kilinor's name did they fight? Lythlet thought, a gnarled knot of anxiety swelling in the pit of her stomach. A quick glance at Una, inconsolably crying as she held her catatonic brother's head in her hands, told Lythlet not to bother her.

Desil pressed his hands over Una's. "He'll be all right," Desil said, looking worriedly at her. Una only sobbed harder, hugging her brother tighter.

The servants chased them away once more, and Lythlet and Desil wound their way toward the fighting grounds.

"A miserably quick match!" Master Dothilos shouted, voice becoming clearer as they neared the end of the corridor. "Let us pray we see more promise in our next contestants: Desil Demothi and Lythlet Tairel!"

The resounding echoes of "Tairel" were swallowed by a bellowing horn. Unseen hands wound up the portcullis before them.

"*Hoo-rah, hoo-rah, hoo-rah,*" the audience chanted, feet stamping in tempo. It was deafening, a far cry from the barren soundscape the arena had been just hours prior. Somehow, it reminded her of the guttural chanting mourners declaimed at funerals, magnified a hundred times.

As if they're welcoming conquessors to their graves.

She stole an anxious glance at Desil, and together they plunged into the arena.

Bright baltascar lights overwhelmed her, addling her senses. Was she really buried deep beneath the heart of the city, far away from real sunlight? It felt like the wrath of a desert sun was upon her shoulders.

The chanting faded with a gesture from Master Dothilos, who stood upon a podium by the spectator seats. A rumble of private chatter remained throughout the crowd, some whooping at the sight of Desil.

"Demothi, Demothi!" they hollered, and he bowed politely in their direction.

Less than a quarter of the seats were filled, but for such a large arena, that was still a remarkable crowd, hundreds of spectators staring down at them. All at once, eyes slitted over in merciless mercantilism homed in on her, weighing her value as they weighed coins in their hands. Some frantically rifled through their beaded coin purses to make last-minute bets with the bookies trawling through the aisles. A man with a scarred face stopped one for what seemed to be a friendly chat, no coins exchanging hands.

Her gut clenched tightly. She was no more than a commodity stripped naked before a hungry market, a racehorse they would ruthlessly beat to the finish line if it meant they'd win.

Everything dissolved into a wordless mass of noise in Lythlet's head. She took a deep breath, trying to steady herself, suddenly intensely aware of how tightly her lungs were caged against her ribs. She steeled her gaze onwards, curious about the spectators. These were folk gambling their coin on the odds of her surviving or not—what were they like?

Many were clearly highborn peers, citizens hailing from the richer sectors of Setgad, evident from their garments and the guards seated by them. Outrageous golden filigree necklaces, ornate diamond-studded pendant watches—even those with more subdued fashion choices carried an aura foreign to Lythlet, one of self-assured dignity that permeated the way they held themselves.

Usually unbothered by her garb, Lythlet smoothed down her threadbare, ill-fitting blouse. She was a slumdog through and through, and she hated how obvious it was.

"Ladies and gentlemen, the conquessor we've all been waiting for! Desil Demothi, brawler extraordinaire, the king of the square of Chuol Ward! But first, the oath! By the blood of your ancestors, do you proud Ederi children vow to salt the earth with the blood of the demons that once gave death upon your ancestors?"

Not knowing what to say, Lythlet grunted wordlessly in answer.

Meanwhile, Desil shouted, making the sign of oath-swearing to the match-master, two fingers of his left hand crossed over two fingers of his right: "Witness me, upon the blood of my ancestors!"

"Then bring out the beast!" Master Dothilos said silkily into his trumpet.

Desil shifted his stance, raising his sword in the air, and Lythlet followed a heartbeat later, spear aimed at the rising gate.

No hands could be seen turning the wheels of the portcullis, but up it rose. A jangle of chains and a loud snarl sounded in the distance. Lythlet fidgeted at the noise, bracing herself. Then—a violent snap of metal shattering.

A massive blur of black rampaged through the hole. Clad in neither fur nor feathers, nor any material Lythlet had ever seen before in her life, the quadrupedal beast's edges seemed like smoke made solid, squirming unsettlingly like a silhouette wavering in flickering firelight.

What the devil is that thing?

It turned toward them, that great hulking black beast, and leaped. With just a few breathless bounds, it had crossed the arena, coming upon her like a storm cloud falling across a meadow.

She rammed her spear forth, but it nimbly sidestepped her attack. Up close, she noticed that although it had a lupine snout and four paws, it had neither a visible mouth nor claws. *How does it attack?*

It leaped once more at her, knocking the spear clean from her grip and smashing into her torso. A most disturbing sensation overwhelmed her, of an amalgamation of a million worms squirming against her flesh, her skin being sucked into an unfathomable abyss. She shrieked, terrified at the violation, and flung herself backward. But the beast stayed glued to her, melting into her like wax onto a candelabra. She fell to the ground, clawing furiously at her skin, trying to peel off the beast and its squirming edges, but to no avail.

Then Desil loomed behind the beast, sword raised. He rammed the blade down, and it caught in the beast's side hard enough to knock it off Lythlet.

"*Hoo-rah!*" roared the spectators.

Lythlet scrambled to her feet, relieved to be free. She spotted her spear resting near the perimeter and ran to fetch it. Keeping Desil in the periphery of her vision, she watched as he slashed at the beast. His sword had collided directly with it, yet when Desil plucked his blade out, no blood spilled.

Does it not bleed? Can it not die?

Indeed, no matter how many times Desil slashed, landing strike after strike, the beast remained unbothered, wrenching itself free from the blade. Then it sprang forward in one great leap through the air, crashing into Desil's side, knocking him to the ground. His sword flew out of his grasp, skittering just beyond his reach. The beast scrambled atop Desil's chest and lowered its mouthless maw to his face.

Desil screamed, muffled, the beast melting onto him in a viscous grotesquery.

Lythlet sprinted forward with her spear, and she stabbed the beast in the side. Her spear returned bloodless, as if stabbing a rubber sheet with a bare finger. But her thrust knocked it off Desil, forcing it to roll over some paces away until it lay sprawled over the ground, winded. It coughed as it tried to catch its breath, the unsettling smoke encapsulating its form twitching violently.

Lythlet pulled Desil up, and together in wordless agreement, they proceeded with the most natural solution to their predicament: they ran away like cowards.

They dashed for the scaffolding circling the arena, scrambling upon the nearest one and climbing upwards until they were made safe by a good height, crouching on separate but neighboring platforms.

As they leaned against the wall, panting to catch their breath, the match-master spoke into his horn. "Spectators! As regular conquessor aficionados will know, Desil Demothi and Lythlet Tairel are taking on none other than the native sentari—not an easy target for mere first-rounders! The great Oraanu poet Uzunaeri called the sentari the most wretched of the sun-cursed beings, for it lives as a bottomless abyss of hunger. And if our conquessors aren't careful, they just might join the little beastie in the abyss if they let it touch them for too long! Shall we see how the brawling champion of Chuol Ward handles the beast?"

"Sentari," Lythlet murmured. It held no meaning, but to know the name of her enemy gave a small dose of comfort.

On a neighboring platform, Desil rubbed his face. "What the devil is that thing? It felt like leeches were wriggling all over my face when it touched me. I think I blacked out for a second right before you rescued me, if that's what the match-master means by joining it in the abyss. Seems like it can steal your consciousness if it's on your face too long, if not worse. Is that how Taovi ended up like that?"

"It hasn't bled a single drop either."

"It can't be immortal, can it?"

"Impossible," she said, more out of hope than confidence. But as she thought on it, it made sense. "This match has to be winnable in some way, otherwise the bullish spectators would be outraged. Why would they bid their hard-earned coin on an unwinnable match? Master Dothilos is a merchant in the end, and he can't disappoint his customers. So we must be able to kill it in some way to make it fair for the bulls."

The beast had gathered itself to its feet and was snarling as it rounded the ground below them.

Lythlet stared at it, confused. "Doesn't it look different somehow?"

Desil peered over the edge. "Not in any way I can see. Why?"

"I can't put my finger on it. It just seems changed somehow."

She stared at the beast roving below them harder, trying to deduce what was bothering her.

After a moment, she said, hesitantly, "Didn't it look bigger when it had just emerged?"

Desil frowned. "Couldn't it just be that we're farther away from it now?"

She shook her head, more determined. "Look at its snout. Earlier, I couldn't see anything beyond the black smoke—not a single flicker of teeth nor tongue. But now I see some hints of white and pink appearing beneath its maw."

His eyes widened. "You're right. What's happening to it?"

"I don't know, but our time to strike may be fast approaching," she said hopefully.

No sooner had she spoken did the sentari decide it was its own time to strike. It launched off its powerful hind legs, making a nearly vertical leap up toward the ledge Lythlet was on.

A cry of surprise ripped from her as its maw neared, but she slammed her spear against the beast's skull. It tumbled from the blow but regained its bearings for another leap. As horrible a sight the sentari had been wreathed in thick, impenetrable smoke, it was no better in its shrunken form. Its newly visible fangs were gnashing at her, oversized eyeballs almost popping out of its skull, and the remaining smoke around it twitched like live leeches in a bucket.

Claws latched onto her ledge as it began to pull itself up, but she whirled the haft of her spear around to crack against its skull twice. Then she rammed the blade down at its paws, not quite piercing the shadow, but shocking it enough to send it to the ground in a brutal fall. No blood stained the tip of her spear, but she was certain she was coming closer toward its fragile flesh.

The sentari lay on the ground, panting pathetically.

"Now's our chance," Lythlet shouted to Desil.

But out of the corner of her eye, she noticed Master Dothilos raising his hands. He clapped twice, crisply, the sound echoing through his speaking-trumpet.

A moment later, more baltascar lights were switched on, bulbs buried in the uppermost walls beside the bamboo platforms they took refuge on. One was right next to where Lythlet squatted, and she blinked in confusion, eyes adjusting to the heightened brightness.

Why? It was plenty bright enough already.

She turned her attention back to the beast, ready to dive down with her spear while it was still downed on the ground.

Except it wasn't.

She shrieked as it launched at her face, making yet another vertical leap. This time, it had no issue catching onto her ledge, and it began pulling itself up.

To her horror, it had somehow grown, returning to a hulking beast of shadow.

Knowing better than to fight it now, Lythlet ran away, springing from platform to platform. She soon reached the highest possible platform, and there was nowhere to jump but down. *Unless—*

She stared at the yutrela bamboo poles in the center of the arena, swaying majestically without a breeze.

The sentari roared as it closed in, paws smashing against platform after platform. Just before its smoke-writhing maw crashed into her, Lythlet sprinted off the ledge. She flew through the air, then wrapped her limbs around the thick bamboo pole. It lurched forward, swaying precariously and groaning like a wounded beast. She thought of climbing higher but wasn't sure if she could: the common minstra poles she'd scaled before were thin and elegant, but these yutrela poles were thick enough to feel as though she were awkwardly embracing a large fellow.

Swaying to and fro, she saw the sentari leaping to join her on the bamboo, but it slipped, failing to find purchase, and crashed to the ground.

Good riddance.

It lay there, panting hard. The tip of its pink tongue flopped out of its mouth.

It's smaller again, she thought, perplexed. *Why does it keep shrinking and growing in turns? There must be a pattern somewhere, but what?*

The sentari rose, sluggishly, teeth and tongue peeking out from the smoke. It faced her, and though it had no expression she could decipher, something in its bearing made it look exhausted.

To her relief, it turned away from her, likely deciding climbing bamboo poles was beyond its abilities. Instead, it looked around and caught sight of Desil still poised on a ledge. It lumbered toward him, every step looking like a miserable slog.

The sentari seemed so small and weak then that Lythlet almost pitied it. "Give it a quick death, Desil."

He nodded, sword ready to strike. He crouched by the platform's edge, waiting for it to draw close enough for him to jump down and behead it in one clean swipe.

But as the sentari approached Desil, a slow, uneasy step from it became a steady footfall, then a heavy stride, then a mighty leap.

It grew again, she thought in horror as its squirming smoke swelled in wild, flaring bulges.

Restored to full strength, the sentari leaped up at Desil. He stabbed his blade into the beast's head, coming away bloodless. The falling beast then snagged at the hem of Desil's trousers, pulling him off the ledge.

He yelled as he crashed onto the ground, sword tumbling far out of his grasp. With a swift hind kick, the sentari sent it farther away, and jumped on him.

The cords of Desil's muscles bulged as he gripped the beast by the neck and slammed it into the wall, pulling it off him. Rising to his feet, he balled his fists before him, brawler's instinct kicking in. The sentari made several attempts to latch onto him, but he wrestled it off every time, slamming it down into the ground, up against the wall, into the edge of a low platform.

But this will be the first fight he cannot win, Lythlet thought, *not against a beast impenetrable by blade, let alone bare fist.*

Then, witnessing the harsh baltascar light falling and fading over them as Desil attempted to retrieve his sword from the shade of a platform, only to be blocked by the beast, her eyes widened. The pattern had unraveled before her.

"Keep it out of the shadows, Desil!" she shouted at the top of her lungs. "It fades slowly under the sun and grows quickly under shadow."

That explained why the beast had been enormous during its debut—it had just come out of a dark, shadowy corridor. Prolonged exposure to the baltascar lights had made it shrink over time. But then Master Dothilos had issued the order for more lights to be switched on—which made little sense at first, until she realized the baltascar bulbs were all positioned right above the bamboo ledges on the wall, their shadows to be thrown out at steeper angles to cast a far-reaching darkness over the arena.

Chasing her on the topmost ledges where there hadn't been shade had made it smaller, but now on the ground with plenty of patches of darkness to recover in, it was at full strength.

"Bring it toward me," she shouted, waving at Desil. There was a ring of undisturbed light just outside the yutrela poles, which only cast their shadows toward the inner circle.

Desil nodded and ran toward it, baiting the sentari into following him.

He'll finish this easily, Lythlet thought, relieved. As long as it was kept under the sun—or rather, the baltascar lights—the sentari would weaken to the point a blade could penetrate its smoke. Desil was strong enough that even with a bit of shadow cloaking the sentari, he'd be able to pierce it.

Except, she realized then, that Desil still hadn't retrieved his sword. The sentari had been intelligent enough to block him every time he tried to scrabble for it.

"Take my spear," she shouted, stretching it out toward him.

But the sentari turned and nipped at it, almost wrenching it from her grasp. Desil choked it backward in time, and Lythlet retracted the weapon.

"It's too clever, Lytha," Desil shouted, kicking the beast to the ground with his boot. "It'll just steal the spear away."

Then I'll kill it myself. We'll wait for its shadow to fade enough for me to pierce its flesh. But two things made her heart sink: the sentari was doubling its attempts on Desil, snarling nastily as it swiped its exposed claws at him, and Desil's steps were turning sluggish, wearied by their prolonged game of chase. *They're both on their last legs—and the beast is turning fiercer, giving one last fight before it dies, while Desil isn't going to last much longer. We can't wait until the sentari's shadows fade enough to show its flesh. But striking now would be pointless—I need something to put more pressure behind my strike to break its shadow.*

An idea took root as she stared up at the height of the yutrela poles. "Eight seconds of control over the cosmoscape," she recounted from the tale of Atena. It was a wild bet to make, especially when Master Dothilos himself couldn't confirm if the legend of the yutrela was true, but she decided it was a bet she had to make.

She had to figure out a way to climb to the top, despite how much more unwieldy it was than the minstra bamboo she was used to, despite the fact she had to somehow hold on to her spear throughout her ascent. Or, she realized, she could make the spear work to her benefit.

She turned the haft horizontal and arranged it behind the bamboo pole. Then *tock!*—she tucked her spear into the nearest notch above and hoisted herself upwards with her weapon as leverage. *Tock, tock, tock,* drummed her spear against the bamboo, a metronome setting the rhythm for her ascent. The tempo hastened as she adjusted to the shifting weight of the bamboo.

Up and up she went, childhood memories calming her adrenaline. Funeral bells were ringing, the mystic drums banging, the mourning company praying for the white wind to guide the spirit of the deceased to the afterlife. She would be paid a few pennies after a funeral, sometimes even a full dumasi coin if it were a richer family. How much could she earn today if she put on a good show?

Pum, pum, pum, went the death drum of her memories, *pum, pum, pum.*

The bottom of her boots caught neatly in the notches of the tree, and soon she reached the summit of the yutrela, flat at the top and just wide enough for her to squeeze both boots on it, surrounded by scant leaves clinging onto life.

She balanced herself upright on the trembling bamboo, standing in the zenith of the roofless arena. She could see all of Inejio laid out before her like a living map, baltascar-laden pillars bookmarking the overrun ruins of her ancestors for leagues around. There she stood, caught between the world of her forgotten lowborn ancestors and the world of the thriving highborn.

A wave of surprise washed over the spectators below, their loud murmurs reaching Lythlet's ears.

"Well, would you look at that? Who would've thought our little bookkeeper would have such a knack for climbing trees? The last reported conquessor to fully scale the yutrela was six decades ago. *Hoo-rah!*" Master Dothilos roared, leading them in a round of cheers.

Ordinarily, Lythlet would have shrunk her shoulders at so many strangers paying attention to her at once, but something else preoccupied her mind.

What am I meant to pray for? She stamped one foot on the flat summit, gauging if any new sensations overcame her. She'd stolen an abridged version of the tale of Atena, and it had simply summarized that portion of the huntress's adventure with a worthless '*she lifted her heart to the heavens, and the heavens responded in kind*'.

Desperate, Lythlet steepled her hands together, clapping thrice. *Please reveal unto me the map of the cosmoscape, O Great Divine.*

Nothing.

Pretty please, she tried once more, feeling very silly.

She felt perfectly normal, and that was a perfectly horrid thing to be at the moment. If she leaped down now with her spear, she would most certainly have enough thrust behind her to penetrate the sentari's shadowy shield, but she'd be crushed on the ground upon impact as well.

Desil hadn't even noticed what she'd accomplished. The sentari kept him busy, darting around. Then it sprang for his side in one tremendous blow, and he fell to his knees. He raised his fists, but the beast's mouthless snout smashed against his face. A muffled scream reached Lythlet's ears.

Desil's fist bounced uselessly off the sentari's neck, and his fingers tried gripping at its head to pull it off. But the sentari stayed steady, leeching off his face, and within moments, Desil's arms fell slack by his side.

Spare him—take my life if you must! she thought, gripped with sheer panic at the sight. Spear in hand, she shifted her weight to spring through the air, ready to fling herself at the sentari with no care for what would happen afterwards.

In that moment, the heavens took hold of her.

Triumphant melodies of golden strings roared in her ears, the ostinato overlaying the sensation of many fingers sinking through her scalp, teasing the contours of her brain into a new shape. A surge of unfathomable spirit thundered through her mortal flesh, and within the trappings of her skull, the divine map of the cosmoscape unfurled like a pennant fluttering in a spring breeze.

All at once, Lythlet was overcome with the matchless excitement of every child's first foray into horology, the sheer magic of lifting a clock's face for the first time and discovering the spinning gears hidden within—understanding that time was not controlled by the two spinning hands on the surface, but by a complex mechanism of pinions and wheels and springs beneath.

Now the cogwheels of gravity had been unveiled to Lythlet, and an instinctual understanding of how to alter the pattern of the world around her stamped itself on her mind—like winding a watch crown to effect one's will upon the mainspring, so, too, could she twist the gravitational fields around her, distorting the force at which she moved through the world.

She surged to the ground, spear tip pointed earthwards at the sentari, divine music roaring in her ears as she propelled forward. She sensed the presence of her spear as a separate entity from her, a creature with its own rhythm, its own soul, its own gravitational field. She flung it down, plucking at the meridian network of the cosmoscape as one would pluck a chord from an eight-stringed izitana, heightening the weight of gravity upon her weapon. It sped to the earth with an impossible force, and penetrated deep into the sentari's belly, ramming past the squirming shadows to the red flesh within. The shadow beast reeled away from Desil, giving him the scant few seconds he needed to scramble backward. An anguished howl escaped the beast's jaws, and blood spilled forth.

The sanded ground rushed upwards to break Lythlet, but she took a deep breath, plucking at another set of meridians along the cosmoscape, those which governed her own orbit. With a single thought, she broke her momentum, floating midair for fractions of a second and tilting herself upright. Barely a plume of dust rose as she landed on the ground with the lightest touch possible.

At that moment, the map scrolled itself tightly within her mind, the cosmoscape regressing back into an ineffable mystery, the otherworldly sensation of transcending mortal limitations into one of the invisible pathways of the universe vanishing entirely from her soul. The thrumming, divine ostinato quietened, fading into silence. She gasped, suddenly feeling very alone, very mortal, very ordinary once more.

Desil stared in momentary shock.

The sentari stumbled toward them, her spear still lodged in its gut. Shadows rippled and shuddered. Its pupils constricted as they fell upon Lythlet. Rearing back, it sprang at her, bloodied fangs on full display. Unarmed and still reeling from her brief traverse through the cosmoscape, she could do nothing but raise her arm to protect her face.

But Desil stepped in, and with one swift stroke of the blade he'd just retrieved, he sent its head rolling and its spirit off into the great unknown.

The beast collapsed to the ground. One by one, the shadows worming around it extinguished as if by a gust of wind, and within seconds, all that remained was a skinned red-raw creature lying lifeless on the ground.

As if the world were reawakening, the spectators burst into a flurry of excitement, their shrieks and applause deafening. Curiosity getting the better of her, Lythlet raised her head.

Hoo-rah, hoo-rah, hoo-rah crescendoed in an arc above her, the echoing voices loud enough to lift her spirits heavenward. The audience was clapping, stomping their feet, celebrating before her in dizzying displays of joy and rage. She stared at the uproar, and then shifted to hide behind Desil.

"An unbelievable performance from our two brand-new conquessors!" the match-master bellowed into his horn. "A stunning blow from Lythlet Tairel—when was the last time we had someone dare to scale the yutrela, much less ride it down to deliver a legendary strike from the heavens? The divine knows it was guiding her descent just now as she manipulated the cosmoscape! And as expected from the beloved brawler, Desil Demothi delighted us with his nimble sparring with the beast to buy time for her ascent! Ladies and gentlemen, your winners for today—two slumdogs making quick work of their first match! I'm sure all who've put their money on the name of Desil Demothi must be praising their wardens."

A flurry of noisy *hoo-rahs* affirmed the match-master's claim.

"No doubt this duo is one to keep an eye on. We'll have their next match scheduled and announced in a few days! Take a bow, champions!"

Desil bent over in a perfect arc while Lythlet weakly bobbed her head. She was too flustered, too intrigued by the mass and tangle of people staring and cheering at her. *For* her.

"Any final words?" Master Dothilos appealed.

Desil shouted, "Thank you for your spectatorship and your support! We shall return!" He gave another sweeping bow, his foot nudging Lythlet to join him. With their heads inches away from the ground, he spared a glance and a wink at her.

She nodded back, still bewildered by the noise.

"Let's go," he whispered into her ear, and she followed him to the armory.

Immediately, he slumped on the bench against a wall, crumpling as she grabbed rags hanging by the washing alcove. She tossed one to Desil and wiped her face with the other.

"I can't believe you climbed all the way up there. I can't believe you *jumped* from all the way up there!" Desil said, arm resting on a drawn-up knee, sword and rag neglected by his side. "You floated down like a feather—how the devil was that possible?"

"Apparently the legends are true," Lythlet said quietly, also reeling from what she'd just done. "The divine really do reward you if you reach the summit of the yutrela. I prayed for you to live, and it rewarded me in return."

"A pure-hearted prayer that doesn't benefit the one praying," he remarked with a knowing smile, making her wonder if she had inadvertently tapped into some sacred teaching. "Can you still do it?"

She shook her head. The map of the cosmoscape had furled away to the heavens, and the ink that had been so clear to her just moments ago had faded into nothingness. "Eight seconds only." All divine blessings came in eights, if folklore was to be believed, whether it be eight seconds, eight minutes, or eight hours.

Desil shook his head in disbelief. "Still incredible. You got a divine touchstone to actually work!"

She blushed happily. "I wonder how much was bid on us today. The match-master said it was more than usual."

"If the jackpot proves substantial," he asked hesitantly, "are you willing to continue conquessing? The match-master has more or less confirmed we'll be invited to the arena again."

"If this indeed turns out to be the best way to repay our debt to Tucoras, then yes, I think we have no choice but to continue."

Master Dothilos appeared by the doorway. "Bravo, champions! My servants will bring along your jackpot shortly, but I wanted to congratulate you first. Desil, my boy, I expected as much from you. You stole the hearts of half the spectators, and the other half will learn why soon enough. And you!" He turned to Lythlet, and she stood reluctantly. "Outstanding, dear girl. You certainly were keeping a few things up your sleeve, weren't you? Cosmoscape aside, your skill with both bamboo and spear gave me quite the shock! I must hear more."

Revealing a pinch more information wouldn't hurt. "Desil and I used to sell our free time to funerals, joining the mourning companies. He'd bang a drum while I'd climb the minstra poles and..." She mimed waving a pennant.

"And your familiarity with the spear? You performed some deft spearwork from the ledges when the beast was harassing you. You're rough and you lack the finesse of better spearmaidens, but there was a beautiful savagery to the way you fought."

"My father," Lythlet said, softly, clipped. Simply referring to him was enough to mute her spirit.

The match-master's eyes were bright, shining with anticipation. "Yes? What was he? A famous swordsman? A hired arm by the Court? A mercenary from the wildlands, perhaps?"

"He was a blacksmith." She was not eager to offer more, recalling how quick Master Dothilos had been to insult her parents when he knew nothing.

"Is getting answers out of her always like pulling teeth?" the match-master asked as an aside to Desil, who reluctantly bobbed his head. "He was a blacksmith *and*—"

"That was all he was. After school, I would sit in his smithy, and he would keep me busy that way. A spear in my hand..." She drifted off, deciding that was enough for him to know.

Master Dothilos waited for her to continue, and after a moment's silence, gave up with a disappointed sigh. "So reckless parenting made you the way you are. There's even less for me to work with than I'd expected." His eyes brightened. "Hold on now, did he ever beat you? Abused children get so much sympathy from the crowd. They make for such compelling characters. Everyone loves making themselves feel better by supporting one—"

"No," she snapped. "Do not slander him. He was my father, even if he did not know how to be one. Why do you pry so hard for a tale to sell to the spectators? I imagine you the sort to craft whatever lie pleases you anyway."

"Because the best tales are the ones rooted in truth. Embellished heavily, of course, but always with two feet on the ground. I'm simply trying to dig your truth out, Lythlet."

"There's nothing more I will give you. If you must forge a narrative of pain to pull in more coin, do as you will, but do not slander my father." The last few words poured out of her like fire from a brazier, the fervency taking even herself aback.

To her surprise, the match-master paused, staring at her thoughtfully. "Very well. Anyway, masterful use of the yutrela. Proving the legends true once and for all! Might be the only prayer I've ever seen answered in my whole damn life. I daresay bids for your next round may be something to look forward to." Master Dothilos patted their backs. "Always delightful to have competent young blood around. Makes me smile—makes me rich!"

CHAPTER SIX

THE POET AND THE RUFFIAN

THUMBING THROUGH THE master bidding ledger, Lythlet tallied the sums at the frenetic pace all her years as a money-minder had trained in her. Meanwhile, Desil counted the jackpot they'd been given. It wasn't long before both arrived at the final sum: eighteen black valirs, which would satisfy Tucoras for a month and keep them fed and housed for the next few weeks.

Lythlet stared at the tiny mountain of coins in Desil's hands, astounded. *It used to take me six weeks at the hive-workshop to make that much, and I just made it all in less than an hour. To think we may make even more the next round.*

"I trust you are satisfied with the records," said the servant who'd given Lythlet the ledger, waiting with arms crossed over her slim chest. "Master Dothilos instructed us to provide you with the master bidding ledger. He seemed quite convinced that as a bookkeeper, you'd be keen on auditing the records yourself."

Lythlet returned the thick black book. "Everything seems to be in order." She was a master at detecting incongruences in an account—almost all the jobs she had worked at involved forging them, after all—but the bidding ledger was air-tight, the sums sensible and adding up to a jackpot even she was content with.

The servant gave a thin, knowing smile. "You will find that Master Dothilos is surprisingly honest. He doesn't skimp when it comes to paying his conquessors."

Despite all appearances of being a swindler and being quite assuredly a crook in the eyes of the white law, they left unsaid.

"What happened to the pair who fought before us?" she asked. "Taovi and Una."

The servant blinked. She lowered her eyes momentarily, and that pause told Lythlet she would hate to hear the answer.

"I strongly recommend you learn not to ask too many questions," the servant said at last, giving her a small smile.

Lythlet bowed her head, intuiting the wisdom of that. *I see the difficulty in finding conquessors capable of progressing beyond the first round.*

Lythlet and Desil left the arena, navigating its tunnels until they emerged into the wispily lit ruins of Inejio Setgad. Spectators loitered around, waving excitedly at the sight of them.

"Good show, good show! Never thought I'd witness someone scale the bamboo in my lifetime," said a plump fellow, his calloused palms rough to the touch as he shook their hands.

Lythlet gave a nervous smile, not knowing how to respond, too overwhelmed by the crowd.

"Made a pretty bit of change thanks to you two," said a redheaded woman, grinning appreciatively. To Desil, she added, "I saw a match of yours back at the brawlers' square. When I heard you were joining the conquessorial arena, I knew better than to bid against you."

More than half the praise referenced Desil's brawling days, and he received it graciously. But his smile grew more and more pinched as the references piled up, his discomfort becoming palpable.

It must be horrible being famous for something you're ashamed of. Feeling sorry for him and knowing he was too polite to extricate himself from the situation, Lythlet grabbed his hand and wriggled her way through the crowd, pulling him along. Some tried to stop them; she shooed them away like they were sewer rats.

Lythlet shook her head at the crowd they'd left behind. "No sense of personal space."

Desil chuckled, but he looked grateful.

"It only gets worse after this," warned a young Ederi fellow, joining their side with a wink.

Lythlet scowled, hoping he'd read the room and leave. She recognized him from her study of the audience during the prayer: he had been the spectator chatting with a bookie without placing any bets. His was a roughly cut brown face, scarred in spots all over, but there remained a certain charm to his ugliness; his bright brown eyes matched a jaunty smile.

He clapped them on their backs. "A well-fought match! Hell of an experience fighting in the arena, isn't it? The gates rolling up, your heart pounding like a battle-drum, and out pops the beast for your killing."

Desil tilted his head thoughtfully. "You've participated in a match before?"

The spectator bowed, his smile lengthening. "A long time ago. I'm Ilden Highvind—"

"The Ruffian!" Desil cried, shaking his hand. At Lythlet's vacant stare, he explained, "The Poet and the Ruffian were the last conquessors to make it all the way to the twelfth round two years ago or so. Shunvi Tanna and Ilden Highvind, the only two champions in many years."

"High praise indeed to be remembered after all this time," said Ilden modestly, even as he looked pleased with himself. "My fighting days are long behind me. It's entertaining enough being on the spectators' side of things, anyhow. Master Dothilos lets me spectate without paying the entrance fee. Say, if you two have the time to spare, there's a humble feast you're cordially invited to. I imagine you're not familiar with Inejio. I could show you around."

Desil glanced hopefully at Lythlet. Were she alone, she would have declined, all too keenly aware a lone woman mingling with strangers with so much coin hidden in her bag was asking to be held at knifepoint. But she afforded him a relenting nod; should things turn sour, Desil was more than capable of protecting them both.

He's fortunate he never has to worry about these things, she mused.

Ilden was well-versed in the twisting roads of Inejio Setgad, roads that had grown organically as a city demanded, not artificially designed into straight lines by fastidious city planners. As they went along a single path of the sprawling sector, he pointed out hidden landmarks: "That mossy little hill there holds the remnants of a keystone shrine. You can dig around and still find old prayer runes and warden effigies to this day. That big ol' bungalow there by the river? Apparently belonged to one of Setgad's founding families. Not too shabby, if you look past the wear and tear, but hardly compares to the estates up in Central now, aye?"

He paused, raising an eyebrow at a small, rising hill in the distance where a crowd congregated. Judging from their tailored clothing, they were highborn peers from Central. "Hmm. They're here again. Haven't the foggiest what those highborn folk are doing there—sightseers checking out the river below? No matter, let's keep to our path. Now, you see that road over there? Follow it all the way down, make a sharp right and keep to it, and it'll bring you to an alley behind a ginhouse in Northeast. An *excellent* ginhouse, I should say. Here we are!"

They stopped in front of a long gray building that might have been an inn centuries ago. Webs of ivy dotted with white flowers crept in tangles over crumbling stone walls. Shingles lay shattered on the ground, and the windows were cracked, but a warm, yellow light glowed from within.

Ilden opened the door, sending the hinge squealing. From inside drifted loud yells and laughter. He ushered them in and said, with great gusto in the vein of Master Dothilos, "Welcome, welcome! Come on through into the Homely Home of Inejio!"

They came to a large, shabby hall with a massive table. Half the ceiling was missing, the wall at the far end had been smashed through entirely, and rubble lay in tidied piles at the corners. Hive-lanterns on the table radiated brightly, the hardworking bees emitting a whirring noise. Long benches flanked the table, and sitting upon them were a few dozen people.

A dark-skinned Ederi woman came toward them, carrying a tray filled with a massive uncooked chicken. Her big brown eyes were warm and welcoming. "Was wondering when you'd show up, Ilden."

He lit up at her greeting. "Where's Shunvi?"

"Out the back, helping the boys pluck some smugglesleaf from the garden. He'll be in after checking on the bread." She nodded a sharp chin in Lythlet and Desil's direction. "Friends of yours?"

"Conquessors of the week, Naya," Ilden introduced, hands on their shoulders. "Lythlet Tairel by my left, Desil Demothi on my right. Naya here runs the Homely Home and keeps us stitched together with good food and good company. And it looks like she's on her way to roasting that chook."

"That I am," said Naya, hefting the tray in her hands. "Shunvi helped me carry the other three you bought to the kitchens earlier. Hold the fort down while I'm out back, all right?"

"Yes, ma'am," said Ilden, looking at her with bright-eyed devotion. "I'll have the table ready by the time you're back."

Once Naya had left, Ilden pulled Desil close, a solemn look on his face. "Listen, I genuinely can't wait to become good chums with you, but I just want you to know that I'm sweet on Naya, and if you use that ridiculously well-proportioned face of yours to woo her, I will actually eat you alive."

Desil burst out laughing. "She's all yours, mate."

"Ah, good," Ilden said, relieved. He nudged them forward. "Take a seat."

Lythlet swiftly snatched the spot by Desil's side. She was getting nervous with such a large crowd of strangers surrounding her. There were maybe thirty people in the room of all ages, of all races, of all shapes and sizes—now thirty-one, as a tall Oraanu man appeared at the end of the hall.

Ilden waved at him. "Shunvi, come meet today's conquessors!"

Ilden's friend came strolling down the hall, carrying a loaf of bread and a bottle of wine in his pale arms. He wore an eclectic mix of Oraanu and Ederi fashion—the modern Oraanu high fashion made its appearance in the black silk robe embroidered with yellow suns and flowers draped over his trim figure. He had left it untied, the usual sash on the waist missing, so that it revealed the Ederi sensibility underneath: the suspenders strapping down a low-necked shirt to his slim-fitting breeches, which disappeared into a pair of knee-length black boots. A long-stemmed wooden pipe was tied to one of his belt loops, bouncing off his thigh. He made the combination look effortlessly natural as he swept toward them with a slow grace rarely found in folk of the south.

"Well met," he said, red lips curling in stark contrast to his milk-white complexion. Shunvi's dark monolidded eyes were so sharply pointed by the edges it rendered his gaze intimidating, but they softened and crinkled as he smiled.

"You ought to have come spectate today, Shunvi," said Ilden, after introducing Lythlet and Desil. "An incredible match for a bunch of first-rounders. Say, which part of Setgad are you two from?"

"Southeast," Desil said.

"A-ha, fellow slumdogs!" Ilden paused and turned to her. "Wait, Lythlet, are you from there, too? I thought you'd be from elsewhere. You speak differently."

She blushed. "No, I'm from Southeast."

"My bad. Well, I was from there—Tresta Ward—but Shunvi and I have made a home for ourselves up in Northeast now."

Desil let out a low, wistful whistle. "From the slums to the Sector of Stone and Steel. Well done."

Setgadians often gloated to outsiders about the city-state's design, regurgitating a nebulously cited factoid that cartographers have always been fond of drawing Setgad on their maps of the greater Edesvena continent—there was something aesthetically pleasing in the way the outer boundaries of the city's four larger sectors came together to form a precise diamond.

Within the rhombus of the city, a total of five sectors were cut out: four of equal size, and the last a round, elevated platform occupying the center. The highborn peers and their descendants had the privilege of living there in Central Setgad, the Sector of the White Sun. Those of a lower class, still wealthy enough that the comfort of not just themselves but of their next generation was secured, found housing in Northeast, the Sector of Stone and Steel, and Northwest, the Sector of the Hawkers.

But all Lythlet had ever known were the southern sectors, renowned for their squalor and their neglect. Life thrived in Southwest and Southeast amidst outbreaks of rusted roofs and rotting shacks, always in full view of the Tower of Setgad gleaming in Central.

"Oh, my journey was bumpier than that," said Ilden. "A bad bout of the ekelenzi flu in my grandfather's youth left him hacking up his lungs for the rest of his life. Medicine used to cost no more than a penny back in the day, he'd always say, but with Governor Matheranos whittling away subsidies year by year, the health wards would demand more and more coin for the same thing, and he'd have to take out loans from scumbags to make ends meet. He passed away when I was young and left me more than a dozen usurers demanding their coins back to deal with. So I came down here to hide from them and the census scribes."

"You were unregistered?"

"Nearly everyone here is. The Homely Home's a safehouse for the unregistered, one of many scattered around Inejio. I lived here for a stint, and that's when I learned about the arena. Soon as I heard about the money to be won, I registered as a sole conquessor, then Master Dothilos paired me with Shunvi. I couldn't have been luckier, honestly. Best partner I could've hoped for."

Shunvi tossed him a hunk of bread by way of gratitude, and he heartily tore it open, stuffing his mouth with a tuft of soft, white crumb. Shunvi broke a couple more pieces off, passing them to Lythlet and Desil.

Between swallows, Ilden continued, "Thought he was the silliest git first time we met. He'd spend all his time doodling away in his conspiracy journal—"

"Not a conspiracy journal," Shunvi said blithely. "Just a log of thoughts and keen observations."

Ilden eyed him with a fond smile. "He fills up book after book with the nuttiest of ideas. Latest thing that's keeping him entertained is trying to crack the case on who the Phantom is."

With shameless confidence, Shunvi said, "The clues are falling into place, and it won't be long before I figure out their identity."

"His last three suspects all turned out to have rock-solid alibis," Ilden whispered to Lythlet and Desil. "And his current suspect is none other than Corio Brandolas."

Desil choked back laughter as Lythlet contemplated the notion that the controversial leader of the opposition party might spend his free time masquerading as the headline-grabbing thief who had captured the entire city's attention for the past couple of years.

"It makes perfect sense," Shunvi said, unbothered by Desil's incredulity in a manner that hinted he was used to it. "The man's a firebrand trying to tear down Governor Matheranos on the grounds of corruption, doing his utmost to build a platform as hero to the oppressed—what does he *not* have in common with the Phantom, who steals from the richest in our city? Many of whom are or have been affiliated with the United Setgad Party throughout Matheranos's two terms?"

Ilden was rolling his eyes, ready to retort, when Lythlet spoke up thoughtfully, piecing together the scant kernels of relevant trivia she'd picked up from gazette reports of the Phantom with Master Winaro's political rants during his readthrough of Corio Brandolas's book: "There was an unusually long break in the Phantom's heists in the months before and after the publication of *The Setgad Dilemma*. Perhaps Corio found his schedule too demanding to be carrying out heists then, if he truly is the Phantom."

Shunvi stared in silence at her, dumbfounded. It seemed as though this was the first time anyone had ever listened to his theories without condescension. A rapt light entered his eyes. "Precisely!"

"Oh." Ilden blanched. "Oh, no. Please don't encourage him. Good grief, he's never going to shut up now. Anyhow! What was I talking about? Ah, yes, Shunvi and I, when we first met! We spent a few rounds butting our heads against each other in the arena, but soon we grokked how the other fought, and we've been inseparable since. Once Shunvi and I made it through the twelfth round, we pooled our jackpots together and sprang for a life up in Northeast. I even had enough to cover all the debt I was running from."

Envy and admiration entwined within Lythlet as she pondered if this was where the road of a conquessor would lead her. *To a life in the north amongst the highborn? To a life free from humiliation, free from being hounded by loan sharks and violent employers?*

She leaned in, seizing the opportunity to pick their brains. "Could I ask: did the match-master ever give any hints to help you prepare for your matches?"

Ilden shook his head. "Master Dothilos would sooner give up his title than help you. It doesn't do him much good to be on your side, after all."

"But why wouldn't he?" said Desil, puzzled. "If he struggles to find quality conquessors of late, surely quietly helping them wouldn't hurt."

"If there's one thing you ought to know about Master Dothilos," Shunvi said, "it's that he's of good repute amongst those of ill repute. He won't cheat you on what he owes you, nor will he break his unspoken contract with the spectators. They trust their bids aren't being wasted on a manipulated puppet show. It's ill-advised to anger gambling folk, after all."

Lythlet nodded. "It also brings the match-master no benefit if too many bids are in our favor." At Desil's lost expression, she continued, "It's different from brawling. You earned the same amount of coin no matter how many people bid on or against you. But in conquessing, we receive a cut of only the bulls' bids—meaning those who've bet on us winning. The more people bid *against* us, the less Master Dothilos is obligated to give us. What works as an incentive for us is a drain on his own potential profit."

"Quite right," said Shunvi. "The master wants the spectators to see you struggling out in the arena, and if he can constantly put you on the brink of death, all the better for him. Come, Ilden, I believe you've forgotten something! Naya told me you were meant to set the table—"

Ilden rose from his seat with a yelp, turning to a rickety old cupboard and pulling out stacks of chipped porcelain tableware. Shunvi joined him, helping to arrange plates, cutleries, and teacups.

"And something extra for our celebrating conquessors," said Shunvi, handing Lythlet and Desil a short-stemmed goblet each. He uncorked the wine bottle he'd been carrying and held back one of his long silk sleeves as he reached for Desil's glass. "A customer of mine gifted this to me just the other day, and I thought to pass it on to Naya as a treat. But she wouldn't mind sharing with you two."

Desil covered the glass with his hand. "Many thanks, but I won't be drinking." He tapped the rosaries on his wrist.

"A man who keeps the vow of temperance," Shunvi said in admiration.

"*Profane not thy flesh, lest thy thoughts and words manifest in profanity*," recited Desil, hands pressed together and brought up to his forehead. With a sheepish smile, he continued, "Just a vow I keep for myself—no judgment upon those who partake otherwise, of course."

"I look forward to attending your inking ceremony one day," Shunvi said graciously, referring to the initiation trial monks and the particularly devout underwent, reciting scriptures from the Poetics by heart as sacred designs were hand tapped into their backs permanently. Moving on, he tilted the bottle toward Lythlet. "And you, madam?"

Lythlet waved her glass toward him impatiently, no future in liturgical rites awaiting her.

He laughed and filled it up. His smile widened further as she took a deep gulp and unleashed a loud, satisfied sigh. "Always makes me happy seeing someone enjoy a good drink."

Ilden prodded Lythlet's arm. "Fancy a guess at what Shunvi does now?"

She shied away from his touch, unused to strangers making contact. "He works at—no, he owns an eatery." She stopped, tilting her head thoughtfully. "Not an eatery. A teahouse."

They stared at her.

"How did you know I own a teahouse?" asked Shunvi, bemused, his dark eyes warm in the yellow hivelight.

"You won the final jackpot. You're far too rich to work at someone else's establishment, so you must have set up your own. You spoke just now of having customers of your own as well."

"But how did you know it was a teahouse?" pressed Ilden.

She pointed at Shunvi's meticulously laid out crockery. "He put his teacup on the right and that small fork right under it, the way a teahouse sets it for patrons who want to order some small dishes to go with their teapot. Eateries position it differently."

"I could simply be an enthusiast."

"You could," she agreed. "But you set your place so precisely without looking, as a man does when doing something rote, something he's done a thousand times, just to get the task done and over with to attend to more important matters. You even rotated your teacup in a full circle when you set it down, which tells me your teahouses are the high-end, traditional type catering to highbrow patrons."

Shunvi gave her an impressed look, eyes wide with growing fascination. "I own two teahouses, one in Northeast, the other in Central."

She bowed her head. "I know only because Desil works at a teahouse, and I've seen this arrangement many times. I read about the teacup rotation ritual from a chef's guide I once borrowed." *Borrowed*, she said; *stole*, she meant.

"She's just being modest," said Desil. "She can—how does that saying go? That Oratha proverb, something about letters and wax?"

"*To glimpse a letter's wax seal and unravel the message within?*" proposed Shunvi.

"That's the one. She's the sort who can manage that, sussing out patterns most ignore. Ilden, you saw how she was in the arena, figuring out what made the sentari grow and shrink."

"Lucky guesses," she said. "You only remember when I guess correctly and forget when I don't."

Ilden slammed his fist on the table. "I propose a game. You know *terrilus*?"

She jumped, taken aback by the noise. "The card game?"

"Ah, so you do know it. Now you have no excuse. Let's play it, you and Shunvi and I. Only I'm going to tell you upfront that Shunvi and I have rigged it in our favor. We know our deck thoroughly, and we've long identified little marks that give away its face. One of us holds the golden ship. It's up to you to guess who. As is customary, we must place a wager."

"No, thank you," she said, even as Ilden dug around in a drawer behind him, retrieving a deck of cards.

Ilden shuffled the cards briskly. "Come now. We don't intend to cheat your coin from you. We only want to see how savvy you truly are. This is a friendly match, and it needn't be much. A penny," he suggested.

"No."

"I won't refill your glass if you don't play." Shunvi tapped the rim of her glass with the wine bottle.

She gave a beleaguered sigh, leaning forward at last. "Fine."

He laughed incredulously. "I meant that as a joke."

Desil rolled his eyes as he dug through his own pocket to retrieve a coin, ready to front her wager. "She's a cheapskate who loves her drink."

"Can we play, too?" A boy peered at them from the table's edge. Alongside him popped up more heads, his brothers, equally blond and equally scruffy. "We haven't any coin, though."

Ilden raised an eyebrow at Lythlet. "Can they? I'm willing to exempt wee tots from bidding."

She nodded. "I don't need their wagers."

The boys whooped, and all waited in anticipation as Ilden dealt the cards into six piles.

Lythlet picked up her deck. An assortment of blues, greens, and yellows, ship wheels and thirteen-pointed suns and checkered moons met her eyes.

"No golden ship, yes?" Ilden checked.

"None indeed."

"Before we deal our cards, shall we up the stakes? How quickly can you determine who holds the golden ship? I'm willing to bet you won't find out at all." He tossed a golden-copper dumasi onto the table.

"And I bet you will find out, but not within the first four rounds." Shunvi threw a matching coin into the growing pile.

"Well?" Desil prompted, smiling at her encouragingly, fingers clasping a modest spira ready to be sown in the gambling pot.

All sense of modesty and shyness went flying out the window—

there was a puzzle at hand, and her mind came alive with the sheer excitement of potentially solving it. "I wager I'll answer your riddle before we deal the first round."

Desil laughed at her sudden brazenness, dropping his coin into the pile. "Nothing better than when she goes for broke!"

But Ilden shook his head. "Play it seriously. You can't know who holds the golden ship already."

"You're right. I haven't solved who has the golden ship, but I'm certain neither you nor Shunvi hold it. You've done this before, clearly, and it would be all too simple for either of you to have the card. But when you suggested we play a game, you slammed your fist upon the table noisily. Rudely," she added as an afterthought. "And I noticed those boys in the corner, one nudging the other two before you had even mentioned the name *terrilus,* as if it was a cue they were familiar with. Then they came to ask if they could join. I wouldn't be surprised if this is a common game you play with them to bully newcomers—"

"Not bully, no," interrupted Ilden.

"We are gentlemen at our cores, after all," added Shunvi.

"Well, he is," Ilden conceded. "You'd have to be much drunker to ever consider me one. We just want to have a bit of cheeky fun every now and then."

"Much cheek you have. But I am convinced one of the three holds the golden ship." She gestured to the blond brothers.

Neither Ilden nor Shunvi nor the boys spoke then, refusing to incriminate themselves, staring at her with varying levels of caution.

Desil leaned in. "Which of the three? The one who asked to join?"

Ilden waved at him to stay silent, to not pollute the game with his counsel, and Desil reluctantly withdrew.

Lythlet retreated into quiet contemplation, resting her cards face down on the table and burying her face into her hands so she could think without the distraction of so many eyes on her. At length, she raised her head. "May I request that he who does not hold the golden ship raise his hand?"

"What?" With an incredulous laugh, Ilden shot his hand into the air. He looked at all the other raised hands, at all the heads swiveling to confirm they were not alone. "You can't expect that to work, not if you genuinely believe us to be grifting masterminds."

Lythlet ignored him, staring at each of them in turn, then at last patting Desil on the back.

She held herself expressionless, but he knew what that meant. He burst into a bright grin. "You've figured it out, haven't you?"

Ilden scoffed in disbelief.

"Well, who is it?" asked Shunvi with an intrigued smile, ink-dark eyes twinkling with delight.

She pointed at the leftmost of the trio, a small, cherubic creature with lovely red cheeks.

"Him?" Ilden jabbed his finger at the boy. "Not the one next to him, the one who asked to join?"

Lythlet nodded firmly.

Ilden threw his hands up in the air. "I have no idea how you came to this conclusion, but—Alemandro, go on, reveal your cards."

A bashful smile, a splay of cards, and half-hidden beneath a pattern of red suns peeked the golden ship.

"You beauty!" Desil whooped, palms thumping the table. He leaned over to kiss the crown of Lythlet's head as the rest of the table burst into cries of excitement.

A laugh borne of pure relief sprung from Lythlet, but she quickly muted it as dozens of eyes returned from the golden card to her.

"All right, well done, you caught where I planted the ship," groaned Ilden. "Now tell me how you knew? You've mastered the gambler's face, and one can hardly guess what you're thinking at any time. Little Ale-boy raised his hand, too, at your strange question."

"Of course he did. Everyone did. No one in on your game would be foolish enough to out himself, especially not the boy." The boy looked sheepish, but Lythlet gave him a nod of solemn respect.

"Then why the question?"

"Because upon asking," she retraced her logic, "each and every one of you raised your hand and looked around, checking on one another. Except him. He alone looked straight at me, with no need to confirm the reactions of others. He knew what was in his hand, he knew he alone was lying."

"Well done," Desil crowed, scooping the coins close and splitting the pile with her. They clinked into her palm, and she cupped them protectively.

Ilden commiserated with the boys. "Better luck next time. Mind your acting, Alemandro."

"You did very well," assured Desil, ruffling the boy's hair as they scooted back to their corner.

"Your prize, madam." Shunvi held his silk sleeve back as he filled her glass with more blood-red wine. With an eager expression, he spoke, "Would you be willing to have a look at my notes on the Phantom one day? I simply must get your thoughts on whether you think I'm on the right track or not."

"Don't badger her with your silly conspiracy theories! Come, next up, a drinking game," Ilden proposed, rubbing his hands together slyly.

"That's enough, boys," said Naya, re-entering the hall with a heavy tray bearing one whole chicken, now roasted to a crispy golden-brown. A couple of boys and girls came in behind her, carrying the rest of the roasted chickens, small bowls of green smugglesleaf and Jhosper berries, and platters of freshly baked bread. She turned a kind eye toward Lythlet and Desil. "A good meal here will warm your bellies and get you ready to head back to wherever you call home. You're welcome to rest upstairs if you can find a spare cot."

"Thank you," Desil said, beaming. He stood and leaned over the table, passing her a knife to carve the chicken with. "How much do we owe for the food?"

"Nothing," she said sunnily.

"We couldn't take your food for free," Desil insisted.

She grinned, rapt with him. "Well, aren't you sweet? Don't you worry about it."

"The Homely Home grows a generous crop in its garden all year round, thanks to the baltascar pillars," Shunvi explained. "Besides that, Ilden and I like to chip in every so often to provide for their necessities."

"'Every so often' is much too modest for all these lads do for us. We'd be done for without them bankrolling us," Naya said with a laugh. Then she winked at Desil. "We haven't much down here but good cheer and spirit, and that means we have plenty to go around. You bring your handsome face around whenever you want."

Glaring at Desil with a hatred that could power a baltascar bulb or two, Ilden looked ready to fling his fork at him.

Desil seated himself nervously before an oblivious Naya, as Shunvi gently edged all potential projectiles beyond Ilden's reach.

CHAPTER SEVEN

TAZKAR, OF STONE AND EARTH

THE DATE OF their second match came racing in on the heels of Calaro, the final month of a bright spring.

"Your insignias, please," Master Dothilos said briskly, ready to jot their answers onto a scrap of parchment. "Who are your wardens?"

"Kilinor," Lythlet answered. She was sitting on the bench in the armory, fist clenched tightly around her polearm.

"Fits you perfectly," the match-master guffawed, stealing a look at her, pale blue eyes eerie in the light. "Daughter of the warden of grief and mourners."

"And hope," Desil added, juggling a bag of slingstones he'd picked from the arsenal.

"A nonsensical combination, if you ask me. Ought to be his twin sister governing over hope instead. Ashentoth's the one presiding over the dawning sun and revelry and all that hogwash—hope would be a logical extension. Yet we're meant to believe Kilinor, that gloomy little ghoul watching over the setting sun, is the one in charge of hope?"

"But it makes perfect sense," Desil argued. "Hope in times of happiness isn't hope—it's expectation. It's only when things are at their bleakest that you find hope unadulterated. That's what Kilinor and his setting sun is meant to remind you. As it says in the Poetics: '*for hope begotten under a dawning sun is a spineless creature. A dawning sun may bring relief that the terrors of the night have ended, but hark! a setting sun shall sunder thy joy, and ye of weak minds shall return to despair once more. But thou whose hope gestates under times of grief and lamentation, know that Kilinor stands before thee. Thy gray grief weighs upon him; he shall illuminate it. Thy woeful lamentations are heard; he shall quiet them. Let his gentle hand kindle in thyself the audacity to hope for better times even when the world strives against you.*'"

Lythlet never knew how he could recite all that off the top of his head and mean every single word, but she had always admired him for his conviction.

Evidently Master Dothilos did not share the same sentiment, staring at Desil contemptuously. "Pious, aren't you? Haven't heard a sermon like that in years. Can't say I care for the drivel from the Poetics."

"Do you doubt the existence of the divine unknown?" said Desil, a touch surprised. "Even after seeing Lythlet harness the powers of the cosmoscape in the last match?"

"I don't go to the extent of the divine-denier cults, if that's what you suspect. It's not the existence of the immortal divine I question, but rather their relevance to my life. Call me a heretic, but I'm of the mind that in their traversal of the universe, they discovered our little planet and decided to populate it with us silly mortals to entertain them. They then established an arbitrary infrastructure that allowed some of us to interface with the elemental meridian networks through bloodrights or divine touchstones—not so much as an act of mercy as written in the Poetics, but more out of perverse curiosity to see what we'd do with it—and they've since collectively decided to bugger off out of boredom and leave us to fend for ourselves.

"I'm not in the habit of wasting my precious time worshipping those who've abandoned me, so no, I care very little for the Poetics and the mysteries of the universe. Honestly, all that fickle old magic nonsense of saying the right prayer at the right time and place or whatnot doesn't appeal to me, and individual bloodright powers have never even been a possibility for us in this part of the world—but the solid science of tempering baltascar into reliably harnessing the powers of the meridian networks is the way of the future by my reckoning. We're on the cusp of a scientific revolution, mark my words, and the old ways will rot into obsolescence within generations."

Lythlet listened in quiet fascination and observed Desil visibly decide to hold his tongue—strong were his convictions, but stronger yet was his ability to discern when a discussion would only devolve into fruitless argument.

The awkward silence glanced off Master Dothilos, who glibly resumed his prior line of questioning, this time targeted toward Desil. "You're a ward of Tazkar, I recall from our interview—hah, of course you are. Big, handsome bloke who'd rather pray at a shrine than knuckle another bloody? I can almost picture you standing poised like a Tazkar effigy, hammer in one hand, *hista* flower in the other. But let me find a way to put some bite in your history. I don't want the spectators to come away thinking you're some spineless craven-heart. I wonder," he said, a strange glint entering his eyes, "if you've truly always kept to the path of peacekeeping in your heart, O darling of the brawlers' square."

Desil paled, lowering the bag of slingstones and looking away uncomfortably.

Rude of the match-master to provoke Desil, when he knows he's ashamed of his brawling past, Lythlet thought with ire. She intervened with a distraction: "Why do you want to know our insignias?"

"Today's match is dedicated to Tazkar. It'd be charming to mention Desil's a ward of his, wouldn't it? I'll keep your insignia in mind for the Kilinor match—if you last that long. Now, I'll be on my way. The match is about to begin, so head down to the gate."

He left without so much as a farewell.

As they made their way down the corridor, Lythlet nudged Desil's side. "You really have the Poetics down by heart."

He smiled sheepishly. "Not all of it. Only bits and pieces. Those verses just now were some I took comfort in recently."

Desil had always been devout, but he'd doubled his fervor the past year once he quit brawling. His shrine visits had multiplied, and she would stumble across him praying at home every so often, drawing the rite of forgiveness into the air. She had told him before she didn't think he needed to apologize so much for brawling, that surely the divine could make an exception for debt-ridden slumdogs with no other alternatives, but he hadn't agreed, nor had he stopped.

She gave a wan smile, then noticed the gray smudges staining his forehead. "You still have prayer ash on your face."

"Do I?" Desil rubbed his skin, checking his fingers for dusty residue. His *thank you* was knifed through by the match-master's booming voice.

"*—Desil Demothi and Lythlet Tairel!*"

Lythlet reached over with her sleeve to swipe at the last dot of ash, and with no more time to spare, they marched forth into the sun-bright arena, polearm and sword raised in the harsh light.

Steady, Lythlet told herself as her nerves came rearing back to life at the sight of the crowd. It had doubled from the last match, more seats filled than ever. Two men caught her gaze: Ilden and Shunvi seated up the back, waving at her eagerly. She returned a shy wave of her own.

"Today, in honor of Tazkar, He of Stone and Earth, they will embark upon a fight to the death—"

A cheer erupted from the stands. "*Hoo-rah, hoo-rah, hoo-rah!*"

"—and we shall watch these proud Ederi children prove their

quality!" The match-master's roaring voice gave way to silence, and he bowed his head, reciting the Prayer of the Peacemakers:

✳ *O Mighty Tazkar* ✳
Make me an instrument of thy discerning strength
To live ever-wielding the duality of mankind in the name of righteous
goodness

In the ensuing twenty-four seconds of silent prayer, Desil tapped the lone colored rune bead on his wrist, a jade-green one bearing Tazkar's insignia: a loop spiraling inwards before abruptly hooking out.

"Now, spectators," said the match-master into his speaking-trumpet, ending the silent prayer, "Desil Demothi, our champion brawler who graduated from the brawling square in search of greater challenges, is a ward of none other than Tazkar!"

As the match-master continued his spiel about Desil's brawling history, Lythlet turned to Desil with a wry look. "He's not even introducing me."

"He might not know what to say," Desil reasoned gently. "He doesn't know very much about you, after all."

"I suppose it's better to be ignored than be the subject of his puffery," she comforted herself.

Echoes of the match-master's baritone sliced her thoughts in half. "By the blood of your ancestors, do you proud Ederi children vow to salt the earth with the blood of the demons that once gave death upon your ancestors?"

"Witness me, upon the blood of my ancestors!" Desil roared, fingers crossed in oath-swearing.

Lythlet, knowing her response didn't matter, whiffled out a string of utterly incomprehensible gibberish, hands held forth and fingers crossed perfunctorily.

Either he hadn't heard her, or he simply didn't care, for Master Dothilos gave a grand smile, casting his eyes to the eager spectators surrounding him. "Then," he articulated precisely, elegantly, coyly, "shall we bring out the beast?"

The portcullis began to grind upwards.

Putting aside her wounded ego, Lythlet snapped to attention, trepidation rising in tempo with the gates.

Forth from the black abyss lolloped the strangest creature Lythlet could have ever imagined in all her years. It had an equine physique, but bloated abnormally with muscles. The thin layer of gray fur covering it didn't do much to soften its menacing appearance—especially not where two necks erupted from its form.

The long faces attached to either end were an exercise in wild contrast. One stared out through bulging black eyes that darted from one end of the arena to the other in fractions of a second. A thick glistening strand of yellow-tinged saliva dripped from its open maw.

The other head was turned a semicircle away, and it arced back to face them at a maddeningly slow pace. Solemn blue eyes were etched deep into an angled skull, glazed as though looking without seeing.

Then it met Lythlet's gaze, its blue eyes piercing her. Something unnatural speared her mind, and she choked, lungs seizing as frost spread through her skull like dye diffusing into water.

Fangs revealed at last, the beast trundled forward toward her.

Lythlet was pinned to her spot, ice searing her with pain so acute she couldn't move. Closer and closer, the strikingly blue eyes came.

"Run!" Desil cried, alarmed by her lack of reaction. He grabbed her by the arm, jerking her backward, and she tumbled to the ground, catching herself halfway—she could move again, the ice retracting its frigid claws from her skull.

Desil dragged her to her feet. "Quickly, before it comes!"

The audience was noisier than usual; excited cries rang out, outraged shouts amidst them.

"Yes, spectacular spectators," Master Dothilos's cloying voice echoed around the ring, chasing Lythlet as she kept a wide berth from the monster, "as the more seasoned amongst you may recognize, this is no easy fiend, especially not for mere second-rounders! Four years have passed since last this mighty beast served as a conquessor's foe, and we could not resist bringing it back for one more match! Will they have better luck than the previous conquessors? That is in their power to determine, under the guidance of Tazkar divine! Now for front-row spectators, I can see you fidgeting. Only the mildest of caution is necessary, my good gentlemen and gentleladies: no flame could possibly reach us at this height."

Flame?

As if in answer, the beast-head with bulging black eyes spread its jaws wide in their direction, and a volley of fire spiraled out toward them.

Lythlet screamed as she ducked to one side, Desil rolling to the other. A blast of solar orange consumed her vision, separating them. The heat singed her, but she had dodged in time to avoid the worst of it.

The fire died as the beast turned away to hack a glob of molten spit onto the sand.

On the other side, Desil was furiously patting sand onto his sleeve, which had caught fire. She took one step toward him, but fell backward, gasping as the heated sand nearly burned her foot through the flimsy soles of her worn-out boots.

The baltascar pendant pressed cool against her chest, and the temptation to forfeit rose.

But she pushed the thought out of her head. *Not yet. We may yet have a chance.*

"Desil," Lythlet hollered. She couldn't reach him, not with the burning sand dividing them.

He held up the blackened tatters of his sleeve in answer. "All's well."

No time to even breathe a sigh of relief, she said, "The other head, the calmer one with blue eyes, does something when you look into its eyes. Frost in your skull. I don't know what it is, but avoid its gaze."

"Oh-ho!" the match-master's amused voice rang through the arena. "Any sharp-eared spectator catch that? The ugly lass just shared a clever tidbit: never look into the eyes of the Sentinel. It normally takes a while for conquessors to suss out the source of the frost-burn in their heads. Much like the mind-melders amongst our Anvari ancestors who knew how to navigate the psychescape, the Sentinel knows how to pierce one's mind and maim from a distance."

"Sentinel," Lythlet repeated under her breath. *Is that what the beast is named?*

She kept her distance from Desil, gesturing at him to do the same. The burning sands between them threatened to melt the soles off their boots, and if fire were to be unleashed, the two of them clinging together in close quarters seemed decidedly unwise.

As if enjoying the scenery, the frost-burner's gaze slowly roved around the arena. Meanwhile, its wild fire-spitting brother was taking a break, drooling slavishly at empty air while twitching its head around every so often. Its gaze met hers, bulging black eyes threatening to pop free of their sockets, and she raised her spear in apprehension. Yet it made no move toward her, no attempt to burn her where she stood.

Lythlet frowned. She struggled to understand the beast, its lapse in ferocity, its dumb stillness. Unlike the sentari of last month, which had ripped around the arena unceasingly, this new monster was staying put where it stood.

It seems to be a beast of no brain, not even one between the two of them. And for that, she could not detect any patterns to decode.

As she studied the twain-beast, the slow, tedious swerves of the blue-eyed head finally narrowed onto Desil. Her mouth opened to issue a warning, but she shut it; he was already carefully avoiding its frost-burn gaze.

But then the beast galloped forth, suddenly awakened from its stupor, its long, skinny legs kicking up dust. Rather than the agony of frost unseen, the singe of fire was upon Desil as the manic head reared back and spat a flare at him.

He dashed away frantically, and the beast chased after him, lightning-quick, closing in on him until he swung himself up a bamboo ledge, climbing out of reach and continuing his escape along the ledges. Thankfully, the platforms were made of fire-resistant minstra bamboo.

How are we to kill a beast whose one head unleashes fire while the other drills ice into our skulls?

She furrowed her eyebrows, mind pacing through an avalanche of thoughts, trying to deduce a pattern. It had looked at her, yet it hadn't attacked—the fire-spitting one, at least. On the other hand, the frost-burner had been immediate in its pursuit once its eyes rested upon Desil.

Her eyes widened. The more she let her thoughts unravel, the more sense it made.

"The fire-breather is blind," she shouted. "Only the frost-burner sees, and it tells its brother what to do. Stay out of the frost-burner's sight. Two ledges above you will get you beyond its vision where it stands, so long as you squat low and press yourself against the wall."

Desil obeyed, leaping up a nearby ledge and jumping across to a higher one. From her end of the arena, she ran forward to make her own ascent, climbing the first platform off the ground, then haphazardly leaping to others as the frost-burner's gaze approached her, it having given up on Desil.

She crept from ledge to ledge, flattening herself whenever those blue eyes lingered near her. At last, she met Desil at one end of the wall, their ledges a mere arm-span apart.

"Now what? We know one's blind, the other not. But that's not enough to put out fires and melt ice-burn." Desil's words were broken up by panting, exhaustion from dodging and running creeping up on him.

"There's something else," she said. "It can't hear, neither of them. I was shouting at you, and not once did it react."

Desil considered that, slowly nodding. "You're right. We ought to pity the tragic beast. A single pair of seeing eyes, no working ears."

"It must rely on other senses then. It can't survive if it hasn't other things to compensate. Smell—no, not that I've noticed. Touch—touch?" She dragged her finger through the air, retracing her earlier route. "It paid me no mind until I started running for the ledges."

"You think it hunts its prey through vibrations in the ground? It must be very sensitive to detect that—we're not quite galumphing beasts."

She nodded. "That's why we've been up here for a minute and it hasn't moved a bit. It can't see us anymore, not from this angle, and we haven't been thumping our feet against the ground for it to follow." Her forehead creased. "But what can we do now, knowing all this? If we leave the ledges to fight it, it'll know where we are, and we're roasted on the spot. It's not possible to sneak up behind it."

"The yutrela," Desil suggested, nodding at the massive bamboo poles. "Channel the cosmoscape once again."

She calculated the possibilities. "No, the roots make the ground tremble when they sway. The beast will know something's happening around there. Master Dothilos mentioned they lack the fire resistance of minstra poles, so I'd rather not be stuck climbing one when the fire-breather unleashes a blast at it."

She buried her head in her hands, trying to steady her thoughts. A surefire way to victory was still beyond her, but she could feel it close, her fingertips scrabbling against a slippery edge. Nothing riled her up more than being so close to success and not claiming it.

Her head shot up, an idea taking hold.

"What is it?" The excitement in Desil's voice was palpable.

"That bag of slingstones you were playing with earlier in the armory. Did you take it?"

He withdrew the pouch from his pocket, lumps of jagged rocks outlined against the cloth.

"Lure the beast in," she commanded. She pointed at the stones tumbling out as he loosened the string choking the bag's neck. "One by one."

His expression wavered in confusion for a moment, but a smile brightened his face as he caught on. His large hand wrapped around one heavy rock, and he flung it to the ground. It skipped twice before coming to a stop.

The beast responded immediately, darting forth toward them blindly.

Desil flung another stone down, and the beast scrambled closer.

Another, and closer.

One more. And then—

Without a word, Lythlet jumped off the ledge, polearm pointed earthward. It rammed into the beast from above, her weight driving her spear deep, crushing bone and tearing flesh, a gush of blood spraying over her.

The beast lurched downwards, but she remained straddled on its broad back. Fire erupted as she wrenched the spear out only to plunge it in once more. It reared its head back at her, the heat coming dangerously close. She jerked aside, missing the flame by inches, strands of her hair singeing with a sour smell.

The beast buckled, then reared back wildly, an awful braying sound echoing from its throats. It tried to fling her off, but her spear was a foot deep in it, and her grip was stubborn. More and more scorching flames flew wildly around, and she ducked and dodged every single burst.

One hand securing the spear embedded in beast flesh, she ripped out the spare knife she had kept in her belt and drove it over and over into the fire-breather's neck. But the blade was too short, and though blackish blood spilled over her hand and coated her fingers, she succeeded only in enraging the beast further.

Then a long blade came down, cutting through the fire-breather's head until it rolled lifelessly on the ground.

Desil had leaped down from the ledge after her, sword at the ready. His arm was raised now, muscles rippling as it brought the blade down to the remaining neck.

But the frost-burner suddenly swerved with before-unseen fervor and met his gaze.

Fortune switched in that whiplash of a second.

A pained sound jerked from Desil's throat, sword tumbling from his grasp. He took a stumbling step backward, then froze like a man turned into a statue. He twitched, red veins staining the white of his eyes. He groaned in sheer, overwhelming agony.

A rumble of concerned cries from the spectators closed in on them.

Lythlet stared in horror. She ripped her pole free, slamming the bladed edge against the ice-burner, newfound strength helping her tear through flesh and bone. She hacked away, not strong enough to kill in a single strike as Desil had, but desperate savagery consumed her. A dozen times she drove the blade into it until at last the creature's head tumbled to the ground, white bone and frayed ligaments exposed, a spurt of blood tainting the yellow dust of the ground.

A cry of relief ripped from her, and she slammed her spear into the ground, burying the red-stained blade deep as she slumped against it.

Hoo-rah, hoo-rah, she heard, piercing the buzzing din in her ears. Clapping hands, stomping feet, *hoo-rah, hoo-rah.*

Her lungs struggled to keep up with her adrenaline, a dizziness threatening her body, but she managed to weave one coherent thought out.

Something's wrong.

The audience was cheering, but there was something strangely restrained to it. Half-hearted, somehow. She looked up. Some looked back at her.

Most looked beyond her.

She turned around warily.

Desil was slouched over on the ground, not moving.

"Well, well, well," Master Dothilos leered into his trumpet, voice slithering restlessly against her nerves.

Her boots stirred up dust as she tumbled to his side.

"Desil?" She rolled him over and grabbed his head.

His cheeks were freezing to the touch, and she recoiled in shock. The olivastro undertone of his skin had been blanched white. His breath steamed out in cold, wispy clouds, and his reddened eyes were lifeless.

She slapped him, calling his name.

He stared beyond her.

She fell back, horrified.

They had beheaded the beast twice over, and it lay in a fetid heap a pace away, blood leaking profusely onto the sanded ground. The frost consuming his mind and flesh should have melted when his gaze with the beast broke. If not then, then with the beast's death.

The spectator stands had fallen alarmingly silent.

Master Dothilos smiled at her, chin resting on palm. He raised his trumpet. "It dawns upon the ugly lass the match is far from over. I doubt even our savviest spectator knows what's happening—it's not a frequent sight, this here! I myself have only witnessed it once before, a long time ago."

Her spirits rose. The match-master knew what was wrong. He could rescue Desil.

But Master Dothilos only turned to the audience. "Spectators, now's the time to extend your bets! Will Lythlet Tairel solve this riddle, or will she forfeit? There's not a lot of time left before the thread of her dearest friend's life is severed. As Desil Demothi is unable to forfeit, hers alone will suffice, if she so chooses. Get your coins ready! My men are coming around to collect your bets."

Lythlet fought the urge to wrench her spear from the ground and throw it at him.

Calm down. She had no time to waste. She needed to think.

She patted Desil's back, begging into his ear, "Wake up." She tried to rub his cheeks to warm him, but the chill was unbearable on her bare skin.

Her frost-burn had ended the moment she broke her gaze with the Sentinel. What was different now?

I killed it before it broke its gaze, she realized. *Its spell, its bloodright, whatever it is—it did not finish on proper terms.*

"Tick tock, tick tock!" jeered the match-master.

A flash of anger, then an inward reminder she must stay calm.

On a hunch, she retrieved her spear and dove toward the beast-head rolled on its side. Those blue eyes were now powerless in death except to one. She plunged the tip into the eyeballs, gouging them out of their sockets, too desperate to mind the gore spilling over her hands. They were plum-sized in her grip, and she stabbed them each, popping them furiously until ichor ran all over her arms in a rapidly congealing mess. She looked back at Desil.

He remained still.

A sob escaped her unwillingly.

"Tick tock, tick tock! Time's running out to place your bets, spectacular spectators!"

She had no inkling what else to pursue. It had made sense to destroy the eyes as a last resort. What else could kill a beast and its poisoned sight, if not beheading it, if not blinding it?

"Tick tock, tick tock!" The spectators had joined in now.

Forfeit. I must forfeit and let the match-master save Desil before it's too late.

As she reached for the baltascar pendant, a miserable thought took hold, not for the first time, not for the last time: *slumdogs chasing their own tails in a circle.* No matter how hard she fought, no matter how clever she pushed herself to be, this was where all her efforts would lead her. She stared up at the audience, the racket of highborn peers, seeing clearer than ever they cared not a whit for either her or Desil. Her value existed only if she could entertain them; her survival mattered only if they could profit from it.

On the verge of tears, her eyes flashed to Ilden and Shunvi. But they only stared, confounded, faces screwed up in concern at Desil. Shunvi shook his head pityingly; he had no answer.

She tugged on the necklace, the cord almost coming undone. But she stopped.

Up in the stands, at the furthest row back, there was a primly dressed black-haired man. He was sitting by himself, waving conspicuously at her. He made gestures, small, too subtle for her to understand. He continued, miming stabbing downwards. He then thumped at the square of his breast, where his heart—

The eyes carry the curse, but it begins deeper within.

She flung away the collapsed eyeballs, tossed aside the bleeding head on her lap, and darted to the body of the slain beast. Approximating where its heart was, she buried the blade of her polearm into it.

Nothing happened. A faint, icy breath escaped Desil's lips, and his chest slowed. It wouldn't be long until his last breath.

Lythlet wrested her pole out, swapping it for the small knife. She had more finesse with it, ramming it into flesh, rending it asunder. Blood spilled freely over her hands, muddying her fingers with its stickiness, and she dug through rough muscle and hard bone with both hands. Her fingers wrapped around a small fluid-filled sac, and she squished it aside—and there was the heart, still squirming in its fleshy cavern.

She ripped it out, arteries pulsing violently in her grasp, and pierced it with the knife.

When Desil cried out, her own heart stopped, and her hands shook, grip loosening on the knife's hilt. Steeling her nerves, she tightened it once more, delivering another stab, pushing the blade in to the hilt, the tip peeking out the other side.

Desil heaved a huge breath, his broad chest swelling with life at last.

She threw aside the punctured organ, dashing to cradle him.

His cheek was still cool, but she could feel warm blood flushing beneath the skin.

"Lythlet," he groaned, "it feels like I've been pulled out of a winter lake—"

Bursting into tears, she buried her face into her hands soaked with blackish blood and congealing ichor.

He grabbed her to comfort her, but his words were drowned out by cheers from above. The spectators clapped their hands and stomped their feet, a cacophony of *hoo-rah! hoo-rah! hoo-rah!* pressing deep into her eardrums.

Above the clamor, Master Dothilos's silky voice rose, "Bravo! I'm sure most of us were expecting Lythlet Tairel to forfeit at any moment. A very perceptive strike indeed, searching for the beast's heart. I would have thought she'd give up after trying the anzura's eyes, but no! Spectators, would you look at her weeping now? Such heartwarming affection! My, my, my, could we be witnessing a childhood love finally taking root?"

Lythlet wiped her eyes on her sleeve, smearing blood onto it, and held up a hand to make a very rude gesture at the match-master.

Laughter bellowed from the spectators.

Master Dothilos called them for a bow, but she turned on her heels for the gate. The thought of bowing to any of these bastards infuriated her.

Desil gave a quick bob of his head to appease the crowd and trailed after her.

CHAPTER EIGHT

SOCK PUPPETS

A PLAIN-CLOTHED PHYSIC was waiting for them, and he handed over tubs of sweet-smelling salve to coat their burns. He tended to Desil first, checking him over for any permanent wounds the beast had rendered.

"Lythlet," Desil called weakly from where he lay. He held out his arm, sleeve pulled back to reveal a white bone rosary soaked red with blood. "If you could, please."

She took it to the basin in an alcove at the back, cupping water from a pail to rinse it. Her thumb drifted over the lone jade-green bead carved with Tazkar's spiraling insignia—an indicator that Desil was his ward—then over the remaining twelve ivory ones, each representing a different prayer.

Fellowship, she read the rune off one bead, *diligence,* another. *Justice* was one of the Four Grails—which of the Eight Virtues did it require? She scrunched her nose, digging deep into her memory.

Her head was a jumble of mismatched prayer formulas, knowledge dulled from much too infrequent shrine visits. The only thing she could confidently recite was that amongst the twelve, fellowship was considered the preeminent prayer—though she couldn't quite understand the theology behind it.

Surely honor or bravery would be of greatest importance? Why consider the vow of fellowship the most sacred to make to another after that of matrimony and filial piety?

Leaving the question unanswered, she set aside the cleansed bracelet, then rinsed the blood and ichor off herself. Towel in hand to wipe herself dry, she sat on the bench, eyeing the physic apprehensively. If he was servicing the conquessorial arena, she doubted he was accredited by the Einveldi Court. He was likely bound under the Eza instead.

The physic left after Lythlet declined an examination.

"You still have blood on your face." Desil took the towel from her and dabbed her swollen eyes gently.

"Thank you." She stared down the corridor leading to the arena. It appeared an entirely different world, one completely disconnected from her daily existence, and now, sitting in the dimness of the armory, she could not fathom how she'd survived out there. "I haven't cried so much in a long time. Last was the day I left your home when we were children."

Pity crept into his eyes. "I know."

A long, shuddering breath escaped her. "You're all right?"

"The physic says so, though I need plenty of rest."

"Good." She took the crimson-soaked towel back. *So much blood.* She spread it out and folded it neatly, needing something to occupy her hands.

"What's on your mind?" he pushed gently.

"I thought you were about to die," she said in a small voice.

He stroked her back. "You saved me before it was too late."

"But I didn't save you with my own skill," she said quietly, casting a glance at the door to ensure they were alone. "Someone helped me."

"Who?"

"A spectator. Black hair. Highborn, by the looks of it. He was sitting by himself in the furthest row, so no one noticed him showing me what to do."

An intrigued look on his face, Desil was about to ask something, but she gestured for him to shut his mouth as the door slid open.

In strode Master Dothilos and a servant, the latter carrying a tied pouch that clinked with every step.

"My champions!" Master Dothilos roared, clapping his hands as he approached. "A stunning show—by far the best I could have ever hoped for from raw debuts! Dare I admit my faith was faltering? I feared I'd be left carrying Desil's frozen corpse out of the arena! You've astounded the spectators, my dears, and I am proud to deliver your prize." He snapped his fingers, and the servant stepped forth, holding out the pouch.

Lythlet rose to accept it. Weighing it in her hand, she was amazed at the considerable bulk. She passed it on to Desil. "The master bidding ledger?"

Master Dothilos handed it to her with a knowing smile.

Lythlet flipped through it, checking the records of every bet placed that morning. Balancing and totaling the sums scrawled in smudged ink and small handwriting, she came to the same number as Desil, who was laboriously counting the coins under his breath.

"That's thirty-seven black valirs and twenty-seven... eight... nine dumasi—ah, no, thirty-eight full black valirs." He was nowhere near as quick with numbers as she was, but she respected his effort.

She sat down, overwhelmed. "We won thirty-eight black valirs?" A veritable fortune to a slumdog. It would take out yet another substantial chunk of Desil's debt to Tucoras.

"Quite a sum compared to the last jackpot, isn't it? Lythlet's stunt with the yutrela last month fetched generous attention. And after today's show, I imagine spectators are more eager than ever to witness your next round. That, my dears, is what we call growing a stable of loyal bidders."

"Well, that's good," she said, still stunned.

"It is indeed. I see a spark in the two of you I haven't seen in a while, not since the days of the Poet and the Ruffian. Ah, those two were truly majestic to behold. The crowds they drew! The Poet is a world-class beauty by any measure—there was this ineffable grace to the way he fought. Brought to mind all those heroes of yore the Oraanu poets speak of. Bit batty in the head though—one time, I had a peek into that ratty old journal he used to tote around between fights, and what did I see? *Things to Do Once I'm Governor of Setgad,* and top of the list was *normalize teahouse cats.* But perhaps that touch of oddness was why he got along so well with his partner, the Ruffian. A lovable rascal, that one. Used to complain to me about receiving second billing, but always in good fun. He knew how to throw caution to the wind and fight like a madman. But you two may yet surpass them given enough time—"

"I do not wish to continue," spoke Lythlet abruptly.

Both Master Dothilos and Desil turned to her in surprise.

"What's this now?" said Master Dothilos, eyebrows rising.

"As I spoke. I will withdraw."

Desil stared at her hesitantly, expression cloudy with confusion. But after belabored thought, he sat down by her side. "*We* will withdraw."

The match-master looked flabbergasted. "Are you not thrilled with your jackpot? Did I not just say you've done a remarkable job for second-rounders? That you have the potential for much more?"

"We won by the skin of our teeth today. I will not risk Desil's life once more, not for coin, and most certainly not for the entertainment of your spectators."

He considered her gravely, his blue eyes making her feel like an insect put under a shard of glass and a noontime sun. Disappointment flickered over his face, then he appraised her for a moment longer with—pity?

"Come," he said, demeanor softening. His hand was warm as

it rested on her shoulder. "I understand your decision. It was an emotional match, and your spirits were put to the test."

"I won't change my mind," she said, suspicious of his kindness.

"And I will respect that. But please, allow me this. I shall schedule your next match and send your invitations. Should you decline, I'll make no further contact with you. Your supporters will inevitably grumble, but I'll do my utmost to appease them. Simply allow me to send the invitation. Refuse then, if you will." He stuck out his hand amiably.

A sensible request. Lythlet shook it. "Very well."

"May I ask something?" he said. "How did you deduce the key to ending the anzura's frost-burn was to finish off the heart?"

She contemplated the benefits of being honest and found them lacking. "I could think of nothing else," she answered, meeting his gaze with a pretense of forlornness. "I tried the eyes, as that made the most sense. When that failed, I guessed I had to dig deeper to end it. Even if the eyes carried the curse, it must originate from deeper within. After all, our ancestors may have used their hands as conduits of their bloodrights, but those weren't the source of their divine blessings—their hearts were, the heavens hearing the most desperate cries of their hearts and answering their prayers. So I searched for the heart and struck gold."

If he were at all suspicious, Master Dothilos made no show of it, simply nodding in response. "Very keen of you. You've been nothing but surprise after surprise. Perhaps I ought to expect better of you from now on—should you choose to stay."

Despite knowing better, Lythlet found herself flushing with pride.

If only he didn't sound so genuine, she thought ruefully.

THE SPECTATORS DEPARTED the arena in slow streams, dissolving into the ruins of Inejio, fading into unseen paths that would take them home.

As Desil leaned on her for support, a few straggling spectators took the opportunity to squawk excitedly at them like seagulls.

"You won me a full white valir," a woman whooped, enthusiastically shaking Lythlet's hand.

"Had me worried toward the end there," said a young man strolling past, taking a brief moment to clap Lythlet's back. "Thought I was about to lose my week's pay in yet another bad bet till you stabbed the demon's heart. Bless you, lass."

She flushed even more, quietly noticing how so many were praising her in comparison to the last match. She whispered to Desil as they walked along at a pace he could handle, "I don't know how you cope with this. Being recognized and praised by strangers. But I suppose you're used to it from your brawling days."

"Somewhat," Desil dismissed half-heartedly. "But seeing how well you're doing, you ought to get used to it."

She shook her head with the slightest pinch of regret. "No more after this."

"You're certain?"

She nodded. "I only cared for the coin to begin with. It gave me hope we could repay your debt to Tucoras sooner. But now I've come to count the cost, and I'm not willing to pay it with your life." She paused, noticing a spectator veering toward them. She jabbed her elbow into Desil. "It's him—the one who helped me."

The black-haired man was tall in stature, clad in neat clothing befitting those of considerable status. Nothing ostentatious, but the tailored cut of his cloak gave away his wealth, as did the slick pomaded parting of his thick hair.

They stood at attention and bowed as he drew near.

"I owe you my life, sir," Desil said.

"And my gratitude for saving my friend's life," Lythlet added, head tilted to the ground, hand pressed to her heart.

The spectator waved at them to rise. "Please, not at all. I'm glad to see you're both well."

"To whom do we owe our gratitude?" Desil asked.

"I am Saevem Arthil." The spectator bowed slightly, tapping his heart in return. "The anzura was a seasonal menace to my hometown Trinevalta. They're tricky beasts, and I knew you wouldn't figure out what to do in time, so I felt compelled to help."

Lythlet now noticed Saevem had the slightest accent that reared its head at certain words, curling them into something more genteel than the usual Setgadian-flavored Vasté. "I hope we helped you win your bet, Master Arthil."

Master Arthil blinked. "Pardon?"

"You bet on us, didn't you? That's why you helped us win."

"Oh, I placed no bets today," he said, looking as if the idea had never crossed his mind.

A non-gambling spectator? She hadn't expected this, but then again, it wasn't as if he were the first. Ilden, and likely Shunvi, was purely spectating with no coin on the line.

"Well, Master Arthil, if you ever have need of us, let us know and we'll repay our debt to you," she said.

"Come to The Steam Dragon down in Southeast, and I'll treat you to a fine meal," said Desil.

Master Arthil raised a brow, a glint coming into his eyes. "I may take you up on that. Will you two be continuing in the arena?"

She shook her head immediately.

"We've decided to decline our next invitation when it arrives," Desil said, an apologetic look on his face.

Master Arthil's smile faded into disappointment. "So soon?"

Was he hoping to start bidding on us from the next round onwards?

"It's much too risky for us to continue," she explained. "If we get another wild beast with a trick I cannot solve, I cannot hope for another spectator to pity us enough to help."

"I understand," Master Arthil said, sympathy and disappointment mingling in his gaze. "I'd sincerely love to see you two continue as conquessors, but I wish you the best in your endeavors." He bowed and took his leave, carving his own path out of the ruins.

As Lythlet and Desil trudged along, her hefting his weight on her shoulder, Desil asked, "Say, what *is* the beast we fought called? Master Dothilos and Master Arthil have called it both an anzura and a Sentinel."

"Allow me," Ilden said, springing toward them from one of the arena's many exits, cloak half slipping from his shoulders. His brooch had been too carelessly clasped, he himself too unbothered to fix it. Beside him, Shunvi walked tall, cloak impeccably billowing from his slender build. "The beast is named anzura as a whole. But the frost-burning head is the Sentinel—"

Ah, of course, since it sees.

"—while the one that spits fire is called the Reaver. I heard some spectators say as much. Good match, by the way. Having trouble walking there, Demothi?"

"Just a little weary from the match. The physic advised I rest before eating."

"Let's give Lythlet a break. Lean on Ilden and me," said Shunvi, offering his shoulder. As he neared her to guide Desil's arm over his neck, he gave her a strange, nervous look, though she couldn't fathom why.

Ilden went to Desil's other side, supporting his weight. "Oof, you're a heavy one. Awful sorry for not being much help just now, Lythlet. Shunvi and I had never faced an anzura, so we knew nothing of the heart. You seemed like you were on the brink of tears when you looked at me, and Twelve Divine, I am not good at handling crying girls."

Lythlet gave a muffled grunt to dismiss his apology, deeply embarrassed.

"Come," Shunvi gently suggested, taking notice of her discomfort, "let's celebrate at the Homely Home."

ILDEN AND SHUNVI bickered the whole way to the Homely Home, pausing only for Desil to greet Naya in the hall, then hoisting him up the stairs to rest in one of the spare rooms. Flimsy old sleeping cots waited to be used, and children chattered loudly in the corner, playing with dolls desperately in need of stuffing.

Desil exhaled as he curled on a cot, closing his eyes.

Ilden smacked his bottom. "Piece yourself together, Demothi. We've a proper feast waiting downstairs. You'll be sorry to miss out on it."

"Come only when you're rested," said Shunvi, shaking his head. "Don't let Ilden nag you into worse health."

"Nag!" Ilden huffed.

Desil glanced tiredly around. "It seems so empty here today. Last time we came here, we couldn't find a single spare cot to rest on. Even the hall downstairs seems emptier today."

"Haven't heard the news, have you?" said Ilden. "Remember that hill where highborn peers were gathered?"

Lythlet knew what he spoke of, but Desil stared with a vacant expression—a month was long enough for a trivial moment to evaporate from his memory.

"On a hill not too far from the river," went on Ilden in vain, Desil's face not registering the slightest recognition. "Oh, never you mind, I'd probably forget if I were you, too. Anyway, it turns out they're folk from Central who'd come down prospecting for land to develop."

"I'd always wondered why they never bothered doing so earlier," said Shunvi as he puffed up a pillow for Desil. "There's so much land wasted here in Inejio that could be turned into something worthwhile, you'd reckon efforts to reclaim the space would've happened ages ago. But times are a-changing, at long last."

"Now there's a plan to revive the area, section by section, turning it into a sector fit for even the highborn," said Ilden. "Their first stage is a cluster of grand residential flats along the river."

"But what about the unregistered?" Desil said. "Surely that means they can't seek refuge here anymore?"

"That was our fear, too," Shunvi said, "but there was an announcement."

"The highborn need labor for their building efforts, don't they?" Ilden said. "So the master-builder's put out the call for workers, and they've allowed the unregistered to join. A very rare opportunity that doesn't bar them. They even offer a salary of— brace yourselves—a whole black valir for a fortnight of labor! I know this seems meager now that you've been exposed to the riches of your jackpots, but—"

"It's still a fortune to us," cut in Lythlet quietly. "That is indeed very generous pay."

"But that's not all. Westiro Asa, the master-builder, has issued a bold promise: whoever joins now and continues until the end of the building efforts will be granted an additional bonus."

"What?"

"It's no secret most of the unregistered fell off the census because of petty debts they had to run from. But should you be one of the lucky early birds committing themselves to the master-builder's cause, they promise to entirely erase your debt on your behalf upon completion of the flats, which they've projected to be two years out."

"That's incredible," said Desil, eyes widening. "The unregistered could reenter the city overground and live a free life again."

Shunvi nodded. "Nearly every unregistered we know from every safehouse in Inejio has joined the building crew. They're glad for the opportunity, as you can imagine."

Lythlet listened skeptically. *It seems too good to be true.* "Can these Central folk keep their promises, though?"

"I would imagine easily so. The profit they'd make from the sale of a single flat will be more than enough to cover the debt of dozens."

"These life-ruining debts of the unregistered are minuscule in the eyes of the wealthy," said Ilden, obliviously preaching to two debt-ridden slumdogs. "I myself was running from a debt of no more than six white valirs, a sum those fat coin purses up in Central could pay without blinking. And word travels of the master-builder having members of the United Setgad Party as the primary investment sources of the project. Certainly, such well-acquainted persons would have the funds to pay out their promises."

"What about you, Naya?" said Desil as she appeared in the doorway, blanket in hand. "Are you holding up well, looking after all these children on your own while their guardians are off at the construction?"

"As well as I can," she said. "At the very least, all's bright on the financial front. Between the folks here finally having some dependable income to spare and Shunvi and Ilden paying for the Homely Home's necessities, we're well taken care of nowadays. But if you ever find time on your hands, I'd be glad to have you help watch over the little ones."

"Absolutely!" he said sunnily. He'd always been a gem at handling children, Lythlet had seen time and time again.

She beamed, utterly unaware of the man observing this interaction with growing dismay.

The moment she left for the dining hall, Ilden slugged Desil in the face with a pillow. "Bastard!"

"Calm down, I'm not after her," Desil insisted.

"I know, I know." Ilden sighed, smoothing the pillow out. "And even if you were, if Naya chooses you, then it's only fair I respect her choice."

"That's very mature of you," Desil admired.

"I didn't mean a word of it!" Ilden snapped, flicking Desil's nose. "That's the sort of horseshit Shunvi says to be a gentleman. I *will* eat your face if Naya ever chooses you, and I'll eat it with relish!"

Lythlet slapped Ilden's hands away. "You feral little man," she said crossly. She brushed Desil's forehead, sorry to see him in such a ragged state. "He was seconds from death! What's wrong with you?"

"That'll take a whole day to answer," Shunvi replied, guiding Ilden away from Desil. He gestured at the children playing in the corner of the room. "We'll get them out of here so you can rest."

But Desil shook his head.

"Are you sure? They're making a ruckus."

"Leave them be," he said. "I could use some company, anyway."

"I'll stay with you," Lythlet said.

"Nonsense. You must be starving. I'll be fine. Shunvi, can I leave my friend in your care? I'd ask Ilden, but he won't stop glaring at me with what quite frankly looks like a cannibalistic gleam in his eye."

"Most certainly," Shunvi said, flashing Lythlet a winsome smile. "I've brought another bottle of wine today, if that entices you. This one's a foreign treat—brewed from sugary glutinous rice and fermented by the fine folk in the longhouses down in Anatera. The merchant assured me the pedigree would astound us all." He suddenly flushed red at the ears, and asked, with unexpected shyness, "I've also brought along my journal today. If you're not too weary from the fight, I would love to get your thoughts on the case I've built around the Phantom."

Lythlet gave a hesitant glance at Desil.

"Go on now, you lush!" He shooed her with a laugh.

She sheepishly followed Shunvi out. But right as he made to close the door behind her, she turned to see Desil sitting up in the cot, calling the children over as he bafflingly pulled a spare pair of socks from his satchel over his fists. One of them was Alemandro, the scruffy little blond boy, and Desil playfully bopped him on the nose with his socked hand, making him giggle.

Looking at all those unregistered children, she was reminded of what she was forfeiting. All the riches of conquessorship, the only chance for her to lift herself out of poverty and escape debt so quickly, bypassing the indignity of becoming unregistered, stateless in the eyes of the white law. Outside the arena, she'd never get another opportunity like this again.

But, she thought as she watched Desil through the shrinking gap of the closing door, realizing he was sacrificing his chance to rest to put on a puppet show for the children with his socks, *I will give it up for him.*

CHAPTER NINE

FATHER

THE RICKETY STAIRS of the Homely Home creaked as Shunvi and Ilden led Lythlet down to the dining hall. The table was filling up, empty spots on the benches being plucked up as the seconds went by. Folk continued streaming into the hall, a thicker crowd than she had witnessed the last time.

"A couple of other safehavens are joining us for lunch," Shunvi explained, ushering her to the bench, "so the table will be a pinch crowded today. Naya likes having these big gatherings every so often." He gestured for her to take a seat.

But Lythlet halted, all intelligent thought vanishing. Amongst the unregistered shuffling into the room, she had just spotted a face she hadn't seen in years. A face she had never expected to see here of all places.

"Father?" Her gasp was quiet, veering toward inaudible.

Shunvi startled, following her gaze to a rail-thin middle-aged man gently guiding a woman into the hall.

Flecks of gray were starting to stain his temples, the single indicator it had been years since last they met. But all else remained the same, Father's waiflike figure still all angles and bones jutting from ill-fitting clothes, his skin patchy in spots, his nose permanently red from his awful habit of rubbing it whenever he was nervous. Beside him was Mother, as skeletal as ever, hair unwashed and stringy but tied into the neatest ponytail Father could manage. Father's arm was around her waist protectively as he guided her through the hall.

Ilden thumped her back. "What are you standing around for?"

She ignored him, pushing him aside.

"What's that for?" cried Ilden, shutting up when Shunvi grabbed him aside, a finger pressed to his lips.

She left them behind, forgetting their existence as she approached the couple she was loath to believe was her parents.

Father looked up just then, and it took a moment for him to recognize her. His eyes turned wide, abnormally large in his frail, bone-edged build, and his steps slowed.

It *was* him, she realized with a sinking heart. She was rooted to her spot, casting a quick glance at Mother, whose bowed head gave nothing away.

"Today?" she mouthed soundlessly. A quick shorthand they had developed in her childhood to ask if Mother was well enough for Lythlet to spend time with her.

"Not today," he mouthed back, a firm shake of his head.

She pinched her lips and stepped aside so he could lead Mother upstairs to the cots. Guilt racked her at the sight of several long scars running along Mother's arms, tattletale signs of those troubled days when flesh had become an unbearable cage for her spirit. New scars had been added to the collection, scars that hadn't been there when last Lythlet had visited them.

She had bidden farewell to her home when she was fifteen, knowing her continued presence would only burden them in a way they couldn't cope with financially. She should've returned during the Harvest Holidays to pay her respects, but as the years had gone on, she had never been able to muster the courage to face her family. Whenever she imagined telling them the truth of how poorly her life had wound up, that little voice urging her to visit her parents would be smothered like a candle-flame in a hurricane.

As they vanished upstairs, her mind reeled with a slaughter of questions, eventually settling on the biggest one: were they unregistered?

Dread at the most probable answer rose.

Father soon returned, limping down the stairs. He paused when he reached her, and they loitered by the banisters in silence. He seemed reluctant to meet her eyes.

"Could we talk?" she said, fumbling with her sleeves.

He nodded, and it depressed her to see how hesitant he was.

They departed the dining hall to the Homely Home's western skywell courtyard, deserted at that moment with all inhabitants inside clamoring for food at the feasting table. A single lonely tree grew in the middle of the gray-white courtyard, centuries old with long hanging branches casting grim shadows about.

She sat herself on the stone steps, tucking her legs in primly.

Father crouched beside her to sit, resembling a willow weed bending to the wind, adopting the same posture—legs tucked in tight, as if afraid of touching her.

She swallowed hard, trying to calm herself. The moment did not seem real, so far from all the ways she'd imagined one day reuniting with her parents, a twisted simulacrum of the homecoming she'd hoped to perform one day when her fortunes had rallied. Her surroundings were smudged like a watercolor remastering of reality done in the dreamscape, the light of the baltascar-laden pillars blanching the canvas a dull white.

They said nothing, and that was nothing unusual for them. The courtyard seemed to close in on them, choking into quietness.

Then Father spoke. His voice was a quiet rumble that would have been lost in a crowd, but it was enough then to shatter the familiar silence. "You've grown taller."

"I have." She had taken after his tall, reedy frame in the years since leaving home.

They fell back into a silence as uneasy as it was familiar.

She stared at their knees, a frigid six inches yawning like a canyon between them. She imagined a feeble tightrope stretching between their kneecaps, thin as a spider's leg. That was all their relationship had ever been through her life, a fragile connection built on their shared blood and nothing more.

One of the books Lythlet had stolen in her youth had been a treatise on modern artistic techniques written by a scholar of the inks. Much of it had been too dense for her young mind to understand, but amidst the slurry of techniques like tenebrism and impasto layering, one thing she had grasped was the concept of negative space. That in any artistic composition, a key element was in the absence of things, a story to be told in the undone.

She imagined then a canvas dominated by negative space, that rigid black tightrope the sole presence on it, her waiting at one end, Father at the other, and everything else, any possible words, tumbling over the sides into the white abyss.

"Why are you here?" she gathered the courage to ask, forcing herself onto the tightrope. "Are you unregistered?"

Father stared at his trousers for a long moment, as if its threadbare nature fascinated him. Her questions were teetering into the abyss, saved only when he finally gave a brisk, reluctant nod.

Her heart sank, worst fears confirmed. She fought the urge to cry by examining the mismatched patches she'd sewn into the knees of her trousers.

"Are you, too?" His question came feebly, creeping along the tightrope toward her.

"No. I know some people here, that's all. Desil's resting upstairs."

She didn't dare turn to look at him, but she heard Father heave a soft sigh of relief.

Silence fell. The tightrope lengthened between them, and she gritted her teeth, urging herself to attempt it once more.

"What happened? How long have you been unregistered for?"

"For about a year now," he admitted, shame etched into every syllable. "Mother had a bad day. I almost didn't get her to the health ward in time." His voice choked, and he buried his head in his arms.

Lythlet closed her eyes, recalling those long scars on Mother's arms. "Is she better now?"

"Still has her moments. You know. But nothing as bad as then. We're staying in a safehaven not too far from here. Place used to belong to the first governor of Setgad, that Hemharrow fellow who's Governor Matheranos's ancestor. I think a lot of these folk running safehavens have a sense of humor, 'cause ours has a long and funny name."

"What happened to our house?" Lythlet asked, sneaking a glance at him.

His half-hearted rambling faded into a grimace. "Lost it to a usurer. The health ward fees to keep Mother alive drove us into debt."

Lythlet fought the urge to bury her face in her hands.

She despised that ramshackle hovel she once called home; simply conjuring the mere memory of it would turn her claustrophobic. As ash-hued and unimpressive as a dust rag, sunlight had always made it even more pathetic, no veil of darkness hiding its shortcomings. Inside fared little better: small, dismally gray, awash in shadows, tilting in a way that threatened complete collapse. Worst of all had been the pungent rotting floorboards, the sour earthy smell defining her childhood. Yet knowing all that was gone not because her family had graduated to better things but had spiraled further into poverty was miserable knowledge to bear.

"But I have some good news," Father said into her silence. "I've signed up for the construction happening down at the riverbanks— heard about it? I start tomorrow. Sounds like it's got real promise. As long as I stick it out for two years, they'll pay off our debt, they say."

Lythlet could not muster a smile in response. Father was no longer young. The thought of this willow weed of a man having to perform hard labor for the hope of returning to a proper life aboveground made the weight of her unfulfilled filial piety feel like a cast-iron chain upon her neck.

"Tell me how much you need," she said, facing him properly for the first time since entering that courtyard. "I'll get it for you."

Father's dark eyes flickered at her. "Are you doing well?"

The skepticism in his voice stung.

"Not quite," she faltered. "I have debt of my own to repay."

A worried look crossed Father's eyes. She regretted her honesty and turned away to her knees.

"What kind of debt?"

"Also to a usurer," she muttered. "Also because of health ward fees."

It was uncanny how similar her parents' story was to hers. *Perhaps our bloodline is simply destined for debt and despair*, she thought bitterly.

"Then don't worry about Mother and me," Father said, feigning a smile that only lasted a breath, like the last gasp of sunlight before night conquered the sky. "Take care of yourself instead. Maybe I'll make enough from the flats to help you pay off your debt."

She wanted to argue, but there was no argument to be made. Two members of the Tairel bloodline were seated beside one another, one wishing to fulfill his paternal duty and save his daughter, the other wishing to fulfill her filial piety and save her father—neither having any capacity to do so.

She looked at him and his pitiful visage, and felt a rope of many strings twisting inside her: regret, contrition, and love, a love she had never been able to voice before for fear of being ignored. She said awkwardly, "I'm sorry you've been through so much while I was gone."

He looked surprised at her words. After a moment, he replied,

"I'm sorry for you, too. I suppose that's why you never came to visit us."

They turned away from each other, ending that uncomfortable prolonged gaze.

Once again, negative space dominated the thin black tightrope.

CHAPTER TEN

THE FIRST LESSON

LYTHLET HAD FOUGHT in it twice, but the arena seemed so foreign from the spectator seats. She was used to the texture of the sanded grounds, the sensation of being dwarfed by yutrela poles looming overhead, the burst of baltascar light that washed the world white at some angles.

The seats were a more mundane environment, however. Another duo of conquessors were practicing in the arena, leaping along the ledges, swinging axes and blades.

It was easy to dissociate oneself from the violence from so far above, she realized. To watch without understanding, without sympathy for those below, the way she could witness a spider devouring an ant tangled in its web and not give a damn.

Her thoughts were interrupted by a shadow looming over her. Dread started in her gut.

"I thought it was you," Master Dothilos greeted her cheerfully. "Come to practice, have you? Let those two down there wrap things up first. They just won their first match a fortnight ago— not too shabby a performance, I'll say. They don't quite hold a candle to you and Desil, but I'm glad my spring roster is shaping up with some promising talent. I wonder if any of you will last until the twelfth round."

Competition for the spectators' attention, she mused, only to remind herself she would be taking herself out of the running soon.

"I came only to watch." She tensed as he sat down by her, drawing her shoulders up. Even with her gaze pinned straight ahead, she could feel him carefully examining her.

Her fears only heightened as he opened his mouth. "What happened to your boots?"

The question took her aback. She followed the line of his finger and examined her feet.

Her boots were an old pair, a pinch too tight, the leather scratched and cracked, stained no matter how hard she cleaned them, and water leaked through on rainy days. But the soles were in particularly bad shape. The surface had flattened somewhat, the hobnails sunken in, molded into awkward, unnatural lumps.

"They must have melted during the last match," she realized, rubbing the malformed hobnails. "The sand was hot where the beast breathed fire."

"It'd be dangerous for you to run around in them," said the match-master. "You'd slip and tumble without traction. Get a new pair before the next match."

These boots were awful, but they were still sturdy enough for daily wear in the slums; it would only make sense to spend coin on a new pair if she were to continue conquessing.

Silence resumed over them.

She was usually one to enjoy silence, the peace and tranquility it offered, but this was an entirely different beast. This was a silence that set her on edge, making her want to shuffle a few seats away from the match-master. He still had something to say to her, she could tell as much, but he seemed to be first calculating the wisdom of saying it.

The tension stretched further between them, like a shadow elongating under the dusking sun, until at last he spoke: "It's pronounced te-mer-i-ty."

She had not expected that. "What?"

"Te-mer-i-ty. At your interview, you said tem-*er*-i-ty. The emphasis was wrong."

"Oh," she said, both baffled and embarrassed. "Well, thank you."

"You're welcome." Master Dothilos paused. "I've deduced the reason why you occasionally say unusually archaic things and mispronounce words is because you've picked them out of books."

She started, brow rising. "How did you know?"

"How else could a slumdog know a word like 'temerity'? You used it correctly, so you know the meaning and the right context for it. But you don't know how to say it right, meaning you've never actually heard anyone say it with your own ears."

She blushed. "I suppose I should stop using words like that."

"Nonsense. Why stop? Ambitious words for an ambitious soul. Leave the average ones to average folk. But I've been wondering how a penniless child might've laid her hands on a book to begin with. Multiple books, if I guess correctly. Those are luxuries for the wealthy, after all, and I doubt you had the valir to spare on a book growing up."

Something was odd about his tone. Ordinarily, he would've said something like that with a sneer so contemptuous it turned audible, malice laced between his jagged words. But he said all this simply, as if fueled only by genuine curiosity. When she turned to him, she expected the devious gleam in his eyes, the mocking curl of his lips, the provocative upturn of his nose, yet he was looking at her levelly, clear of all mischief.

She recoiled.

"What's the matter?"

"I've never seen you look so benign before."

He nodded in understanding, a small smile appearing. "I am one man in the arena, another out of it. We must all put on a show in life, and I doubly so in the arena. I must be Master Dothilos to spectators and conquessors alike—arrogant, bombastic, yet utterly magnetic. With new conquessors, I choose to be particularly obnoxious to set the tone for our relationship going forward. They mustn't be under the impression I'm friendly to their cause, after all—they're signing up for a dangerous game, and I need them to know it, even if that means becoming an unbearably antagonistic caricature. But there's no match now, so I come to you as myself. Enough about me. How did you ever get those books?"

She remained wary of him, but the truth was a tale buried so deep in her childhood, it had been rendered harmless by time. "I stole them."

He brightened. "Did you now? How many?"

"Five." *Times ten.* A little caution still seemed prudent.

"What type of books?"

"One was a guide for chefs, from which I learned about cuisines from far-off lands. Another was a book on financial literacy."

"And thus began your career as a bookkeeper. What about the remaining three?"

"Storybooks."

"Ah, legends and myths and all that? What was your favorite?"

"Atena the Huntress," answered Lythlet, an uninhibited, childlike smile growing. She had treasured every page stolen in her youth, because they were hers, some of the very few things she could claim possession of. She would turn them obsessively, running her fingers along every word even without the slightest inkling of its pronunciation.

"Ah, Desil mentioned you built trigger traps when you were young. Modeling yourself after your childhood icon, were you? Any others?"

"Rentavos the Gentleman Thief by Yoshifero Vidana," she went on, eagerness unbridling her tongue. "I stole an illustrated omnibus edition of all the adventures Master Vidana had written to date, and it was wonderful. Rentavos's escapades in Bizarre-Naeveri were my favorite. I stayed up all night with a hive-lantern by my side just to see how he could possibly infiltrate Consul Montevinzi's court and solve the mystery of Beracani's murder in nine hours. I still have his creed memorized by heart—*to be noble of mind and honest of heart, and to stand evermore on the side of justice!*"

Master Dothilos laughed, charmed by her excitement. "Only you could recite that without an ounce of shame."

"Is there something to be ashamed of?" she asked, confused.

He smiled fondly at her. "Perhaps not for you. I'm noticing a trend here—you like the puzzle-solvers, the thinkers, the outwitters."

"They made more sense to me. There'd be patterns to follow in their tales. Clues to pick up and piece together that'd reveal the truth."

"A logical progression of things," he offered.

She nodded. "I always thought there was something divine in a well-formed story. A standard Ederi story structure is done in three acts, and as the Poetics say, three is the number of poetry in motion, be it poetic fortune or poetic justice. That can't be a coincidence."

"A well-written story with a satisfying conclusion, a happy ending—I can see the appeal of that to a resident of the slums. All those stories preaching the great myths of mercy, duty, and justice."

Myths?

Master Dothilos went on, "Who wouldn't want to immerse themselves in a world with that? Least of all a young girl desperate for a good tale to escape her sad little home and troubled parents."

What did he just say? She turned to him, nascent anxiety muting her.

He looked nonchalant. "I was curious, you see. I knew I wouldn't get answers from you, so I had some of my servants investigate your family."

Her heart pounded. "You mustn't involve my father or mother—"

He held up a hand. "I had no such intention whatsoever. I just wanted to know where you came from, what made you the way you are. I assure you, no one even spoke to your parents—they couldn't find them. They simply gathered what bits they could from your childhood neighborhood."

She turned away from him, frightened.

"That hovel of a home must have felt like a cage to you. Hardly looks fit for living in. Little wonder you grew up so miserable with your parents the way they are. It's admirable the lengths your father went to, to provide for your family and escape the pathetic shadow his swindling parents cast over him, but living honestly is a struggle if you're not particularly bright. 'Simple-minded' was what some of your neighbors called him, and we all know what that really means. And your poor mother! I gather she never quite recovered from the awful things she went through with her family as a child. Your neighbors said that even when it wasn't her flesh failing her, her troubled mind would make her take a knife to herself—"

"Please stop."

Her whisper was barely audible, but he had heard. "I'm not saying any of this to make fun of you. I myself can relate—" But he stopped, looking surprised as he read her face. "Some of this is news to you, isn't it?"

She refused to answer.

"Well, which parts? I could tell you more."

She shook her head fiercely. "I am curious. But it isn't right for you to know their secrets to begin with, and if it was too painful for them to share it with their daughter, it would be wrong for me to learn them from you. Don't—" she spluttered for a moment, her stutter returning at the swarming hive of emotions lodged in her throat.

"I promise to tell nobody any of this," he said calmly.

"Do not go after them again," she spat. "They have no part to play in what we're doing. You have no right to their stories."

"I swear to you in the eyes of the Maker and the Merciful I will not. I was curious, and I see now that has offended you. I apologize." He sounded genuinely contrite, like a child realizing his impulses had done wrong.

Is he putting on an act? She honestly couldn't tell, the supposed sincerity in his eyes confounding her.

He continued, "You needn't be so alarmed. I just wanted to understand you, that's all."

"You don't deserve to know anything about me," she said harshly.

"Perhaps I don't," he admitted. "But I must confess, there were things I empathized with."

She glared at him, curious, but unwilling to encourage him.

He fidgeted with the cuffs of his sleeves before speaking quietly, "Like how you were apparently mute as a child. Your neighbors say you didn't speak a word for years. They all thought the demons in your mother's head had made her give birth to an idiot child— but you weren't an idiot. No, you had a tongue, you just didn't know how to use it right. I suppose you grew up in a house of so few words, you just didn't understand the need for them until you were older."

Lythlet nodded, tiredly. She didn't see the point in hiding anything anymore—Master Dothilos knew everything. "I was six when my father realized they had done something wrong with my upbringing. He hoped proper schooling would help me find my tongue. They scrounged together what few coins they had to send me to the nearest one."

"And yet it wasn't an easy journey, was it? I hear it still took some time for you to speak, and your words came slow. A speech impediment, they said."

She reddened and lowered her face.

"But one you overcame in time. Perhaps through the steadfast companionship of a fellow schoolmate and his mother, the schoolmarm?"

"Desil," Lythlet said softly.

"You went to live with them for a time, didn't you?"

"My mother fell sicker than usual." She was certain he already knew this, but perhaps by saying it herself, she could control some part of her narrative. "She could no longer work, and then my parents couldn't afford me. When Desil heard of what we were going through, his family insisted on taking me in. I lived with them for half a year before my mother's condition had improved and my father saved enough to take me back."

"And you went back a child with a fully functioning tongue, at last. One with a rather dramatic way of speaking. Dare I say from listening to Desil's mother read stories to you every night?"

In truth, Lythlet had never pieced this together herself. But it hit her then where her vocal cadence and love for overwrought dialogue came from. "Both his father and mother. They'd take turns telling me stories, encouraging me to read along. It was the first time a voice had ever made so much sense to me. It was language with a pattern I could follow, far from the depressed silence of my father and the demented murmurs of my mother. I can't put into words just how much I loved living with the Demothis, how much I owe them for the brief respite they granted me."

Master Dothilos nodded with a fond smile. "Yes, some stutters are cured by adopting a distinctive manner of speaking. I can attest to that myself."

She stared at him, wide-eyed.

He winked. "You think I've always spoken like this? A mighty baritone that shakes the world with a single syllable? No, my child. Look at you, slouching, mumbling, your gaze dithering about nervously. You're the perfect picture of me when I was young. Part of me wants to run from you for how much you remind me of that time, another part just wants to pity you."

He sighed, hand falling limp by his thigh. "I, too, came from a deeply unhappy family. I was soon abandoned to an orphanage, and in time, I fell further and became unregistered. Yes, my dear, I came from nothing—from your part of the world. I know how it feels to be stuck in an endless rut of poverty, where no matter what choices I made, I would never rise to the level of those highborn folk."

He looked down hesitantly, then spoke again, "I recall from our interview that you have debt. Forgive the discourtesy of my prying, but my servants discovered during their investigation that the debt is under Desil's name. Apparently, it's quite the substantial sum—though I don't know the precise number. Will you be able to afford it without the jackpots?"

Her silence was answer enough.

He frowned. "How large is this debt?"

She grimaced, shaking her head. "The principal was not particularly remarkable. It's the terms of interest that keep us in debt."

"Ah," Master Dothilos said, suddenly understanding. "One of those predatory usurers?"

She nodded.

"What are the terms exactly?"

"One hundred and thirty percent per annum, applied on a bimonthly schedule."

Master Dothilos stared at her in horror. "And Desil was foolish enough to accept this?"

"This was some years ago. He didn't know any better—we were still young, and he had never learned how to interpret a usury contract. They're written in a way to deliberately confuse people, after all. He signed without understanding, and in great desperation."

"Whatever for?"

"For me," she said quietly. "He borrowed that money for me."

"I was wondering why you felt obligated to pay his debt for him. What happened?"

"I'd fallen ill. He carried me to the health ward but could not afford the treatment."

"And standing not too far away was a usurer kindly offering his services," Master Dothilos finished with a grim, knowing look.

She nodded.

"I can't imagine you'd agree to such a loan. Couldn't you have stopped him?"

"I was unconscious. I hadn't eaten for days, and flesh failed me at last."

"What happened to you?"

She fell silent. These questions were unearthing more and more dangerous memories, memories she'd buried a long time ago.

Madam Kovetti.

She had a violent reaction to the name, jerking backward into her seat with a sharp inhale.

Master Dothilos looked at her in concern.

She answered quickly, before he could ask further, "I had a job I couldn't handle the stress of. That's all."

"Ah, my servants did say you had a string of employment under various lowlifes and swindlers—"

Her heart began thumping against her chest, wondering if he knew.

"—but I didn't bother looking into it that deeply." He shrugged. "I figured it was just the typical dodgy bookkeeping."

She nodded, relieved.

He was about to speak further, but she cut him off: "I know what you're trying to do. You're going to say that if I want to pay off Desil's debt, I need to stay in the arena."

"You don't need me to say that for you to know it," the match-master answered easily. "An ordinary job isn't going to cut it, not for the kind of debt he signed on for. And I know you *have* found an ordinary job in the recent weeks—minding the books at an inn, I believe. But that's not going to get you out of debt. Poverty is a vicious cycle, and it's going to take a stunner of a miracle to spring you free from the poverty trap and into the cycle of wealth."

She eyed him. "And now you're going to say conquessing can be that miracle."

He laughed, caught red-handed. "Couldn't it? Weren't you just saying three is the number of poetic fortune? So why not hold on for the third round at least and win another jackpot?"

"Because behind all the lucky and unlucky numbers, there's an important lesson," Lythlet said. "Three may be the number of poetry in motion, but four is the number of death, as it was on the fourth day of creation the first death of a mortal was recorded, mercilessly slain by a wild beast. Eight is the number of divine blessing, for it was on the eighth day of creation that the Sunsmith heard the lamentations of the grieving and granted them bloodrights so they could fend for themselves against the wilderness. But nine is the number of suffering, the number of trials one must endure in the halls of damnation. Three and four, eight and nine—to me, the pattern is clear: taking your good luck too far will lead to your own downfall. I've been lucky so far, but perhaps crossing the line by even one step will turn luck into misery."

"Yet I don't think you truly want to quit, Lythlet. You wouldn't be here otherwise, searching for something to justify staying. I still think of what you said during your interview, when I pushed you for the truth. *I just want to be happier.* A perfectly daft answer, I thought at the time. But now I realize you were being honest on a level most people wouldn't dare approach. You harbor a quiet dream within, and you wish for the chance to realize it."

"Dreams are dangerous for slumdogs," she said stiffly. "Dreams are hope, and we are not allowed that privilege."

He flashed her a pitying expression. "Sad words to hear from someone so young. Yet so familiar, so bitterly familiar. But indulge me, please. You must have one dream, however small it may be."

The first thing that came to her mind was, *I'd like to pay off my parents' debt and return them to a life aboveground*, but it felt much too personal to share.

So she shyly pointed up above.

He followed her finger until he was staring at the dark underside of Central. A smile grew on his face. "Now that's a proper dream. No gold nor gems for you—you're not the type to care for trinkets. You want to belong to Central. Well, what's keeping you from there? Reap every coin you can from these matches and earn your seat amongst the highborn."

"Even if I were to have all the gold in the world, they'd never accept me."

"Hmm?"

"I know how I come across," she said, more bitterness spilling out of her than she would've liked. "I saw the notes you took of me during our interview, and I can't even argue with them. I know how I look; a schoolmate once said I had a face made to be beaten. I know how I sound, prone to stutters, odd in my word choice. *Idiot child*, I was called in my youth. I know how I act, utterly lacking in social grace, shying away from attention, slouching into myself if I ever get it, always incapable of picking up the subtle cues others intuit unless I tell myself it's a puzzle to be solved and devote my full attention to unraveling it. I rely entirely on the charity of the naturally affable taking me under their wing and protecting me from the worst. Small wonder the only friend who's ever tolerated me long enough to remain one is Desil alone. How would the highborn ever accept me into their world?"

"It's not easy," he said, "but it's not impossible. I can attest to that myself. Rub shoulders with any highborn who comes your way, see who sticks and who you can discard when the time is right. The art of social climbing is a game in the end, and though you may think it beyond you at this moment, I'd like to remind you that you've already proven yourself to be quite savvy at games."

But she shook her head and pointed to the fighting grounds. "I'm not even human to the spectators when I'm down there. They judge me like I'm a beast of burden they're considering buying. The bulls only support me so they can fatten their coin purses even more, while the bears anticipate me failing, if not dying, for their profit. Somehow, I despise them even more than I despise you—you lead them, but you're nothing more than a shameless hawker peddling his wares, willing to say anything to get their coin. But them—how can they laugh and clap as I weep and bleed on the ground?"

Master Dothilos looked at her thoughtfully, as if her words had stirred something in him. "Because they genuinely don't consider your dignity to be as important as their entertainment. Unless your life can be packaged into something entertaining with a nice moral about how working hard will get you all your dreams, they aren't willing to extend any sympathy to you. All those stories you grew up reading, would their heroes return to an impoverished life filled with debt? No, somehow or other, their deeds would always be rewarded financially: a pot of gold at the end of their journey or royalty seeing their worth and marrying them. There's an implicit message to all these stories: so long as you strive hard enough, you will be rewarded with all the money you need."

"And if I'm poor and miserable, it's because I've done nothing to deserve more than that," she said bitterly.

He nodded. "It's not about morality for them—it's about doing your damnedest to succeed, whether by fair means or foul. Highborns weigh the concept of individual agency heavily, and the stories they're willing to pass on to their children are rife with it. They want to believe they deserve the success they have now, after all. But agency is, in fact, a rare privilege, and having it already means you were born to the right person. Anyone who buys into the concept of a meritocracy is someone naïve to the workings of the world. What option have you ever had but poverty, Lythlet? Did you have a hand in the makings of your fate? Did you get to choose a mother who was whole of mind, a father who wasn't a halfwit? You didn't even have a say in your friend dragging your life down with a fool's debt. That scar on your forehead—am I right in guessing a former employer gave it to you?"

She stared at him with wide eyes. "Yes."

"A second guess: he was not the first employer to be violent with you."

She nodded, bewildered. The match-master was truly perceptive. Hive-Master Winaro had been the worst of them, but she could trace a long string of violent bosses through the years, from debt collectors to scam-peddlers.

"As I suspected. Now for my final guess: you didn't quit upon first signs of abuse, because you desperately needed the coin and were willing to put aside your safety for it."

She nodded.

He sighed. "I'm sorry, my girl. Yours is a familiar story for our part of the world. But those spoiled, coddled highborn who have never once known poverty would never believe it. I can already hear some of them saying, '*Well, why didn't she just find another job?*' As if opportunities were countless for a slumdog of low education and no connections, especially in this crippled economy! '*Well, she just has to try harder! She's being too passive and helpless!*' An utterly idiotic, privileged mindset. Like warmongers who've never fought a battle in their lives, they will demand you work harder without understanding you've already worked harder than them, but it's the age-old systems built up around you that make it impossible to escape poverty. Ultimately, all that separates us from the highborn is nothing more than luck, the fortune of being born to the right person in the right part of the city."

He chuckled suddenly, struck by a thought. "Yes, it's not easy for lowborn like us to find our feet amongst highborn circles—they're absurd folk who speak of family jewels and leaving behind legacies. Legacies! All my mother ever left me was a piss-stained blanket on the doorstep of the orphanage. What did yours ever leave you but a wounded heart? Nothing! And that is a concept they cannot conceive of at all: that there are people in this world with truly nothing to fall back on, but to hope they stumble upon a lucky opportunity. The naivety of the highborn is utterly infuriating."

She listened silently, reeling at how every word resonated with her soul, him so easily articulating a truth she'd long harbored in her vindictive heart.

"I think," he continued slowly, "that's why I've found myself intrigued by you. There's a palpable fury inside you, despite your moments of shying away like a meek little mouse. I've seen the way you look when the spectators cheer for you after you've won. Your façade cracks for a heartbeat, and there's wonder in your eyes— shock! Confusion! You can't believe what you're seeing, what you're hearing. But above all, there's a glint of something magical in you. Something I felt, too, that set my path ablaze, that's led me from a life of fear into a life of riches."

She waited, anxious at what the answer might be.

He reached over and brushed her hair; she stiffened at the touch. "Ambition. The brief, nascent stirrings of it. It's taking root in you like an itch you can't scratch. You heard them praise you, you pondered your own success, and you thought, *what if I could keep winning?* From one slumdog to another, I would dearly love to see someone like you rise the ranks and prove every one of those insufferable fools in Central wrong."

She looked down at her knees, finding it impossible to maintain contact with his pale blue eyes. Master Dothilos had spoken not as a match-master, but as one who had lived as a downtrodden boy with nothing to hope for.

"You are cunning with your words, Master Dothilos," Lythlet said quietly. "But I know you flatter me only so I'll accept your invitation to the next round."

He laughed, shaking his head. "Silver-tongued I may be, but the ingots gleam true. I haven't lied to you, not even once. We're not friends, and I doubt you'll ever let me be one. But friendship is cheap, meaningless without weight behind it. Partnership—

now that's something I bequeath only upon worthy people. We could have that, you and I. A mutually beneficial agreement in the arena. I saw the way you puzzled your way through the sentari and the anzura. You have a clever mind, and the ambition to match. But there's something you must learn to complete the trifecta: *conviction*." He emphasized the word in a way that made it echo through her eardrum.

"Conviction in what?" She waved her hand over the arena. "In a game that demands I put not just my life on the line, but that of my dearest friend?"

"Conviction in *yourself*. That you deserve to stand proudly before the highborn and be judged, not as a measly little mongrel who's crawled out of the slums, but as someone worthy of attention. Yes, you'll be entering a game of high risk. But isn't high risk, high reward a basic maxim of investing? Some things are worth making the leap for. Our Anvari ancestors—what was the great equalizer for them?"

She hesitated, thinking. "Their bloodrights."

He nodded, and his approving smile calmed her. "Very good. You could be the poorest boy from the lowliest village, but who would spit in your face if you had the bloodright to draw fire from thin air and rain terror upon your enemies? You could be a withered old woman who's lost everything in the world, but who would dare cross you if you knew how to traverse the geoscape and crush stone with sight alone? No matter who you were or where you came from, if you were blessed with a bloodright, you could make it in the world. Yet our ancestors, once they were forced to become Exiles fleeing to the west, chose to stay here in Edesvena, a land that stifles the use of their bloodrights. Why would they give up such power?"

"They had nowhere else to go—their prison island had sunk, and the Anvar motherland wouldn't accept them back, not for their crimes," recited Lythlet, school-day memories flooding back. "So they sailed here in desperation and found the nomadic Oraanu clans willing to receive them as long-lost brothers and sisters. I suppose after a long, arduous journey with many sunken ships, they were relieved to finally find a refuge."

"You think of their decision as an act of exhaustion, of resignation. But what if I told you it was conviction? Because although they had to sacrifice their bloodrights, they nonetheless knew they couldn't squander this rare opportunity for a yet-to-be-written future. The Oraanu were welcoming them to their new home, agreeing to work with them in establishing cities around the holy lands that sun-cursed beasts would naturally avoid without the meddling of arena-operating mortals like me. Even if they had traveled farther west, they couldn't be certain they'd receive such a hospitable welcome again. And they knew—they had the *conviction*—that even without their bloodrights, they would find a way to survive and prosper here. No longer were they reviled Exiles nor petty criminals—they declared themselves Ederi, People of the New Home."

He laid a hand on her, gripping both her arm and her attention. "What would you like to be seen as, Lythlet? Know what you want, and you shall have the conviction to mold your destiny, to craft whatever identity you want the highborn to behold you with."

She was startled by the question. "Anything but an idiot child," she said after a moment's thought. "I need no sainthood; I need no lofty praise. I only ever wanted to be seen as an interesting character, not one so easily relegated to the sidelines. Call me a thief or a liar, and I'll gladly take those instead."

He blinked at her curiously, her last statement taking him by surprise.

"Thieves fascinate people," she explained. "Rentavos the Gentleman Thief is a beloved fictional character for a reason, boasting the perfect combination of intrigue and skill. Meanwhile in real life, the Phantom sweeps the city into a fervor every time they strike, everyone wondering who lies beneath the mask, in awe of their impossible heists. And what is a liar but someone with secrets to keep and a guileful imagination? They're hiding something, and nothing riles people up more than a desperation to uncover someone else's secrets. Look at how you couldn't resist digging into my past! If I had simply told you who I was in our interview, would you have cared about me? But a thief, a liar! Aren't these so much more interesting archetypes to study than the shy, stuttering child of lowborn parents?"

His befuddlement shifted into a smile. "Only you could provide me with so unexpected an answer. The way your mind works is a puzzle in itself, and yet so captivating in its oddness. A thief and a liar—my word, the highborn would certainly find that story a seductive tale. Someone desperate enough to sink to immoral lows to control the arc of her story. The *agency* you'd display to them! I can already imagine them being tickled by your audacity, charmed by your rejection of passivity."

He leaned back in his seat, head tilted up to the underside of Central. Lingering deep in thought for moments, he exhaled deeply. "My dear Lythlet, I, too, am a fellow child of lowborn parents, once racked with so much doubt and self-loathing he only whispered, never daring to raise his voice lest he be struck. And yet, I had three things that pulled me up from the trappings of my life: a clever mind, a startling level of ambition, and the conviction that I deserved a place in this city. I earned my way amongst the highborn—I gave them no choice but to accept me. And thus, I made it."

He gazed at her, pale eyes piercing like needles. He did not need to say the next four words, but even unspoken, they haunted her on her journey home.

And so could you.

CHAPTER ELEVEN

THE BESTIARY

A FULL WEEK passed under the misery of dark, gray clouds and endless summer rain. The third round was inching closer and closer, and Lythlet was yet of two minds.

Clutching the mail she'd picked up from Faravind Post, she made her way to Nestali Road, a street flanked by triple-story terraced shophouses, each painted a different color, chipped and weathered by the passage of decades. The Steam Dragon occupied a lot flanked by a fortune-teller and a clothier.

"Good afternoon, Schwala," Lythlet greeted the teahouse dog, stepping over the threshold. It was past teatime, and the teahouse was half-empty. She seated herself on a stone stool and patted her lap to welcome Schwala and his wagging tail closer. "Have you seen Desil?"

Not in the least bit concerned with her inquiry, Schwala simply huffed and pressed his muzzle into Lythlet's hand for the requisite number of scritchy-scratchies.

No thanks to him, she caught sight of Desil running around the back of the teahouse, and he joined them after a moment, looking frazzled with his apron tossed over his shoulder. He set a pot and some spare teacups on the table.

"Break time, Schwala-wala," he sang wearily, kicking off a sandal to scratch the dog's belly with his toes.

Schwala panted appreciatively, freckled tongue flopping out.

"You look tired," Lythlet remarked, pouring hot tea into his cup first, and then hers.

Desil gave her a wan smile. "We ran out of sairan and orange rikri halfway through teatime, so I had to run down to the suppliers and hoist back a couple of leaf-tanks. It was a nightmare running around in the storm."

Lythlet took a sip, closing her eyes as the bitterness invaded her tongue, slowly diffusing into a pleasant aftertaste. She rummaged through her bag. "I went to Faravind's earlier. Your parents wrote to us."

Desil's face brightened as she handed him a letter. A comfortable lull fell as he read it. She'd already read hers; Auntie Arathel's letter had been nothing short of heartwarming, filled with small, cozy adventures the schoolmarm encountered with her pupils, save for a brief mention of how she feared the United Setgad Party's proposed budget revision for Southeastern schools would mean even fewer sheets of parchment and charcoal styluses to go around.

Desil put down his letter and bumped her elbow. "Do me a favor, will you, and write back to my mother? Ma was asking me to have a nag at you—"

"I will, I will. I'll sneak in some time when I head back to work this evening."

"Much obliged."

"There was something else at Faravind's," she said, pulling out a card. "Master Dothilos's invitation."

Desil eyed it. "Have you sent off our refusal?"

"No. We've three days to respond."

"Do you need that long? You seemed so set on quitting last we spoke."

Last they spoke had been the previous match. She hadn't broached the question with him since, preferring to mull it over privately.

At her silence, he said, slowly, "You want to continue, don't you?"

She nodded shamefacedly at her teacup. "I want to pay off your debt to Tucoras once and for all, and if my calculations are correct, we may be able to accomplish it with just two more jackpots. Can you believe that? Two months and we'll be done with this debt that's been crippling us for years."

"You have the heart to continue, so let's," he encouraged.

"I only wish we had some way to prepare ourselves. I am not you, Desil, I can't win with brute strength alone. I must use my mind—but some beasts are just impossible to solve, especially when our backs are driven into a corner, and I don't have time to think." *I'm not silly enough to hear one speech from Master Dothilos and be swayed into risking Desil's life again—I need more to have the conviction to be a conquessor.*

"Have you thought of getting into contact with Ilden and Shunvi?"

"To ask what they fought and how? Certainly, but they would only know what they'd faced before or seen in other matches—they didn't know about the anzura, did they? And from what they told me, they faced only big, hulking beasts. I have an inkling that Master Dothilos is less interested in testing my strength than my mettle. He may throw trickier monsters our way."

"Still, we're short on options, so it can't hurt."

She grunted unhappily, flicking her now empty cup. "But it seems the logical choice is to quit now and save ourselves the heartache."

They both fell silent, neither having any good ideas.

Two plates clinked onto their table, one filled with fried rice cakes, the other shelled prawns drowned in starfruit juice and herbs. Mister Millidin gave a bashful smile before leaving for the kitchens.

"Thank you," Lythlet said before cramming her mouth full. Starfruits were imported from the southern islands of the Ora Empire, and they came at a steep cost. To be given such a treat was an honor, and her gaze followed him as he joined his wife to help her at the back of the teahouse.

"I want that," she whispered wistfully.

"A husband?" Desil said, surprised as his eyes fell upon the eternally shy, freckle-faced Mister Millidin.

"I'm looking at Madame Millidin."

"A wife?" he said, even more perplexed.

"*Freedom*," she said, frustrated. "Madame Millidin can rest knowing she provides for herself, her husband, and their children. She'll never have to fear being beaten by an ill-tempered boss, nor forced to make a decision she disagrees with by an employer threatening her livelihood. She has a freedom I've never had."

Desil wore a look of concern. "Has the inn been treating you well?"

She rested a hand on his arm. "I'm fine."

"So you said for months until you revealed Valanti had been beating you."

"I mean it this time. I'm not being treated badly." Still she hesitated. "But Master Winaro did not start violent either. It grew as a weed, hidden at first before it spread everywhere. And I fear..." She drifted off.

"You fear it could start again in anyone." He looked at her sadly, leaning over to kiss her head. He'd always been sympathetic to her problems—there were commonplace threats she faced in the slums that he as a broad-built, imposing lad would never have to fear. "You really have had the worst luck. Valanti was one thing, but then there were those usurers before him that gave you those bruises."

"And before them were the fortune-telling scammers," she added, grimacing, thinking of all the times she'd had her ears twisted and slapped.

"And the *other* pair of swindlers before them. And then of course, the brothel—"

Lythlet laid a hand on his. She murmured, quietly, yet warningly, "We agreed to never mention Madam Kovetti again."

Desil pinched his lips together, nodding in complete understanding. "Sorry."

Customers filtered in as they spoke, and amongst them was a party of one.

Lythlet's eyes widened. It was Saevem Arthil in a custom-cut cloak, a gilded brooch clasped across his chest, clutching a package in his arms.

"I am looking for a Desil Demothi," he was saying to one of Desil's green-aproned colleagues, who pointed at Lythlet's table in answer.

They rose as he approached, bowing. "Come for a meal, Master Arthil?" said Desil, smiling.

"Please, call me Saevem," he said, brushing off the title.

Lythlet and Desil bowed again, the generosity of his gesture not escaping them.

"May we take a more private table?" Saevem requested, eyeing one at the back, partitioned away by florid mother-of-pearl screens.

Desil made the arrangements, and it wasn't long before all three of them were seated in the private enclosure. A brand-new steaming pot of tea was delivered by Madame Millidin, and Desil filled Saevem's teacup first.

"We're glad to see you again, Mas—Saevem," he said.

"And I you," Saevem replied perfunctorily. "I did not come for tea and snacks, however. I have a merchant's deal I would like to propose."

Lythlet and Desil exchanged glances at each other.

"What sort of deal?" Lythlet said cautiously.

"One we can both benefit enormously from." He set his teacup down and leveled with them. "I would like to request that you stay in the arena."

"Master Arthil—"

"Saevem."

"Saevem," she corrected herself, unused to a highborn being so unostentatious, "as I mentioned before, this is no longer a gamble I am willing to make. I cannot risk Desil's life, nor my own, for the sake of some coins."

"Would this put your fears to rest?" He held out the item he'd been clutching, a thick package bound in cheap, unmarked parchment and tied with a brown string.

She yanked the string loose and unfolded the parchment until she discovered the object within: a bulky, black leather-bound book. The cover was textured, golden letters gleaming crisply on it, crammed together like a cluster of lightning-bees.

"'*An Annotated Compendium of the Modern Beast by Scholar Yavida Lewenskiros*,'" Lythlet read the title aloud.

It needed no explanation, but perhaps the shock on her face drove Saevem to speak: "It's a bestiary."

"Goodness, there are hundreds of beasts in here," Desil said in growing excitement as he riffled the pages. "Or thousands, even. And there are diagrams and annotations everywhere."

Lythlet gawked. A book of this quality, with perfect ink drawings on fine vellum, was not easily found, much less purchased, by even the wealthy. None of the books she had ever stolen, not even those from the richest households of the southern sectors, came close.

"I never imagined there were so many different sorts of sun-cursed beasties out there." Desil jabbed at a page. "Look here, a nine-headed dragon-snake. *Venomous, and can only be slain when the one mother head has been isolated from the body.* I hope we don't get that—snakes spook me."

"Shush now, you'll jinx us," she scolded. "I'm unlucky enough for that to happen."

She turned to the next page: a lifelike rendition of a furry bugbear with pitch-black eyes and two arched horns protruding from the crown of its head greeted her.

For all of Master Dothilos's theatrics about sun-cursed beasts, playing into the fears of the religious and the superstitious that they were demonic hellspawn sent by the Scorned One to plague mortalkind, this bestiary took another tack: it made it emphatically clear these were no more than exotic animals from the wilderness— that these ephemeral creatures could have their oddities studied, dissected into bare-bones facts and observations, and have their mystique and terror stripped away through rigorous research.

Lythlet peeled her eyes away from the fascinating ink drawings of creatures she had never heard of to Saevem.

"You're giving this to us?"

He nodded. "I will, if this is what you need to stay in the games."

"So you really are a bull," Lythlet remarked, flipping through the pages.

Saevem blinked. "Pardon?"

"A bull," she repeated. At his blank expression, she continued, "As opposed to a bear?"

"Ah," he said, nodding politely, clearly not understanding.

Strange how he could be such an ardent supporter, gifting them so luxurious a resource, yet not know even basic arena nomenclature.

"What do you want in exchange?" she said. It no longer seemed likely he was doing this purely to profit from their victories.

He folded his hands together. "Two things. The first being your agreement that we keep this confidential."

She nodded. This would be to both their benefits: Master Dothilos would likely confiscate the book if he knew about it, and Saevem would suffer a horde of angry bearish spectators descending upon him, furious that he'd upset their odds.

"The second being that, when the time comes, I will request your help on a certain matter. And when that happens, I would appreciate if you recalled the debt you owe me."

She stared at him. "This is much too vague for me to agree to."

"I am not at liberty to divulge much information at this moment," he said, apologetically. "All I can say is that your connection to

Master Dothilos is precisely what I need to avenge a dear friend's murder. But perhaps this will convince you I am no conman." He reached into his pocket and withdrew a calling card. Fingers delicately pinching the topmost corners, he held it before her.

Her fingers met the bottom two corners, and she bowed her head as she tugged on it—but to no avail. He did not release the card, and she then understood she was meant only to look upon it.

It bore no name nor designation and was blank but for a single symbol stamped on the front. A diamond, not filled with the Fated Ship as the United Setgad Party chose for their emblem, but by a single long-stalked *hista*, the flower of peace and one of the symbols of Tazkar.

The symbol was oddly familiar.

Then it hit her—she had seen it while idly browsing Master Winaro's copy of *The Setgad Dilemma* during the rare moments of quiet in the hive-workshop. It was the symbol the Coalition of Hope had co-opted for their political gerrymandering as they challenged Governor Matheranos's reign over Setgad for next year's election.

Lythlet raised her head, shocked. "Are you working for Corio Brandolas?" *What the devil would the opposition leader want with us? With conquessing?*

Saevem nodded. He quickly returned the card to his pocket, casting a furtive look around. "We seek allies. I can say no more at this time but know that the Coalition of Hope will care for those who serve us. Now, will you stay in the games?"

It remained a cryptic request, yet she considered the situation: this was a highborn offering her something she desperately needed just as she needed it. Master Dothilos's advice reverberated through her thoughts, that his success had depended upon rubbing shoulders with whatever highborn came his way. Were she to not only win the favor of a highborn like Saevem but also ingratiate herself to the needs of a political firebrand and possibly the next Governor of Setgad like Corio Brandolas, the rewards would be unimaginable. Of course, the odds were certainly unfavorable, but the notion of high risk, high reward remained at the forefront of her mind.

She cast a tentative glance at Desil, then down at the bestiary. Her thumb traced the thick ink lines constructing the monsters, and a smile finally tugged her thin lips. "This is what I've been looking for, Desil." She looked up and met his gaze, the fires of hope and ambition swelling in her heart.

Desil grinned. "I think it's time you replied to that invitation."

CHAPTER TWELVE

DIRANTAS, OF THE DARKEST NIGHT AND THE TRICKSTERS

THE FIRST WEEK of Andachi hosted their third match, dedicated to the warden Dirantas, He Who Mastered the Night and Dreams.

Lythlet had forced Desil to go to the arena earlier than usual, although they had little to do but wait in the armory as spectators filled the seats. But she'd woken in a fit of fear, and sleep had been impossible to return to, so she'd dragged him awake and out the door, allowing him a brief shrine visit along the way.

The bestiary was at home; she couldn't risk Master Dothilos spotting it and confiscating it. All she could do now was churn through the entries she had memorized, mentally recreating the lavishly colored drawings and detailed notes.

She had spent every minute she could studying. There hadn't been enough time between the demands of work and home to go through every single cataloged creature, but by ruling out the beasts unlikely to appear and prioritizing creatures native to the northern territory of Edesvena, she'd made her way through the bestiary, taking notes and reciting facts under her breath as she went about her day.

But was it enough?

It was the height of irony that she would feel most anxious when most prepared. The past two matches had relied on luck and instinct. What had she to prove then? She had only wanted to bring home the jackpots. But today was an opportunity to prove her conviction was not misplaced, to determine if the newfound fire within her soul could light a path out of the desert.

Desil gently nudged her flame-blighted boot with the tip of his. "Deep breath, Lytha. In and out."

"Is it obvious I'm worried?"

He laughed, loud and clear, and took a seat beside her. "When are you not? But you're worse now than ever. Come, you've done all you could for today's match. Now we take it one step at a time."

She exhaled heavily, pulse pounding like a festival drum. She listened to the rising rumble of voices from the arena, wondering how many spectators had come to witness the match.

As if to distract her, Desil began slashing his sword at empty air, practicing. "This blade reminds me of all those stories Ma used to read us about those ancient warriors and their sacred swords. They always had special names, didn't they? How about I call this one the Silent Stinger?"

"You haven't half the wit of Malovis the Starlight Journeyer to steal the name of her blade."

He clucked his tongue. "Let me have my fun. You mind your own weapon instead. Go on, name it."

Lythlet appraised her spear. There was nothing special about it, no markings, no ornamentations on its sturdy shaft. But it served her well, and she had grown fond enough to treat the matter with gravity. "I shall call her Spear."

"What?"

"It's a good, uncomplicated name for a good, uncomplicated spear."

"No, it's n—oh, never mind. You're happy enough, I can see that. I dread the day you name your children, but I look forward to playing with little Son and Daughter whenever they come along.

Honestly, it's a good thing I told you to name our lightning-bees at home after your favorite characters, otherwise Rentavos and Beracani would be Sassy Bee and Neurotic Bee."

She laughed at last, and it was like pressure being released from a valve. She turned to him, smiling. "Thank you, Desil."

He smiled back.

THE SILENT PRAYER to Dirantas was underway, Master Dothilos having just finished reciting the Prayer of the Quick-Witted. Nearly every Ederi spectator had their head bowed, their first two fingers brushing their lips, then their brow, while the Oraanu amongst the audience waited silently out of respect. Though they shared a belief in the Sunsmith and the Moonmachinist, the latter being the much beloved Matron they worshipped at their moon-temples, the Oraanu diverged on the finer details of the religious canon, making no prayers to the wardens.

Lythlet scanned the seats, spotting Shunvi and Ilden, both waving when they got her attention. She hoped to see Saevem to offer a nod of gratitude but couldn't find him in the thickening sea of strangers. There were more spectators than ever, and nearly half of all the seats were filled.

Many to disappoint if I fail to perform well, she thought nervously.

"May Dirantas witness us today," Master Dothilos said, drawing the prayer to an end, his magnified baritone consuming all thought. "Spectators, we're all familiar with Desil Demothi, darling of the brawlers, are we not?"

The crowd *hoo-rah*ed, stamping their feet. Desil gave a gracious bow, but his smile was tight, uneasy.

"But so little do we know of Lythlet Tairel! Well, spectators, it's only fair she gets her story heard after proving herself a worthy conquessor the last two matches. And what a story it is—the story of a girl with nothing to her name!"

Lythlet's head shot up, heart swerving from an anxious drumbeat to a thundering march. She grabbed Desil's arm as a thousand stares attacked her, then hid behind him. She dropped her eyes from their penetrating gazes, counting the grains of sand before her, desperately hoping the moment would pass.

"It's all right," he soothed, though he, too, looked wary.

Despite her flagrant discomfort, Master Dothilos continued, "Born to a luckless pair in the slums of Southwest, she was given a name that belied her mother's true fears: *Lythlet*, Candle-Flame, small, flickering, not long for this world.

"One glance, and we can all guess how difficult her life must have been. An ugly whelp of the slums, beaten and bruised into keeping her head down, scarred by a wretched world. Yet I'm not about to tell you the story of a girl defeated by life. I'm here to tell you about a girl who refused to stay down. Meek and unassuming she may seem, we who have witnessed her first and second matches know better now than to underestimate her! Remember how she toppled the sentari, remember how she outfoxed the anzura! Remember how she stood upon the yutrela and commanded the heavens to reveal the cosmoscape unto her! She is by far the brightest, most perceptive mind we've seen in the arena in a long time, a thinker who worships the classics, a student of the scholars of yore. Yet higher learning was never on the cards for her. No schoolhouse for her, not for a slumdog whelp without even two pennies to rub together—but in her youth, she buried herself in books, scrounging together an education by her own means. But hold on now! We're talking about a girl with nothing to her name, nothing to her family's! How came she upon these books?" The match-master swiveled, finger stretched toward her, eyes condemning her where she stood. "THIEF!"

"*THIEF!*" the spectators echoed, obeying his cue.

She stared, dumbfounded, goose pimples rising.

"Yes, my dear spectators. Before us stands a girl so thirsty for knowledge she would pilfer tome after tome from the shelves of the rich and the poor and everything in between. Come, my girl. Tell us how many you stole in your life."

What number had I given him? "Five," she shouted nervously.

The match-master laughed, the majestic sound echoing around the arena. "A cunning answer from a girl wise enough to hide her youthful misdemeanors." Then he raised his finger and jabbed it in her direction.

"LIAR!" he bellowed, a velvet baritone.

"LIAR!" the spectators echoed, a horde of delighted wildfolk spellbound by his story.

"She's not fool enough to reveal all her secrets to us, not someone who unleashes surprise after surprise every match, but I know it. Hundreds! Hundreds of tomes disappearing off shelves all over the city! The watchmen were once sent after her, and they beat her blue and bloody in punishment. But did she stop? No! Still, she persisted, the hunger to survive and prosper thrumming through her veins. Here stands before you a girl determined to prove that who she is, is greater than where she hails from! A girl who decided when young that she would not be held back by the circumstances of her birth—if she had to lie, cheat, or steal to better her standing in the world, damn the heavens and the chains binding her to the hellscape of the slums, she *would*."

Master Dothilos held his hands out with seraphic inspiration, trapping the spectators with the empyrean thunder of his voice. "And come she now, spear in hand, with nothing more than an earnest wish: to prove her name wrong, to show that she cannot be so easily defeated by life itself. Not she, not a thief on a quest to claim her future! Not she, not a guileful liar with a hundred secrets up her sleeve! Not a girl who's never been afraid of being BEATEN!"

"BEATEN!"

"BRUISED!"

"BRUISED!"

"Not a girl who refuses to surrender! Not a girl who stands before you now as a CONQUESSOR!"

"*CONQUESSOR!*" The chorus of a thousand-strong rang like bells in her ears, deafening, overwhelming, making her tremble from her core.

With nothing but voice alone, the match-master had given birth to the energy thrumming in the arena. It was not he who had stamped the first foot, nor he who had uttered the first *hoo-rah*, but it started nonetheless for him, for the transformative fiction he crafted that cast her as a wily protagonist seizing the reins of her life.

The stares of thousands on her had felt like a suffocating noose just moments prior—but now the knot strangling her neck loosened, and a swift flame rose in her.

I deserve to be here, a voice inside her spoke to the spectators with an even-keeled conviction. *I deserve to be seen by you. I deserve to have you know my name.*

"By the blood of your ancestors, do you proud Ederi children vow to salt the earth with the blood of the demons that once gave death upon your ancestors?"

Feet planted apart, Lythlet raised her hands. Two fingers crossed over two fingers, she swore the oath back at Master Dothilos: "Witness me, upon the blood of my ancestors!"

Master Dothilos cast a bright smile at her, an eyebrow crooked skyward. He bowed deeply, flamboyantly, to her, and she knew at that moment, he was welcoming her to their partnership.

"Then release the beast!" he said into his speaking-trumpet.

As the gates ground upwards, metal grumbling and creaking, Lythlet pushed all distraction from her mind.

Remember the compendium!

Page upon page flew through her mind as she stared into the now gateless abyss, illustrations of beasts waxing and waning in her imagination.

It came then: the soft padding of feet bumbling across the sanded ground.

A tiny little monster emerged from the darkness, scrabbling across the ground clumsily, leaving claw marks behind. Wrapped in a halo of brown fur, it had a flat face with two large black pupils. It froze mid-step when it caught sight of them, then plopped its round bottom on the sandy ground, stunned by their presence.

"Lythlet?" said Desil hesitantly, with a hint of confusion.

Oh no. She could read his thoughts; the two of them were hopelessly susceptible to the small and the furry. *It's rather adorable.*

"Are we supposed to kill it?" His sword was already lowering.

"Wait," she commanded, clenching her spear. "This match is dedicated to the warden of tricksters, is it not?"

She glared at the beast, waiting for its secret to unravel. She could not recall anything so small and underwhelming from the bestiary, but she hadn't had the time to look at every page. Her eyes traced its rounded belly, its cherubic snub of a nose, the tiny little stumps starting to grow from the crown of its head—

"Bugbear."

No sooner had she spoken did the young bugbear shriek, an awful cry warbling from its furry throat.

Thunder rolled forth, thunder from the deep. From the abyss beyond came a roar, a stampede, and at last the true bugbear emerged, a hundred times larger than its offspring. The earth trembled as it dashed to the cub's side.

Lythlet pulled Desil back, trepidation rising. "Mind the horns. They like to gore their prey."

"What else?"

"Avoid the cub at all costs. Killing it will only enrage her."

"We've an issue then. They don't seem easily parted." He pointed at the mother bear gently ushering her cub underneath the safe stretch of her belly with her paw. He frowned, reluctance washing over him. "Must we kill them? It's no more than a mother protecting her child."

She had been thinking the same, but the weight of the spectators' stares forced her to reconsider. "These are dangerous beasts, Desil. Same as the sentari, same as the anzura. We came to slay sun-cursed hellspawn, and so we must. We're not allowed to spare pity on one just because they look comelier than the others we've encountered."

His sword remained tilted to the ground. "I haven't the heart to do this, Lytha."

Something deep within her tightened. "Would you have us forfeit?"

He did not answer.

From above, Master Dothilos's gaze burned into her. *He must wonder why we've yet to make our move. Surely no other conquessor would wait so long—most would strike the cub the moment it stumbled out.*

"We're being silly, Desil. These aren't sun-blest animals, sweet and harmless like a bitch and her whelps sent by the heavens to aid us in our mortal toil. Sun-cursed devils, isn't that what the Poetics would call them instead?" she reasoned, pulling from what little she could recall of the religious canon. "Monstrosities set loose in our land by the Scorned One to try us, to sully the Sunsmith and Moonmachinist's good creation."

For once, the religious appeal failed to strike gold with Desil. "They aren't even approaching us," he argued, slowly raising a hand to his forfeit pendant, the other sheathing his sword.

She opened her mouth, torn between debating further and acquiescing, but a bone-shaking howl interrupted, followed by the earth trembling.

Perhaps it was reacting to the violent flicker of light reflecting on Desil's sword as he moved to sheathe it, perhaps it was no more than beastly instinct driving it to attack—but the bear charged at last, and she charged with a fury, ginormous paws throwing up storms of dust toward them.

They split paths, Desil darting down one side of the arena,

Lythlet skirting the edge opposite, clambering upon the elevated platforms rimming the arena. Higher and higher she climbed, hoping for a good vantage point.

"Seven tons," she murmured breathlessly, rattling off bestiary notes as she jumped from scaffold to scaffold. She grabbed onto a lone bamboo shaft jutting out of the wall, swinging from one platform to another. "Not to be confused with the bogbear native to the southwest. Fiercely protective of its young. Often depicted with two horns, but some subspecies will grow up to six." The bugbear below was the classic dual horn, however.

She stayed high, watching Desil scramble to safety on a platform. But the bugbear followed him closely, the cub straggling at its rear, and he struggled to lengthen the distance between them. The bugbear went on its hind legs, long claws stretched toward Desil, missing him by what seemed like minuscule gaps of sheer luck. One paw smashed effortlessly through a corner of the platform he was trapped on, shattering its edge. The bugbear struck again, demolishing another corner.

Lythlet pulled out the bag of slingstones—after the last match, it seemed useful to have at all times—and started pelting the bugbear, hoping to distract her.

The bugbear turned around, narrowed its bottomless black eyes on Lythlet, and rampaged toward her. But Lythlet was high beyond the bugbear's reach. The beast roared, smashing the lower platforms into fragments.

Desil panted, arriving on Lythlet's ledge. "Forget what I said about it being no more than a mother protecting her child. I thought she was about to gut me until you took her away!"

"It has a temper," Lythlet agreed, holding onto her ledge. The bugbear was fruitlessly clobbering the walls of the arena beneath them, making everything near them vibrate.

"What do we do?"

"The bestiary had little to offer by way of defeating it."

He looked disappointed. "Nothing at all?"

"Well, there was one part I couldn't understand," Lythlet said slowly. "An offhand note. '*True to its name, the bugbear finds extraordinary comfort and grows deeply drowsy in the presence of summer's most disagreeable creature.*'"

Desil raised a brow, impressed at her memory. "What's it supposed to mean?"

She shook her head, lost. "Most entries were straightforward, but some had vague notes like that. Scholar Lewenskiros is a polymath who's written scholarly compendiums on several other fields, and sometimes he writes in a way that seems to be referencing one of his other books."

"Cheeky."

"But effective marketing," said Lythlet begrudgingly, wishing she had a complete library of Scholar Yavida Lewenskiros's work. "While we're stuck up here, let's put our heads together and decipher the note. It may be useful. *True to its name*, it says. I think it must be referring to the *bug* part of it—there are dozens of sun-cursed beasts with *bear* in their names, so it makes more sense for it to be referencing the most unique aspect."

Desil nodded. "All right, that makes sense. And what's this about summer's most disagreeable creature?"

They sat there, stumped, deep in thought, holding onto their shaking platforms. Lythlet's mind raced. Summer had descended swiftly over Setgad, the days turning sweltering. Her kataka flat was humid at all hours of the day, and she felt sticky and awful constantly. Moreover, her sleep was frequently interrupted by some very unwelcome guests flying in through the gaps in their walls—

"Mosquitoes."

Desil stared at her like she'd lost her mind, then widened his eyes. "Mosquitoes! Brilliant! But what can we do with this? We can't summon a swarm of mosquitoes to assist us. Not sure I'd want to, anyway. My arm's still red and itchy thanks to the one bothering us last night."

"Maybe we needn't actually have those pests here. We just need to make the bugbear think they are, then it'll calm down enough for us to kill it." She pointed at the yutrela poles. "Remember the tale of Atena and how she hid in the forest from the first of the Heavenly Dragons?"

"By using a yutrela leaf the way Pa used to make music on a gumleaf?" Desil's father had had the knack of taking the common gumleaf and humming a vibrating tune out of it. Desil could never achieve more than blowing the leaf out of his grasp, but his father had better luck teaching Lythlet a few sound variations.

"The tale does say she used it to make a sound akin to the hum of insects."

"Do you think it really works?"

"The best tales are the ones rooted in truth, and Atena must be a legend for a reason."

He smiled. "There's something rather daring about you today. Go on! Best you have a go before the bugbear destroys more of the arena."

Lythlet sprang from platform to platform, rising in an arc that brought her near the height of the spectator stands. Keeping her momentum, she launched herself at the yutrela poles, grasping one, her weight sending it swaying back and forth. The groaning of the bamboo was akin to the yawn of giants, and the bugbear jolted, turning.

Terror crept through Lythlet as the bugbear loped toward the bamboo ring, toward her.

Her hands scrabbled around the bamboo notches and hoisted herself up, feet securing her weight. But one boot suddenly gave way, sending her swaying precariously through the air.

She cursed her thriftiness; her lousy pair of damaged boots with the tractionless hobnails had made her slip. Heaving herself up, she steadied herself, wrapping her legs around the pole until it stabilized.

A terrified shriek tore from her as the bugbear smashed its paw against the bamboo, sending a ripple through it. It did not break, but Lythlet couldn't risk it further. She may have had an inkling of mercy for the bugbear, but the feeling was decidedly not mutual. She hoisted herself upwards in a surge of adrenaline until the top.

Planting her feet on the flat surface, she perched her weight with delicate balance. She plucked one of the sparse leaves at the top, pressing it against her lips. She blew once, and nothing but wind came out.

Out of practice, she cursed herself. Fortunately, Desil began distracting the bugbear, shouting and making a racket from his end. She had a few more seconds to spare, recollecting the techniques Uncle Bezil had taught her. She sealed her lips with the leaf, took a deep breath, and hummed against it.

A loud, eerie, high-pitched vibration sounded, like a mass of mosquitoes were swarming around her head.

The effects were instantaneous: the bugbear paused, then set its paw down mid-lope and yawned. Desil raised his head and stared at Lythlet with an incredulous grin.

She ran out of breath and inhaled.

In that brief second, the bugbear reared back to life, and it turned back to the bamboo ring, letting out a savage yowl as it bashed its paw against the pole Lythlet was on.

She lost her breath to a shriek as she nearly fell over, the bamboo wobbling. She clapped her lips to the leaf and hummed again, returning the bugbear to its trance. But she couldn't risk it returning to its senses the next time she took a breath.

Eight seconds from the moment I leave the top, she reminded herself, ready to invoke the divine touchstone.

Lythlet rose to her feet, spear ready, tip down, leaf still vibrating against her mouth. She shut her eyes momentarily to pray: *May Desil always find happiness in this world*, and with the map of the cosmoscape unfurling in her mind once again, she leaped off the bamboo, riding her spear to the ground, wind rushing past her ears. Music with a cosmic resonance roared in her eardrums, a bacchanalia of euphoric strings vibrating all over her body. She drilled the polearm into the back of the bugbear, and with a single thought, she molded the laws of gravity around her, slowing her descent in the nick of time to fall cushioned in the bugbear's massive furry form.

Crying out in pain, the bugbear reared on its hind legs, and Lythlet clung on to her spear. Her yutrela leaf was accomplishing nothing now, so she let it flutter away, fading simultaneously with the cosmoscape's golden melody as the eighth second came to pass. The world whirled around as the bugbear trampled the ground, but she held tight. Her hand shot forth to the bugbear's horn, a massive rough thing, and holding onto that as leverage, she ripped her spear out and plunged it into the neck of the beast several times, ripping its throat apart. The cries turned garbled, gasping, melting into a choked whimper.

Almost!

Once more: a hand on the horn, a spear pulled free, and its bloodied tip thrust in one final blow.

At long last, the bugbear collapsed on the ground, bloodied and breathless. Lythlet yanked her spear free and slid off, boots touching the sands as the spectators burst into loud applause.

"Desil?" The beast was so large, she could not see around the corpse.

He came toward her, sword resting in its sheath, arms cradling the tiny bugbear cub to his chest.

She started. "What are you doing?"

The spectators' cheers nearly drowned her voice out.

"I didn't want a child to witness its mother's death, the poor babe." His guilty look pressed heavily on her.

"The mother came first for us," she reminded. "She would have eaten us in a heartbeat, if not gored us into pieces. We killed her to protect ourselves."

"I know," he said grimly. The cub took to playfully gnawing his hand with its toothless gums, and he yelped, prying his hand free, a ring reddening on the back of his hand.

"Be careful," she tried. "It's still a sun-cursed beast."

"I will. It didn't mean to, I'm sure. Unless it truly is in their nature to turn violent, predestined by the great unknown to always walk down a path with no redemption. Or is there a way for it to rise beyond its making, to triumph over the temptation to fall prey to its base instincts?" He sounded oddly solemn, genuinely contemplating the question with a troubled expression. He rubbed behind its ear, smiling bitterly as it let out a growly purr.

"Rare, is it not?" Master Dothilos interrupted. "That the conquessor leads by slaying the mother. In the past, most struck the cub first, and learned only too late the terror they've brought upon themselves when the mother arrives. Rarer yet to see one conquessor alone defeat the bugbear while the other cuddles the cub! But conquessors, don't forget! Two beasts were sent to you, and two beasts are meant to be slain."

"*Two to be slain!*" the spectators roared in agreement.

Blood drained from Desil's face, and Lythlet grimaced.

"Give it a quick death," she said quietly.

"I can't," he said.

"*Two to be slain!*" the spectators demanded.

"We won't get our jackpot if we don't. All our efforts will be for naught if we let that cub go. And Master Dothilos will only have his servants slaughter it afterwards anyway."

"Lytha," he said, apologetically.

"Then I'll do it," she said with great reluctance. "Look away."

Desil gripped the little thing tightly, but loosened his hold with a resigned look, letting her take it.

The cub squirmed in her hands, letting out an uncomfortable growl.

Sun-cursed beast. Sun-cursed beast. Sun-cursed beast. She had to convince herself of this. She had to mentally transpose herself back up to the spectator seats, to capture the alienating distance that rendered the violence of the arena entertaining rather than savage, to shear away the empathy induced by proximity and dissociate herself from what she was being called to do.

"*Two to be slain!*" the spectators demanded. "*Two to be slain!*"

"I'm sorry, little bear," she started, feeling awful nonetheless.

I'll do it quickly, she promised herself. *It will be merciful. The way Madame Millidin kills chickens—one swift strike to the head. It's a cub without a mother, it has little future anyway.*

It whined, and she struggled to keep her grip on its fidgeting sides. It flailed its paws at her, and a claw cut through her arm, making her cry out in pain. The cub fell to the ground, her grip weakened. With remarkable dexterity, it sprang up from its bottom and scaled her legs like she was a tree, claws ripping holes into her clothes.

She raised her spear high over her head defensively, alarmed at what was happening.

Big black eyes loomed close as it neared her head, jaws spreading wide in obvious threat—and its gums closed in on her hair, yanking it hard by the roots.

She screamed, the familiar pain thrusting her backward in time.

The bugbear vanished and it was her alone, her of the long distant past. Her little self at age six, new to the schoolhouse, tongue still fat and limp behind teeth just beginning to loosen from pink gums.

A miserable day of feeling like an otherworldly creature forced into mimicking her schoolmates to get by had thankfully come to an end, and all she wanted was to go home. She knew the path herself; she knew her parents couldn't come to fetch her. She'd stepped out of the schoolhouse, out onto the unpaved dirt road it sat on, and headed toward home.

Then someone had bumped her shoulder. An older schoolmate, one who sat a few rows behind her in the one-roomed schoolhouse that serviced a dozen of the slum wards. He was only two, three years older than her, but he seemed gigantic then.

"Why don't you talk normally?" he demanded. "Why do you just stare at us? It's very rude."

She pushed past him, pressing on for home.

He yanked on her hair, pulling her back. She had screamed—the same scream she was hearing now, a shrill high-pitched wail.

"So you *can* make some noise." He let go for a moment, but only to sink his hand deeper into her hair to grab the roots. He pulled again, and she screamed louder. "I heard your mother has some demons in her. Is that why you can't talk?"

He had kept at it for much longer. Pulling her hair, yanking her lips apart, ramming his fingers inside her mouth to feel her tongue—"You have a tongue, so why don't you use it?"—playing with her like she were an insect he wanted to dissect.

"Tell me to stop, and I will," he said after a while, as if he were doing her a favor. "Just use your mouth and say stop and I will."

"S-s-s—" was all she managed to get out, tongue not obeying her mind.

He frowned. "Why are you like this? It's just one word, it's not difficult." He shook her small head by the roots of her hair, forcing another incoherent scream out of her.

The boy had paused then for a moment, his grip on her hair turning still. She thought he was about to let go, but he was staring at something. She turned her eyes to follow his gaze.

There was another boy watching them. Also from the schoolhouse, also from a few rows behind Lythlet, where the older children sat. He met her eyes. Saw her hair in disarray, a rough hand submerged in it. Noticed her tearstained cheeks. Heard her stuttering, incoherent plea, filled with clumsy but desperate hope, "S-s-s—"

And he walked away.

She watched him leave with a sinking heart.

The first boy went back to pulling her hair, then her lips,

squeezing them into shapes, trying to train her to say 'stop', acting as though he were performing an act of charity. Eventually, he gave up, dropping her to the ground and walking away.

She had cried on that unpaved road for hours, rubbing her sore scalp, spitting out the taste of the boy's unwashed fingers. Back in her empty home with the rotting floorboards, she had cried some more. But when her parents came home, she had said nothing to them. She couldn't.

Screams flooded her ears, those of distant memories, those of the present, those of a bugbear.

Lythlet plunged her spear in and out, in and out, trying to get the deafening noise to stop. And then it was no longer the bugbear screaming, nor her as a child, nor her in the present. The bully was kneeling before her, and she pierced him through the face over and over again. She was returning the favor, targeting his tongue, tearing out the back of his throat, rendering him the one incapable of saying a simple word. Then it was the second boy's turn, the one who had seen her and abandoned her, who had within the span of five seconds told her without speaking a single word that she had not been worth his time.

Her little self killed them swiftly, killed them brutally.

"Lythlet." A hand rested on her shoulder.

She froze, spear halting midair. Her eyes were wide open, mind returned to reality. It was Desil, his face concerned, frightened.

The bugbear cub was silent now. It had no choice but to be; there was not very much of it left intact. A smear of bloody flesh was heaped before her like some grotesque offering.

Stunned, she reached forth. There had been a beast here just moments ago—where had it gone? Her fingers came into contact with a bloodied patch of serrated fur, and then something hard. She pulled it out. It was stained pink from the gore, but it was a little white stump—the would-be horn of the bugbear cub.

She stared at it, horrified at what she had done. Horrified at the blinding rage that had consumed her.

"*Hoo-rah! Hoo-rah! Hoo-rah!*" She looked up, stunned. Her mind had somehow erased the presence of the thousands of people with her for those brief moments she'd regressed into memories. The audience cheered all around them, feet stamping, hands clapping, *hoo-rahs* erupting.

Master Dothilos looked approvingly down at her. "Well done."

She bowed in response, the smoothness of the action surprising her.

CHAPTER THIRTEEN

THE SECOND LESSON

"MY CHAMPIONS!" MASTER Dothilos crossed the threshold of the armory with arms spread wide. "A marvelous show, one of the more thrilling performances of late. Here's your well-earned jackpot—and the ledger, too."

Needing something to occupy her mind, to erase the memory of the smear of pink flesh and the bloodied white horn now resting in her pocket, Lythlet wrangled with the ledger, flipping through the pages. The way the odds had been stacked, there had been an equal number bidding against them as there had been for. She returned the ledger, confident that the numbers made sense.

"I imagine you've been keeping track," Master Dothilos said, "but this is more than double what you made the last round. You're drawing more bullish spectators at a rate simply uncommon for third-rounders, and you're keeping them on your side. After your performance today, I wouldn't be surprised if the number spikes even higher next month."

"We might fill up more than half the seats," she said, a thrill of victory sweeping through her.

Master Dothilos smiled. "You've answered my question before I even asked it. I'm glad you'll be accepting my next invitation. The two of you are exactly what I've been looking for: a pair worth marketing. I've commissioned handbills to advertise your matches, so your extended presence will be required one of these days for the inkmaster to capture your likeness. And," he added with an eager glint in his eyes, "I've already devised a name for your duo."

"A name?"

"I only bother investing the effort into pairs I foresee a bright future for. I remain proud to this day of the Poet and the Ruffian— those boys got a fair share of fame for their names alone. Spectators would cheer at the mere mention of it."

"Well, what is it?" she asked, curious.

"The Rose and the Thorn," he said, the epithets trickling out of him in dulcet tones.

Lythlet and Desil swapped curious glances at each other as they considered this.

"Who's who?" asked Desil politely.

"The Rose could be none other than you, that much is obvious to anyone with eyes. The ladies in the stands have been very vocal with their affection for you, as have some rather overenthusiastic men."

Lythlet rocked her head from side to side. *The Thorn*, she mouthed. She didn't mind it, yet it lacked a certain something, though she knew not what.

When she looked up, Master Dothilos was glancing at her thoughtfully. Then he turned to Desil. "Why don't you go wash up? You're still covered in sand and, I regret to inform, you reek of sweat."

With a sheepish expression, Desil left to the washing alcove.

Immediately, Master Dothilos spun on his heels to Lythlet. "May I borrow you for a moment? I thought we might have a wee chat today. Follow me this way. It's a shortcut to the stands—ah, isn't it much airier here? The armory was too stuffy for my liking. Have a seat, make yourself comfortable."

Sitting with her hands folded on her lap, she stared at the arena below. Master Dothilos's servants were chopping up the mother bugbear into smaller pieces to carry across the sands, a gruesome and laborious effort that would consume them for hours. She turned away from the gore and dragged the toe of her dusty, stained boots around in circles on the ground.

"You've yet to replace those horrid boots, haven't you?" commented Master Dothilos wryly, seating himself beside her. "I noticed you slipped on the yutrela because of them. You really ought to use the jackpot to invest in a new pair."

"I know," she said. "But I fear I won't have much coin left after I pay the loan shark next week."

The match-master looked sympathetic. "You know, if you had told me three months ago that you'd be the one worth keeping my eye on and not Desil, I would've laughed in your face. Truly, what a uniquely clever mind you have. I assume you borrowed inspiration from the tale of your beloved Atena today, using the yutrela leaf to lull the bugbear into a state of calm. And then your utterly savage display at the end, ripping the bugbear cub into pieces. Magnificent, precisely what the spectators needed to see to trust you've the brutality needed for these games. Desil, on the other hand, has been unremarkable. I'm not saying he doesn't have his own appeal: the spectators still love him for both his brawling reputation and his good looks. But not me. There doesn't seem to be much beneath the surface, and I'm not interested in someone as vapid and witless as him. You, though—now that's a story I want to work with. A genuine underdog without even a pretty smile to fall back on, nothing but her own brains keeping her alive. Well done, Lythlet, for discovering your conviction. You're starting to stand a little taller, a little prouder."

She smiled, silently squeezing her knees. Praise was a rare treat for her. "I enjoyed how you framed my story at the beginning."

He laughed. "Thief! Liar! I ought to thank you for the inspiration. It gave you an angle the spectators could respect. Who doesn't love the tale of an ambitious underdog, someone defying the odds life has beset them with? And I barely had to lie to do so! Remember what I told you? The best stories are those rooted in truth, embellished only for entertainment's sake."

"Is that why you said I stole hundreds of books?"

"Sounds far more impressive than five, doesn't it? Not that you had told me the truth then—no need to panic, Lythlet. I knew you were lying. You're a cautious creature, and you know better than to be wholly honest with me. Yes, hundreds of books! Stolen by a little girl whose own parents bleakly named her Candle-Flame, a little thief in the slums desperate for an opportunity to improve her standing in a wicked world. What a premise you've given me to work with. The spectators loved every morsel of it."

She considered then the power of storytelling in the right hands, how Master Dothilos had taken her truth and made it palatable, entertaining, empowering to the masses. "Thank you," she said sincerely.

His warm smile stretched further, the light reflecting off his hair in golden rays. "Although I cannot officially be on your side, know that I am not your enemy either. I'm simply someone who wants the honor of working alongside you. May I ask what happened when it came to slaughtering the bugbear cub?"

She blinked. The horn stub in her pocket seemed to grow extra jags, digging into her thigh. It hadn't felt right to drop it back into the bleeding heap of mangled flesh, so she'd taken it, though she had yet to decide what to do with it.

"It seemed like something came over you after it attacked you. You were screaming like a savage as you thrust your spear in and out—a stunning sight that'll go down in the annals of conquessing, truly—but I daresay you weren't angry enough at the cub to warrant such a display."

She fell silent, embarrassed. "I saw a memory then. A bully from schooldays. I saw him there, and one other."

"What did they do to you?"

She recounted the incident to him, rage resurfacing as she spoke. She clutched at her knees, bunching the thin, drab fabric of her trousers in her fingers to keep her emotions in check. "It kept happening for weeks," she finished quietly. "That boy would hunt me down every day to taunt me and pull on my hair and my tongue. He even got some of his friends to join a couple of times. Until one day, Desil caught the bully red-handed and chased him away for good. I'd never seen Desil so upset, swinging his fists at that boy to teach him a lesson. Then he helped me up from the ground, dusted the dirt off my clothes, and asked if I was all right. I couldn't answer, of course. But he just held my hand and led me to a seat inside. We became friends after that, and he refused to let me out of his sight at the schoolhouse." She smiled softly at the memory. "He really is a good soul. He holds true to the highest commandment of the Poetics: *to love a soul in spite of its vessel.*"

"Does he now?" said Master Dothilos with a faint, inscrutable smile. After a brief pause, he asked, "What's that bully up to now, do you know?"

"Dead, I hope," she blurted out, and blushed. Desil would've scolded her for wishing death on someone; there was most certainly a verse in the Poetics condemning it as uncouth.

But Master Dothilos burst out laughing, delighted. "Well, I hope so, too, for your sake. Very good."

"Good?" she said, surprised.

"That anger in you is a gift. Use it wisely, and it'll propel you to new heights." Master Dothilos hesitated, drawing his lips into a grim line. "Can I share something with you? Something secret."

She nodded.

He took off his cloak and untucked his dress shirt from his breeches. He clutched the hem in his fist and lifted it, revealing a pale palette of scars splattered across his torso in brutal lines.

She stared incredulously at the lacework of old lacerations.

He spoke, "Our stories run parallel to one another—*thief, liar, beaten, bruised!* You're not the only one who's been savaged by the world." He tapped her forehead, where the scar Master Winaro had given her remained.

"Who did that to you?" she asked.

He fell silent. "A very bad man," he said at last.

She looked at him with pity. "I'm sorry. Did he give you that burn on your arm as well?"

Master Dothilos started at her question, staring at the reddened patch of mottled skin on his arm. It had come into sight when he removed his cloak. For a second, she thought he looked rather sad looking upon it. But then he hardened, saying quietly, "No, this was someone else. A traitor, someone who tried to destroy me when I was on the cusp of digging myself out of poverty. You see, Lythlet, escaping the cycle of poverty won't be easy. Obstacles will pop up at every turn: those above you will try to hobble your ascent and invasion into their territory, all while your peers try to tear you down in jealousy, in a deep desperation to ensure you don't succeed before they've gotten the chance to. That's when you'll have to rely on the very thing I taught you: conviction. You must steadfastly believe you are on the right track, or you'll inevitably be pushed and dragged down by everyone else. But I have a second lesson for you if you're willing to learn."

She leaned forward. "What?"

He smiled. "Always a pleasure having a keen student. Tell me, how did you kill the bugbear today?"

She frowned at the simplicity of the question. "I stabbed it."

He shook his head. "You stabbed it, but would a single stab from an undernourished woman like you kill a mighty bugbear? Desil might have been able to pull it off with his brute strength, but you're not him. How did you kill the bugbear?"

She furrowed her brows. She had jumped from the yutrela. "Gravity," she tried, "speed, velocity, momentum—"

"Mo-men-tum!" he repeated, enunciating every syllable into a divine melody. "The mass of an object multiplied by its velocity, as per the workings of Scholar Rossova, and the most powerful force to have by one's side. Now, what's one of the requirements of momentum?"

"I didn't get to attend school consistently," she said, sheepishly. "We couldn't afford it. They might've taught this while I was gone."

"That's perfectly fine," he assured her. "The answer I'm looking for is *direction*. Momentum requires one direction of travel. To leap from the slums into the highborn circles, you're going to require a tremendous amount of intentional momentum, and you cannot waver for even a split second in your conviction that you deserve what you seek. A crossbow bolt only has power as long as it's focused on its target as it zips along from string to prey. A grand tale like those you used to read must hurtle from beginning to end with a sense of momentum behind every scene. Would the adventures of Rentavos the Gentleman Thief be half as exciting if he sat down for a very long, pointless cup of tea in the middle of a heist instead of getting on with the story?"

"Rentavos actually did have many long teatime chats with his confidants in the unabridged versions," Lythlet corrected modestly. "I always thought those slow, slice-of-life vignettes were charming and cozy."

"Well, that's because you had no friends in real life besides Desil, so you wanted to experience camaraderie vicariously through them," he said bluntly. She shut up at that.

He's not wrong, she thought sadly.

He went on, undistracted: "From now on, everything you do must induce forward momentum. Anything that hinders you is the devil, and you must exorcise them before they send you spiraling in the wrong direction. Your rage at that bully—use it. Get drunk on it and come back to the next match ready to slaughter a beast with that anger. Think of everyone who has ever belittled and beaten you, and slaughter each and every one of them in your mind."

"Did the spectators really enjoy watching me kill the cub so cruelly?" she asked quietly. "Had they no pity for it?"

He burst out laughing. "My dear, these people mount the heads of bugbears on their walls and stuff their cubs to showcase their wealth. *Pity?* Oh, Lythlet, you have severely overestimated the quality of the spectators. They're literally folk who choose to spend their weekends watching slumdogs get slaughtered by wild beasts! No, they have no mercy, nor should you. It may be a fine, noble quality in those storybooks you grew up stealing, but the serpent you call mercy is nothing more than a fairytale notion that sinks its venomous fangs into the young, weakening them to the brutality of the world. Don't let lofty ideals poison your cunning, dear girl. Stubbornly sticking to childish creeds will get you nowhere—learn to cunningly adapt to the world around you instead."

One argument floated to the top of her mind, but she left it unvoiced, fearing she'd come across as childish: *isn't one who lives like that no longer in possession of a moral compass but a moral weathervane?*

"You needn't have mercy for the beasts, anyway," Master Dothilos continued. "They wouldn't have any for you. Just like I wouldn't expect you to have any mercy for those in your past who hurt you. Why should you? Hate them, despise them, treat them with the contempt they deserve. I'm not going to implore you to love thy enemy, I'm not one of those barmy reciters of the Poetics—no offense to Desil, of course. That pure, unfiltered rage you channeled today was a gift to behold, and I want you to hold on to it. After all, far more satisfying than succeeding despite your naysayers is to succeed *in* spite of them."

"I wonder why the cub suddenly attacked me," she said, still bothered by what had happened. She circled her finger over the jagged lump in her pocket.

Master Dothilos reached over for a lock of her hair, holding it between them. "Same color," he murmured, glancing sideways into the arena. His gaze led to the mother bugbear's corpse being heaved out in chunks.

She paled. "Did it think I was its mother?"

"I doubt so. But perhaps it thought it could play with you the way it usually does. They like to yank on their mother's fur to get their attention."

She buried her face in her hands.

"Don't feel too bad, Lythlet. Those beasties don't know their own strength, and I don't doubt you had no choice but to kill it." He reached over and raised her chin, guiding her gaze from the ground to the height of the arena, to the now empty seats covered in the glaze of Inejio's baltascar lights. "Forget all that. Nothing but inconsequential trivialities. Look at all these seats instead. Stay with me a few more rounds, and you'll be staring at an arena filled to the brim with people who've heard your name. Those who bid against you, those who doubt you—prove them wrong. Make them recognize you as a thorn in their side, one they cannot ignore."

She could not unsee what he had shown her: the vision of thousands, tens of thousands overflowing the arena, calling her name, cheering, whooping—every soul knowing her, every soul unwittingly contributing to her coffers.

"Consider me a merchant extraordinaire of entertainment, and I'm about to make it possible for you to leave your mark on the canvas of revolution. You put in your blood, sweat, and tears, and I'll transform your story into the *zigatanos*, the spirit of the age," Master Dothilos promised. He seemed the type to slip in Vas Terrim words whenever he wanted to show off his prowess. "The Rose and the Thorn! You may get second billing, but don't think you're any lesser for it. It has more *oomph* at the end, does it not?"

She wavered.

"Come, girl, look at me. What's the matter?"

"I think it's missing something." His baritone made it velvet, the syllables rolling off the tongue like golden syrup, but it sounded lackluster when anyone else said it.

He laughed shortly. "Not my best work, you mean to say? But a prickly girl with a spear, none too pleasant to look at—what could fit you better?" He spoke benignly, yet his words were clipped minutely. Few would notice, but Lythlet had spent enough time around bad-tempered men to recognize one on the brink of losing his.

He's sensitive to criticism.

"Well," she said cautiously, tiptoeing around that temper, "the Thorn may suit me, but as you say, am I not more than an ugly, unpleasant girl? I am cunning and I am quick—I am nothing if not a golden bet to make."

He paused at her words, something new washing over him. "Yes," he said, nodding slowly, "you're on to something. The Thorn is too plain, too single-faceted for someone of your caliber. A golden bet to make deserves a royal name, does it not? What say you if we call you the Golden Thorn?"

Lythlet smoothed down her shirt, staring at the bloodstains as she dwelled on it. "The Golden Thorn." The syllables tumbled out easily; it was no longer his voice alone making it sound dulcet.

Against her will, a smile tugged on her lips.

Grokking her silence, Master Dothilos grinned. "My dear girl, you and I are about to begin something wonderful."

CHAPTER FOURTEEN

A FUNERAL FOR SMALL THINGS

DESIL DID NOT speak to her on their journey home.

He's upset at the way I killed the cub, Lythlet guessed. *He never would've let me kill it if I was going to do it that way.*

Had she really done anything wrong? It was a task that needed to be done by either one of them and she had simply stepped up in his stead. The spectators loved her for it, and she'd secured the jackpot and their goodwill as a result. But she couldn't quite shake the feeling that Desil wasn't wrong either—his was probably the most humane of all the reactions in that arena.

They came to the rope ladder leading up to their kataka flat, and as she brushed her hand against it, she remembered what was in her pocket—the last remains of the cub. She paused. What should she do with it?

The answer came to her, and she let go of the ladder. Quietly, she said, "You head up first. I have some business to take care of down here."

He looked concernedly at her but nodded.

Curving around the massive trunk, she came to a secluded corner at the edge of the kataka premises and squatted there on her heels to dig through the earth with her bare fingers. Her fingernails were caked with dirt by the time she'd created a small hole. She brushed it off before diving a hand into her pocket, digging out the horn stub.

The jagged edges pinched the skin of her fingers.

Gently pushing it into the earth, she said, "I'm sorry, little bear. I did not understand that you only meant to play."

She was glad she was alone. Master Dothilos would've scoffed at the idea of having remorse for the death of a wild, unthinking beast, as would all the spectators.

"May the white wind guide your soul through the abyss, that you shall find rest in the halls of healing," she continued anyway, reciting the prayers she'd heard so often at Ederi funerals growing up.

Another absurd thing to say—these prayers were not meant for sun-cursed beasts, who had no redeemable souls. No amount of guidance would ever lead them to the halls of healing. Yet Lythlet did not feel right simply saying nothing. *It's not so easy abandoning mercy*, she realized, *even knowing I should*.

Lythlet was drawing the rite of mercy in the air, twirling her first two fingers in a loop before touching them to the palm of her other hand, when she felt a presence lurking over her shoulder. She turned, frightened.

It was Desil, staring at her wide-eyed. "I was worried about you, so I came back down. What are you doing?"

"Nothing," she said, embarrassed. Then, sheepishly: "I'm holding a funeral."

He sank down on his knees, peering into the hole at the horn. "For the cub?"

She nodded, blushing. "I know it's silly."

"A little," he agreed, giving her a small smile. But he sat on his haunches beside her and drew a rite of mercy of his own.

She took comfort in his presence, and they sat side by side for a long while, drawing the appropriate rites, of mercy, grief, divine intervention, and remembrance.

"I thought you were angry at me for killing it the way I did," she said when they'd finished.

He paused before responding. "I was just surprised at how enraged you became. You normally kill the beasts as cleanly as you can, but you kept attacking the cub long after it had died. You weren't yourself, and that scared me. Was I seeing a side of you I never knew existed, I wondered."

"I'm no more capable of hiding a predilection for violence than you are," she said to soothe him, but he seemed unconvinced—even a little apprehensive now, she realized from his tense shoulders. In hindsight, perhaps it was distasteful to dismiss his concern so flippantly, especially to one who so despised the concept of petty violence against his fellow man. She bowed her head, solemn again. "Desil, did I commit a sin today? I know one of the high commandments of the Poetics is to take not what cannot be returned by thine own hand."

He sat quietly, and at long last, he shook his head. "You took the life of a sun-cursed beast, and that is not a sin. No bloodguilt lays upon you."

She nodded, relieved. "It's not like I killed a man," she comforted herself.

Desil kept quiet, staring at the horn. After a moment, he raised his head. "Where did you and the match-master disappear to while I was washing up?"

"Up to the stands. He wanted to talk." She faltered. She did not want to recount the match-master's cruel words about him. "He was very complimentary of us. Said we've the makings of champion conquessors."

"We or you?"

The question surprised her. She cast a cautious glance, but he didn't seem upset. "Me," she admitted.

He nodded, and she struggled to read his tone. "I thought as much. I barely fought today, anyway." Silent for a moment, he then resumed: "Be careful with him, Lythlet. I think it's plain enough to the both of us he's not a good man."

She glanced up at him. "He's a swindler through and through, and I'd be the last to say he's a pure-hearted fellow. But getting on his good side would only help us in the arena—and perhaps beyond, if he were to set us up with the right connections in life."

Desil ran a hand through his hair, clearly unhappy with her response. "I know. But he's just—I don't get a good feeling about him, that's all. Try not to talk too much with him."

She pinched her lips and nodded—not in agreement, but in understanding. *Desil means well, but if I were to listen to him, I'd been crippling our conquessing careers. All I need to do now is maintain my conviction and my momentum, and we'll both be set up for brighter futures.*

She began pushing dirt into the hole, burying the white horn once and for all. As the dirt filled up layer by layer, she threw in a few more things: the image of those two little boys she'd brutally stabbed—*may the white wind guide your souls*—and the bitter sadness of the aggrieved child she had been. A funeral for one became a funeral for many small things, and soon she was trying to heap into that hole anything that bothered her.

At long last, she was done. Desil pulled her to her feet, and they grappled their way up to their kataka flat. Inside, she thumbed through their jackpot once again, counting every coin. Every single coin, from the humble penny to the awe-inspiring white valir, was a symbol of the spectators' faith in her.

I may not like what I became in the arena, she thought to herself, *but I do like how I was rewarded for it.*

CHAPTER FIFTEEN

THE GIRL WHO DRANK STARS

THAT NIGHT, DIRANTAS sent a dream chasing after Lythlet.

The little prison island Nazao was sinking into the ocean. Waves of violent black water swirled around it, an inky soup rising and falling like a bolt of forgotten laundry fluttering in the storm. On the shores, Lythlet watched as ship after ship departed, plunging into the ocean to find a new home.

Above the Fated Ships rolled clouds of black thunder, coruscant veins of lightning hanging beneath, swaying in equal parts threatening and theatrical—they rather resembled Oraanu wind chimes dangling off the eaves of Setgadian houses.

Thousands of Exiles were fleeing; thousands would sink in the perilous journey, innumerable bloodlines buried at the bottom of the fathomless ocean. But dangerous as the journey was, all coveted the chance to escape certain death, and Lythlet was no exception.

Yet no ship would let her board, each turning her away.

"Please," she begged one, then another.

"*Thief! Liar! Beaten! Bruised!*" they denied her, setting sail for the west one by one.

The storm was closing in on her, the island beneath her disappearing inch by inch. She stared heavenwards, and in the eye of the storm was a fragment of the unsullied sky. Stars dotted the firmament like candles lit in the distance.

Then one flickered, twinkling coyly, before streaking southwards in a spiral.

Lythlet's eyes widened—were she to catch that star, she'd need not a ship, nor need she beg for passage. She elbowed her way through the remaining Exiles, navigating through the marching mess of embarking men and women and children alike, pale and dark and every shade in between. Her feet scraped against strands of weeds and fronds of bracken as she ran from the sandy shore.

The star was reaching the island, a violent yellow amongst the black backdrop. It burnt a golden streak across a gusty field of tall grass, and she threw herself after it, catching it in her hand. It was alive, untamed and as wild as a breathing beast. Fire burned from within, searing to the touch, yet without scorching her, a fire birthed from divinity—the Star of Fate. She wrestled with it, subjugating it to her will. Raising it to her lips, she tipped it into her mouth, drinking the starlight, the flame of heavens flooding her until all within her was golden.

Walk upon water, daughter of Kilinor.

At once, the eye of the storm widened, storm clouds parting above her. The stars of the night sky wheeled in concentric circles, she at the center of a vortex of destined greatness. Time and space coalesced into her, until it was her alone with the night, steps leaving a trail of fire the darkness could not quench.

She turned the seas golden in her wake as she crossed into the new world.

LYTHLET SNAPPED HER eyes wide open, the worn-out wooden boards of the ceiling staring back. Her mind was still, her thoughts lucid, as though the dream had been nothing more than a daylight wandering of the mind.

Could it have been a vision?

She sat up, staring out the window at the waking world, the rising sun, and the Tower of Setgad piercing the heavens in the distance. The guilloche sun symbol gleamed on the Tower, sunlight making the golden-white flames dance free from the borders of the diamond, flames impossible to cage and beautiful for that violent ambition. She smiled. In both dreamscape and the waking world, she remained one and the same, captain of her fate and fortune.

"Good morning," she said to a city on the cusp of recognizing her as a protagonist at last.

"THAT'S SIX WHITE valirs," said Lythlet, beaming as she poured the coins into Tucoras's palm.

The loan shark stared with barely concealed disbelief. It was an easy pile to count, but he made a great show of thumbing through every single coin individually, biting into them to check their authenticity. At last conceding he was not being cheated, he shoved the coins into his pocket. He regarded Lythlet and Desil with an impressed look. "That's another six white off your debt. Next month will be five white valirs due—"

"And then my debt will be paid in full," said Desil, grinning.

Tucoras nodded. His lackeys stood behind him dumbly; they'd not been given anything to do in the past few months, with Lythlet and Desil paying off their debt and more so easily every time. He reluctantly turned to leave but paused. "How in the name of the Sunsmith are the two of you making so much?" he blurted out. "You went from struggling to pay me spiras and dumasi to handing over full white valirs."

Lythlet and Desil exchanged a look, a satisfied glint in their eyes.

"We made some very wise investments," she answered, "and we're now reaping the rewards."

Tucoras sidled up to her. "Well, if this investment of yours is still open to newcomers, I would love to be introduced to your people. I could help you, you know. I have connections of my own you may find beneficial—"

"We'll think about it," said Lythlet, fighting the urge to crow in the man's face. He'd treated them like beggars to spit on for years, and now here he was, practically crawling on his knees to be let in on their success.

Life really is different when people know you have coin to your name.

A KNOCK ON the door of her kataka flat startled her.

"Expedited delivery for Lythlet Tairel!" hollered a voice from the other side.

Eyebrows furrowing, she peeked suspiciously through the window. Faravind Post never delivered directly to the kataka flats. The risk of the delivery-carriers being robbed of all their parcels ran too high otherwise. One had to pick up their mail from their offices instead to ensure the safety of one's own possessions.

But true enough, it was a man clad in a Post cloak, a winged envelope stitched into its back. His face was red, sweat dripping from his jaw; the climb up the ladder had winded him. He noticed her through the window and held up her parcel as a token of goodwill. "I have a long and busy day ahead of me, miss. I'd appreciate it if you took this off my hands."

She waved at him to leave it by the door. She was not foolish enough to open her door to a stranger, least of all without Desil at home, and it was not impossible for a common thief to procure an official cloak through underhanded channels.

With an impatient shrug, he did so and returned to the ladder with an unsubtle groan.

Once certain the man had gone, she opened the door, snatched the parcel inwards, and shut the door firmly, lock clicking in place.

What in the name of the Twelve Divine could this be?

One had to pay a premium to have Faravind deliver a package directly to a recipient living in Southeast, yet she couldn't imagine who would bother doing so for her.

A scrap of paper slid out on top of the unopened box.

Lythlet,

A gift you must never speak of to anyone else. Consider this a necessity in times to come, when I no longer want to see you stumbling and slipping. You can't afford to lose momentum now. You have some time to break them in.

Yours truly,

Not quite a friend, but most certainly a partner

She lifted the lid disbelievingly. *Master Dothilos?*

A pair of fine, luxuriously supple leather boots rested snugly in the box. She ran her fingers over the threaded seams, all precisely stitched in even lines by expert hands. There was the shoemaker's stamp imprinted on the side, an elaborate crisscrossing pattern of stars. Lythlet intentionally kept herself unfamiliar with the ever-changing fashions of the highborn, ignorance being the best defense against envy, but even she could tell these were no commonplace boots.

The hobnails at the bottom were defined, especially compared to the pair currently on her feet. She touched her own soles, marveling at how used she'd gotten to the fire-flattened nubs, then ripped off her boots to pull the new pair on. She tightened the laces, the leather taking shape around her calves, forming a perfect fit. *How would he know my size?*

She grabbed the note again, hovering between joy and disbelief. There was something written on the back.

P.S. I know you well enough to guess the inquisitive nature of your thoughts. If you must know, there were some of your footprints left in the arena, pressed into the sand, and I had them sampled for your size.

She laughed, touched by the thought and effort that had gone into this.

She was not naïve: Master Dothilos was not a man of charity. He was a merchant first and foremost, and he counted his costs dearly. There would be unspoken expectations behind such a generous gift—but he would only cast such expectations upon a person with something to offer. One who deserved further thought.

And that, she thought proudly, *is what I have become.*

CHAPTER SIXTEEN

A POET'S GIFT

As SUMMER THICKENED over Setgad, the sun turning unbearably oppressive with every new dawn and the heat deepening into a wretched humidity that saw them constantly soaked with sweat, Lythlet doubled her efforts in studying the bestiary.

She read and she read, from dawn until dusk by the sun, then by hivelight until sleep claimed her. She read at home, she read at work when she could escape notice, she read while eating at The Steam Dragon. She sorted the beasts into little rooms in her mind to keep them tidy, drafted mnemonics to make sense of them, and recited their entries word for word as if she were a living compendium.

Desil teased her obsessiveness, but the wardens had bestowed upon her this rare opportunity to uplift herself, and she was not about to squander it.

There had been no delay in their response to the fourth invitation. In a match dedicated to Nalepos, warden of still waters and deep meditation, the match-master had dredged a redivira from the wetlands.

"Cut off the hands quickly," Lythlet had whispered to Desil, and they had done just so, avoiding its deceptively short and blunt claws as recommended by the bestiary. Beneath those claws were needle-thin hooks that could grapple them and tear their skin into shreds, but dismembering the monster rendered it harmless.

Hoo-rah! The Rose and the Golden Thorn! Hoo-rah!

Lythlet carried the echoes of those cheers home, letting them ring in her ears and mute the memories of those who had cursed her, belittled her, and beaten her over the years. But nothing could compare to the joy she took in handing over the last five white valirs to Tucoras—and in him once again trying pathetically to curry their favor.

She went a few nights later to The Steam Dragon, bestiary squeezed into a haversack. Right as her foot was about to cross the threshold through the moon-shaped entrance, a man stopped her.

"Saevem?" she said, surprised.

"I was hoping to catch you here," he said, towering over her. "How fare your matches?"

"Very well, thanks to your gift," she said with a bright smile, bowing before him. "It's kept us alive for two matches now. I've gotten very good at swiftly coming up with lies of how I'd deduced the beast's weakness whenever the match-master inquires what inspired the killing blow."

He looked pleased. "Wonderful. Has Master Dothilos begun introducing you to anyone?"

She raised a brow at the odd question. "No. Why?"

"Oh," he said with a disappointed pinch to his lips. "I've heard that when Master Dothilos takes a liking to a conquessor, he becomes keen on introducing them to his circle."

"Be that as it may, he has made no introductions on my behalf," she answered. Who could she possibly meet through Master Dothilos that would help Saevem avenge the death of his friend? "If you're interested in his connections, why haven't you tried cozying up to the match-master yourself?"

Saevem shook his head. "I am aware the man has spies of his own—he's a cunning fellow who'd be sure to root out my links to the Coalition of Hope quickly, try as I might to keep my identity private. Anyhow, I hope you continue your winning streak, Miss Tairel. And when the time comes, please—remember me."

Remember the debt you owe me, she interpreted.

She nodded, bowing as he took his leave, then finally crossing The Steam Dragon's threshold. Schwala wagged his tri-colored tail at the sight of her, waiting by her side as she scanned for an empty spot.

"Miss Tairel!" Ilden greeted, startling her. "What a coincidence! Grab a seat, won't you?"

He sat at a stone table in the center of the room filled with two pots of tea and a few side dishes, most already empty. Shunvi was by his side. Apropos of the summer's high fashion, his silken robes had been retired after spring, and he now wore a loose thigh-length apricot-colored cotton robe for the evening, black Ederi-style breeches covering his legs.

Lythlet pulled up a chair. She had envisioned a quiet, intense session reviewing the bestiary with Desil during his break, but it seemed unlikely she'd have that opportunity with these two around.

Immediately, the men leaned in.

"That fellow you were talking to just now—do you know who he is?" pried Shunvi.

"He came over to Shunvi's teahouse months ago, and he hounded us with some odd questions," said Ilden. "We couldn't make head nor tail of what he wanted from us. He seemed curious if we were close to Master Dothilos, and when he found out we haven't had much contact with the man since our matches, he left with a glum look. What's he after?"

"I don't know," stammered Lythlet. The first part of Saevem's bargain flooded her mind—she was to keep this confidential. "He's simply a bullish spectator, as far as I know. He recognized me and had some nice things to say."

"Is that so?" said Ilden, looking slightly disappointed. "Well, no matter. We came down to give Demothi a surprise. He's rushing around now, but he says he'll join us later."

Glimpses of Desil's unruly brown ponytail could be seen bobbing around the kitchen.

Shunvi prodded an empty plate. "Shall we order more dishes? I'm partial to the soy roasted mushrooms myself. Perhaps some balsamic plum pork?"

"More sea urchins!" Ilden demanded, scanning the metal menu grafted onto the wall to the right. "Order what you'd like, Lythlet. We haven't celebrated your recent victory yet, so let's get to it now. Our treat tonight!"

"He means *my* treat, seeing how he's conveniently forgotten his coin purse," said Shunvi with an eviscerating side-eye. "But please, help yourself. We've a pot of broken jasmine here. Care to try a cup?"

"Say no," warned Ilden. "The tea's as pungent as the pit latrine back in Tresta Ward."

"You uncultured swine." Shunvi punctuated his words with a deep sip from his cup.

She smiled. "I'll try some. You lads order what you want. I'm fine with anything."

As Shunvi flagged down an apron-clad boy and ordered more dishes, with many suggestions front-loaded by Ilden, the latter suddenly became distracted by Lythlet's boots.

"Those are new, aren't they?" Ilden said, wide-eyed. "That starry etching on the side—they're one of Master Sayino's goods! Those cost a bloody fortune! Can't believe you even managed to snag a pair before they sold out. Sunsmith, I'd kill for a pair of Sayino boots."

She flushed happily, gratitude toward Master Dothilos swelling.

Moments later, Desil appeared from behind, shunting plates of Shunvi's recent order onto the table, then seating himself with a relieved groan. He lifted the apron over his neck to officially signal his rest.

"Welcome," said Shunvi, clapping Desil on the back. "It's been ages since we were last gathered. We didn't get to catch your fourth match."

Ilden added, "I heard it was quite the show, but Shunvi and Naya would've roasted me alive if I left them alone in the Homely Home with all those tykes. Their guardians are all busy building the flats along the river, so we're helping Naya look after the young ones."

"*I'm* helping," said Shunvi wryly. "You spend most of your time bothering Naya."

"Lies and slander. I expected better of you, Shunvi Tanna."

Shunvi ignored him, turning back to Lythlet. "I was very stirred by what Master Dothilos shared of your past at your third match. Knowing the match-master, it's a story that's been embellished— but the root of it is true, isn't it? You really did go around stealing books?"

She nodded with a small, embarrassed laugh.

He grinned and leaned behind to fetch something from his bag. "I happened to pass by a bookshop recently and thought of a gift for you and Desil."

"A gift?"

"One for your cultural enrichment, book thief. *Mot chin soe nak*—'flowers fade quickly, but a well-bound book will last you decades.' I thought someone like you would appreciate this." His smile broadened at her surprise as he thrust a thick leather-bound book before them.

"'*Five Classic Oraanu Legends — A Vasté-Oratha Bilingual Edition for Young Scholars,*'" Desil read the cover aloud, a grin on his face.

Lythlet flipped through it, excited. One page would be written in common Vasté, and the next would be in the dense logographs that made up the Oratha tongue. This brand-new book was nothing but pure amusement—a luxury she hadn't been allowed for a long time. "It has the tale of Atena," she said, delightedly skimming the pages of the first story.

"Do you like her, too?" Shunvi said brightly. "Her and General Lauturo were some of my favorite stories to read."

"Oh, yes, very much. Atena the Huntress and Rentavos the Gentleman Thief are my two favorite characters."

A light entered Shunvi's dark eyes at the mention of the latter. "*To be noble of mind and honest of heart, and to stand evermore on the side of justice!*" The Poet, ever composed compared to Ilden's feral nature, began chattering excitedly like a child discovering a kindred spirit. "I love all of Master Vidana's works. I attended a public reading of his at the Library of Athernara a year ago, and he was brilliant. Apparently, he's taken a break from the Gentleman Thief series and has been working on a war epic releasing next year or so, though he was awfully secretive about the details. Man has the presence of a mountain. He must have been a menace back in his military days! Did you ever read Rentavos's escapades in Bizarre-Naeveri, by the way? Those were my favorites."

All at once, an eager discussion broke out between the two.

Beside them, Ilden and Desil cast awkward glances at each other.

"Shunvi's going to be at this for a while," said Ilden with a sigh. He nudged Desil in the side. "You another lover of those booky-books?"

"I much prefer being read to than reading," Desil admitted.

"Attaboy. Shunvi's all about that la-di-da nonsense he digs out of old books. Thinks they enrich his spirit and broaden his mind or whatever. What a dull boy. I haven't an inkling what all the girls see in him, but women can be blind. Hand me that plate of sea urchins, would you, Fair Rose? I could eat a whole bowl of these babies."

"Not with my coin purse, you won't," Shunvi interrupted with a scowl. "You always order them whenever I'm the one paying."

"Oops," said Ilden, not even feigning an ounce of contrition as he made a grabbing motion for the most expensive plate on that table.

Desil pushed it toward him. "Have at it."

"I like how you're not even blinking at the name, Fair Rose," said Ilden impishly, scooping a generous mound of sea urchin onto his fork.

Desil sighed, beleaguered. "Haven't had much choice but to get used to it. The Rose itself was plenty embarrassing on its own, but now half the crowd's added Fair to it for reasons beyond me."

"Your fanatics are indeed obsessive," Ilden concurred, laughing without the faintest hint of sympathy. "Just the other day, I was speaking to quite the enthusiastic fellow who seems intent on proposing courtship to you any day now. Shall I introduce you to him? You've mentioned having acolyte-leanings before, so if you're all right with men, I may very well be introducing you to your future husband. He's quite handsome—if you squint."

Laughing, Desil offered a noncommittal nod. "With such high praise, how could I possibly say no?"

"Wonderful! I'll set something up," Ilden said, merrily shoveling more than his fair share of sea urchins into his mouth. Lythlet felt quite confident that he would most certainly forget to arrange anything.

Shunvi leaned behind to reach for something. "Have you seen your handbills, Lythlet? They're starting to go up around the city. We spotted one in Inejio."

"Oh!" Her hand was trembling as she took it. "I didn't know they were done. Master Dothilos said it'd take some time for the inkmaster to make enough copies."

Large flamboyant handwriting headlined the poster: **THE ROSE AND THE GOLDEN THORN — A GOLDEN BET TO MAKE!** Beneath was the inkmaster's rendition of Lythlet and Desil, a precise likeness with bold lines and vivid colors done by hands that had spent decades practicing their craft.

Desil leaned over to peer at the handbill, bursting into a laugh at his portrait. "I really am long due for a haircut." He rubbed self-consciously at the messy ponytail he'd recently started sporting to keep his curls out of his face.

"I'll give you a trim later," she promised, smoothing out the creases of the handbill carefully. She stared at the poster, and her own face stared back, a face that had never held much meaning before—now reproduced on parchment for the city to know she was a person worth taking note of.

"May I keep this?" she asked shyly.

"No," returned Ilden immediately, a cheeky smile curled on his jaw.

"Ignore him," spoke Shunvi kindly. "It's yours now. You'll see plenty more, I reckon. Half the city will be coated under these."

She smiled appreciatively, continuing her efforts in smoothing out the creases. Desil's debt had been repaid in full, and now she was free to dream of what she could do with her future jackpots and fame. Her mind was reeling with all the possibilities her life was about to take next, the horizons of her ambition shifting as she indulged in it. "I know it's silly, but somehow this feels as precious to me as a jackpot."

"Not silly at all," Shunvi assured. He raised his teacup at her, and she toasted him back.

But as she stared at the poster, at the curl of red paint around her lips, the haphazard spackling of brown dots over her cheeks, and the shaded concave of her bony cheeks, she felt something tugging her back to reality. Gray-watercolor memories weighed her down. Father, Mother, and the haunting notion of home they had always represented throughout the years, dispossessed as they now were—hollow and ramshackle, yet ever-damning her for her failure to surpass them. Yet filial piety seemed less like a prison sentence now—it took on a new shape in that moment, transforming into an opportunity to prove herself.

She could not keep looking forward without looking back even once.

Tentatively, fretfully, she thought for the first time in many years: *Perhaps it's time for my long-awaited homecoming.*

And then hopefully—a quiet, desperate hope: *Perhaps I won't be a burden to them this time.*

CHAPTER SEVENTEEN

HOMECOMING

THE HOME FOR Temporarily Embarrassed Highborns was the safehaven Father and Mother had sought refuge in, and it had taken up residence in the abandoned mansion once belonging to Governor Hemharrow Corinthos, the first governor of Setgad. Though rundown by time and pillagers, some of the estate's former majesty remained intact, evident from its tall brownstone exterior with granite quoins and gabled dormers.

But where tall iron gates should have stood was now empty space, the estate free for all to enter. In the middle of the sandy road that led to the mansion's entrance stood a statue of Hemharrow Corinthos, dwarfing Lythlet.

There really is a resemblance between Corinthos and Governor Matheranos, Lythlet thought, admiring the artistry of the white stone statue. The incumbent Governor Matheranos was a descendant of Corinthos through his maternal line—a link frequently boasted about by his supporters in the United Setgad Party. She knelt to the plinth and brushed the plaque free from dirt-ridden vines.

Here stands Hemharrow Corinthos, firstborn son of Harrowtar Corinthos and Mythleta Varinos. Appointed Governor of Setgad by the Einveldi Court under the auspices of the Ora Empire on the 8th of Marben, in the twenty-eighth year of the Sephir Circuit, it is his divine duty to serve the people of Setgad with utmost honor.

Based on the few history lessons she had the chance to enjoy in her fragmented schooldays, Lythlet recalled the impact Governor Corinthos had made on the then-burgeoning city-state of Setgad. Brokering the relationship between the citizens of Setgad and the Twelve Judges of the Einveldi Court, he had instated the notion of a democracy by successfully convincing the latter that future governors ought to be elected by the people, not handpicked by the Court alone. Thus, he founded the United Setgad Party, and under his leadership, Setgad had grown into one of the most prosperous city-states on the continent. He'd garnered so much public adulation in his early years that when the city-state held its first elections at the end of his appointed term, he won in a landslide victory. A second landslide victory occurred eight years later, and a third would've happened had he not decided his twenty-fourth year as governor was to be his last, thus setting the precedent for every governor elected after him.

"*Otara menaré,*" Lythlet said, patting the statue's feet. *You've worked hard*, it meant in Vas Terrim, one of the few sentences every person, low- or highborn, could not escape life without knowing.

She circled around the statue, heading deeper into the estate, hunting for her parents.

An unregistered woman taking rest in the gardens answered her question about Father's whereabouts with a finger pointed at the long colonnade running around the estate's grounds. Following the yellowing columns, Lythlet spotted Father leaning against one, staring at a pair of birds nesting in a dried-up fountain.

"Father," Lythlet greeted him, hands together behind her back. She shielded her trembling as best she could.

He turned, surprised. Before he could greet her, he coughed into his raggedy sleeve.

"Are you sick?" she said, worried.

"Just a mild cough I've picked up recently."

She frowned. "Has the construction been hard for you?"

"It's fine," he said firmly.

She knew not to push it further—she'd hurt his pride if she insinuated he was anything less than capable of the work. And despite his cough, something about Father did seem hale and sturdy then, a fresh scent lingering about him that reminded Lythlet of the far-off fields of harvest. Perhaps the construction had given him new purpose, something to cultivate his strength.

"Did you come to visit us?" he asked.

She nodded bashfully. Tentatively, she asked, "Today?"

A warm smile crept onto Father's sunspotted face. "Today."

Her heart flushed with relief, the unfamiliar sight of his smile calming her fears.

They went together through the portico of the mansion, past its wide double doors with stained-glass windows, and up several staircases until they reached the attic. Eaves slanting overhead, the room was lit by a dormer window at the far end. Much of the room was taken up by mountains of boxes and supplies, but a small, lumpy mattress had been shoved against the side of one wall. In the corner of the room, Mother was sweeping, battling dust bunnies with a broomstick, and she looked up at Lythlet in surprise.

Mother looked as thin and stretched out as ever, like a hairpin pulled so far in the wrong direction it was on the verge of snapping in two, yet her eyes were lucid, bright, and brown. Lythlet felt her emotions overrun at the sight of her mother whole of mind and spirit.

"Lythlet, it's been so long," Mother croaked, laying the broomstick against the wall and gesturing her to sit on the bed.

But Lythlet went before her and prostrated herself on the ground—the proper ritual greeting a child owed their parents after a prolonged absence. In hindsight, she should've bowed to Father like so when they'd met in the Homely Home, but she had been too flustered then to even consider the appropriate customs.

"To your good health," she wished, forehead pressed to the backs of her hands.

No reply came, but she lifted her head to see Mother offering a hand to help her up. She took it, fondly thumbing the bony bumps beneath Mother's fragile skin.

Mother guided her toward the mattress. She sat on it, while Lythlet sat on the floor, cross-legged.

Father had gone to a corner to rifle around inside a box, and he came back again with other things, plying the floor before the mattress with small cartons, some half-empty, some filled to the brim. Dried sour plums drenched in both sugar and salt; roasted brown mangos; many little tins of *tapuri,* fried, crunchy noodles coated in spices. Snacks that were cheap and could last forever, snacks she had enjoyed in her childhood.

"Some things we saved from the house when we had to leave. Take some home later," said Father quietly, gesturing at the food.

She popped open the lid of one tin of *tapuri.* It was stale, bought some time ago, but the pink crescent peach seasoning remained sweet on her tongue. "Why did you get so many?" Father and Mother did not like crescent-peach-flavored *tapuri* as much as she had.

They looked lost as to how to reply, and she regretted her question. It grieved her to try to understand their silence, to solve the unspoken riddles of two detached souls. She made to say something else when Father finally spoke.

"In case you ever came back."

Her throat tightened. "I'm sorry I never did."

Mother met her gaze with a slight shake of her head. "You've been busy. Father said you've been struggling with some debt, too."

She wiped her seasoning-covered fingers on her trousers, straightening her back. "That's what I've come to talk about. I have good news: I've paid off my debts. And I vow to pay off yours, too."

Father and Mother exchanged a surprised glance with each other, uncertain for a moment.

"You don't have to," Mother said, doubt evident in her voice.

"We'll do it on our own," Father said, hacking a cough into his palm. "It's no small sum, and it's our own business to take care of. I'm earning good money at the flats, and my debt will be repaid in two years."

"Two years isn't soon enough," Lythlet said. "I don't want you to struggle at the flats for that long. Tell me the sum, and I'll have it paid off by the end of this year."

"Lythlet," Father said delicately, "you mustn't make a promise you cannot keep."

"But I can, Father. I've come into some wealth recently." She rifled through her haversack and took out a silver chain, presenting it to him. "A gift for you—for your birthday next week."

Both Father and Mother stared wide-eyed at the chain. It gleamed handsomely even in the dull light. There was a small charm attached to it, that of a five-petalled *neira* flower—his first-moon flower, something she had in common with him. It was a gift she had poured much thought into; she had considered simply offering money, food, or clothing, but knew something so blatant would offend his pride. But this, masquerading as a birthday gift, was a *reshunzi* chain, a complex Oraanu creation where the links could be broken up and sold individually to pawnshops for nearly par value, should her parents have need for smaller allotments of coin. Thrifty as she usually was, Lythlet had gone above and beyond to procure this, borrowing from Desil's share of the recent jackpot to afford it.

"You could wear it around your ankle, under your sock, if you're worried about others spotting it," she said. "It's thin and lightweight, and won't burden you as you walk."

Yet he made no move to accept it, simply staring at it dumbly. *Does he not like it?*

Disappointed and baffled by their collective lack of reaction, Lythlet wavered. They sat a mere arm's length away, yet silence stretched as a desert between them. She saw now a three-way tightrope between them, that miserable black line suffocating under the weight of the indomitable negative space.

Lythlet took a deep breath. "Please," she said quietly, determined not to surrender so easily this time, "tell me what you're thinking."

Father spoke fearfully, "Can you really give us this? It looks so expensive."

She dug deeper beneath the surface of his question, and realized then why they'd been so tentative, so skeptical thus far. They must have thought she'd stolen it the way she'd stolen as a child.

"I can. I promise you I can. I got lucky with an investment," she said carefully, "and I purchased the chain with my own coin fair and square."

She had never lied to him, not even in her youth, and her unwavering answer was enough to convince him then. The lines in his face softened, a cloud being whipped away from his mind with a gentle hand. "Thank you," he said at last. "You... you've been doing well."

"I have."

"*Otara menaré*," he said.

Her shoulders heaved in relief, the sheer honor of hearing her father say this to her overwhelming her.

"*Tolliënimhé ristellë rimmonim*," she whispered back instinctively, bowing her head, "*rimmonim napei gineret tolliënim.*" *We who will not forget you, you who have come before us.* It was an old-fashioned response, a ritualistic expression of gratitude and filial piety that most folk nowadays had foregone for truncated options. But Lythlet was old-fashioned for her time, and there was no response more perfect for her to commemorate this moment.

"If you will not let me pay off your debt, then very well," she said, voice bolstered by her resolve. "Pay it off with your own work, Father. But I promise I'll make my riches sooner than later, and I'll buy you a proper home aboveground to return to. A home better than the one we had before—better than anything you've ever imagined."

They looked at her with a brand-new light in their eyes, one that took a moment for her to decipher—it was faith.

For the first time in her life, they had faith in her.

The three-way tightrope was no longer alone on the canvas, buffeted by the walls of a white canyon. The negative space was now splashed with flickers of this moment: the soft brown of Father's and Mother's proud eyes, the glinting silver of the *neira* charm dangling from the chain, the pink-and-orange flecks of the *tapuri* seasoning—and with a broad brushstroke, Lythlet added the dawning golden touch of her conviction.

CHAPTER EIGHTEEN

RUNNING FAST

LYTHLET'S DEBT OF gratitude to Saevem deepened as *An Annotated Compendium of the Modern Beast* proved its worth match after match.

The fifth match had been none other than Desil's much feared nine-headed dragon-snake, and though the arena had transformed into a filthy, blood-stained mess by the end, with all nine heads dissected and their wriggling brains strewn everywhere, the Rose and the Golden Thorn had yet another decisive victory under their belts.

The sixth match had been a mire-ogre, a great lumpy beast that scurried around spitting muddy balls of gas in their direction that would explode upon contact. Desil used the sling to fire rocks at them, popping them before they could reach either him or Lythlet, carving a path for her to dive forward and stab the mire-ogre. Not even Master Dothilos's sonorous baritone could survive the flood of cheers from the audience when she was done slaughtering the ogre, their calls for the Golden Thorn sending shivers down her spine.

See me, hear me, know me, she thought proudly.

The bidding ledger had become so thick with entries with new spectators chipping in their coins, Lythlet could no longer feasibly keep the sums in her head. She reveled in the jackpot instead, letting the coins slip through her fingers, then scooping them up once more to savor their rough-cut edges. Knowing every single one belonged to her and Desil, not a single one going to wind up in Tucoras's oily hands, gave her an unspeakable joy.

"The Rose and the Golden Thorn," said Master Dothilos, clapping his hands together thrice as he entered the armory. "I simply cannot say how honored I am to have you two as the rising legends of my roster this year. The other promising duo forfeited their third match, and all other conquessors so far have failed to triumph in even their first round. There really is something special about the Rose and the Golden Thorn. Could I borrow you two for just a spell before you go? There are some spectators dying to meet you."

He whisked them through the maze of hidden halls tucked far beneath the spectator stands. Massive statues of the Twelve Wardens were poised by every doorway, their mighty physiques making the corridors seem narrow and tight. Soon they came to a high-roofed atrium, the entrance flanked by fair-haired Ashentoth, warden of the dawning sun and merriment. Across the other end of the hall, the exit was guarded by her soulbound lover Shiratoth, warden of all that flowed, be it an inspired thought, the ceaseless rhythm of time, or—the much prayed-for—prosperity and fortune. She stood shrouded in white robes, ebony hair accented by a white feather tucked into her braid. Veins of baltascar ran through the grand fan-vaulted ceiling, lighting up the venue with a soft, pearlescent glow.

A chorus of *hoo-rahs* heralded their entrance. There were dozens of spectators waiting there, and Master Dothilos led Lythlet and Desil through. The match-master was clearly popular amongst the crowd, all the guests affectionately hailing him by nicknames, him effortlessly appeasing their need for conversation with a few glib words.

Lythlet observed him in quiet awe. It was hard to believe this was ever an orphan boy who struggled to make himself heard and respected—he wove his way around the highborns like he was above all of them.

One day, she thought, almost immediately laughing at herself for even imagining she could reach the heights of Master Dothilos's hierarchical accomplishments. But despite her disbelief, there were glimpses of hope for her: many highborn approached her, congratulating her, telling her how they adored seeing someone so savagely ambitious succeed in the arena.

After a few minutes of awkward, stilted conversation with some fellows, the match-master tapped Lythlet on the arm and led her away by the elbow.

"Come, my girl. I can see you're struggling. Vapid he may be, I'm grateful Desil has the social mores you lack." He nodded at the distance, where Desil was enthusiastically entertaining a conversation with a bright-eyed middle-aged woman wearing a blinding golden filigree over her chest.

"Are all of these spectators highborn?"

"Indeed. Those pink, chubby fellows you were just talking to are brothers who own a spectacularly profitable range of businesses all over the city—inherited from their grandmother, of course. That woman Desil's with is the gazette-master of the *Twelvemonth Sun*. Tackily fond of gold, I can tell you that. I once got into a horrendous fight with her ridiculously violent cat, but I'll save that story for another time."

"And you all travel in the same circles?" She thought of the question Saevem had broached her with recently: *has Master Dothilos begun introducing you to anyone?* Who was she meant to pay attention to here? she wondered.

"The webs of the elite intersect heavily, my dear. They may be insufferable at times, but there are benefits to rubbing elbows with them, as we've discussed." The baltascar light glinted off his pale blue eyes. "They find me a vital part of their lives now, most of them. The arena is simply one aspect of my success. A small one, in fact—the greater part is my knowing the right people."

She eyed him sideways. It was hopelessly evident he was a man who sought validation and approval from others and boasted the moment he got it.

He retreated with her to a corner and gave her a goblet and a platter of dried fruits from a small table.

"Do you drink?"

She answered by gulping away, nose wrinkling happily at the shock of alcohol.

"Good. Desil declined my offer." He took a sip from his own, the lump in his throat bobbing. "Ah, that hits the spot. How goes your debt to the usurer?"

She beamed. "Paid in full with the jackpot from the fourth match. You should have seen him during our final payment, meekly begging to know how I'd made so much coin. This is the same man who had no compunction in stomping on me as if I were an insect, in ordering his henchmen to bruise Desil and me black and blue the one time we ran late in our payment, in painting our walls with vulgar threats whenever he felt like it."

"Nothing I love more than a tale of righteous vengeance." He toasted her goblet with a grin, and they drank deeply. "It feels wonderful putting people in their place, doesn't it? In this world, you need coin and clout to do it, and now you have both. You see, my dear? Wasn't I right when I said conquessing is your way out of poverty?"

She bowed to him. "I thank you for everything you've done to make this possible."

"You're most welcome, Lythlet. It's my pleasure to work with someone so capable. Which brings me to something I must discuss with you." He set his goblet down and sat beside her on the marble bench. "You've worked as the bookkeeper for some rather unsavory folks, yes?"

She looked at him questioningly, resting her goblet on the table before nodding.

"And you've learned the clever tricks they use in their books to either hide or exaggerate their profits?"

"I have," she confirmed hesitantly. "But why do you ask?"

"I require your expertise, my dear girl. You see, my—how shall I put it—benefactor has made a request, and I need help fulfilling it. He believes he's being cheated by someone whose profits he gets a cut of, the sum of which has been dropping suspiciously low as of late. The accused fellow has provided his ledgers in rebuttal. I have them here with me."

He gave her a pair of small but densely filled ledgers, minute details scribbled over every page.

"A dogfighting ring?" she said with distaste, catching sight of transaction details while riffling through the pages.

"Indeed. But my benefactor is not so convinced by these numbers. He suspects the ringmaster is skimping on his end of the deal and underreporting his income."

She nodded, intuiting the conundrum. "Your benefactor believes the ringmaster is keeping two sets of books, and the ledgers with the real numbers are hidden away."

"Lovely deduction, my dear. You truly do know a thing or two about accounting fraud."

"One of the first things I had to learn if I wanted to keep my job," she muttered, stroking the spines of the ledgers. Something bothered her. "Who is this benefactor?"

"You needn't concern yourself with that."

His evasive answer only confirmed her guess. "What is it you're asking me to do?" she asked warily.

"Find the real ledgers, if there are any. Compare the numbers and see if they match up. Then report your findings, and I'll settle my benefactor's concerns."

But she shook her head, thinking of a reply that would save both their faces. "Forgive me, Master Dothilos, but I fear I can be of no help. Perhaps one of your servants—"

"I have nowhere else to turn," he pressed. His troubled blue eyes were framed by a furrowed brow. "This must be done soon, and I cannot spare any of my very busy servants on this. Summer is always a pivotal season in marketing, and you being precisely at the midpoint of your conquessorial career means I must have all hands on deck promoting your remaining matches. Momentum, my dear: I'm trying to create it for you."

She knew what he was doing—hinting at how she ought to repay his efforts in like. If there was one thing life had taught her, it was the importance of repaying her debts.

But she avoided his gaze, remaining hesitant.

He leaned closer. "What are you concerned about?"

She said quietly, "You're trying to hide that your benefactor is the Eza. I fear becoming entangled in something dangerous." Who else could stake a claim in another man's business so easily and have enough clout over Master Dothilos to drag him into this? Unease settled over her, her grip on the ledgers slackening. She was already loosely connected to the Eza through the conquessorial bloodsport; tightening the bind seemed foolish.

The match-master's eyes widened. With a small smile, he said, in careful, clipped words, "My, aren't you clever? Yes, as long as I'm under the aegis of the Eza, I must grant any favor he demands. He knows I'm a man with many connections in both highborn and lowborn worlds, and he frequently requires me to find the right person for whatever odd jobs he throws my way. But if you help me resolve this issue quickly, the Eza needn't know of your involvement at all, and I'll remain in his good books. Otherwise— well, I fear what might happen if I fail him. I think you know how merciless the Eza can be." He glanced nervously down at himself, and Lythlet recalled the elaborate lacework of scars on his torso.

Tendrils of guilt gripped her heart, tightening. She *did* owe the match-master much gratitude; the happiness of recent times wouldn't have been possible without him. "It's not in my constitution to abandon those I'm indebted to, Master Dothilos. I'll see what I can do."

He breathed out in relief. "Thank you so much. I'm glad to have someone like you on my side."

She nodded. "If the ringmaster's hidden his books too well, what should I do?"

Master Dothilos smiled dryly. "You have a violent reputation now, Golden Thorn. Use it boldly, use it freely. Cause a ruckus, if you want. Bring your spear along if you wish to add weight to your threat. It may spook him to see you in full conquessorial regalia."

Her eyes widened. "You want me to threaten the ringmaster?" She breathed out. "I suppose that could be done. Desil and I will work something out, and I'll report back to you with our findings."

The match-master looked confused. "Desil?"

"If it comes down to threatening the ringmaster, I think a former brawling champion would have a role to play."

"He's far too soft-hearted for this matter," the match-master said skeptically. "Allow me to find you someone better suited for the job—I know plenty of fellows with the muscle required for this business. They're well-acquainted with the Eza and won't hesitate the way Desil likely would."

He raised a fair point. Desil would be aghast at the notion of threatening another, of wielding his strength in a way that violated any one of his Twelve Prayers.

Yet the logic of his proposal battled her loyalty. She thought of how in their interview with Master Dothilos, Desil hadn't hesitated for even a heartbeat to sign up jointly with her. "I've always done everything with Desil. Somehow I feel guilty pairing up with someone else," she admitted.

"Don't. Just because you're friends does not mean you owe him your everlasting loyalty to the point of making insensible decisions. The boy may be twice your size, but he has half your wit. It hasn't escaped my notice, nor the spectators', that you're the one directing Desil in the arena. Even if he lands the killing blow, we see how you whisper in his ear beforehand. For all the years he's been by your side, have you reaped any great reward from his companionship? This is the same boy who trapped you in a fool's debt for years."

"He gave me love in times when I needed it."

"You are young, and you've yet to learn the cheapness of love," he chastised. "For his naivety, you spent years in debt, your future robbed from you until you joined my arena. I worry about you yoking yourself to someone so intellectually inept and utterly unambitious compared to you. He may be a fellow slumdog, but he has been privileged in ways you never were: fair of face in a world of vanity, well-loved from young and constantly told so by a father and mother who were whole of mind, and blessed with a natural strength to keep him safe in a city filled with petty violence. Yet by having all these blessings, he was robbed of the chance to learn spite, to practice doubt, to be fueled by the thickest oil of them all: sheer, undying lust for revenge. You have this. You have many to prove wrong, and the Twelve Divine know there's no better motivation for success than a love-starved childhood."

"I think you can stop now," she said as politely as she could. Hearing him dismantle Desil so thoroughly brought her to the cusp of anger, though she found herself incapable of poking holes in his argument, much to her dismay.

Master Dothilos laughed shortly. "Forgive me," he said, clearly not meaning it. "I get carried away sometimes. I just want you to keep in mind the most important thing: momentum. In all those storybooks you read, I suppose friendship was some powerful, unifying bond between characters, but most friendships don't amount to that in reality. Some friendships are, in fact, hindrances rather than help, and in this business with the ringmaster, I fear

Desil with his piety and soft-hearted nature will simply slow you down. Perhaps he was good to you as a child, saving you from schoolyard bullies and petty menaces. But in the real world with grown-up terrors and grown-up problems, he has yet to prove his value. It may be time for you to consider how much stronger you may be alone, away from him, and graduate onto more beneficial connections."

"His friendship has been an anchor in a drifting ocean throughout the years," she argued.

"An anchor," said Master Dothilos wryly, "is precisely what kills momentum."

"SOMETHING'S BOTHERING YOU," Desil said by way of greeting as Lythlet crossed the threshold into The Steam Dragon, a large wooden mallet resting on his shoulder.

"*Woof*," Schwala agreed, nuzzling his forehead into her hand and whining until she started scratching him.

"Busy day," she said, not quite lying. The inn she minded the books at had been hectic, new receipts in need of logging being shoved before her face all day long, as visitors from other city-states took advantage of the long summer days to come and holiday in the Diamond City. But in truth, work paled in comparison to the ceaseless cogitation she'd engaged in for days now, thoughts spiraling in circles as she mulled over the task Master Dothilos had assigned to her. He had left open his offer to introduce a partner to her, and she'd yet to decide if she was taking him up on it.

Desil hefted the mallet on his shoulder, leading her to an empty table. "I'm afraid I've to help Madame Millidin pound out some rice cakes, so I can't keep you company. But here, take your mind off things with this." From a drawer, he withdrew Shunvi's gift to them, the thick bilingual storybook, and plopped it in front of her.

"I'd been wondering where this had gone."

"I've been reading it during my breaks. A much easier read than the bestiary, I can tell you that." He laughed sheepishly. "If only I weren't too slow-witted to memorize that the way you have."

"You're not slow-witted," she said firmly.

"Don't bother," he dismissed. "I get every beast confused with another, and I certainly can't recite all the nitty-gritty details on them the way you can."

"You just need to know how to prioritize your efforts," Lythlet said. "The arena can hold neither water nor airborne beasts, so don't bother with those pages. I used to only study creatures native to our region, since it seemed unlikely Master Dothilos would fork out extra for an exotic breed from far away on early-rounders. But now that we've reached the midpoint, he's likely willing to draw more from his coffers in the name of a good show, so I've been expanding my study to the beasts plaguing the east and south, as well as those from the Ora Islands."

"The fact you can strategize like this shows why you're a better conquessor than me," he said. "Without you whispering in my ear during our matches, I'd have been wiped out a long time ago."

It troubled her to hear him repeat Master Dothilos's criticisms.

"That's not true," she began.

But he interrupted her, smoothing out his apron. "I need to head back to the kitchens now before the madame scolds me for disappearing. I'll get someone to bring you some tea."

A teapot came within minutes, delivered by another teahouse worker. She poured a cup for herself, breathing in the steam—ulaberry tea, sweet and blood-red with petals floating atop it, the most fragrant of the summer berries. Schwala laid himself flat on his back by her feet, subtly demanding she rub his white tummy.

Five Classic Oraanu Legends sat in front of her, a dainty green bookmark tucked in between the pages Desil had left off.

She flipped through the Vasté pages, smiling fondly at the first legend, that of Atena, daughter of lowborn farmers who earned first the trust then the fealty of the Four Dragons of the Heavenly Mountains. Atena's ingenuity with trigger traps had always inspired Lythlet to imagine wild inventions of her own, spending lonely childhood days scraping together oddball contraptions out of anything she could find.

　She read the story aloud to Schwala in bits and pieces, then reached the second legend, the one Shunvi had so earnestly recommended, its title emblazoned in beautiful cursive script across the top of one page.

GENERAL LAUTURO AND THE NINETY-NINTH NIGHT OF DARKNESS

in which the esteemed general conceives of his twenty-third principle:

> *A battle fought with deception is a battle won before a single drop of blood spills. Cast shadows where nobody stands, and your enemies will quail before you.*

> *And so it was that in the autumn of 191, Emperor Edavo XIII, the Chosen of the Crescent Moon, commanded General Lauturo to rage into a war that could leave neither side unharmed. But secretly unto himself, the general thought there was another way, a way that would spare his soldiers from needless death.*

> *On the eve of his army's departure, he held a great feast for all, and secretly seeped into each of their goblets the essence of the yurarani herb. His soldiers raised their goblets to him over and over, proclaiming their ceaseless loyalty to him, unwittingly surrendering themselves to a deep, undisturbed slumber for a moon and a sun, their heads drooping lower one by one.*

> *But when General Lauturo left the feasting tent for his horse, a blade pressed into his back.*

> *"May the moon bleed upon you tonight for your betrayal, Lauturo," cursed his assailant in the night. "What madness has befallen you, my brother? Did you set them to slumber*

so that you may flee? The Five-Masked Devil terrorizes our empire, and you choose to aid his efforts?"

For it was Lieutenant Jinvi, sworn brother of General Lauturo since his first full moon.

"Jinvi," the general said heavily. "Of all nights you would choose temperance, it had to be tonight."

"Explain yourself!" the lieutenant demanded, sword pressing deeper into his sworn brother's robes. "Why leave without a word, sneaking into this corpse-night as a thief runs from the master of a house?"

"Jinvi, Jinvi, friend before mountains and stars, brother beyond mortal bonds, you need not doubt me tonight. I have sent our soldiers to a harmless sleep. A corpse-night it is, but the Matron guides my path, and she has shown me the moonlit way to the Five-Masked Devil. Watch for the high noon, for return I shall with the devil's skull clutched in my fist."

"But why go you alone, Lauturo? Let us follow you there— let me follow you there. Command me to fight by your side to the ends of this world, and I will obey every time."

"Brother Jinvi, truly no man possesses greater loyalty than you. Yet there are battles that must be fought with silent haste in the dark of night, and thus I choose a road that admits only one. Two visions did the Matron unveil to me as I prayed at the moon-temple. In one, I ride alone to the Five-Masked Devil, and without word of my approach reaching the Devil's ear, I end his terror. In the other, I am aided by another, and we become thwarted by the Devil's forces. So it is that if you come with me, you will die with me. Says the Matron unto us: if you want to run fast, you must run alone. Jinvi, despair not! I will return, and we shall feast in victory."

Lieutenant Jinvi bowed his head and knelt to the general. "Two oaths I make unto you: that I shall await your return, and that I shall avenge the lack of it. May the Matron render

the second unneeded, Lauturo. Ride swiftly, and return once
more the pride of our people."

The tale continued for much longer, but Lythlet sat back, letting
the book fall shut, Desil's bookmark unmoved.

"*If you want to run fast, you must run alone,*" Lythlet muttered
under her breath. It seemed a fortuitous whim of the divine that
she would read this today of all days.

"Pardon?" said Desil, seating himself beside her, mallet-less. He
didn't lift his apron, indicating he was still on duty, but business
had quietened enough for him to rest.

She tapped the book. "General Lauturo has some words of
wisdom."

"Solid story. Really enjoyed that one. When he confronts the
Five-Masked Devil and realizes—"

She delivered a swift, chopping motion to his hand. "I haven't
read that far yet, so shush before you ruin it for me."

He clamped his lips together and mimed weaving a threaded
needle up and down through his lips. He only broke his silence
to say, "Naya and the two lads have asked for our help in looking
after the little ones at the Homely Home again. I was thinking of
going on Nichavind. You've time off that day, haven't you?"

Lythlet paused. She had thought Nichavind ideal to visit the
ringmaster. She opened her mouth, about to finally tell him of
Master Dothilos's request—then halted.

If I want to run fast, I must run alone.

"I'm afraid I can't," she said after a moment, apologetic. "I've
work to do that day. But give my regards to the Homely Home."

CHAPTER NINETEEN

THE PRINCIPLES OF GENERAL LAUTURO

Lorent Bicarda was not exactly the most personable companion, but Lythlet understood at first sight why Master Dothilos had paired him up with her. He was a broad-shouldered brute with many scars pockmarking his face, his ears cauliflowered to a grotesque degree, and his knuckles seemingly permanently swollen. He spoke purely in grunts and shrugs, and she decided very early on to keep conversation minimal between them for the sake of her own sanity.

But having him as an escort made Hiligna Ward a little less daunting: it was a part of town best described as seedy after sunfall, and little better in daylight.

They passed rows of dilapidated, abandoned shacks which soon gave way to fields of weed and red-raw earth, occasionally punctuated by a lone building in equal amounts of neglect. Eventually, she came upon a long and wide-gabled storehouse— the address of Khavi Monul's dogfighting ring.

Remembering a technique from one of Rentavos's heists, she stepped only upon the stones dotting the landscape, preventing her tracks from being left in the soil. She passed the same trivia on to Lorent, who glared at her before reluctantly tiptoeing upon the same stones she did.

Master Dothilos had assured her the entire area would be empty so early in the day, as dogfighting took its spectators only at night. Nonetheless, Lythlet remained on guard, peering around for any unwanted persons, straining her ears for voices, footsteps, stray coughs. All she could hear were snuffling noises, but those were distinctively canine.

At the door, she pulled out a lock pick. *It's been a while, old friend*, she thought fondly at it, one of the two she'd bought as a child, spending the entire fee earned as a funeral flag-bearer on them. The lock popped open after a few seconds of fiddling around.

Few windows lined the building, and the interior was dim, drenched in shadows from every angle. A single desk and a cupboard were all that filled the ringmaster's administrative quarters. But search as she might, with Lorent standing guard mutely, she could find nothing of value, neither records nor clues of Khavi Monul's black tax evasion. The only thing of merit was a memorandum written in fat, brash letters left on a desk:

DO NOT FORGET:
MEETING WITH E.M.
NICHAVIND HALF PAST NOON
HIS OFFICE

Lythlet peeked at her pendant watch. It was a couple of hours away from high noon.

Very good. He won't be home then. I'll investigate the rest of this storehouse, and if there's nothing here, I'll head over there. She turned to the only other door at the end of the room, and the knob gave way immediately.

A thoroughly bare room greeted her, the flooring removed to

reveal dry red earth underneath, a wooden enclosure forming a ring in the center—the fighting pits for the dogs.

She crossed the room, anger and disgust welling up at the faint trails of blood staining the earth. There was another door, and she pushed at it.

The hinges squealed, and a chorus of barks and yelps overwhelmed her, the sheer volume drowning out all thought.

Both the administrative quarters and fighting pits had been dire and dim, but they were kept respectably tidy, all things considered. The kennels, however, were a shamble of stink and rot, the only things gleaming in the barren light being metal bars caging row after row of hounds.

A foul stench forced her hand over her nose, yet she wished she could cover both ears as well. Scores of canines were driven wild at the sight of her, and they sent their cages rattling in metallic excitement, echoing alongside their growls and yelps.

She was not naïve to the realities of dogfighting, but to see the beasts firsthand, housed in their own filth with barely enough room to lay on their bellies, awoke misery in her gut. These were sun-blest animals, created to be sweet and docile, yet dogfighting handlers had starved and beaten them to induce aggression, feeding them a steady diet of ill roots and powders to force them into beastly proportions.

Pity took over her, and she went toward the nearest cage, pulling out her lock pick.

But the hound within lurched forward, a brown beast swathed in abnormal bundles of muscle and sinew. Even on all fours, it came to the height of her ribs, and it snarled at her, dirty yellow fangs gnashing at the bars. She stopped in her tracks, silently regarding it, weary with helplessness.

The pick in her hand felt as worthless as a twig. There was no feasible way to unlock the cage and not have the hound maul her where she stood. It was a beast so damaged by its own life, so trapped in the cycle of torture and starvation, it could never have freedom.

"I don't know how I can help you," she spoke quietly to it, apologetic. She could barely hear herself over its snarling.

Reluctantly, she stepped away from the cage.

If only there were some way I could shut this whole monstrous ring down. But turning to the watchmen for help would be in vain. She had been disappointed by the city's withered justice system one too many times in her life to have any hope in them. Even if she were to alert them of what was happening within this storehouse, the ringmaster could easily bribe his way out of gaol.

She gave one last glance at the sea of rusted cages and the hulking beasts within, the stench of unwashed filth permeating the walls.

"This is not the life you were meant to live," she whispered sadly to them, turning to go.

The hounds were unceasing in their growling, their baying. But somewhere in the din, a high-pitched squeal made her pause. She strained her ears, listening curiously. Her footsteps led her to the back of the room.

One cage was separate from the others.

"Little ones," she exclaimed, bending down to greet the litter squished inside. It was a pack of black and brown pups, too young to have seen a full moon. They yipped at her, clumsy paws stepping over one another in the crowded excrement-smeared cage. Likely a new acquisition of the ringmaster, yet untouched by harsh hands. Either they would be trained and damaged to join his kennel, or used as bait in a match, thrown into the wooden pits for the bigger hounds to tear apart and feed themselves with.

"I can help you yet," she said with a growing smile. Perhaps saving these pups would help her atone for what she had done to the bugbear cub in some small way. She hadn't quite shaken off the shame of that match, despite Desil's assurance she had not marred her divine record with bloodguilt.

"Leave them be," Lorent said, startling her. She'd almost forgotten he was there, so mindlessly quiet was he.

"Master Dothilos told me I could cause a ruckus if I wished, and I think seeing his business get meddled with might spook the ringmaster into obeying the Eza," she argued, refusing to admit that mercy was simply getting the better of her.

He shrugged disinterestedly, receding back into silence, arms crossed over his burly chest. She was quite certain he suffered some degree of brain damage.

With no assistance from Lorent, she dragged the heavy iron cage across the floor with all her strength, sweat running down her arms. She kicked open the door leading outside, sunlight flooding the kennel. She winced, having grown used to the dimness, but continued heaving the cage out. Once clear of the room, she knelt and finally, with overwhelming relief that she could be useful at last, withdrew her lock pick.

The latch on the cage loosened, and she delivered each pup one by one into the open field, their furry bodies snug in her hands.

"You'll have to run now," she ordered, watching with relief as they bounded away. "Go as far as you can. The streets of Setgad may have problems of their own, but you'll find much better lives there than in this awful place."

A weight brushed against her foot, and she looked down at a very small, very quiet pitch-black pup clinging to her ankles. It looked up at her with its big brown eyes and wagged its tail once.

"Aren't you a tiny thing! Were you the runt of the litter?"

"ROO."

"Goodness, what a peculiar noise that was," said Lythlet, privately charmed. There really was no other word for the sound that had come out of the pup's throat: it was a polite, truncated howl that sounded more like a mild request than anything else. "Do you not know how to bark properly?"

"ROO," the pup replied politely once again.

"That's all right, it took me a long time to learn how to speak properly, too. Now, carry on," Lythlet said. "Your brothers and sisters are leaving you behind."

She tried to help the pup along, carrying it across the field, but when she set it down, it only rested its little head on her boot, staring at her with drooping eyes, making her heart ache.

"I have an errand to run, and you're taking up a lot of my time." She wagged her finger weakly, trying to sound cross but failing. "I can't keep you, if that's what you're hoping for—the kataka flats are no place for a pup. *Shoo!*"

But she gave the pup only a few seconds of failure before scooping it up into her hand and blowing a kiss at its dirty face. "You won't last a day out in the city if you're going to be like this, you silly runt. Come, we must hurry."

THE STEAM DRAGON opened late every other Nichavind, lifting their shutters at noon instead of the usual seven a.m. start. When Lythlet arrived—alone, as she had sent Lorent ahead to meet her at Ringmaster Khavi Monul's private residences, not wanting to be bothered by his hulking presence—she had to squat low to enter the small gap beneath a semi-lifted shutter.

Schwala wagged his tail at her, then froze, spellbound by the puppy in her arms.

On a grand pearl-inlaid table in a private room at the back, Madame and Mister Millidin were enjoying a tender, private meal, sharing tea and a plate of golden honey-egg biscuits with each other.

Shy, freckle-faced Mister Millidin was the first to notice Lythlet peeking at them from behind a screen. "A puppy?" he said, delighted. He rose, stretching his skinny arms out to her, and sat back down with the pup cradled in his arms like a baby. He made soft woofing noises at it, leaving his wife to handle the business end of the matter, as usual.

Madame Millidin, with a smoking pipe in one hand and clay curlers still wound up in her white-streaked hair, stared at Lythlet with one eyebrow raised in an aggressive prompt.

"I found that pup abandoned in the streets," Lythlet lied, nervous. "I'd like to keep her, but the kataka flats wouldn't be safe—she might tumble over, and when she's full-grown, I'll struggle to carry her up and down the ladder. I was hoping…"

"Eh, all right," Madame Millidin said easily, relaxing her brow and feeding the pup a puffy biscuit off her plate. "We'll keep her here. Schwala could use a friend anyway, that fat old laggard. But it is upon you to be her master. See to it you eventually find a home on the ground so you can take her in."

Lythlet stroked the pup's ears, smiling quietly. "That future may not be too far off." With her future jackpots, she'd finally be able to afford a proper house.

Keenly aware of the trickling sands of time, she nonetheless lingered a minute to introduce Schwala to his new companion. He stared at the puppy as if he wasn't sure what she was, then nosed her bum, his tail finally starting to sway again. Lythlet petted their heads.

"Thought of a name yet?" Madame Millidin tossed her two remaining puffy biscuits at the dogs.

Lythlet stared at the tiny pup happily nipping at the treat with her sharp little fangs. She thought of how small the pup was, how comfortably snug it was in her hand, how sweet and innocent it was. She thought for a long time, and at long last, she said with an inspired smile:

"Runt. Her name is Runt."

MASTER DOTHILOS HAD given her the home address of Ringmaster Khavi Monul, in case her investigation at his storehouse led to nothing. It was in Minatu Ward, a respectable area a short walk away from the governor's southern precinct.

What Lythlet envied most was not the size of the houses, generous as they were, but the fact they were landed. Built with their foundations in the ground—with plenty of space for a hound to frolic about—not dangling up in a tree with a wearisome rope ladder.

Her arrival in Minatu Ward had been well timed, just a minute past high noon. She found Lorent poised covertly by a street corner, and he gestured for her to peer around. She caught sight of two Oraanu men departing Monul's residence, one a short, well-dressed fellow who was most likely Khavi Monul, the other a big, muscled bloke who appeared to be his personal guard, rivaling Lorent's imposing stature. Once they'd cleared the street, she went forth and used her lockpick to break into his house.

Lorent stood watch by the entrance as she swept through Monul's residence. An hour of fruitlessly scavenging his plentiful rooms ended with her back in the private study, scowling at the impressive library of books stretching high to the ceiling. *Ledgers, notes, journals, something! The ringmaster ought to be punished for his kennels, and if it could be brutally meted out by the Eza, that'd be justice fair and square.*

She skimmed the shelves once more, hoping for something out of the ordinary. His books were meticulously cataloged, arranged by area of interest, and then alphabetically. There was a section on entomology, a total of fifteen books—which included, much to Lythlet's private amusement, *An Annotated Compendium of the Modern Insect* by Scholar Yavida Lewenskiros—and then a section on culinary creations. Then there was a row of tomes dedicated to the adventures of General Lauturo. Try as she might to focus on her duty at hand, Lythlet couldn't help but paw at them. Shunvi's book had whetted her appetite for more of the general's journeys.

She flipped through *Arctora Principalis: An Academic Treatise on the Modern Applicability of the Principles of General Lauturo*, finding a thoroughly uninteresting dissertation that sucked any sense of adventure out of the legend. Wondering at the ability of some scholars to render anything joyless, she slid it back onto the shelf and skimmed along the spines of the rest of the collection.

Her fingers twitched as memories of her childhood pastime crept up on her—surely it couldn't hurt to pinch a book or two for her own collection. A ringmaster who abused dogs didn't exactly deserve mercy from her. She ran her hand along the tops of the books, letting her heart lead her to her next treasure. It came to pause over *The*

Principles of General Lauturo, the dust jacket protruding rather oddly from it.

Curiosity piqued, she pulled *The Principles* out, removed the dust jacket, and cackled with unexpected triumph. Revealed was Monul's current-year ledger.

Who would've thought my sticky fingers would crack the case? she thought, plucking out the rest of the Lauturo-themed books, examining the contents of each. Half of them were legitimate tomes dedicated to the general's impressive life, but the others were ledgers spanning years and years of records.

Comparing them with the false ledgers the ringmaster had supplied the Eza, a giddy smile bloomed on her sallow cheeks as she unpacked the fraudulent transaction records, the clever expenses made up to hide profits, the debts fabricated to skim more off the top for himself.

She returned to the foyer, reuniting with dull old Lorent. "Evidence procured," she announced, raising the ledgers. "Now we move on to the next act: confronting the man himself. His massive companion won't be easy for us to spook, though. I was thinking, if you give me enough time to build a trigger trap, we could invoke General Lauturo's twenty-third principle: *a battle fought with deception is a battle won before a single drop of blood spills. Cast shadows where nobody stands, and—*"

"Just let me smash their faces in," Lorent interrupted impatiently.

"Fine," said Lythlet bitterly, shoulders drooping. *Desil would've indulge my imagination a little longer.*

"YOUR MASTER SENDS his greetings, Master Monul." Lythlet rose from the settee in the foyer to give a polite bow, hand twirling through the air in faux formality. Lorent stood immovably by her side, looking like an ancient statue.

Across the foyer, by the entrance, Ringmaster Khavi Monul and his guard reeled in surprise. The ringmaster was a stout, snub-nosed man who rather ironically resembled a dog—one of those breeds with a squashed-in face. His companion, on the other hand, was a tall, burly man whose arms were corded through with absurd muscles, a dead-even match for Lorent.

"Who the devil are you?" Monul demanded.

"No more than an appreciator of your fine bookkeeping skills, Master Monul." She held forth the two ledgers Master Dothilos had given her.

At the sight of that, Monul stilled.

"You have been accused of keeping two sets of books. The ones I hold now are forgeries you concocted in efforts to keep more coin for yourself. What say you to these claims?"

"I've just explained myself to him," he cried. "Why must I repeat myself?"

"Because you have not explained yourself to me," she answered, although she did not wholly understand his words. *Has he just met with the Eza? He was off meeting a fellow whose initials are E.M., I recall from that note in his office.*

He huffed. "As I've just explained, his suspicions are completely unfounded. I would *never* be so low as to cheat him of my profits. I'm an honest man, and I won't have you stand in my own home, accusing me of lies—"

Lythlet patiently pulled out *The Principles of General Lauturo*, brandishing it as if she were a merchant hawking a book.

Khavi Monul silenced, wearing the expression of a dog getting caught eating something he shouldn't. "That's just one of my favorite books," he tried weakly.

"It's your current-year ledger," she said flatly. "The real one, clearly stating that you've underreported your profit this quarter by a truly brazen seventy-five percent. Sunsmith and the Twelve, you're going to be roasted alive for that."

He fidgeted, growing frustrated as the seconds ticked by. "Why were you sent here instead of the watchmen?" he said at last, looking irritated at her.

His question made little sense at first, but it was simple to reason with. *The Eza must call his guards the watchmen, too.*

"Because I am better than the watchmen," she replied simply.

I sound just like Rentavos the Gentleman Thief, she thought gleefully.

He squinted. "I recognize you. I've seen your handbills posted around. You're that conquessor everyone's been talking about. The Golden Thorn. Can't escape a conversation nowadays without hearing of your fights."

She flushed proudly, but kept still, trying to remain impassive.

"So you were pulled in through Master Dothilos," Monul mused. "How that man has clambered into everyone's good graces never fails to amaze me. Mark me, that man's words may be silver, but they come from a forked tongue."

"Enough," Lythlet resumed, picking up the reins of the conversation. "I will deliver these books as proof of your crime, but you have been granted one mercy. Remit what you owe immediately, go bow before your master and beg for his forgiveness, and no harm will come your way."

Monul closed his eyes, brow furrowing, jaw clenched. Then his eyes opened, glinting. He raised his left hand, and his muscled companion stiffened, taking one heavy-footed step forward and balling his fists up by his chest.

She observed calmly. "If you intend on killing me before I can deliver these books to your master, you must know that my death itself will implicate you."

Monul laughed. "And what of it? I can flee the city with all the coin I've saved before anyone catches wind of your death. Ozori here was a champion brawler back in his day—he'll make short work of you and your friend."

Lythlet opened her mouth, ready to retort, but Lorent sprang to life then, whipping forward like a bolt of lightning and clocking Ozori right in the face.

Crashing into the door behind him, Ozori regained his footing just in time for Lorent to smash a vase against his ear. Porcelain shattered in a rain over his blood-splattered face as he collapsed to the ground, knocked out. Snatching at one of the falling porcelain shards, Lorent then held it against Monul's neck, a pinprick of blood appearing on the man's pale skin. He drew close until he was a mere inch away from the ringmaster's face, eyes wild as a beast's as he spat out the next few words.

"I'll drag you straight to the Eza right now, you worthless piece of dogshit. And if you ever forget to pay your dues again, the Eza will send me out again, and I'll gladly hunt you down like the pathetic weasel you are. Think of running away, and I'll shove your scrawny little rodent body into a bait-bag and feed you straight to your own bloody hounds."

The sheer fear in Monul's eyes was enough to confirm he had learned the error of his ways.

Goodness, Lythlet thought, privately impressed by Lorent's sudden verbal abilities, *this face-smashing business is certainly more efficient than my trigger trap idea would've been.*

"MY DEAR GIRL, I am glad to see you return. What's that dust jacket you're waving around?" Master Dothilos rose from his seat in his office, welcoming her.

"Just a bit of cultural enrichment I picked up," she said cheerfully, "right before Lorent went off and delivered Monul to the Eza with the real ledgers I found." Not that she had expected or desired otherwise, but Master Dothilos had made it clear beforehand that only Lorent was sanctioned to meet with the Eza, so she had happily foisted the rest of the dirty business onto the man's shoulders.

The match-master's confusion faded, and a bright smile expanded across his angular face. "You *are* a wonder, my girl. I knew you could do it." He clapped her on the back fondly.

She beamed with pride, glad to have been of use.

He cocked his head. "Was Lorent good to work with?"

"Not the brightest baltascar bulb in the room, but he certainly knows how to threaten a man."

"I imagine he did a much better job than Desil would've."

She opened her mouth to argue, but miserably could not find the words to dispel the subtly smug comment. It was true. Perhaps Desil would've stepped in to defend her if it came to blows, but drawing things to a swift conclusion by preemptively attacking and threatening others would not have been his modus operandi.

"Go home now," Master Dothilos said with a smile as gentle as the sun after a storm. He needn't say more; he had already proven his point. "I'll see you next month."

CHAPTER TWENTY

THE THIRD LESSON

THE MONTH OF Kalijean marked the delayed onslaught of autumn. Summer faded almost overnight, sun-bright red conquering the green in the foliage of the kataka flats.

The fast-broaching chill of the changing seasons demanded work on their part: Lythlet and Desil spent a whole day spreading pages of the *Daily Diamond* in a thick layer over the floor for extra insulation. When the city was on the cusp of winter, they would add straw mats, but for the meantime, they fell asleep next to baltascar-block printed headlines of *HARVEST PARADE PREPARATIONS UNDERWAY; THE PHANTOM STRIKES AGAIN—THE JEWEL OF ARKANTA GONE MISSING!; MATHERANOS VS BRANDOLAS: WHAT YOU NEED TO KNOW FOR THE ELECTION; 16 YEARS WITH GOVERNOR MATHERANOS—A RETROSPECTIVE; MATHERANOS: LOWER TAX RATES FOR NORTHERN AND CENTRAL SECTORS IN THIRD TERM;* and *A MEOWRACLE: HERO CAT SAVES CHILD FROM DEADLY BALCONY TUMBLE!*

Besides exciting headlines of successful Phantom heists and heroic cats, and mind-numbingly tedious political journalism,

Kalijean brought, too, the seventh match of the Rose and the Golden Thorn. A pair of kaebinas were their foes, small, twee creatures with round, protruding bellies and stubby limbs. Yet much like Lythlet, what they lacked in strength, they compensated with speed and wickedness. They bolted around the arena, using their tails to whip merciless bruises into Lythlet and Desil, then vanished into thin air, roaming the arena invisibly until their next attack.

Although quite possibly the most irritating match thus far, *An Annotated Compendium of the Modern Beast* had taught Lythlet how to lure the beasts into a distracted stupor. Knife in hand, she dragged the blade across her forearm, wincing as a trail of blood appeared. In an instant, the kaebinas were upon her, feasting on her offering. Desil then snatched them by their tails and sent their heads tumbling to the yellow sands with a swipe of his blade.

"Up and up," Desil whispered into her ear as the spectators cheered.

"Up and up," she echoed in agreement, heart light, head giddy.

That was the way her year had been progressing, one victory leading to another, an infinite unfolding of coin spilling into her jackpots. Praise, endless praise, for the Golden Thorn—she had a legion of fanatics calling her name now. Never before had her life been so gratifying, her hard work being rewarded on a monthly basis with deafening *hoo-rahs* and plentiful coin.

As Desil washed himself by the alcove, Master Dothilos arrived. She rose in greeting, glad to share her celebration with him.

"May I borrow your company for a moment?" he said with a thin smile.

Something sharp in his gaze made her falter. "Is something the matter?"

"Just a little business I wish to discuss."

She trailed after him in silence, disappearing through the warren of corridors. He may have been genteel with his words, but she knew a practiced smile when she saw one. Something was bothering him. *Perhaps another demand from the Eza?*

Soon they emerged into the spectator stands, not too far from his pedestal, his speaking-trumpet resting upon it.

"My dear girl," began the match-master, the endearment lacking the usual affection, "I thought I'd inform you that the Eza was very pleased with how the Khavi Monul affair was handled. He's paid his dues and seemed adequately humbled by you and Lorent."

"I'm glad to hear it." Relief seeped into her, but she held it at bay, yet sensing a tension to the man.

He did not continue, staring at her with an inscrutable expression. It may have been a trick of the baltascar light, but his eyes appeared unsettlingly bluer then.

Hesitantly, she spoke, "Yes?"

"Although the ringmaster was repentant to the Eza, he did have one complaint. He discovered an empty cage in his kennels, and deduced it was your deed." His baritone was as sharp as a blade fresh from the forge.

She said nothing, uncertain where this was going.

"Did you let loose a cage of pups when you visited the kennels?"

At length, she answered, "Yes."

"Did I tell you to do that?"

Lythlet had thought the truth harmless, yet something intangible had clearly fractured between them. She drew back an inch, fearing that temper of his she'd only ever seen brief glimpses of thus far. "You told me I could cause a ruckus to threaten the man—"

"Then scatter his papers and knock over a vase or two—why upon the Sunsmith and the Moonmachinist would you take it upon yourself to free a bitch's litter?" he snapped. "My instructions were to find proof of Monul's misdeeds and threaten him, not to impact his ring's bottom line."

"I didn't know you cared for his operations—"

"To hell with him, I don't give a damn what goes on in his kennels. But my opinion doesn't matter as much as the Eza's." He turned away from her, pulling his dress shirt out of his trousers and up to his neck. Layered over the intricate lacework of age-old scars, four ugly, fresh streaks of red threaded across his back, the skin bruised black and yellow where it had been broken. "I was flogged four times for your impudence."

"I'm sorry," she said, horrified. "I had no idea—"

"No idea?" He pulled his shirt over the lacerations, laughing in a way that made her feel small. "You had no idea there would be repercussions for meddling in the business of a man who's making the Eza plenty of coin? Lythlet, I think it's time for your third lesson."

Despite the palpable tension between them, she couldn't help but listen eagerly. The third lesson—she'd been looking forward to this, wondering if it were ever coming. Poetry in motion, poetry in wisdom, it was here at last.

"First," he said, a finger springing out of his fist, "you learned conviction, to know with every fiber of your soul that you deserve what you want. Then, you learned momentum, the importance of not looking back and letting things get in your way. Now, you must learn the most vital lesson there is if you want to abandon the stench of the slums and join the circle of elites: you must learn not to cross the line. You must never violate the hierarchy you exist in."

"Isn't that contradictory?" she said hesitantly. "How can I rise in the world without violating hierarchies?"

"When you rise in status and clout, you naturally shift your position up the hierarchy in a sensible fashion. That is natural: a child becomes a man, and in doing so, gains the abilities afforded only to a man. But if a child tries to prematurely assume the respect granted only to a man, he will be ridiculed and punished for it. Thus must you always be aware of your position in this world relative to the position of others. Let's use this situation with Monul as an example. You were sent as a delegate of mine, so you must consider *my* ranking. Am I above or below Monul in the eyes of the Eza?"

"Above?" she guessed.

Master Dothilos laughed acerbically. "Wrong. Dogfighting is an extremely profitable and stable venture all year round, as I'm sure you learned from rummaging through his records. Meanwhile, conquessing has its seasons of profitability—when my roster is beset by a string of poor performers, I have less to offer financially to the Eza, though I remain in his favor by providing my services as a middleman for his odd jobs, introducing the right people with the right skills for whatsoever he requires. Only when I'm blessed by better contestants who draw in more spectators do my profits balloon to the point that Monul's steady cashflow looks meager in comparison. In the grand scheme of things, I am of equal importance to Monul in the eyes of the Eza. We both provide him with very generous dues in exchange for his protection, so there is a limit to what I can do to Monul. The Eza would have forgiven the actions you took to investigate Monul's accounts, given the circumstances, but his pardon vanishes once you meddle with Monul's profit-making ventures."

"But those pups were trapped in a tiny cage, covered in their own filth," she defended herself. "Had I left them there, they would've been tortured or used as bait for the fighting hounds to tear apart. How could I have turned a blind eye?"

"Silence! Now is the time for you to learn, not to argue. By stealing from Monul's kennels, he was able to lodge a complaint against me. He spent a fair amount of coin on those pups, apparently, and it'll cost him a pretty penny to replace them. Obviously, this expense will impact his profits, which means his future dues to the Eza will shrink."

He leaned forth, grabbing her by the shoulders threateningly. "And do you have any idea how foolish it is to take coin out of the pockets of those above you?"

"I'm s-sorry," she said, trying to keep her re-emerging stutter under control. His rage was becoming bitterly familiar, harkening to all those in the past who had found pleasure in watching her shrink before it. "I just felt bad—"

"What did I tell you last time?" he snapped. "Leave mercy to the realm of folklore and fiction. Look at you. So clever with cheap tricks, yet so foolish with the world. Let me guess: you had mercy for those innocent little pups, you felt you had a duty to save them, and you thought you'd bring justice to a nasty, wicked man like Monul by freeing them. You fool. It seems all your success in the arena has gone to your head, and you've forgotten you live in the real world, one that has no place for those fanciful myths."

"They're not myths," she said quietly.

"I'm terribly sorry, you must be right," he condescended. "You certainly would know better than I. Why wouldn't you? Look at how marvelously your life went the last time you worked so hard to uphold those virtues!"

She stared at him questioningly.

"Once upon a time," he began, "there was an ugly, stuttering girl stumbling her way through the slums. Oh, she was wretched, oh, she was poor! But she had good morals by her side, a merciful heart, a strong sense of duty, and a great love for justice! She was in great need to earn a living, however, and blessings upon blessings, she found a marvelously paying bookkeeping job at a high-class brothel—"

Her heart stopped. She turned to stare at him in horror.

"—owned by a woman named Madam Kovetti."

"How do you know this?" Lythlet demanded, terrified. "You said you didn't bother looking into the work I've done."

"I lied," he snarled in her face. "I know everything about you and your miserable little life. I know what you found, I know what you did, I know what happened."

Her pulse quickened. She had buried those memories deep inside, locked them up tight in a cage and suffocated them under mundane routine, but they came rushing back like a thunderstorm pelting a moon-temple rock garden into disarray.

Master Dothilos cared not, continuing, "You were there for only a fortnight. Startlingly short, especially considering how generously Madam Kovetti pays her staff. You must have kept your head down the first week. I doubt she would've let you know too much so soon. But you were bright even then, and you must have caught on quickly that it was no ordinary brothel she ran."

Lythlet rose to leave, feeling herself getting sick, but Master Dothilos yanked her by the arm back into her seat.

"When did you find out?" His breath was hot on her face.

"The day I quit," she gasped, trying to pull her arm free in vain.

"Your conscience could not support you working there any longer, could it?" he sneered.

"How could it?" she cried.

Madam Kovetti had always been coy with the details, giving her no more than plain numbers she had to record in the ledgers. Her brothel catered to an exclusive clientele, exclusive enough that only senior bookkeepers were allowed to handle any transactions involving their names, while Lythlet dealt with petty cash and minor expenses. The brothel had been so large it was easy for her to be sequestered away in the administration quarters.

"We keep this door locked at all times for the sake of my girls' privacy," Madam Kovetti had explained silkily, tapping the door bridging the administration quarters to the rest of the brothel. "They don't enjoy being bothered in their free time."

Not being one drawn to social situations herself, Lythlet hadn't thought much of it. Until one day—

Try as she might to suppress them, snatches of memory came back to her in a vulgar pastiche: an early morn, the sky weakly lit in gray colors. Herself the first to arrive in the administrative quarters, a tidily kept wing of the brothel filled with ledgers and drawers. The door to the rest of the brothel left unlocked for the first time in her brief tenure, a bit of curiosity.

First: a small storage room filled with chests of drawers, within them vials of strange yellow liquid. She'd plucked one up, given it a good shake to investigate it, but returned it none the wiser.

Further down a corridor, then another, and another. A web of dark hallways, a staircase leading down—

Fragile bodies, fragile minds.

"What you saw must have disgusted you," said the match-master presently. "A den of children kept hostage and drugged out of their wits for the pleasure of adults. Girls even younger than you had been, boys whose voices would not deepen for years, lives sold into a trade that would break them irreparably."

"It was not just what I saw," she muttered.

The worst memory of them all rose to the surface: that of a closed door.

No more than a four-paneled plank of solid wood in front of her, with a shining golden knob waiting to be twisted. She could see nothing of what was behind it—but she could hear everything. Every revolting bit of it: the grotesque combination of one crying out in pleasure as another cried out in pain.

White-hot fury had ignited in her. She reached for the knob; it was locked. She rattled it harder, shrieking at it, demanding the man inside open it. Then she had taken to kicking the door, throwing her weight against it. She wanted to break it down, pick up whatever fragments it'd shatter into and use them to bludgeon the man to death.

Then her collar was tugged up high against her throat, making it hard to breathe.

"Whoa-ho! You're not supposed to be here!" It was one of the brothel guards, a massive fellow who had always been friendly to her in their sparse interactions. He dragged her back like she was feather-light, all the way to the administrative quarters. Before shutting the door, he said in a sheepish voice, "Listen, I won't tell Madam Kovetti you saw anything, and you don't tell her I left this door unlocked. We'll keep our jobs, and she'll be none the wiser. Are we square?"

Her mind was racing, rage making her tremble. But she was not a fool—she knew rushing headfirst back into the brothel would be fruitless. There were too many guards; she'd never be able to save all those children single-handedly. No, there was a better way.

"Square," she had agreed, waiting for him to close the door to the brothel. A firm, sturdy click indicated the lock was in place. Then she'd grabbed her bags and gone out the other door, the one that led back to the rest of the city.

"Now when you left the brothel, you didn't simply return home, did you?" said the match-master in the present. "No, you went straight to the watchmen. You reported what you knew. What you found. What a good citizen you are, my dear."

How does Master Dothilos know so much? The Eza must have spies in the ranks of the watchmen for him to know all this.

But her bewilderment fell lifeless to the wayside at his next words: "And then what happened?"

Blood drained, her face left a pallor as memories coursed through.

"What happened?" he pressed, a sneer on his face. "You gave the watchmen everything they needed to investigate the brothel and put an end to that woman's business. You delivered straight into their hands all the evidence they could hope for to rescue those poor boys and girls, to stave off the trade of future younglings. What happened?"

She withdrew into silence, but he tightened his painful grip on her arm. She knew from experience she would discover bruises there the next day.

"What happened?" he repeated through clenched teeth.

"Nothing," she whispered. "Nothing happened."

"Nothing!" The match-master finally released her arm. "The watchmen did nothing. Business went on as usual. Madam Kovetti still runs the brothel to this day! You even went to the watchmen again a few days later in utter confusion as to why nothing had been done. And what happened? You got the beating of your lifetime and then they threw you out! *That* is what you get for all your mercy. *That* is how you're rewarded for the duty you felt toward those children. *That* is the justice of our world—one great big lie!"

"But I had to try. If you were me, would you have sat back idly and let her continue unhindered?"

"I assure you, I despise Madam Kovetti and what she does. I'll celebrate the day she dies, and I'll only attend her funeral if it's open-casket so I can spit at her corpse," he spoke with a venom that was utterly genuine. "But the fact remains that no matter how much you disapprove of their actions, you cannot cross the line. You will never be rewarded for your good intentions, not the way those heroes you wasted your childhood reading about always were. You certainly weren't: the whole debacle depressed you to the point it wrecked your appetite, you starved yourself for days until you fainted, and then Desil had to carry you to the health ward—and there he signed his life and yours into a fool's debt to that loan shark! By sticking your nose into places it didn't belong, you ruined your own life. And I am not talking about your starvation nor Desil's debt."

She stared at him questioningly.

"Did you not wonder why Madam Kovetti was never investigated?"

"Because the watchmen are failures at their duty to protect our society."

He laughed. "You're not wrong, but you miss the fact that perhaps even their hands were tied. Madam Kovetti is a woman protected by those with power, those profiting greatly from her continued business. She may be despicable, but she knows how to pay her dues on time."

Lythlet paused. "You mean she was protected by the Eza?"

He nodded grimly. "Madam Kovetti is one of the most profitable earners in the Eza's stable. She ranks high over most in his eyes."

Lythlet buried her face in her hands.

He continued, a coy tone behind his words, "Once you recovered, you were then under the employ of a pair of swindlers for long months. I don't think you're one to condone scamming the slow-witted and the elderly. May I ask why you continued to serve under them?"

"I could find no other work," she answered warily, wondering what he was getting at. "No one else would hire me, no matter how long I searched. Desil and I were so hard up for coin to pay off Tucoras, I had no choice."

"Do you think that was a coincidence?"

She froze. She had suspected her foul luck in the past was unusual, the fact that nearly every single one of her employers had been violent, scheming lowlifes oddly coincidental—but what was he implying?

Master Dothilos sighed. "That's what happens when you meddle in the business of a powerful woman with powerful connections. You're lucky Madam Kovetti decided to only punish your employment opportunities rather than end your life outright. I suppose she didn't think you were a threat worth stamping out entirely. After all, all you had done was report her to people with no actual power to stop her. So, you were blacklisted by most and condemned to working for the lowest of the low, any scumbag with a reputation for treating their staff poorly and violently, until she stopped caring enough to punish you any longer. It was only this year you began working at the inn, right? The only boss you've ever had who hasn't beaten you over petty matters?"

Lythlet sat there, winded. Had she truly suffered for years for doing what was right? Something that hadn't even amounted to any justice in the end?

"Do you understand now, Lythlet? Imagine how much easier your life would have been had you never meddled in Kovetti's business. If you hadn't the stomach to continue working for her, I would understand."

Her shoulders sagged, weariness consuming her. "But I should've just quit and kept my mouth shut?"

"Precisely," he said. "Don't let storybook ideals destroy your life. Consider instead what *is* actually written into the laws of nature: the predator-prey relationship. The strong eat the weak, the weak eat the weaker. Now, do you want to be prey?"

"No," she answered mindlessly, knowing it was the answer he sought. "But if that means I must play the role of a predator and destroy another for my own success, I want no part in it."

"What if I told you there was a third way?" he said, a gleam in his eye. "Symbiosis is another thing written into the laws of nature. Forging a mutually beneficial relationship with someone above you will grant you many benefits without you needing to dirty your hands. I refuse to fraternize with Madam Kovetti— the one time I had to attend a gala she was present at, I spat in her glass while it was unattended. But I do associate myself with others even higher than her. The Eza himself, for example, as well as many others. And in doing so, I've been able to carve out some status and success for myself."

"I understand," she said, wishing she did not.

He nodded, pleased for the first time that meeting. "Very good. You see, you're forming a symbiotic relationship with me, too. I take care of you, I guide you and teach you the ways of the world, and thus you have the opportunity to grow. In exchange, you work hard in the arena and assist me in occasional favors outside it."

"Master Dothilos," she said, tiredly, "with all due respect, I think it best if you refrain from asking any further favors from me."

His gaze quavered, a dozen emotions running through, too quickly for her to pick apart. At last, he spoke, in a gentle tone she knew better than to read as genuine, "Do not be disheartened, girl. These immortal wheels of corruption turn as cogs, and they will continue to turn whether you're in it or not, so you might as well reap your own reward from it. Follow me and I will guide you along."

His words rang hollow, and she slipped deeper into a gray mood. "You're asking me to turn a blind eye to any injustice I encounter as long as they're committed by someone high in the hierarchy of society. I cannot. I *will* not. I have been the ignored victim many times in my life, and nothing hurts more than to have your pain seen and heard but brushed aside as meaningless. The bully who pulled my tongue out when I was six—I hate him as much as that boy who walked away from me when I needed his help. Hive-Master Winaro, who beat me and threw things at me—I hate him as much as his wife who never comforted me in the aftermath. I refuse to choose apathy for the sake of bettering my own standing in this world."

Master Dothilos sighed, shaking his head. "Lythlet, injustice has been woven into the very fabric of our city from the dawn of time. It is a tree, the roots of which are centuries old. Do you think you can reform the watchmen, beseech the Einveldi Court to hear your concerns, and uproot the Eza all by yourself? No, my dear girl. Be wise. All we can do is find a way to survive and prosper within this system."

She did not respond for long moments. She could sense him getting impatient beside her, but she could muster nothing for him. At long last, she nodded quietly.

"Good." He sounded relieved. "So will you be a good girl next time?"

She bristled at the patronization, knowing if she did not demarcate boundaries now, he'd overstep further. "No. I fear more than ever deepening my connection to the Eza. I believe it wise to avoid anything more to do with him beyond conquessing—"

Master Dothilos kicked the seat in front of him, throwing his hands into the air. "You need to work on your sense of gratitude, idiot child," he snapped. "I was whipped four times by the Eza as punishment for your meddling in Monul's business. Are you foolish enough to defy me further when I could demand four whiplashes on you in return?"

She fell dead silent, that murderous look in his eyes telling her to believe that threat.

He was red in the face, seething with a vitriolic rage, eyes darkening in malevolence the longer he looked at her. It was then she saw Master Dothilos for who he truly was. He was a man who put on airs, who flaunted his highborn connections, who frequently launched into long speeches to prove his intellectual capabilities, a man so ardently desperate for worldly validation. But underneath all that remained the boy he had once and always been, an angry, lonely boy who felt cast aside in a world that seemed impenetrable for the likes of someone as broken as him, and to have his self-made success and standing threatened for even a second turned him incorrigibly furious. Fresh off a flogging, he desperately needed to feel superior to somebody in that moment, and she had the misfortune of being in the wrong place at the wrong time.

"Do not forget I've made you what you are—how dare you think you can now betray me?" the match-master said, voice shaking with a visceral rage barely concealed. His attempt to regain his restraint was obvious as he forced the next few words out with an unnatural evenness. "I could very easily decide you're unfit to be invited to the next round and cut short your conquessorial career right here."

"You wouldn't do that," said Lythlet, flustered. "You earn an enormous amount of coin from my matches—more than what you offer Desil and me as jackpots. You're not foolish enough to cut off your own profits."

"And you're not foolish enough to think that's the worst I could do to you," he countered viciously. "Shall I call upon the usurer your parents owe a whole gold coin's worth of debt to?"

Lythlet stiffened. "What?"

"Did you think I wouldn't discover this? I could so very easily share your parents' whereabouts with their usurer, who has been waiting rather impatiently for his money to be returned. But then again, I needn't go through the usurer at all if I wanted to ruin your parents' life. I could simply make my case to the Eza, and your beloved father and mother shall be funneled into the underworld quicker than you can blink. Perhaps they'll find new purpose in their lives as mules for the euphoria-inducers. Or shall we let your mother enter one of the newborn-trafficking syndicates? She has a few childbearing years left in her—"

"Don't you dare!" Lythlet roared.

He sneered, satisfied with her reaction. "Ah, does that cross the line? Very well. I am a merchant, and I am always open to negotiation. We could settle on something milder—a classic torture session, how about that? Your fragile little mother wouldn't last an hour. Your dim-witted father might survive longer—which is unfortunate for him. The Eza told me recently he's become fond of one particular persuasion technique: hammering bamboo toothpicks beneath his victim's nails. Requires very little materials, yet it's startlingly effective at breaking them."

"You—you, don't—" she stammered, paling.

"What? I don't what?" he goaded haughtily. "I don't know that they're currently seeking refuge in the Home for Temporarily Embarrassed Highborns? I don't know they've been given a room up in the attic? I don't know that your father has been toiling away at the riverside flats in hopes his debt will be repaid in two years?"

She stared at him, horrified at the knowledge he wielded like a hatchet. Any protest she uttered would anger him further, and her entire life had taught her the dangers of provoking a bitter man nursing a wounded ego.

"Come, girl," said the match-master, sounding much calmer. Evidently, he felt the balance of power had been restored, his mood bettering in turn. He patted her knee, his touch less fond and more condescending. "There may be some frustration between us right now, but let us put aside this fight. I will do nothing so long as you give me no reason to do anything. I see so much potential in you, I only want to help you harvest it. I wouldn't bother with anyone else. You understand that, don't you?"

All goodwill he had built with her had diminished the moment he threatened her, yet instinct told her those last few lines were genuine. Somehow, that only stung harder, knowing there was a part of him that genuinely respected her potential, that truly wanted her to succeed—but only on his terms, not hers.

"You understand, don't you?" he repeated harshly, eyes penetrating. "You understand that even if you pull out of the arena, I won't let you go? I've invested my time and money in you, and I don't enjoy the prospect of them failing to bear fruit."

She looked at him, knowing the role she now had to play to survive—knowing the lines she had to observe and obey.

"I do," she said, defeated.

THE HOMELY HOME, ever-bright with yellow hive-lanterns, was now as familiar to her as home. She had memorized the name of every child that crossed the threshold, she could map the holes in the ceiling with her eyes closed, she could wend her way through the garden of greens for whatever herb or vegetable Naya requested. But on that day, the chatter enveloping her was unintelligible, the food tasteless, the air stale.

Lythlet could only quietly watch Desil give a boy a piggyback ride at the far end of the hall.

She hadn't mustered the spirit to tell him what had happened. It had been the same when Hive-Master Winaro began beating her: she'd kept it from Desil not out of malice or mistrust, but simply overwhelming exhaustion. It seemed easier to keep silent than to explain everything from the beginning, especially when there was no way Desil could help without getting into trouble himself. She had tumbled into a trap all by herself, by letting Master Dothilos weave a narrative of kinship between them, deceiving her with support and encouragement until she had fallen in debt to him.

She buried her head in her arms, ashamed of herself. *Perhaps they were right, those who once called me idiot child.*

"Are you well?" asked Shunvi, peering at her. A child rested on his lap, sleepy from a belly full of food. "You seem troubled."

She was sorely tempted to tell him everything. But in what way could he help? Instead, she regarded the sleeping child. "Where's his mother?"

"Working at the flats. Their hours grow longer and longer lately. My leg's gone numb." He chuckled, stroking the boy's head.

"I'll carry him to the cots," offered Lythlet, but he shook his head.

"He'll wake if I move an inch. Perhaps you ought to go and rest though. You seem wearier than usual after a match."

"No need." After a moment, she asked, carefully so as to mask her intentions, "Shunvi, did the match-master ever communicate with you beyond the arena? About things other than fighting?"

He turned to her in surprise. "In a manner of speaking, if we count plain and simple blackmail."

Her heart raced. "What happened?"

"It was a vague threat, and it's possible I inferred the worst. But it was after Ilden and I had won our final jackpot at the twelfth match. I'd begun my first teahouse in Northeast, and Master Dothilos came visiting. He said he'd be keenly watching us, hoping we wouldn't forget what we owed him—and that he'd be happy to remind us if we ever did." He frowned, black eyebrows furrowing. "I may have been reading too much into it, but it was so odd, I thought he was trying to demand a cut of my profits."

"Then what happened?"

His answer surprised her. "Nothing. He left us alone after that, never bothered us again. For a long time, I kept waiting for the pin to drop, but for some reason, he never made good on his threat. Perhaps it really had simply been my imagination."

Lythlet sat quietly, considering this. Master Dothilos was a man who deeply prized his connections; it seemed odd the match-master would let them off the hook so easily. *Perhaps he felt there was greater value in letting Shunvi's teahouses thrive, so that he could one day flaunt to the other highborns his connections to a famous teahouse-master?*

A second, grimmer possibility arose. *Or perhaps he realized neither Shunvi nor Ilden were as broken as I am to be so easily ensnared by his poisoned praise, and there were greater fools to be preyed upon, such as yours truly.*

A commotion was spreading, drawing her from ruminating further. Children were scrambling to the corner where Desil sat as he announced he was about to spook them with ghost stories. Naya and Ilden joined his side, dimming a couple of lanterns by tossing old rags over them. Even the child on Shunvi's lap raised his head, woken by the noise, and left to join.

The classic Ederi story of frangipani-scented ghosts was soon complicated with furious widow spirits and cursed blood-drinking men, but the young audience reacted in piecemeal to every part of the nonsensical story with much enthusiasm, gasping and shivering. Logic was not the strong point of Desil's storytelling skills—but his dramatic gestures and facial expressions carried the tale far, and not least of his efforts was him fighting to keep a smile from breaking free whenever a child squealed and hid their face behind tiny hands.

If there was one gift Desil had, it was to stir in Lythlet a burning nostalgia for times she had taken for granted, of late nights swapping tales as nonsensical as this with Desil in his family's home, of childhood days when she had yet to learn the evils of the world.

Lythlet thought of the lost children of Kovetti's brothel once more, those she had failed to rescue. They needed no ghost stories; they needed no more horror in their lives. The way their city was set up, with a justice system withered by those who knew where to funnel bribes to, there was nothing she could do to save them.

As the little ones of the Homely Home shrieked in terror at Desil's story, she thought with a heavy heart, *What a blessing it is that there remain children more scared of ghosts than of the world around them.*

CHAPTER TWENTY-ONE

IZANTAS, OF THE STORM AND THE FURY

"LYTHLET?" DESIL CALLED, holding forth a piece of mail he'd collected from Faravind's. "What's this about a second Inejio arena?"

Lythlet, setting aside the thick woolen blankets she'd been folding, peered over his shoulder at the invitation card.

Your next match has been arranged for 11:00 a.m. on Septavind, the 2nd of Sotoye. It will be held in the second Inejio arena. Meet my servant at the headquarters at 9:30 a.m., and you shall be escorted there. Your timeliness is appreciated.

"I'm not sure," she said, an unsettling feeling coming over her.

That feeling did not leave her, and it only worsened on their match day when they met with one of the match-master's servants and asked about it.

"The match-master," the servant said, avoiding their gazes as he ushered them down to the basement, "believes you two are adequately skilled for the river arena. We haven't hosted matches there in a long time, but your successes of late have impelled him to open it once more."

Desil stiffened. "River arena?"

"Is it *by* the river, you mean, or..." Lythlet was too nervous to finish.

The servant did not answer, his expression dark.

In Inejio, he led them along an unfamiliar path twisting and turning through the sprawling remnants of their ancestors' homes, until the ivy-covered structures gave way to the river gashing through. The water glimmered eerily in the pale baltascar light of the pillars, glimpses of shiny scales reflecting off it. Dread rose in Lythlet with every step they took along the rock-laden bank.

It was not long before the river arena loomed before them. Its construction was identical to the usual one: a tall roofless circle decorated with glassless windows and flying buttresses. But there remained one notable difference, a single factor that made Lythlet's stomach drop like a stone.

The arena was not landed in solid earth, but built to stretch across the waters, spread over the river's surface like a bizarrely pompous bridge.

Desil hooked a hand around her elbow. There was a slight tremble in his grip, and her heart pounded in answer. *There must be solid ground for us to fight on. Master Dothilos couldn't be so unreasonable—could he?*

She contemplated the answer to that with a sinking feeling.

"In we go," said the servant solemnly, ushering them through the corridors to the armory. "Await Master Dothilos's cue."

"Desil," Lythlet called in a shaky voice as he reached for his usual sword, "I think it best if you chose something else today. A long-reaching weapon. There's a harpoon at the end of the wall. I'll maintain my spear. And perhaps we should bring hatchets and knives, as many as we can carry."

Desil pinched his lips together as he plucked two hatchets off the wall. He glanced uncertainly at her. "You don't truly think we're meant to go into the water, do you? There must be some sort of solid foundation built over the river, right?"

Neither of them could swim. The Ederi had never been fond of water, not with their history of sinking ships and ocean-swallowed islands. Her ancestors had survived tumultuous seas and an ocean with a will of its own to reach Edesvena, and they had no love of water to pass on to their descendants.

Desil took her silence grimly—then hope flickered in his eyes. "Did you ever look into the sea beasts in the bestiary?"

She buried her face in her hands in answer. Not once had she imagined the possibility of a river arena.

He sat down next to her, winded.

THERE MUST BE *solid foundation, there must be.*

They waited in the gated corridor, listening to the horde of spectators taking their seats, whooping excitedly with loud, shrill voices. Somehow, they took on a hollow quality, like wind blowing through an abandoned house.

The match-master called their names, echoes bouncing down to them as the gate lifted. Desil reached over to give her hand a tight squeeze, and out they strode into the bright arena.

Once her eyes had adjusted to the baltascar lights, Lythlet cursed, her worst fears realized in that single instant.

The gray cement bank they stood upon ended an arm-span out, giving way entirely to a massive pool of water.

For once, Desil did not partake in the prayer Master Dothilos now led, one to Izantas, He of the Storm and the Fury. "How are we supposed to fight here?" he hissed, eyes wide with fear.

She bit her lip, frantically scanning the rest of the arena.

No yutrela, none to scale, no hope of a familiar divine touchstone to even remotely alter the odds in their favor. Small bamboo platforms floated around instead, drifting like lotus leaves growing in a pond. As with the main arena, there were rising protrusions installed all around the walls, wooden shafts jutting out at haphazard angles. She could rely on those, but it would be otherwise impossible to avoid going into the water.

She eyed the match-master up in the stands, half-hidden behind his pedestal.

His grin was on full display, lips drawn wide, teeth flashing in the light. He bellowed into his speaking-trumpet, "Spectacular spectators, behold! Our rising legends stand before you! We haven't had the pleasure of witnessing a river match in many a year—precisely twelve years, three months, and six days ago, if anyone's keeping count. None of us thought it'd ever happen again. Too difficult! Too dangerous! Far too traumatic a struggle for Ederi conquessors! But ladies and gentlemen, times have changed." He lowered his voice, leaning into the trumpet, words taking on a sweet quality. Like flies drawn to a pot of honey, the spectators waited with bated breath. "Not until today do I have conquessors worthy of a river match standing before you. Who else could triumph easily, swiftly, painlessly, but these *invincible* conquessors, the Rose and the Golden Thorn!"

The crowd cheered and stomped their feet.

She stared aghast at the match-master as he turned a sneer in her direction. Even without it, she would have known he had been mocking her. Her fear was tangible, and he relished every moment of it.

He's orchestrated this whole impossible match to put me in my place—to remind me that I am beneath him, and that my success depends upon him.

The forfeit pendant was heavy on her chest, and her hand inched toward it.

"I do have something thrilling to announce," said the match-master. "Indeed, I am not the only one excited for the Rose and the Golden Thorn! Spectators, your bids have been gathered— and yes, some bearish naysayers still linger amongst you. But the Sunsmith Himself can testify that the bulls are out in full force today! For they have put on offer a tremendous reward for the Rose and the Golden Thorn should they win: a jackpot of no less than *seventy-eight white valirs!*"

Her breath hitched and Desil startled. It was an enormous sum, edging closer and closer to the value of a full gold coin.

She lowered her hand from the baltascar pendant. Her heart hardened, fists clenching until her nails had driven deep grooves into her palms.

For the past seven matches, she had struggled and triumphed, building a momentum to earn the spectators' love, their investments into her jackpots swelling as a result. Forfeiting would gain her nothing; she was bound to Master Dothilos either way. This was all she had left to fight for.

I cannot let the match-master destroy my momentum.

"By the blood of your ancestors, do you proud Ederi children vow to salt the river with the blood of the devils of the deep blue that once gave death upon your ancestors?" Master Dothilos's voice loomed.

Desil looked hesitantly at her.

She sympathized with his worries, but she couldn't give up that jackpot, nor could she succumb to the match-master's ploy to destroy her in one fell swoop. "With me, Desil. *Witness me, upon the blood of my ancestors!*"

Their shared cry reverberated against the waters, his voice a touch more reluctant than hers.

She took the first step, leaving the stone-gray embankment and leaping across to a bamboo platform. She wobbled for one precarious moment, but it seemed the platforms were weighed down from underneath, and she didn't topple over.

Once she found her balance, she jumped to another, then another, making her way across the arena. Every leap emboldened her. This match would not be impossible, not as long as she kept her wits about her.

The creak of wooden platforms and the heavy thud of footsteps behind told her Desil had gathered his courage, following her closely.

Lythlet wondered what was waiting for them. She thought of a sea dragon but pushed that out of mind; the arena was enormous, but even it could not hold a sea dragon. A river-troll, perhaps, one of those devils who took pleasure in dragging people into deep waters and holding them until they had drowned.

What other devilries of the deep did she know? None, other than stories she had heard growing up, monsters she wasn't certain truly existed or were merely folklore told to scare children into staying away from the water.

She chewed her bottom lip and braced herself. Desil joined her on a neighboring square of bamboo, and they stood still, waiting expectantly.

From her angle, Lythlet could just barely make out Master Dothilos. He leered down at her, his presence overwhelming; his remarkable ability to make her feel like an insect trapped by a child armed with a magnifying glass and too much time on a hot summer's day had returned.

"We've a special beast today—it wasn't easy bringing him all the way here, but it will be worth it for the Rose and the Golden Thorn! Bring out the beast!" Master Dothilos roared.

She heard the grinding of gears but could see nothing. No gates were visible; everything lay beneath the water's surface.

A mighty splash erupted, and something monstrous leaped in an arc over her.

Lythlet stumbled as the oversized creature gracefully sank back into the water by her left, its greenish-gray skin disappearing from sight, her platform swaying in the ensuing wave.

"Goblin-shark!" Desil shouted.

Her blood turned to ice.

All around them, spectators edged forward on their seats, hoping to catch a clearer sight of the fiend, loud gasps escaping their lips.

Even from the brief sighting, there was no doubt Desil was right. It was a goblin-shark, evident from the green hue of its skin, the serrated dorsal fins, and the red markings on its underside.

Without thinking, she made a series of jumps toward the edge of the arena and clambered up the rising flats on the wall until she was well away from danger—from the water. Desil did the same, always only one step behind her.

"What do we do?" he hissed.

"I don't know." Words she had not uttered in a long time, words she loathed confessing. "What do we know about goblin-sharks?"

"Very aggressive," Desil supplied, looking equally helpless. "I know they're from the sea around the eastern islands of the Ora Empire. I suppose they must be able to survive in freshwater, too, if it's able to swim in this river."

"Interesting, but not something we can work with."

"Back in schooldays, a boy said his brother was out hunting for their meat with one of those Oraanu shark-hunting gangs."

"And?"

"Nothing more."

She winced, peering over the platform's edge. Unfathomable water silenced all the bravado she'd mustered just moments ago. "Will it come out, or are we to go in after it?"

"Surely not," Desil cried. "We're shark feed the moment we plunge into the water. Master Dothilos hasn't lost his mind, has he? He knows we can't swim, he must. Hardly any Ederi can!"

He hasn't lost his mind at all, she thought miserably. *He's simply a vindictive man who wants to make sure I know my place beneath him.*

Lythlet frowned, raising her head. Master Dothilos stared back, fingers steepled together, goading her without a word. He was enjoying every second of their helpless floundering. Every minute longer the spectators watched them hide in the heights was a dent to their reputation and a notch on Master Dothilos's victory belt.

"I think we must forfeit," Desil whispered.

She gripped his wrist fiercely. "We don't. The match-master is testing us, and I refuse to fail. To come this far and end it all without even trying would be foolish."

His lips were pinched, but he nodded hesitantly.

"Stay with me." She led the way, circling the arena with slow, cautious steps, waiting for a monster that refused to emerge.

Master Dothilos's voice reached their ears: "Playing it safe can be wise, but a bit of danger is sometimes what you need to lure in your prey. It's hungry, and it likes to know food's close at hand."

"He wants us back on the platforms," she grimly translated.

With grievous reluctance, they leaped off the wall and landed neatly on separate platforms below. Standing poised side by side, their eyes never left the water, searching for tattletale ripples, their blades shining in the burning light.

There was nothing subtle about the goblin-shark's second appearance, however. It flew out of the waters, diving toward them, jaws spread into a black vacuum ringed by rows and rows of enormous fangs. They ducked down just in time, avoiding its bite by hairstrings.

As it returned underwater, its tail smacked against Lythlet's platform. It dipped over dangerously, and she launched herself at the opposite corner until it righted itself.

"It's coming again," Desil warned.

She crouched down, clutching her spear.

I'll pin it down, she thought desperately, grasping at any idea. The shark was so large, she knew it would take a tedious length of time for them to stab it to death, but she could not conceive of any other alternatives.

She clutched the haft of her spear, and when the goblin-shark emerged once more, she was prepared: her spear lashed out and buried itself deep, piercing the shark until blood sprang from its side.

She had hoped this would make it tumble from the sky onto the platform, where she could pin it down. But as though the spear embedded in it were nothing more than an insect bite, the goblin-shark flew overhead unhindered, dragging her along.

Her world toppled over as her feet flew heavenwards and she crashed into the water headfirst. Water pierced her nose, burning a liquid fire down her lungs.

The goblin-shark snapped its jaws at her, but she clung to her spear at an angle just beyond the reach of its fangs. Going mad with hunger, the shark flipped her round and round. She focused all her might on maintaining her grip, but her lungs screamed for air. Instinct begged her to break through the surface to breathe, but terrified sanity warned if she released her spear, the shark would swallow her in a second.

A great grayish-green darkness grew on the fringes of her senses. A strange sensation in her lungs swelled, her soul fighting with all its might to separate from her flesh. Mind and body tore apart, a tree savagely prized by its roots from earth, her existence vanishing where flesh drowned. The divine were calling her to flee the mortal world—*ride the white wind, child of Kilinor.*

Her hand slipped, and the world came to a halt.

The water was painless.

She could not yet breathe, but there was no need to. She lingered in the realm between life and death, the white stretched-out plane of a single second separating her from the great abyss beyond. All around her, a chorus of gentle murmurs encouraged her to wait for the white wind to carry her away.

It won't be long, child of Kilinor, until your suffering has come to an end. It won't be long, child of Kilinor, until it is time to rest.

Something skittered in her gut.

But now is not my time to rest, she thought. *This is not how I die. This is not how my story comes to an end. Not now, not today, not till I have done justice to the star I swallowed in that dream—and certainly not for Master Dothilos. I will not let him kill my momentum!*

The brief, gray touch of death receded, voices collapsing into silence. She re-rooted her senses, and the world shuddered into motion.

She lunged forward, one hand grabbing back onto the spear, the other fumbling for support. It brushed against the goblin-shark's dorsal fin, and she fought the urge to scream as her hand came away bloody, the fin's serrated edge leaving a jagged wound in her palm. But even as pain threatened to overcome her, a burst of inspiration struck. She stared at the fin once more, suddenly recalling one of the earliest books she'd ever stolen, a chef's guide to exotic cuisine.

The shark jerked violently as a harpoon thrust into its side.

Hands drew Lythlet up, and finally she could breathe again. She drew in air with painful sobs, doubled over on a platform as her eyes and insides burned, coughing violently, spitting out great gobs of water—but she had an idea, and that was all she needed to reinvigorate her.

They did not have to waste time blindly stabbing the beast. She recalled Desil's mention of a shark-hunting gang. He had said it was for their meat, and there had been no time to think deeper on it. But now she recalled from the chef's guide that Oraanu shark meat was often poisonous, unfit for consumption. There was only one part worth harvesting, it had explained—the fins.

She groped for the knife at her waist.

But out of the corner of her eye, she saw Desil, dripping wet and coughing, reaching for his baltascar necklace.

"Stay your hand! I know what we must do," she gasped out in choked, haggard breaths.

He paused, hand falling from the forfeit pendant. "Are you certain?"

She nodded, water-wrecked senses stabilized by newfound confidence.

Relieved she'd stopped him in time, she turned to grin triumphantly up at the podium. *You cannot overcome me so easily, match-master.* This was no longer a match between her and a goblin-shark; this was between her and Master Dothilos.

Master Dothilos's sly grin faded, no longer certain he had the upper hand.

She pulled out her knife, daring the sea-beast to come for her again. She knew how to kill it this time.

But out of the corner of her eye, Desil straightened, hardening his face. To her rising alarm, his hand rose once more, arcing toward his sternum in one smooth gesture.

He wouldn't, she thought, a sickness growing in her gut.

With one effortless movement, the clasp of his pendant snapped, and Desil threw the baltascar to the platform. His boot shattered the glass, and green smoke erupted under his foot, funneling up into the sky.

"Forfeit!" he shouted.

Her eyes widened at the fumes—at what he'd just done.

"Fool!" Her shout was drowned out by the spectators' furor. The clamor of the arena was deafening as the bulls raged and the bears rejoiced.

With a single word, Desil had undone the momentum they had built. Even if she did not forfeit with him, their reputation had been self-smeared as forfeit-keeners, killing the faith the spectators had in them.

What had she been working for that he could so easily destroy in a single breath?

Master Dothilos snapped his fingers, the singular *click* cracking like a whip across Lythlet's eardrums. A chill swept through the audience as the crossbowmen planted around the height of the arena raised their bows, the gleaming tips of their bolts all perfectly aimed at Desil's head, condemning him with contempt of the arena.

Desil stared at her, nonchalantly ignoring his perilous state. He was clearly expecting her to snap her pendant in unison, growing confused the longer she did nothing.

She turned away, too overwhelmed with pain and frustration.

"You're hurt," Desil shouted.

"Have I need for you to tell me of my own pain?" she would have retorted, but her throat stung too much.

On he went, "Forfeit now and we'll end the match. The physic will take care of you."

She pointed her knife at Desil, silently commanding him to draw his remaining weapons, a hatchet and a knife.

Desil obeyed with a horrified expression, conceding to resume the fight.

With that, Master Dothilos snapped his fingers once more, and the crossbowmen lowered their weapons, the contempt of the arena drawn to an end.

Even with his weapons out, Desil still pled in hushed tones, "Forfeit, Lythlet. This match is beyond us."

"It may be beyond you, but it is not beyond me," she mustered the strength to say. It was too late to unmake his mistake, but she had to salvage their legacy. "As I'd just told you, I've figured out what to do."

"You're hurt, and we've both lost our spears," he argued.

As if her flesh supported his reasoning, she doubled over, racked by a violent cough, excess liquid spilling past her lips. She needed rest, desperately, and to clear her lungs and bandage her hand, and something along her calf ached—*but now is not my time to rest.*

One peek into the stands confirmed her suspicions: Master Dothilos was grinning once more, insufferably happy at her misery, at Desil's forfeit, at that one single moment destroying the goodwill of the spectators.

I can still defeat you, she swore fiercely.

The goblin-shark emerged once more, two spears firmly embedded in its side. It lunged for her, but she dodged its attack. Using one of the spears as leverage, she broke its momentum, beaching it on a platform. She had only seconds; the shark would thrash around until it was back in the water. The platform trembled violently as her knife flashed in the air.

She brought the blade against the dorsal fin, the one that had sliced through her palm. Back and forth, she sawed desperately, and she was halfway through before the goblin-shark flung itself back into the water.

Lythlet hissed in impatience. She caught Desil's eye, and he seemed to catch on to what she was doing.

Now you understand, she thought with simmering frustration.

It was easier to track where the goblin-shark was. A thick trail of blood stained the path it cut through the water. Their eyes hunted the pluming red line until it reached the platform Desil stood upon.

Lythlet leaped toward him just in time for the goblin-shark to reappear, no less hungry but all the more clumsy for its injuries. With Desil tugging one of the spears, the shark was beached on a platform again, and there they set upon finning it. Desil raised his hatchet and brought it down on the bit of flesh still connecting the dorsal fin to the body, and it came off with two blows.

The shark thrashed itself around, wriggling closer to the water.

Meanwhile, Lythlet knifed through the goblin-shark's left pectoral fin. Thinner than the dorsal fin, the long chunk of meat soon came away in her hand.

She leaped away in time, narrowly avoiding the bulk of the shark rolling over her as it finally returned to the river. She made her way back to the cement embankment by the gate, crouching, panting heavily. Desil joined her a moment later, and they remained still, watching the rapidly bloodying water.

Lythlet raised the pectoral fin overhead, blood dripping past her fingers onto cement. Desil joined her, a single fist presenting the severed dorsal fin to the spectators.

Shaking with shallow pants, Lythlet glared hard at Master Dothilos, damning him for drawing out his verdict. They knew the truth already: with its major fins hacked off, the goblin-shark could swim no longer, and immobility would bring it death. The water of the arena, rapidly turning a putrid, inky red, vouched for them.

"Bravo," was Master Dothilos's silky congratulations, and a round of shaky applause followed. "I shall concede this as a win."

Lythlet's attention faltered after that. The pain she had been suppressing heightened at full, and she turned, stumbling down the corridor to the armory.

CHAPTER TWENTY-TWO

FORFEIT-KEENERS

LYTHLET COLLAPSED AGAINST the bench in a barrage of coughs, ending with a spit of watery yellow phlegm on the ground.

Desil stroked her back.

"I'm fine," she rasped.

"You're not. Your face is green, your hand's bloody, and your leg's injured, too. I think you may have worsened your wounds when you insisted on fighting."

You should've forfeited with me then, was the unfinished message she read in his eyes, and her lips tightened into a thin line.

Master Dothilos came then with a physic, who sprang to Lythlet's side. There was little water left for her to expel she hadn't already, and the physic gave her a bitter root that would settle both mind and body.

"Will she be all right?" asked Desil.

The physic nodded. "She did not take in a fatal amount of water. The westeaves root will protect her lungs from swelling. I'll give her a pouch of it to chew on for the rest of the week. She needs rest, and a lot of it, but I imagine she'll be fine once the shock has faded." He crouched down, examining her bleeding hand.

"Congratulations," said Master Dothilos once the physic silenced. "As announced, seventy-eight white valirs. Here are the ledgers for the day—though I suppose it can wait until he's done binding your hand. One of the more thrilling matches of the year, while being one of your more disappointing performances."

Lythlet refused to entertain him with a reaction.

"It was quite the spectacle, of course. River matches always are. The spectators were gasping in their seats as you went underwater. Blood started to stain the waters, and everyone was certain you were shark feed until Desil came to your rescue. But I daresay your bullish supporters are disappointed in how much you struggled today—especially with Desil forfeiting. No one enjoys witnessing weakness, not when their coin's on the line."

She didn't need to look to know he was smiling. "But we won. They saw us kill the thing."

"Oh, yes, they did. Very clever, Lythlet, targeting the fins alone. But the masses do not always appreciate brilliance, not if you've weakened their confidence in you beforehand. You see, I've sold you as a golden bet to make—unbeatable, invincible, infallible. Thus, the spectators have begun to have ridiculous expectations of you. Seeing you struggle for even a single moment dashes their confidence. And bullish spectators won't forgive Desil for keening on a forfeit. It's very hard to convince people to continue investing in your partnership when your partner has announced to the world he doesn't have faith you'll succeed. It was a mistake, my dear boy," he said to Desil, "one I fear the Rose and the Golden Thorn will struggle to recover from. Forfeit-keeners are confidence-shakers."

Desil said nothing.

Lythlet shut her eyes, wincing as the physic tended to her leg, binding it up in white linen.

But on the match-master went, "As it has been with previous

forfeit-keeners, I predict many spectators will switch from bullish to bearish—from supporting you to betting against you. I'm sorry to share this, but you need to brace yourselves for a meager jackpot the next round, and possibly onwards, depending on your future performance."

He was not sorry at all. Spectators would still come to their matches, and the match-master's cut would increase instead of hers.

Against her better judgment, Lythlet asked, "How much can we expect our jackpot to drop?"

"If you're lucky, you may suffer your jackpots only halving in value."

"Half if we're lucky!" she cried. It was as if all her efforts in the last few matches had been for naught.

Desil grabbled uselessly at his wet breeches, avoiding her irate gaze, then went to the basins at the far end to wash up.

Master Dothilos knelt by her side, leaning toward her ear. "It's a pity your friend failed you today. It seems he didn't trust you when you begged him not to forfeit. Honestly, after I've spent the whole year nullifying rumors of his cowardly escape from brawling, he repays the favor by forfeiting! Did he forget how damning being held in contempt of the arena would be? How daft can a man be?"

She gritted her teeth. "I can unmake his mistake."

"You can try."

She shrank under his patronizing tone.

A moment of silence. A small smile crept on his face. "I just threw at you the hardest challenge any Ederi conquessor could face, and you survived. You truly are a miracle." He faltered. What he said next, he said with an unfamiliar softness, "I know you don't like me. You don't have to—I wouldn't care for it. I know you fought today not only for the jackpot, but to show your defiance of me. You refuse to succumb to my petty ploys to put you in your place. And truth be told, I find my respect for you only growing as a result. I see your desperation, and I recognize it from my youth.

I struggled, and because of the pain I endured, I grew strong in my convictions and became who I am today. You are so much like me—your anger, your pride, your ambition, your sheer potential."

This blatant brush with the match-master's soul startled her. She thought of his scars, of the little whispers of his past he allowed her a peek at. She did not trust him anymore, not a single bit—but she was certain he truly held a genuine, twisted affection for her, as a father looks upon his prodigal child, wanting only to see them reroute themselves from youthful folly to the golden path they'd laid.

"Keep following in my footsteps, Lythlet. I will guide you through the worst of the world and ensure you emerge wiser and richer." He patted her cheek once more and left her alone with Desil, an uncomfortable silence shrouding them.

OUT INTO THE ruins of Inejio went Lythlet and Desil, not a word uttered between them.

She crushed mossy debris beneath her polished leather boots, the bitter aftertaste of the westeaves root lingering in her mouth. It helped tremendously, eating away almost all pain. But it did not dissolve her fatigue, and she stumbled, collapsing by the side of an unpaved road.

"A moment," she muttered, "just a moment."

"You're still hurt," he said, a hand on her shoulder.

"Just tired." She looked at his hand, resisting the urge to shrug it off.

His fingers tensed—he'd picked up on her anger. "I did what I thought was right, Lytha," he said, retracting his hand. "I forfeited for you."

Frustration had been simmering inside her like a bubbling black cauldron, and his words tipped it over on its side, spilling the contents. She looked up sharply. "But you forfeited *after* I assured you I knew what to do. Why would you do that?"

"When I pulled you out of the water, you were struggling just to breathe. How could I in good conscience let you continue?"

"Of all times to doubt me, you had to choose the worst." The memory of Master Dothilos smugly grinning at her the moment Desil had forfeited made her anger boil over. "I've done all I could for us to succeed this far, for us to survive eight brutal matches, and for you to unmake my efforts with a single breath is infuriating."

His voice raised a notch, Desil said, "Neither of us knew what to do. You haven't studied even a single page of the bestiary on sea beasts—"

"I was able to handle these matches long before we were handed the bestiary. You should have given me the chance to try. We were building a jackpot worth a fortune, and now you've cut us down to half at best."

"All we've lost is a bit of coin in our future jackpots. Has the water addled you so badly that you weigh that heavier than your own life?" he snapped.

She looked at him in disbelief. "A bit of coin? Desil, a bit of coin was what kept us in debt to Tucoras for years. A bit of coin was what destroyed us, until we earned enough to buy our freedom back. It's what separates us slumdogs from the rest of the city. Do you really think we're privileged enough to think a bit of coin is nothing?"

"I'm not arguing with that," he said exasperatedly. "Fine, you were right, and you knew what to do. But I was not wrong in wanting to protect your life. You've lost your head if you think any jackpot is worth dying for."

"It's not just the jackpot, Desil," she said, his short-sightedness frustrating her. "We've lost the confidence of the spectators. All the momentum we've built by winning, you've dashed it into pieces, and now whatever jackpots are up for the taking might not even be worth the effort! You've cost us our reputation, our pride, our ego—"

"Your reputation, your pride, your ego."

His words struck her dumb.

He glared at her. "That's what this is about, isn't it? The coin is one thing, but you've invested yourself in the name of the Golden Thorn so deeply that you cannot bear the thought of the spectators doubting you again, and for that you would risk your life, throwing away all sense for your pride. Why put yourself in so much danger for an audience's accolades? You seek pride from beyond when you should be looking for it from within."

She shook her head, clenching her teeth. "Desil, you with your blessed childhood are the last I will listen to on this. You were told from young that you were loved, wanted, and needed. Can't you realize that all that pride of yours you think comes from within comes from that instead? You're a fool if you think anyone can emerge from a childhood of neglect and belittlement with pride. I was a miserable, mute child whose mother was possessed by a death spirit, whose father was too depressed to ever speak to her. Yet now, when I'm finally being recognized for my effort, for my abilities, you judge me. You lean on me in these matches, depend upon my study of the bestiary, yet when I say I've figured out how to win, you ignore my plea and forfeit."

All anger left him, and he stood there, stunned. At length, he said, quietly, guilt-ridden, "You're right. How foolish I've been to hope you wouldn't notice how much I've been lacking. You are the Golden Thorn, and I am no more than the Rose beside you, ornamental, disposable."

Her rage slowed. It had been a while since she'd seen him look so ashamed, not since his brawling days when he'd come home, jackpot in hand, misery scrawled over his face at what he had done to earn it. Brawling had broken his spirit, and now she had done the same. She reached for him. "Desil, I'm sorry. Let's not fight. I didn't mean a word I said—"

But he edged out of her reach. "You did, even if you won't admit it to yourself. And you would be right to. I have fallen short in many ways, try as I might to hide it."

"That isn't—"

"I am not a fool, Lythlet," he interrupted, "I know you have little need for me nowadays. I can fight by your side, but any other muscled lad would serve the same purpose. I want you to know that I'm sorry. I've failed you in many ways, and I haven't been one you could rely on for a long time. Perhaps in our youth I sufficed, but you've grown beyond that while I haven't, and I have no one to blame but myself."

She was inexplicably saddened by his thoughts. "I never thought that. You've never failed me."

He gave a pained laugh. "Only because you've never put much expectation upon me to begin with. You didn't count on me in the days of Valanti, hiding your bruises without a word to me. You don't count on me now in the arena, for we both know I can't think as quick as you or memorize the bestiary with your ease. Nor do you count on me outside the arena for anything more serious than mindless companionship. And why would you? As you said, our lives were destroyed by my debt to Tucoras, and here I am, once again destroying our future because I haven't the good sense you do. I was good to you when we were children, but I've been nothing but a burden since."

He abruptly took a step back, wiping his tearing eyes. She reached for him, but he turned away violently.

"Desil," she called as he left. She rose but tumbled to the ground, legs yet to recover their strength.

He vanished from sight, turning a corner behind a ramshackle stone building.

Using all her might to heave herself from the ground, she pushed herself to her feet and staggered after him. But he was nowhere to be found.

She stood alone, lost in the ancestral ruins in mind, spirit, and soul.

CHAPTER TWENTY-THREE

RUNNING ALONE

THEIR KATAKA FLAT had always been abysmally small, no more than an inkblot on the canvas of Setgad, yet it seemed absurdly vast and empty to Lythlet in the days that followed, she alone amongst the gazette-and-straw-laden floorboards.

After Desil left her, she had stumbled home and fallen upon her sleeping pallet, exhaustion pulling her headfirst into a dreamless black ocean. A new day had begun by the time she opened her eyes, Desil's pallet untouched.

As the days drew on, the seasons graying beyond the windows, it would remain untouched.

At first, she thought to give him time alone, so that they could temper their moods, but she started worrying about him after a week, when there was no sign of him returning.

She went to The Steam Dragon in search of him, and while feeding Runt—who was undergoing a miraculous growth spurt, more than quadrupling in size—Lythlet learned from Madame Millidin that Desil had requested time off. His other workplace, the metalworks, informed her he'd done the same.

Her last hope was the Homely Home, but she went there only to learn she'd just missed him.

"He came for a spot and played with the children, but went off soon after," Naya said, looking more frazzled than usual, curls escaping the knot tied at the nape of her neck. "He seemed in a glum mood, truth be told. Is all well?"

Lythlet evaded the question, looking around the Home. It seemed quieter than usual, with only a couple of children playing in the courtyard. She had nothing to do, and the thought of returning to her empty home depressed her further.

Naya frowned, the weight of her unspoken questions growing, though she was either too polite or too busy to voice them. "I really must hurry off, but you're welcome to stay, of course. Help yourself to some tea over in that corner. If you need rest, go ahead and borrow my own cot—all the others are taken up by the builders. They're so exhausted by work, they can barely get out of bed. It's ekelenzi flu season as well, and half of them are coughing up a storm. I haven't had much rest thanks to all the caretaking they require—I know it's not their fault, but I'm plain tuckered out."

Guilty about being such a bother, Lythlet assured Naya she could go and attend to more important matters. Once alone, Lythlet found in the corner a glass jug filled to the brim with a brown tea, loose leaves settled at the bottom, and poured some into a chipped mug. With a sip, she placed the ingredients: opalten leaves brewed with longan honey.

Lythlet set her mug down, mood shifting down even more dismal paths. Desil would sometimes make her this tea during her bloodsweek to help her cope better with the cramps. She hadn't even meant to conjure the memory of him up, but so entwined were their lives, it was impossible to avoid thinking of him.

The urge to cry sprang up—she felt like a storm-tossed ship drifting in the boundless seas without an anchor.

* * *

THE CITY HAD never seemed so vast before, so filled with unknown nooks and crannies.

Desil had vanished for a month now, the Harvest Holiday finally beginning. Lythlet was sitting by the ledge outside her flat, legs dangling a hundred arm-spans off the ground, twirling the invitation card for the next match between her fingers. She rested her chin on the railing, staring at the sunset drowning the city in a sea of autumn orange. A cool breeze engulfed her. She ought to fetch her cloak, but she felt too miserable to move.

She had always thought herself a solitary creature, but it seemed even she had her limits, and she had crossed them violently.

The rope ladder twitched.

She eagerly leaned over the edge, hoping it was Desil coming home at last. But to her surprise, it was Shunvi ascending the ladder, pausing to wave at her before latching his hand back on a rung. She waved back, confused, but glad for any companionship.

"Are you well, Lythlet?" he said once he arrived, wiping sweat from his brow. "I wanted to check on you. The river match was simply awful."

"I feel better. I've been resting as much as I can, and the root has done much for my healing."

He sat down next to her, the closest contact she'd had with any other person for the better half of that month. "I'm glad to hear it."

On a hunch, she asked, "Did Naya send you here?"

He smiled. "I'm not her errand boy, if that's what you mean. But she did mention you were distraught last you met. We were worried about you, Naya and Ilden and me."

"I'm fine," she promised, a lifeless assurance.

"Has Desil been taking care of you?"

She hesitated. "I haven't seen him since the last match," she said at last, tense.

Shunvi looked taken aback. His lips parted, questions ready to spring forth, but it seemed he read her stiff demeanor well enough to leave the matter alone. He glanced around awkwardly before nodding at her hands. "What's that you're holding?"

She stilled her idle twirling of the cardstock, holding it out to him. "My invitation to the ninth match," she said bitterly.

"It's in two days," Shunvi said. "Will Desil return by then?"

She avoided his gaze, glancing dourly at the sheets of autumn leaves coating the ground far below. According to the rules, her sole presence would not suffice. She would be disqualified once and for all, and the Golden Thorn would recede from the public eye.

Shunvi exhaled, then clapped his hands together to break the awkward silence. "Are you to be all alone for the Harvest? That simply won't do. Why don't you come up and visit Ilden and me? It's a long journey to Northeast on foot, but I know a shortcut through Inejio. If we leave now, we'll arrive at midnight, and you could stay the night."

Lythlet contemplated the offer. It was charity, plain and simple, and she was such a proud creature, her first instinct was to refuse. But the loneliness had grown unbearable, the weariness of returning to a quiet, empty home day after day twisting her neuroses down paths of endless rumination and regret. So, with a weak smile, she nodded gratefully.

THE POET AND the Ruffian's house was a testament to the riches of Northeast, a pristine white building that would be burglarized thrice a week if it were in the Southern sectors.

"May the Maker unmake you; you certainly know how to show up uninvited," greeted Ilden, jabbing her arm playfully. "I jest, I jest. You're always welcome around here, Lythlet. Doubly so if you ever got Naya to come along with you."

Shunvi waved him down. "She's staying the night," he explained. "We'll watch the parade tomorrow and give her as good a tour of Northeast and Central as we can."

He showed her to her room, and though grateful for his hospitality, Lythlet slept fitfully, plagued by a recurring dream of a swarm of lightning-bees trapping her inside her empty kataka flat, the dark wooden walls closing in like a coffin slamming shut.

THOUGH DESIL WAS nowhere to be seen, there were memories of him to be found everywhere, phantom images flashing in and out as she went about her day.

During a breakfast of fried eggs drizzled with soy sauce lying atop bowls of pork porridge prepared by the men, Lythlet watched enviously as Shunvi and Ilden swapped Harvest gifts with each other: a matching pair of handsomely jeweled hairpins they immediately fastened above their ears. It was a Harvest tradition inspired by the tale of General Lauturo and Lieutenant Jinvi, and any two friends who considered themselves kindred spirits partook in it to show their camaraderie.

"Desil and I do that, too," Lythlet said softly, reminiscing as she stared at the white-gemmed pin resting above the curl of Shunvi's ear. "Every Harvest since we met. But our pins aren't so pretty— they're simple copper pins we reuse every year."

"Cheer up!" said Ilden, who was one of those misguided fellows yet to learn those words were never helpful. "You'll find Desil soon, and then you can wear all the pins you like."

Shunvi jabbed him in the side. "Be a little more sensitive."

"Ah? Ah! Ah… does she want me to hug her or something—"

"No, I do not want you to hug me," Lythlet said crossly, very embarrassed by this ordeal.

"Oh, thank the Sunsmith." Ilden breathed out in relief. "I'm no good at this. Shunvi, you cheer her up. I've got to get ready." He dashed away to his bedroom, returned ten seconds later to retrieve his forgotten indoor slippers from underneath the table, then finally left for good.

"I could take mine off if it bothers you." Shunvi gestured at his hairpin. It matched his Harvest outfit perfectly—a traditional Oraanu silk robe with long, hanging sleeves, midnight blue with a golden floral print, a broad sash fitting him snugly around the waist, the low neckline exposing his strikingly white clavicles.

Shunvi's monstrously fluffy white cat, General Meowturo, sprang upon his shoulder just then, batting the hairpin with its mitten-like paws.

"Naughty general," he scolded, planting the cat onto Lythlet's lap. It sat obediently but continued staring at the hairpin as if it were a lightning-bee it simply had to squish.

She shook her head. "I'm just being silly. Pay no mind to me."

"Absolutely not," he said graciously. "You're in our care today, and I intend on making your first visit to Central as enjoyable as possible."

She smiled gratefully, petting General Meowturo.

THE GOLDEN PEACH was a formidable establishment, a triple-story swallowtail-roofed teahouse decked out with strings of hanging paper lanterns at the eaves and giant pots of variegated bougainvillea at every column. The two teahouse cats Shunvi kept liked to take naps in those pots, curling around the rim and letting their tails dangle over the edges. The teahouse occupied an enviable location on a prime commercial street in Central, and its balconies offered the perfect vantage point to view the Harvest Parade marching through the streets.

Governor Matheranos was at the head of the parade, waving to his constituents while seated upon a traditional palanquin colored by gold leaf, carried upon the backs of a dozen men. The ridge of the arched roof bore thirteen spikes to represent the Sunsmith and the Twelve Wardens, and the moon-shaped windows bore tribute to the Moonmachinist. Intricate carvings ran through the body of the palanquin, showcasing a medley of Ederi and Oraanu influences, fated ships sailing beneath crescent moons.

Lythlet watched quietly as the crowds enthusiastically waved back at their governor, that iconic mane of wild white hair enough for even people from the furthest edge of the throng to recognize him.

Truly the uncrowned king of Setgad, she thought wryly. The man had been in charge of the city-state for sixteen years now, and with the polls indicating a guaranteed win for his third and final term in the coming elections, he was locked in for another eight years. According to the *Twelvemonth Sun*'s recent headlines, his opponent Corio Brandolas's latest accusation of the governor misappropriating funds had been found utterly baseless yet again—the United Setgad Party had issued a notice vindicating Governor Matheranos, making it clear the "extremely minor" financial misconduct had been performed without his knowledge by an underling who'd since been punished.

I wonder what else Saevem and the Coalition of Hope are up to, Lythlet thought, delicately nibbling away at a puffy kaya-infused bun, the gooey filling threatening to spill out of the soft crumb.

Shunvi had done his utmost to make Lythlet as comfortable as possible, providing her balcony table with so many side dishes and pots of exquisite tisanes, there was no hope of her finishing them even with Shunvi and Ilden's assistance. The two men were presently leaning over the balcony to scan the procession that followed after the governor: *rimmonimwen olnarë wariëtel*— the sun-blest beasts who give unto us. Decorated horses led the parade, their long faces marked by flecks of gold, followed by packs of happy hounds with brows dusted with red ash. Shunvi and Ilden took turns elbowing each other, whooping in excitement at the sight of Shunvi's teahouse dog, Little Mushroom, proudly marching in the vanguard with an ashy brow.

"If only I could've trained his cat siblings to march alongside," Shunvi said wistfully.

Try as she might to enjoy the show, memories of Desil continued to assault her, Lythlet trudging from one into another like an inescapable mire. First had been the hairpins, now was the procession of children marching through the street below behind the beasts, decked out in their fineries and carrying large sunflower stalks.

"*Otara menaré, tolliënimhé ristellë rimmonim, rimmonim napei gineret tolliënim,*" the children chanted, a promise from one generation to the previous. *You've worked hard. We who will not forget you, you who have come before us.*

Lythlet and Desil had been thrice picked to join this procession in Southwest in their childhood days. Forced to wake early, then to march through the streets for an hour, waving sunflowers meant to represent how they, too, would grow toward the sun. Desil would wave to his parents when he found them in the crowd; she never bothered looking for hers, knowing they'd never be capable of attending.

Blinking back sudden tears, Lythlet looked away and into the distance, hoping for a distraction. Just behind the opposite row of commercial shophouses was a residential street of massive mansard-roofed mansions, enormous green gardens stretching out between them.

So that's how the highborn live. Little wonder they're happy to keep voting for Matheranos if he keeps their lives as cushy as this, with promises to make it even easier on them with tax cuts and baltascar luxuries. Those majestic houses would dwarf her kataka flat a thousand times over. Even just looking from a distance made her feel like a stray dog that had stumbled somewhere it did not belong.

She cocked her head at one curious sight: in the wide green gardens of one mansion stood a tree with a small wooden enclosure built into it. "Shunvi, what is that? It looks like a shorter version of my kataka flat, but why have they need for one? There's a perfectly fine mansion beside it."

Shunvi peered in the direction of her outstretched finger. "Those are playhouses for children—what they call a 'treehouse'. They're meant to imitate your kataka flats without requiring the same effort to climb as high."

"They're a new thing that the highborns have taken a fancy to this year," Ilden added. "I reckon it won't be another year before the trend dies out, though."

She stared at him blankly. "The highborn find such things enjoyable?"

Shunvi nodded reluctantly. "The concept of living up in a tree is intriguingly foreign to them."

It struck her hard then, that emblems of her hardships could be easily reduced into tokens of amusement for the highborn.

Something else about the mansion caught her eye then: a dark-blue Oraanu cloth talisman swaying in the breeze from the mansion's eaves—yet another reminder of Desil.

It was an Oraanu tradition, hanging a talisman to announce to the neighborhood the arrival of a newborn child, and Ederis had long adopted it, too, as their cultures had borrowed piecemeal from one another over generations of living side by side. Upon Desil's insistence, the Demothis had hung one for her when she went to live with them—he had wanted her to know she had found a home away from home, that she would be family to him from that day onwards.

The memory made her heart ache, and her anxiety over tomorrow's match heightened. With no word from Desil, she had no inkling what was to happen with her conquessorship—and more importantly, with their friendship.

"Shunvi, Ilden, I thank you for your hospitality, but I think it's time for me to return home," she said, rising from her seat, feeling suffocated in that thoroughly unfamiliar place. Being surrounded by highborns and Centralite luxuries made her feel like a trespasser.

"So soon?" said Shunvi, surprised. "But I was hoping to take you to the Library of Athernara afterwards—you'd love it, I'm sure. I wanted to show you some more of Yoshifero Vidana's works besides his Gentlemen Thief series."

"Forget libraries, you can't leave without watching the fireworks at midnight," Ilden argued. "They're the highlight of the whole day!"

But she shook her head, "I'm feeling tired. I ought to go give my parents their Harvest greetings, and then have an early night. I have a match tomorrow, after all."

Shunvi hesitated but nodded downheartedly. "Would you allow me to accompany you home at least?"

"You won't be back in time for the fireworks then," she demurred with a polite bow of her head. "I'll be fine alone. Ilden was complaining last night that I've stolen you from him, and I think you ought to attend to your needy friend."

Shunvi punched a sheepishly smiling Ilden in the shoulder. "Come back and join us if you change your mind."

She nodded, forcing a smile, and left the grand teahouse behind for a journey that stretched long over the evergreen weed-strewn roads of Inejio.

CHAPTER TWENTY-FOUR

MOTHER

THE HOME FOR Temporarily Embarrassed Highborns was eerily quiet as Lythlet trekked through its dusty corridors and unpolished marble stairs to the uppermost floor. The attic door was open, watery light spilling from the dormer window.

Lythlet stepped inside, eyes adjusting to the dimness. A cough caught her attention. Father was asleep on the mattress, curled toward the wall. His shoulders heaved with yet another cough, but he returned to a restless doze.

Mother was closer to Lythlet, sitting upright on the mattress, rail-thin knees hooked over the edge, still as a stone guardian. Her face was void of any expression as she registered Lythlet's presence.

Lythlet's heart sank, recognizing this familiar sight.

"Today?" she whispered tepidly, already knowing the answer.

Silence.

Mother's eyes flitted left to right in an aimless gaze, the way they always did when her mind was overrun with ill spirits. She lingered like a ghost in her own bed, hidden in the shadows with a demon spirit whispering in her skull. Breathing without living, looking without seeing—she *was* without *being*.

Lythlet lowered her head, already exhausted by the visit. "I've come to give my Harvest greetings, Mother," she murmured. She went on her knees before the blank-faced creature and performed the ritual of filial piety, a complex series of bows punctuated by verbose well-wishes for the wellbeing and prosperity of her elders.

There was one final act to this greeting. She was to take her mother's hand in hers, press it to her forehead, then kiss it before uttering her final wish for Mother's good health.

Don't, warned a voice inside just as she reached for Mother. Her fingers brushed Mother's bony hand, hoping to feel her warmth—the warmth of a loved one, any loved one.

She did, a soft spark that made her feel some semblance of home, a dash of golden honey on the sparse canvas.

Then Mother slapped her hand, eyes flitting around nervously, not seeing anything Lythlet could. She began chanting a slurred incantation under her breath with a tinge of irate frustration, drawing the rite of exorcism with harried hands.

"Sorry," Lythlet stammered, withdrawing her stinging hand in a panic. "I'm sorry, so sorry." She fled backward with her head bowed, like a crab scuttling away for cover. She shut her eyes, tears spilling out. Memories rippled across the red undersides of her eyelids of every single time this had happened before.

She shouldn't have hoped for anything different this time. But she craved a loving touch so much, her better judgment had been subdued.

After a moment, she raised her head to gaze upon her mother, blank-faced as ever, completely unaware of how much she had just wounded her daughter. A fleet of conflicted emotions sailed right through her—disappointment, anger, frustration, contrition—before she settled on resignation.

"It's not your fault you're like this. I'm sorry for crossing the line," she said, hushed, words falling in vain on the ears of a possessed woman. Then she realized this was a blessing—she could say anything then, and nothing would matter.

"I've made the terrible mistake of trusting someone I shouldn't have, Mother," she admitted. "And now I've endangered you and Father. I fear there's no way for me to unmake my mistake."

Not a single reaction.

In that room defined by negative space, in that moment defined by what was unsaid, Lythlet reached deep into the silence of her soul, and something reached back. A brand-new idea, one final scheme. A desperate gambit she could employ, the only one that would guarantee Father and Mother's safety.

She let out a deep exhalation, trying to gather her courage before this woman she loved. She forced a grim smile onto her lips as she rose from the floor. "But don't worry, Mother. I won't let anyone hurt you."

Before leaving, she tiptoed around the head of the mattress to tuck Father in, pulling the blanket up to his shoulders. He coughed once more, his breath warm on her hand, and she felt pity for him. He must be weary from the construction. His forehead didn't burn with a fever, but his persistent cough made her wonder if he'd caught the season's flu. A faint smell wafted from him, familiar, yet one she could not place. It was pleasant, a scent that once again drew to her mind the bucolic, far-off fields of harvest, yet discomfort stirred in her, the hair on her arms rising.

I'm certain I've breathed that scent before.

He stirred then, on the brink of waking, and she backed away, not wanting to disturb him further.

LYTHLET ARRIVED AT the kataka flats long after sunfall, stars blinking overhead, cresting a full moon. All her neighbors were out on their ledges to enjoy the fireworks that would begin on the dot of midnight. She watched enviously as families and friends jostled on their ledges, yelling at one another to make space.

Her ledge was almost empty except for her and her hive-lantern in its glass casing. She stared at the lightning-bees with quiet affection.

She lifted the lid and reached in to gently stroke the fuzzy bees. "Thank you for your companionship, Rentavos, Beracani, Truvelio, Nuneca. You, too, Yoshifero. Don't bully the others so much when I'm gone." They scuttled over her hand, familiar with her touch, their bright bioluminescent flesh limning her fingers red.

She withdrew her hand and was about to shut the lid when she paused. *Perhaps not*, she thought, leaving the lid tipped upwards. *Desil might not return soon. Best I give the little bumbles a chance to fly off once their hive begins rotting.*

The first firework of the Harvest whistled into the air, bursting into hundreds of orange flowers, marking the midnight hour. A second explosion followed, erupting into white snow that flaked into vanishment. One by one, the Oraanu pyrotechnists painted the midnight with their fireworks.

It was beauty beyond measure. She lifted her gaze to the looming darkness of night, to the terrific bursts of fire-flowers erupting in the sky, breaking the stretch of Dirantas's might. She watched on the brink of tears that would not come, understanding this would be the last Harvest fireworks she'd ever witness. But weeping would require an energy she no longer had. She felt truly, utterly, irredeemably empty, like a cask that had been tipped over for days until every drop of wine had leaked out and evaporated into thin air.

The fireworks were far from over, but she decided to turn in—there was no point wasting her time watching a show she was not enjoying. She left the hive-lantern outside, little Rentavos and Yoshifero squabbling in buzzing staccato beats, lid left tilted vertically.

CHAPTER TWENTY-FIVE

A DEATH TO SPITE BULLS AND BEARS

LYTHLET STOOD BEHIND the shut arena gates, waiting for Master Dothilos to call for her. She was alone, spear in hand, knives by her belt, a pouch of stones strung to her hip.

She looked behind, down the length of the dim corridor that would return her to the armory. She imagined Desil emerging from the end, rushing toward her, smile on his face, sword in its sheath, stopping by her side to wait together, but that phantom of him faded into the shadows of the corridor.

He will not come, she thought sadly.

"*...and Lythlet Tairel!*" Master Dothilos bellowed then, summoning her presence.

She heaved a grim sigh, rubbing her face tiredly. Then she straightened her back and strode out into the yellow sands. All eyes were drawn to her, her sole presence stirring murmurs from the spectators.

"Stand you alone, Golden Thorn?" spoke the match-master. "Where is the Rose?"

She knew him well enough to know his feigned curiosity masked delight, his blue eyes twinkling.

The spectators remained hushed, leaning forward in their seats.

"I have come alone," she shouted.

"You understand, of course, given your nomination as a joint conquessor, your partner's implicit forfeiture is your own?"

She drew a deep breath. "Then so be it."

Scores of cries erupted, but Master Dothilos raised his hand, shushing the spectators without a word. "What a tragically anticlimactic end! To think you've come so far, only to diminish due to the Rose's tardiness."

But what he said next took the audience aback.

"Spectators!" he roared. "Shall we consider something new today? It would be a shame to have the legacy of the Golden Thorn come to such an end. We're not fond of companionless matches here—yet a single rule alone may be bent for a rising legend! What say you if we invite the Golden Thorn to stand alone today?"

HOO-RAH! HOO-RAH! HOO-RAH! came their answer, and the arena trembled beneath their stamping feet.

"Your voices have been heard!" said Master Dothilos with a deep, booming laugh. "And what of yours, Golden Thorn? Stand you before us now to fight a beast with your sole might?"

Lythlet stared grimly at him. She had guessed he'd be willing to twist a single rule as such, in order to preserve his standing as the grandmaster of entertainment.

She bowed, head nearly sweeping the sand. "As the spectators will it."

Master Dothilos beamed as he flipped open the nigh pristine copy of the Poetics on his lectern. He said nothing for a moment, but his eyes spoke well enough. *You never fail me*, they said. *You never fail to put on a good show.*

The prayer and the meditation came to an end, and every single spectating soul waited with bated breath as Master Dothilos initiated the oath: "By the blood of your ancestor, do you, child of Kilinor, vow to stand alone and salt the earth with the blood of the demons that once gave death upon your ancestors?"

"Witness me," she began, overlapping her fingers into a cross for the oath-swearing sign, every word growing in strength as she sealed her fate to the whims of the world, "upon the blood of my ancestors!"

The gates rolled up, metallic screeches jarring her eardrums.

Pum-pum-pum, came thundering footsteps, and the beast emerged.

A perversion of a man stood before Lythlet, thrice her height and swollen with crimson muscles. It stood headless, neck opened to the world, but its hands juggled three different-colored heads: one yellow as sunshine, one green as a spring meadow, one blue as a summer sky. All three heads smiled at her, long red tongues wagging loose from toothless mouths.

"The sannassan," Lythlet recognized, reciting bestiary notes quietly. "A fearsome beast native to the Havaleighan region. Possessing three heads it can rotate between, its abilities alter according to which it elects to wear. Yellow, and its jaws will stretch wide enough to eat any foe. Green, and it sprouts extra limbs that it uses to restrain and twist its victim into condensed helical shapes for future consumption. Blue, and it spews a poison that paralyzes any living creature."

Heads juggling through the air, the beast stood still, observing her just as she observed it. Then it flung its sunshine-yellow head high up into the air, and it arced back down to land perfectly on its outstretched neck. The green and blue heads flew up into the sky in smaller, separate arcs, coming to rest on each of the sannassan's formidable shoulders, like birds perching on a branch.

Instinctively, the roots of a scheme to defeat it burrowed into her brain—then she stopped. She pushed all that logic and reasoning out, reminding herself of the final gambit she'd decided to enact today.

She eyed the spectators, all watching her with bated breath. Bulls and bears, opposing forces united in one thing: they desired to have her suffer for their entertainment. In her own pettiness, she realized this was a golden opportunity to end things on her own terms and make their lives miserable in the process—to die as a thorn splintered in their sides, to die a death that would spite both bear and bull.

Lythlet held her head high and flung her spear to the ground.

The spectators gasped.

She stepped toward the sannassan, undaunted. It stared at her, curious, but certainly not about to fight a willing victim. When she came within grasp, it moved swiftly, grabbing her by her hair, twisting it around its fist, and lifting her high into the air. That familiar pain coursed through her from her scalp downwards, and she almost slipped backwards into brutal childhood memories. But she took a deep breath, steeling her senses, and simply stared as the beast opened its jaws. Wider and wider, its lips stretched, revealing a toothless pink cavern with a long, slithering tongue.

The sannassan grabbed her boots in its other hand, holding them tight, and jammed them into its mouth.

Lythlet did not resist.

The audience stirred; more gasps, more nervous rumblings.

Her feet were fully lodged into the beast's throat, toes squishing against the fleshy pink confines of its esophagus. Saliva lubricated her journey southwards, the sannassan pushing her deeper, jaw unhinging slowly to accommodate her shins.

Featuring a most unique biology, the sannassan lacks the usual complex digestive systems of the common beast. Nor does it possess teeth to grind its prey, instead electing to swallow its victim whole, storing it in the hollow space that can be considered its stomach. At the bottom of the space sloshes inches of acid that slowly digests the contents, providing the sannassan with a steady flow of nourishment fresh from a live source.

It would be a lie to say she wasn't afraid—had she the choice, she would've preferred a quick death as opposed to slowly being digested over the course of days. But this was the best, most spiteful

death she could think of at the moment—to die before either bull
or bear could be satisfied, before the ten-minute mark that allowed
bears to profit off her death, to make them all lose their coin and
turn their rage toward Master Dothilos.

"Fight!" the audience shrieked at her. "Fight!"

She turned to Master Dothilos, and he stared at her, truly at a
loss for words. No glib twist of sentences springing easily from his
lips, no calm manipulation of the scenario to make it palatable to
the audience. No—thousands of spectators were watching her be
eaten alive.

"Fight!" screamed the audience louder as her knees popped past
the sannassan's lips. Many rose from their seats, burying their
hands into their hair in alarm, stomping their feet in frustration. A
few ran to the parapet at the edge of the spectator stands, leaning
over to scream at her, voices lost amidst the din of the deafening
arena.

She watched the spectators disinterestedly, privately relishing
their growing dismay. The sannassan was delicately shifting its jaw
around to fit her widening thighs. One hand was still tangled in
her hair, and the pain of her scalp being pulled tight was almost
unbearable, tears blurring her vision.

But Lythlet's eyes widened as she made out one spectator
climbing over the parapet's railing, narrowly missing the spikes
rimming the top. They were cloaked, the hood pulled up over
their head. Edging themselves along the inch of floor surrounding
the parapet, they then slid down a sloping rail, nearly slipping
and crashing to an early death on the ground. But they caught
themselves in time, balancing upright and jumping to a slat of
bamboo protruding from the wall.

"Spectators, you were all informed to never enter the fighting
grounds!" Master Dothilos roared at once, outraged. If the cloaked
spectator heard at all, they made no sign of it, running forth to
fetch Lythlet's spear.

What in the name of Kilinor does this fool think they're doing?
Lythlet thought, alarmed. Once the sannassan was done with her,
it'd happily add this spectator to its menu. She slipped further
down the beast's gullet, an awful mucous coating more of her
body.

"Spectator, you are not to interfere with the fight!" Master
Dothilos warned with leonine gravitas. Were it not for his speaking-
trumpet, Lythlet would've struggled to hear him—between the
outraged cries of the spectators and the nasty gurgling sound the
sannassan made as its jaw stretched to inhuman proportions, it
was almost impossible to make much out. "Lay down the weapon!"

The cloaked spectator ignored him, sprinting forth and piercing
the spear into the back of the sannassan's thigh. No scream could
the beast emit with Lythlet half-lodged in it, but its throat vibrated
around her like an earthquake. Its hand released her hair at last,
and relief caressed her aching scalp as she stared down at the
spectator, taking in their oddly familiar silhouette through her
tear-blurred vision.

Lythlet froze, trying to suppress that flicker of hope.

She knew this trespasser, but she had imagined meeting him so
often over the past few weeks, she no longer trusted herself.

Master Dothilos's fury was palpable, the echoes of his baritone
nearly shattering his speaking-trumpet. "Guards, loose your bolts
at that spectator!"

Crossbows were raised, cocked, and loaded, metallic bolt tips
glinting as they took aim at the intruder.

The spectator spun to the podium, reaching for the brooch
clasping his cloak and snapping it. "I am no spectator!" The
garment fluttered to the sand, and a swell of cheers erupted from
the spectators, the clamor sweeping all around the arena.

Despite her current predicament with the sannassan, Lythlet
burst into a smile.

It was Desil, panting, face red, unruly brown curls cascading free
from the hood.

The sannassan, seemingly realizing it was running out of time, began pushing her into its mouth hurriedly.

Desil turned back to Lythlet. "Fight, you fool, fight! I swear upon the Sunsmith that I'll chase you down this beast's gullet if you don't!"

He means it, she thought, wide-eyed. *He really will throw himself in after me.*

She sprang into action. Ripping the knife from her belt, she sliced the wrist of the massive hand holding her waist, working it back and forth until it detached from the rest of the arm.

With its one remaining hand, the sannassan tried to cram her into its mouth, but Desil pierced its shoulder, and the arm fell limp. Meanwhile, Lythlet stabbed the sannassan's yellow eye, twisting the knife around to scramble the beast's brain. It twitched like a lightning-struck creature, but its lips remained squeezed tight around her hips, holding her like a vise.

Desil climbed the beast's back, and bracing himself by planting his feet apart, he sank his fingers into the sannassan's nostrils and pulled the head back. His biceps bulged with the effort, but soon he'd forced its jaw wide enough for her to pull herself out. She fell onto the ground half-coated in saliva.

He pulled her to her feet. "We haven't defeated it yet, have we?"

She shook her head. "We need to take care of the remaining two heads."

"How?"

She had already concocted this idea before her suicide attempt; she just didn't think she'd put it to use. "We make it take care of itself. I'll yank off the green head, you handle the blue. Then pull its upper lip back as far as you can, Desil."

As if some adhesive were keeping its heads on its shoulders, Lythlet struggled as she tugged at the green head, resorting to using her knife to cut it free. Then, with a nod at Desil, they pried the beast's yellow lips as far apart as they could. She shoved the green head into its throat, reaching as far in as she possibly could, dropping it into the vat of acid. Then he did the same with the blue head, depositing it into the beast's own gullet, force-feeding it to itself.

The beast slumped on the ground, digesting itself helplessly.

The spectators burst into *hoo-rahs*, and Desil threw himself onto Lythlet, wrapping his arms around her and knocking her to the ground. "You're a fool and a half, Lytha! What were you thinking? Why didn't you fight?"

Sand stuck to her cheek, and it was perhaps only then it really sunk in that Desil was back.

"I didn't think you'd come," she said, not hearing his question.

"That's a terrible reason to let yourself be eaten alive," he cried.

His question finally registered. "I wanted to die a death that would spite both the bulls and the bears."

"Also a terrible reason!"

"Ladies and gentlemen, another match won by the Rose and the Golden Thorn!" Master Dothilos announced, the spectators cheering even louder. He seemed restored to the glory of his glibness. "Except only one oath sworn today! Dare I determine this to be an illegal victory?"

Desil raised his head from the ground. "Damn you and your cockheaded oath, match-master," he roared, pointing at the podium with a censorious finger. "You cannot play with our lives like this, you feckless bastard!"

Lythlet blinked, a bewildered curl to her lips. At least three of those words had never been uttered before by Desil for as long as she'd known him. *Poetry in profanity*, she thought, almost wanting to applaud him.

Master Dothilos, too, needed a moment to compose himself. "Oh my," he said with an incredulous smile, a hint of admiration dancing in his eyes, "it seems the Rose has grown a few thorns of his own! But, my dear boy, you shouldn't interrupt me. What I was about to say was: yes, this may indeed be an illegal victory—" he held up both hands to assuage the audience's rising cries "—

but have we not already bent a rule today by allowing the Golden Thorn to stand alone? What's another bent rule in the face of such a legendary match from the Rose and the Golden Thorn? Hoorah! Rise and take a bow, my champions!"

DESIL CARRIED HER to the armory, hugging her tight to his chest. "You madwoman," he kept muttering as he laid her on the bench. He knelt beside her, looking exhausted. "I thought you'd forfeit the match straightaway, to be honest. But when you swore the oath, well, I figured you'd actually *fight* and not just let yourself be eaten. You terrify me, Lytha. I can't bear the thought of you dying, and here you are, happily throwing yourself into the jaws of a beast!"

He palmed his own face, exhausted. "I'm sorry," he said after a moment, "for everything I said that day. I was being unfair to you—of course, you have every right to be proud of yourself after all you've been through. I've just been feeling so lost with myself lately, I took it out on you. I was wrong to put that burden on you. I may envy you, but I love you, and I'm proud to see you do well."

"I'm sorry, too," she said, hurriedly. "I said some cruel things to you. And you were right, even if I didn't want to admit it—I have been keeping much from you because I didn't think you could help. But it's unfair of me to think that without even giving you the chance. In the end, you are the one I trust the most in this world, and I think of you as my soulmate, my brother beyond mortal bonds. Running through life without you by my side is, frankly speaking, quite miserable."

Her words made him smile. "I feel much the same. I spent the month in the cloisters of a shrine in Southwest. Would you believe I finally got started on my inking?"

She gawked as he turned and raised his linen shirt, revealing a small segment of an ornate black-ink vine drawn into a single ridge of his spine. "Goodness, you've always talked about doing it. How was it?"

"Unbelievably awful," he confessed with a sheepish laugh. "Felt like my skin was tearing apart. There's a reason why I only have this little bit done after a whole month. Every single session, I'd show up with all the scriptures memorized, the words clear as day in my head, ready to recite them to the shrine-master who's wielding a tiny mallet and this wooden tool with a needle coming out of it—but the moment the needle jabbed my skin, my mind would go blank with pain, and the shrine-master would pause his tapping, waiting for me to continue to prove I'm worthy of the ink. A single chapter of the Poetics was what got me this little vine— it's going to take me ages to get half my back covered." He paused, glancing at her. "Throughout the ceremonies, I kept thinking that as meaningful as it was for me to finally get my inking started, the fact that you weren't witnessing me recite at least a verse or two made the whole thing fall short of what I had been imagining all my life."

"What good is a victory hollowed out by loneliness? Nectar tastes sweeter when you share it with one you love," she mused. She gave him a rueful smile. "I'll be there for you at the next ceremony."

He returned the smile, lowering his shirt and leaning toward her. "Lytha, do you know why the oath-swearing sign is what it is?" He made it then, crossing two fingers of his left hand over two fingers of his right.

She smiled. "Something from the Poetics?"

He nodded. "It's because two together is always stronger than one alone. If one falls, the other can help them up; if one is cold, the other can keep them warm. A single thread is easily snapped, yet a cord twisted of many strands is not quickly broken. That's why—two fingers of your left bound to two fingers of your right, forming an unbreakable oath."

He held the back of her head, pressing their foreheads together. He remade the sign again, holding it in front of her chest.

"And that's what I want my friendship to be for you. Something you can count on not just in good times, but in bad times, too.

Even when the world overwhelms us, I'll stand by your side and catch you when you fall."

She smiled, eyes brimming with tears. She made an oath-swearing sign of her own and pressed the back of her fingers against his. "And I swear the same oath to you."

There in the dim armory, surrounded by walls of weapons, hounded by echoes of spectators overhead, they clung together, a silent vow stitching the frayed ends of their friendship into a many-threaded cord.

MASTER DOTHILOS CAME then, unaccompanied.

The moment he crossed the threshold, he fixed Lythlet with a distraught look. Without so much as a glance in Desil's direction, he chased him away with a flick of his fingers. "Boy, go wash up."

Desil rose, glaring at him. "I'm not leaving Lythlet with you."

Master Dothilos flung the flimsy jackpot pouch at his chest, snapping, "I said, go and wash up, boy!"

Desil stepped forward, fists curling by his side.

But Lythlet stayed his hand, squeezing his wrist. "It's all right. He won't hurt me here. I want to hear what he has to say."

Casting misgiving eyes, Desil obeyed, heading to the alcove at the back. Cupping water with a pail, he washed himself facing them, keeping them in full view, though he wouldn't be able to hear more than scraps of their conversation.

Master Dothilos and Lythlet stared at one another, neither saying anything. The effortless charisma he'd mustered at the end of the match was gone; he was now deep in contemplation.

At last Master Dothilos spoke, "I thought you had a plan. Even when you cast your spear aside, I thought you had a plan. Even when your feet were jammed down the beast's throat, I thought you had a plan. It was only when you looked at me did I realize you truly had no tricks up your sleeve, no cunning scheme to kill the beast. You only wanted to die. Why would you do that?"

"Because I understand the importance of cutting my losses early before they spiral out of control," she said quietly. "I am ready to throw my life away if it means you'll never have a reason to harm my father and mother."

"That was just a petty threat, no more than that," he snapped. Then he grimaced, looking aside. "I was caught up in the moment. Have the wisdom to know that for the future."

She gazed tiredly at him. "Master Dothilos. You know me better than to think I'll believe that. Men frequently make threats they wholly intend, only claiming they never meant a word of it when it rebounds on them."

"Nothing I said will happen as long as you obey me. Do not throw your life away over petty matters, my dear girl."

"I refuse to live and die on your terms as your cur, Master Dothilos. I will not choose apathy over justice, wealth over duty, wrath over mercy. And I know," she said hurriedly as he opened his mouth, "that you're about to reiterate these things are myths. But I don't agree, and I have no intention of living a life that neglects these things."

He shut his eyes, clearly frustrated, but knowing this was a fruitless path to take. "Believe what you want to believe then, Golden Thorn, but do not be so reckless with your one life."

"You know what I desire then. If you want me to live, then grant me the freedom to live as I will. Promise me you will withdraw the threat of the Eza and leave me and my family be."

He sucked in his breath between his teeth, her plea bitter to his taste. "I will grant you a reprieve, then," he said, "out of consideration for your fragile mental state. Perhaps introducing you to underworld matters alongside your conquessorial career was too much. I'll leave you be until your final match—and then we shall resume."

"That's not enough, Master Dothilos," she said quietly.

He said nothing. The silence between them turned thick as molasses, and in the depths of it, hope bloomed. He could only be quiet because he was considering her plea—his strange affection for her, the genuine kinship of the two browbeaten children found deep within their bitter psyches, was the fulcrum upon which her fate teetered.

Then his eyes darkened, and he stood with a scowl. As he left the room, he tossed back a contemptuous glare. "Do not cross the line, cur."

CHAPTER TWENTY-SIX

THE BEE'S GOLD

THEIR JACKPOT HAD truly been damaged by Desil's forfeit from the river match, presenting a sum infinitely worse than Master Dothilos's projections: a meagre twelve white valirs made their way into their pockets.

"And given how I just attempted suicide in front of every single spectator, we must have chased away every single bull we had left," said Lythlet glumly at the dining table of the Homely Home. "No one in their right minds would consider us worthwhile investment vehicles anymore."

"Oh, I wouldn't be so sure about that," said Shunvi, a conspiratorial glint in his eye.

"Some interesting rumors began pouring out of the arena after your match," said Ilden, a coy smile curling his lips. "Rumors that perhaps it was a semi-scripted fight today, meant to heighten the usual dramatics to get the spectators talking more, so that your last matches draw the biggest crowd possible."

"Why upon the Sunsmith would such rumors spread?"

Ilden grinned and drew a playful rendition of the oath-swearing sign at her, fingers opening and shutting. "Because the Poet and the Ruffian have got your backs. It was Shunvi's idea. The moment the match ended, he realized that despite your victory, bulls' confidence in you would be shakier than ever, and, well, you only have three matches left to reap a jackpot from, so it's all rather bad timing to have the sums plummet now. So we put our best assets together—"

"—that being my love for a good plot twist—" said Shunvi, winking.

"—and my *big* mouth—to perform a little damage control," said Ilden, chomping on a breadstick Shunvi had baked in the Home's oven as if it were his reward. "Shunvi spun a couple of conspiracy theories on the spot into my ear, then I gibbered away like a maniac to anyone who'd listen about how it was all clearly a set-up. Does the arena take us for fools?" he uttered in faux outrage. "Pah, as if the Golden Thorn would let herself get eaten for no bloody reason! And Desil's cloak-brooch had *clearly* been tampered with beforehand just so he could make that ridiculously dashing reveal in front of the whole arena. And did you hear that hideously out-of-character script he screamed at the match-master? *Damn you and your cockheaded oath, bwah!* Such shoddy acting, oof!"

Desil groaned in embarrassment, slinking down in his seat like he wanted to hide. "Must you always mock me so?"

"You're a top bloke, mate. Which means it's my duty to take the piss out of you whenever I can."

"You're both wonderful," said Lythlet, truly grateful. "Thank you so much."

Shunvi smiled. "It won't completely bring bullish sentiment back in your favor, but those who want to believe will believe—especially if you perform well in the next few matches." He dropped his voice and leaned into her ear. "Are you feeling better?"

She nodded subtly. "Somewhat." Her future remained deeply uncertain, volatile with the threat of the Eza imminent—but at the very least, she had a moment to breathe and consider what path to take.

They all helped Naya set the table and apportion the food to the many plates waiting, and just as Lythlet was about to finally take her seat, she noticed something.

She jabbed her finger toward the set of hive-lanterns on the middle of the table. "Your hives are starting to rot."

"Damn it," Naya cursed under her breath. "I've completely forgotten about those—we used to have a fellow staying here who did it for us, but he now works in Shunvi's teahouse."

"That's all right. I picked up a few techniques while working at a hive-workshop, so I could do it for you if you have the tools," Lythlet offered. She reached for a lantern, wanting to get a better idea of how bad the rot was.

She popped the lid of one open, reached inside, and grasped the stem of the hive. The lightning-bees hovered near her hand tentatively. "Don't worry, bumbles," she sang off-key to them, thoroughly unaware of how odd she was being. "My name is Lythlet Tairel, and I am a friend, not a foe." When one eventually landed on her hand in a show of trust, the rest swiftly followed.

"Oh, don't worry about it now," said Naya, waving her off with a smile. "Eat up first."

But Lythlet had frozen. White rot was flaking off the bottom of the hive, a faint amount that wasn't urgent to address just yet. But the smell, this gentle, nutty smell that had always vaguely made her think of hazelnuts—

The memory of her father's sleeping form came to her then, interrupting her. He'd carried a scent she hadn't been able to place, one so utterly familiar it had bothered her, like a jigsaw she was one piece away from solving.

Not this smell—it had been different.

Then her eyes widened as horror seized her, the identity of that scent becoming clear at last.

Rot. It's golden rot. Her mind raced, piecing together the clues. *That's why the master-builder of the riverside flats offers such good terms, saying they'll pay any debt the unregistered hold after two years—the unregistered will turn ash-white from the inside and die before they can collect on it.*

Her stomach churned in disgust as she recalled Shunvi and Ilden mentioning the construction was backed by unnamed politicians.

"Naya," she said, darkening, "all the unregistereds who've been working at the flats. Have they come back smelling different?"

Naya's brown cheeks took on a deep blush. "Goodness, do you mean they reek? We try to keep as clean as we can here, and fortunately the river makes it easy to bathe oneself, but—"

"No, no, the fragrance is pleasant, not foul."

Naya tilted her head, tapping her pointed chin. "Well, yes, everyone working at the flats has been coming back smelling rather nice. I've gotten so used to it, I didn't think of it when you asked. Why?"

"And have they all come down with the ekelenzi flu?"

"Unfortunately, yes, most of them. Whenever we're on the brink of winter, the flu hits us like a brick, and this year's even worse than usual."

Anxiety ignited, and she rose to her feet. "I must go and see my father," she said. "And I think it best if you all come with me."

THE HOME FOR Temporarily Embarrassed Highborns was still asleep on that cool gray noon, barely a soul stirring awake at Lythlet's entrance—they must've crawled out of Inejio to watch the midnight fireworks, and, judging from how deeply many were dozing on the settees and cots laid out in the halls, still needed much more sleep. Lythlet gingerly picked her way up to the attic, trying not to disturb anyone.

Father was awake, thankfully. The man sat alone on the edge of the mattress, half-dazed as though only woken from sleep seconds ago, weariness carved deep into his bronzed skin. He grew flustered at the sight of the five of them entering the room.

"Happy Harvest, Uncle," Desil greeted with a smile, bowing with a palm over his heart. The other three followed, echoing the appropriate albeit casual Harvest greeting for their generation to say to their elders.

"Desil? Is that you?" Father said, wide-eyed. He fumbled with his hands for a second, rising from the mattress. "I'll go get Mother. She's out feeding the birds in the garden—"

"No, I want to talk to you," Lythlet said, urging him back down. She did not want Mother to hear this yet. "I came yesterday while you were asleep, and when I tucked you in, I noticed a scent lingering on you, a scent I detect even now."

He flushed, embarrassed. "I—"

"It is not a matter of cleanliness," she interrupted. "I believe it comes from your clothes. Do you wear this to the building site?"

"Yes. I haven't much else to wear. But—"

"Please pardon me, but I must confirm my suspicions." A furious blush arose in her cheeks as she leaned in. She sniffed at his shoulder, once, twice, and then an extra-long thrice. He stared up at her in bewilderment, and she shuffled backward immediately, bumping into Shunvi, who caught her gently.

"What are you doing?" Father asked, looking uncomfortable. He turned to cough into his sleeve.

But Lythlet regarded him grimly, stomach twisting. Her suspicions had been confirmed—she *did* know that smell—and she had spotted golden-white flecks of dust on his shoulder. "Father, you are in the process of being killed."

What little levity occupying the room dissolved as everyone fell into a tense silence.

Father lowered his arm. "What?"

All eyes were on her as she spoke, pointing at the dust on his clothes. "You are familiar with hive-rot?"

"Of course, there's not a soul who isn't. But this isn't it, I can tell as much."

"No, indeed, it isn't. But this is hive-rot that has been left to linger. Few ever see it, for most tend to their hives and purge the rot long before it comes to that. If not disposed of carefully, the rot continues to fester, turning a shade of yellow. Its scent shifts, too, until the mind struggles to place it."

Father remained silent, a look of confusion on his face.

Lythlet continued, "It's now called golden rot by those in the hive-keeping trade, but once upon a time, it was called the bee's gold for its many uses. A paste with medicinal properties, a fine fermented powder some claimed induced a divine state of consciousness—and for a few decades, it was common practice to mix it with quicklime and ash from the fire-mountains of the South Sea to produce a type of mortar strong enough to set the foundations for a grand house."

It took a few seconds, but his eyes widened at her last words, realization flooding in at last.

Her tone was sober as she continued, "But there is a reason why it fell into disuse. It soon became clear it was a poison upon extended exposure. As with hive-rot, a brief encounter will do little, if anything at all. But drawn out over years, golden rot will remain in you and eat away at your insides. Your cough is but the beginning of much worse."

"How do you know all this?" he asked, alarmed.

"I worked for nearly a year at a hive-master's workshop," she answered. "Though I served as his bookkeeper, I had little choice but to help with his operations, too. He would always stress the importance of the safe disposal of hive-rot to avoid it festering into golden rot. I would wear a shroud to cover my nose and mouth at all times, as did he. I imagine those hiring you did not bother providing you with any."

"No," he spluttered. "They never gave us nothing to protect ourselves."

She nodded, as calmly as she could to avoid adding to his panic, though her insides roiled with rage. "I didn't think so."

"But Master-Builder Asa himself plans to live in one of the flats we construct," he argued. "Surely they wouldn't lace the walls with something so poisonous?"

"Once mixed in and hardened, it is benign. It will not affect the residents, only those who handle it while it remains dust."

His brows furrowed, and skepticism colored his words. "Lythlet, this is ridiculous. They've paid us so well. Why would they be so generous if they plan to kill us?"

For once, his doubt did not hurt her. He was a man clinging to hope, and hope often came in the defiance of truth. "Because what they've given you may seem generous, but it's only a fraction of the profit they will reap in the end. They give you a black valir for a fortnight of labor, and you rejoice, but they have a vault of gold coins in their homes. And their bigger promise lies at the end, does it not? Haven't they promised to aid in the repayment of any debt you hold should you work for them until the end of the construction?"

His face fell. "But you're saying we'll most likely die before we can claim it."

She nodded. "They know the sum of what they've promised, and they have structured it so they will never have to honor it. They prey upon the unregistered for this scheme, knowing you're desperate for employment, but also have no access to the health wards above Inejio. You will grow sicker as the months go by, with no chance to visit a physic and learn the truth."

"No one would do something as monstrous as this—"

"Father," she said delicately but firmly, "the riverside flats are the first step in a plan to gentrify Inejio Setgad into an exclusive haven for the wealthy. The highborn would never accept the unregistered as their neighbors. You know this. Even the mere idea of the unregistered darkening their doorsteps would inevitably lower the value of these flats. I have spent my life working amongst merchants of all sorts, and this is exactly how the master-builder and his investors think. But they cannot have you fleeing elsewhere, aboveground. So they hire you to labor on their flats, which completion will be long enough for you to take a deadly rot within your flesh, and you will die in time for them to sell them."

She turned to the other four, all listening with dismayed faces, and said, "You must tell as many of the unregistereds as you can before it's too late. They must know they're being sacrificed for highborn luxuries."

Anger had reignited in her, fueling her thoughts, but she halted as she turned back. Tears were springing forth from Father's dark eyes.

It was easy to get carried away upon a tide of rage. But it was better, she decided, to stay with a person and their grief. *Wrath serves oneself, mercy serves others.* She softened, crouching to his level. "Father, I'm sorry."

He buried his face in his palms, bloated joints and wrinkled knuckles hiding him. "I am a fool as ever. I thought I'd finally found an opportunity to free myself from my debts and return us to a proper life aboveground, but now you tell me I've made yet another fool's choice."

Lythlet reached out and held his hands, the tightrope shrinking into vanishment. "You are not a fool for wanting the chance to better yourself. You are not a fool for trusting the word of folk who have branded themselves as wiser and more accomplished than you. These highborn masterminds are cunning grifters, and they know how to lead you to your own demise, all while ensuring you never have a chance to look at the map they alone hold in their hands."

Father groaned, pushing her hands away and withdrawing into himself. "I've done nothing but stumble from mistake to mistake. Perhaps my greatest mistake was marrying your mother and bringing you into this world, that the two of you would be damned to a life with a fool of a husband and a father. Had I known better, I never would have had you."

A tremble spread from Lythlet's fingers, and the tightrope

remanifested into a whip lashing her throat. "Never say that again," she said in a shattered voice. "Not to yourself, and never to Mother for she will not understand until it's too late that it's not her existence that burdens you." She wanted to say, *and never to me again, because I won't forgive you twice*, but she knew she'd never be able to get those words out coherently.

A warm hand fell upon her shoulder. She knew it to be Desil's, but she looked away, ashamed of her outburst.

She took a deep, heaving breath, and spoke once more in an even tone. "Mother needs you. She needs you to be whole of mind and spirit. She has always loved you, and so long as you love her, she won't weigh your worth by any other measure. Don't think yourself a failure for struggling to find an easy path in a hard world." Her voice had shattered again midway, but she was determined to guide her father down a road he might not have known existed.

Desil's hand had squeezed tighter in encouragement when she faltered, but now he released it, and she turned to catch his gentle gaze upon her. She looked away, uncomfortable at how vulnerable she'd made herself before an audience.

Father stared. He seemed to know the weight of her plea, to intuit the words stemmed from a wounded heart. "Is it too late for me?"

"How long since you began work at the flats?"

"Five months."

"There is still hope. From my learning under the hive-master, a cough may continue for years, but you won't go the way of the white wind as long as you stop further exposure to the golden rot."

He sat quietly, and she sensed a reluctance in his silence.

She knelt before him, knees pressing into the wooden floorboards. "If you are as I am, you're thinking that you may as well carry on since you've come this far. Earn what wages you can, give it to Mother, and hold out as long as possible so they're forced to pay your debts before you succumb to the golden rot. But Father, your life is worth more than that. You must live for Mother, and more importantly, for yourself."

He hid his face behind one broad palm, until all she could see were tears dripping from his fingers.

"I am sorry," she said once more, lost for clever words.

CHAPTER TWENTY-SEVEN

THE WAY OF THE MERCHANT

ALL FIVE OF them left the attic behind, every one of them deep in thought. Desil's hand remained on her shoulder, squeezing tight. At the foot of the long marble staircase, Naya turned and said, "I'm going to speak with the leader of this safehaven about this golden rot business right away. We need to spread word as quickly as possible."

Lythlet nodded quietly.

"But not all unregistereds belong to a safehouse, and we haven't a way to reach those who don't," Ilden said with a troubled face. "Lythlet's father may refuse to return to the site, but there are hundreds waiting for the chance to replace him and receive his salary instead."

"As long as there remains a bold promise, there will be plenty desperate enough to fall for the master-builder's ploy. The effects of golden rot are slow enough that they'll only regret it when it's too late," Shunvi agreed, dissatisfied.

"Wait!" a voice called out, and Lythlet raised her head to see her father leaning over the banister from above. He waved at her, hobbling around the rim of the railing toward her. "Come back. I want to talk."

She took the steps two at a time to meet him in the middle, a dusty mezzanine outfitted with settees that had long had their stuffing ripped out of them, the others tailing after her. "What about?"

Anger gave Father's voice a rare strain of energy. "Master-Builder Asa. You say the man's been poisoning me as I work for him. I want to stop men like him from ever committing such crimes against the unregistered again. We may be lowborn, but we are people, nonetheless. What can be done about him?"

Lythlet sobered as she sat on the stiff-backed settee. "I fear very little, Father. Even if a miracle were to happen, and we were able to bring the case all the way up to the Einveldi Court, there's little point. You're unregistered, stateless in the eyes of the city, and any damages resulting from the Court will not find its way into your pockets."

"That's fine," he said.

"Will you not grieve the coin you cannot keep?" she asked, surprised.

"It matters more to me that we prevent these highborn from causing any more pain than I be rewarded."

She smiled at him, admiring his honor. As strangled as their relationship was, she knew then with iron-wrought certainty she loved him.

He coughed again, a painful hacking into his sleeve, and he sat hunched over with an unnatural weariness. A weariness he would have attributed to the long, hard hours he worked at the flats, or the ekelenzi, or to a myriad of external factors had Lythlet not told him the truth.

Mercy serves others, she reminded herself. "I can promise you nothing, Father—but I will help you seek the justice you deserve."

Father breathed a sigh of grateful relief.

"But it goes without saying that reporting this scheme to the watchmen would be in vain," she said slowly, thoughts spurring her to fidget in her seat.

Father nodded. "However we may be wronged, the watchmen do not serve us unregistereds. Never have, never will."

"And if rumors of the master-builder having political ties are true, then they'll easily smother any movement stirring within the watchmen."

Father nodded. "There's always talk of Master Asa meeting some bigwig to update them on the construction's progress."

She drummed her fingers on the scratched-up table between them, letting her thoughts unspool. "Then we'll simply have to destroy their whole business another way."

"Destroy?" said Father hesitantly.

"Not with violence," she assured. "Provoke them with even a single instance of aggression, and they'll loudly smear all the unregistered as violent, uncivilized animals who deserve to be culled, and you will garner little sympathy from the rest of the city. No, there is a simpler way."

"What?"

The little cogs of her mind were spinning into action, her tongue unbridling in turn. "The way I know best: the way of the merchant. Investors bankrolled this scheme hoping to make a mountain of profit off these flats—so what if we cut short their road to fortune and devastate them financially? I have worked with grifting folk like them my whole life, and the fragility of their egos cannot be overstated. Scars and bruises bother them momentarily, but the pain and frustration of lost profits, wasted investments, and failed plans will haunt them to their graves. We'll outsmart them at a game they created by utilizing their merchant sensibilities against them and disrupting the supply-demand continuum. Crush all demand for the flats, so that the master-builder will be forced to halt the construction, preventing any unregistered from falling for this scheme again."

"But," said Ilden, perplexed, "how exactly are we going to do that?"

Lythlet leaned back in her seat and covered her face with her hands, wanting to think in darkness. In time, she peeked through her fingers at them. "As always, the easiest way is to prey upon ignorance and ego. These are fancy things built for the highborn in Central, which makes things easier for us. They're folk whose words catch fire quickly. If the highborn hear the flats are constructed with golden rot, they will surely tighten their purse strings in fear and disabuse each other of the notion of purchasing a flat."

Father frowned. "But you said that once hardened into mortar, golden rot's harmless. Why would they care?"

She smiled wryly. "*I* know it's harmless. But few others do, save those in the hive-keeping and architectural trade. The vast majority of the highborn won't know any better. Simply preying upon their ignorance and associating the riverside flats with poisonous hive-rot that's been left to fester will sharply drive down demand. And the next strike will be the most devastating."

"That being?" Shunvi gazed at her keenly, black eyes shining bright.

"We must ensure their pride is thoroughly offended. Educate them not only on the harmful effects of the golden rot, but also its cheapness, and emphasize the absurdity of paying so much coin for a flat built with such poor-quality materials. These elites living above us would never want their names associated with a fool's bargain, and they'd be outraged at the whole thing, that they were about to be taken for halfwits. With us manipulating their ignorance and ego in a two-pronged attack, Master-Builder Asa and his investors will be destroyed, their names publicly shamed for all to see."

"But how exactly will we tell them these things?" Father said. "I must keep low, as must all the unregistered. We cannot simply go into the streets of Central and demand their attention. They'll think we're a nuisance, they always do."

"We need an advocate," she said thoughtfully, then turned glum. "And I regret to say none of us here are suited for it."

"Come now," said Ilden, "Shunvi and I could do it. I'm no longer unregistered, and seeing how Shunvi's the teahouse-master of two reputable establishments, he does have a growing degree of clout in the highborn circles."

"I'm afraid that won't work," said Lythlet regretfully. "We must remember, the master-builder is supported by political investors. Anyone publicly disgracing them would immediately become a target for their wrath, and I fear putting anyone in such danger. The four of us are tied to conquessing, whether past or present, and although bloodsports may be tacitly allowed, it's outlawed on paper. It would be much too easy for any claims we make to be discredited, our reputations smeared, and us thrown into gaol. Shunvi, in particular, I would not advocate raising your voice. They will rip all you've worked for from your hands."

"I can rebuild whatever they destroy," said Shunvi determinedly. "My ego is the least of my concerns."

"But you must think of your teahouse workers. Many of them were unregistered before and have only recently settled into proper lives thanks to you—they will not be left unharmed should you be thrown into gaol," she said, and he reluctantly nodded as he considered her words. "Besides, I think it would be better if we found someone with the expertise and clout to confirm that golden rot is being used at the flats, someone the masses would find truly credible."

"Then bring in the fellow who taught you," Shunvi suggested. "The hive-master."

She shifted uncomfortably. "I must decline. The man used to beat me and fling glass bottles at me in rage, and I robbed him in farewell."

He flushed. "Sorry, I didn't know."

"No, you couldn't have," she assured.

Father stared at her. "Did he really?" he asked quietly. Not out of doubt, she intuited—out of concern.

She nodded reluctantly.

He said nothing, face falling. He reached over to lay a hand on hers, awkward, yet warm.

A silence fell upon the group as each ransacked their own mind for a potential alternative.

After a moment, Ilden tentatively said, "But suppose you tried—"

"Ilden Highvind, if you're about to ask Lythlet to go back to a man who used to beat her, I'll never forgive you," Naya cried.

"I wasn't," said Ilden with a guilty expression strongly suggesting he had been.

"Absolutely not," Desil said. "The man was awful. He's not someone we can reason with anyway. He's your typical old-fashioned Setgadian merchant obsessed with social standing above all, and the last thing he'd ever consider is working with someone he deems beneath him."

"And in his eyes, I don't even rank," Lythlet said quietly. "But the fact remains Hive-Master Winaro is reputable. A mid-tier merchant who is genuinely an expert in his trade and honest in his business practices, commissioned by the government to service the southern sectors. I did the books for him, and he's never cheated even a single penny—his reputation is spotless. A plot to knowingly exploit and murder unwitting workers would be heinous even to him. His one flaw is his temper, and mistreatment of subordinates may be frowned upon, but it's hardly illegal in Setgad. You couldn't throw a stone without hitting an ill-tempered employer down here."

"Lythlet, don't open up old wounds," Shunvi said. "We'll come up with someone else."

But she shook her head. "I know Master Winaro better than anyone. His business, his desires, and his weaknesses. If I play my cards right, he may truly be our best bet."

"But will you be all right seeing him again?" he said in a quiet voice, concerned.

Here, Lythlet kept quiet, struggling under the weight of memories.

She reached up to feel the scar on her forehead, Master Winaro's parting gift from last winter.

"We'll let Lythlet handle this however she's comfortable," Desil said after a pause. "Perhaps we should consider retrieving a sample of the golden rot from the flats to begin with? We'll need one regardless of who we ask for help."

Father opened his mouth, but Lythlet cut him off.

"I don't want you returning there, ever," she said plainly. "Not for a single moment. You've already inhaled enough of the poison into your lungs."

"But the sites are heavily regulated," Father argued. "Only workers are permitted to enter, and even then, only in the strictest capacity."

Ilden, who had shrunk into the deflated settee cushions out of shame from his earlier castigation, popped back to life with a dramatic flair, an eager glint entering his eyes. "Say no more! I think it's time I brought my old friend Marcielot Perryweather back into the game."

All stared blankly at him—all besides Shunvi, who rolled his eyes in full knowledge of what was to come.

THAT EVENING, LYTHLET wandered out to the ledge of their kataka flat and leaned against the wooden railing. Deep in thought, she stared at the city stretched out before her like a map laid flat on a surface. It was the same city as ever, wickedness running through every nook and cranny, but somehow it did not seem as impenetrable as before, not with Desil back by her side.

Before they'd left the safehaven, Father had tugged on Lythlet's sleeve, pulling her away from the others for a moment. "Thank you," he had muttered.

The memory made her smile, as short and simple as it had been.

A chill wind picked up. It was getting dark, the sky turning that rare shade of pink seen only for scant minutes before the sun disappeared.

"Don't stay out too long, Lytha," Desil called, peeping out through the open door. "It's cold tonight. Where's the hive, by the way?"

"Right here." She glanced down at the hive by her feet.

"Here we go," he said, plucking it up. "Looks like Rentavos and the rest are waking up right on time. Come on, fellows, time to lend a little light. How come the lid's been left up?"

She stared at him for a moment, reluctant to answer. "Because I thought I wouldn't be returning home after the match," she finally said, softly.

He lowered the hive-lantern, her words sinking in deep. Lost in silence, his eyes watered. Then he stepped up to her. "Put it down."

"What?"

He held the hive-lantern before her, the light within it slowly growing as bee after bee awoke. "I want you to put it down," he urged.

With a small smile and a brisk flick of her wrist, she set the lid right, covering the bees safely. "There."

Heaving a sigh of relief, he threw his arms around her.

CHAPTER TWENTY-EIGHT

RUNNING TOGETHER

"AIN'T EASY WORK pretending to be hard at work," Ilden quipped, bouncing a cloth-wrapped package in his hands. "But I feigned it long enough to register for the construction under my alter ego and sneak out with this treasure. The flats were blessed by the presence of Marcielot Perryweather but for a day alone! Come, praise me."

"Good work, Perryweather," Lythlet obliged as she plucked the bouncing package from his reach. He had come with Shunvi that morning to her flat, and they sat in a circle on the floor. "Dreadful name, though."

Ilden beamed. "Isn't it simply? If you must know Perryweather's heartbreaking backstory, he's the bastard child of a Central highborn, abandoned as a mere babe to spare his father the shame of an illicit affair. But mark my words, Marcielot will one day ascend the highborn ranks and seek his vengeance. Curse you, Father! Ah, Shunvi and I got up to a lot of silly business after we won our jackpots, and we had to swap between an alias or two to keep our shenanigans under wraps."

"Silly business?" she repeated, blinking at them.

"Oh, just some havoc we used to wreak at the casinos—" he cut himself short as Shunvi shot a glare at him. "Never mind, let's not bring up the past."

"Yes, let's not," Shunvi said, swiftly. "Still, Marcielot wasn't his worst name."

"First time I had to come up with a fake identity, I was put on the spot and blurted out that I was Pompatom Tumblebear. The ego really struggles to survive under the weight of a name so ridiculous."

"Now I wish I'd come along with you to the flats," said Shunvi wistfully. "It's been a while since we had some fun."

Lythlet unraveled the cloth. A fist-sized lump of icterine rock sat in the center of their circle like an offering to the divine. Powder flaked off as she delicately maneuvered it around with a corner of the cloth.

Shunvi leaned forward. "Is it what you think it is?"

"It certainly looks and smells like golden rot to me," she said, nodding. "But I require proper confirmation."

"From the hive-master," he finished tentatively.

A grim feeling settled over her.

"Will you be all right?" Ilden asked sheepishly, as if still guilty for pushing her into it.

It took a moment, but she nodded. "I know what I need to do. You boys run along now. If you want to visit Desil, he's at The Steam Dragon. You might catch him on a break if you're lucky."

"Are you sure you don't want us to come with you?" Shunvi said. "There's no shame in wanting help."

"I'll need some peace and quiet to think through my plan," she said. "We're to establish an ongoing partnership with Master Winaro, and I must find the right words to make him willingly work with us. And I suppose I ought to be brave and go at it myself. As General Lauturo once said, if I want to run fast, I ought to run alone."

Shunvi and Ilden exchanged an uneasy, conflicted glance at each other, but after a moment, they nodded.

BY THE TIME Lythlet reached the doorstep of Master Winaro's hive-workshop, she had mentally prepared and revised a script multiple times, a script she knew would prey upon the hive-master's deepest desires.

Yet her hand trembled with the burden of memory as she looked inside and saw Master Winaro on a stool, delicately carving out hive-rot with a scalpel. Steeling herself, she pushed the door open.

The bell, ever so familiar from her months in the workshop, tinkled, announcing her entrance.

Master Winaro paused his work, lowering the tool. "Welco—" He stopped himself short. A murderous look entered his eyes as he recognized her. "I thought I warned you what would happen if you ever came back here."

She clenched her shaking fists tightly, trying not to let her stutter emerge. "Master Winaro, I have not returned to discuss our past—"

He rose from his seat. "Do you think I give a shit what you've come here for? You disrespected me, and you dare show your face here?" The scalpel flashed in his hand, reflecting the bioluminescent hives surrounding them.

Time should have blunted the edge of her painful memories with Master Winaro, but as she stared into the face of the man who had beaten and belittled her for months, every bit of bravado and dignity she'd accumulated since leaving him evaporated. She could feign ironclad arrogance before a man like Khavi Monul, one who only knew her for her conquessorial achievements. But she could not bluff Master Winaro with a brand-new persona, not a man who knew her woebegone days and erstwhile existence of groveling timidity. He would see through any act she put on now and scorn her harder for it.

"If there's one thing I'll offer you, it's my gratitude that you've returned to the scene of the crime," he spat. "You robbed us, didn't you? I would've dragged you to the watchmen if only I'd found a single scrap of evidence. Did you use my wife's necklace to pay for those boots, you piece of trash?"

"Master Winaro," she tried her script again, syllables slipping into a stutter, "I have come to make a merchant's deal with you—"

"I would sooner slit my own throat than ever think of entertaining a bargain with a slumdog like you. Now leave before I slit yours."

The bell rang once more, a waft of cool wintry air flooding the workshop as the door swung open.

Lythlet stayed still, shrunken, shoulders huddled together. She turned her head away from the newly arrived party, not wanting them to see her trembling lips. Master Winaro, on the other hand, immediately straightened, lowered his scalpel, and bowed deeply in the direction of the newcomers, deep enough to signify they were either upper merchants or highborns.

"Welcome, welcome, sirs," Master Winaro greeted. "Step right this away and I'll assist you. Please, don't let this woman bother you—I was just in the process of having her removed from the premises."

"Hive-master, stay your tongue," said the customer coldly. "I did not come to engage your services, and I'll thank you to spare me your needless salesmanship."

Lythlet startled at the familiar voice. She spun on her heels.

Shunvi was drawn to full height as he glared at Master Winaro with a steel-edged gaze. With his fashionable robes and well-groomed bearing, it was impossible to mistake him as anything beneath an upper merchant—and the haughty upturn of his chin tipped his scales toward highborn. Behind him were Desil and Ilden, each casting concerned looks at her that told her they had overheard Master Winaro's words from the outside.

They must have picked Desil up and tailed me here while I was too caught up with preparations to notice, she realized, heartened by their presence.

A flicker of suspicion wavered in the hive-master's eyes at Shunvi's words. "Who are you?"

"I am Shunvi Tanna, proprietor of The Golden Peach and The Silver Phoenix teahouses in Central and Northeast respectively. I'm sure you've heard of them."

Suspicion vanished, and Master Winaro bowed deeply to his mercantile superior. "An honor to have your presence here, Master Tanna. The reputation of your teahouses precedes you. And your companions?"

Shunvi cast a quick look behind at Desil and Ilden. "This is my family's sworn guardsman Dedaro Demothen and my personal manservant Pompatom Tumblebear. Isn't that right, men?"

"Yes, Master Tanna," Desil barked with a stifled smile.

Shunvi raised his brows at Ilden. "Pompatom, did you hear me?"

"Yes, Master Tanna," Ilden wheezed out with a chagrined smile.

Just like that, Shunvi had solidified his status as a highborn—one with enough means to have a retinue accompanying him at all times.

Impressed, Master Winaro said, "If you did not come here to engage my services, then how may I help you, Master Tanna?"

"I came simply because I could not abide your treatment of this lady," he said sternly, gesturing toward Lythlet. "I could hear your insults and threats through the window, and I found them most shameful."

Master Winaro forced a polite smile. "Master Tanna, your chivalry is most respectable, but you needn't defend this woman. She is far beneath us in station—yours especially."

"A most reprehensible attitude to have, hive-master. It is my duty to defend this lady's honor—"

"She has none," the hive-master interrupted, patience wearing thin. Imperative as it was to show deference to his superiors, his hatred for Lythlet was all-consuming. "Master Tanna, forgive my impertinence, but on what basis do you wish to defend this woman? She is no more than a thief who once worked under me—poorly, if I may add. I strongly suspect she robbed my wife and I when she left us."

Lythlet swore she could see the cogs in Shunvi's head spinning in the split second before he slammed his fist on the counter. "On the basis that a man must defend the honor of his betrothed!"

Lythlet blinked.

His what?

"Your betrothed?" Master Winaro's dumbfounded look vanished into an incredulous laugh. "Master Tanna, I don't know what game you're playing with me, but I'm beginning to doubt you even know this woman's name, let alone your engagement. It seems highly unlikely a man of your standing would choose to wed someone so far beneath you."

"I beg your pardon, sir," said Shunvi, outraged, "but I am most certainly engaged to Lythlet Tairel. And she has told me much about you—about how she suffered greatly at your hands during the seven months she worked as your bookkeeper. She's spoken of your abuse and exploitation, how your childish temper would flare at her whenever you struggled with your own workload, how you would shout and scream at her like a mindless brute, how you would hit her in your worst moments. I know of the bruises she hid so her dearest friend wouldn't worry about her—bruises *you* gave her. Have you the temerity to continue casting aspersions on the woman who shall be my wife?"

He knows how to pronounce temerity, Lythlet thought, unexpectedly delighted by Shunvi's performance.

Master Winaro spluttered wordlessly, thrown off-course. His eyes flickered in a panic between Lythlet and Shunvi. He had just committed the gravest of sins of Setgadian society: to insult the honesty of a man above him, and worse, to insult the virtue of the one he loved.

Shunvi turned and cupped Lythlet's face with impossibly warm hands, the sensation making her stomach flutter with an unfamiliar feeling. *Am I about to be sick?*

"My love," he said with all the subtlety of a sledgehammer, the timbre of his voice deeper than ever, "you must never let anyone speak to you this way again. I know this ghastly man must terrify you, but you're not alone, and none of us will let him harm you. Now, please, say what you've come to say to him."

There was a look in Shunvi's fathomless eyes that made Lythlet's heart pound like a child let loose on a kettledrum. Not love, she knew—but an earnest, wholehearted trust in her.

"Thank you, Shunvi," she said, smiling as he released her face.

If Shunvi's theatrics hadn't been enough, her being on first-name basis with him was enough to convince Master Winaro he had made a great many terrible mistakes that day.

Shunvi delivered a piercing glare to the hive-master. "Let's begin with an apology from you."

Master Winaro flinched. "I apologize for the way I treated you, Lythlet," he said through gritted teeth.

She stared, wide-eyed. Never in her life had she expected Master Winaro to show such deference to her. It didn't matter that he didn't mean the apology—the fact they'd brought him down to this level was a victory in itself, kneecapping a giant that had been looming in the recesses of her worst memories.

But Shunvi tut-tutted, wagging his finger left and right. "Surely you know how inappropriate it is to refer to your superiors without their titles."

Master Winaro blanched. He visibly struggled with the words, "Madame Tanna—"

"She isn't taking my name," said Shunvi, exasperated.

"Forgive me, Madame Tairel," he said, chagrined.

"And remember, my darling," Shunvi gently said, taking Lythlet's hand and looking down at her with a smile, "you no longer need to refer to him as Master."

Lythlet paused, realizing he was right. With their fictional betrothal, Shunvi had just elevated her station above Master Winaro's. He winked at her then, and she fought the urge to crow in laughter with him.

She stole a peek behind at the other two. Ilden paused

contemplating his downfall from Marcielot Perryweather to Pompatom Tumblebear to nod encouragingly at her. Desil, refusing to break character, subtly flashed the oath-swearing sign by his hip. She took a deep breath, feeling her heart quieten, her soul settle.

Far be it for Lythlet to question the wisdom of General Lauturo, but she wondered then if she'd rather rewrite her story into one where she did not have to run alone. All those grand tales she grew up reading always seemed to center around a lone protagonist— but perhaps life was better lived recognizing the small but certain happiness in having others to run together with, that the spirit of collectivism that had always seemed so foreign to her would not slow her down but pick her up whenever she stumbled.

Raising her head, she met Master Winaro's gaze calmly, courage restored. "Valanti, I've come today to offer you a merchant's deal."

"That being what, Madame Tairel?"

"First, I must ask you to identify this substance." She took from her pocket the wrapped sample Ilden had stolen and set it before him.

Valanti glanced suspiciously at it, flicking the corners of the cloth apart until the yellow block sat before him. He adjusted the magnifying bifocals on his nose and jabbed the sample with a long pair of metallic tongs. After a moment, he looked up sharply and hissed, "This is golden rot. How came you to possess this?"

Lythlet exchanged a glance with the three men, all heartened by the confirmation.

"Riverside flats are being built for the highborn in Inejio," she explained. "And this is being used in their construction."

The hive-master startled, understanding the implication. "The builders are being exposed to this every day? A year of huffing in this dust, and they'll be wheezing themselves into an early grave."

She nodded. "These builders are unregistered, with neither the watchmen nor the health wards as recourse. They're being tricked into early deaths for the sake of the completion of these flats."

"Who is the master-builder?"

"A fellow named Westiro Asa."

Valanti frowned, eyes clouding over in recognition. "I'm familiar with the man. A few of my friends in the architectural trade have mentioned him before—never for anything good. I can't say I'm surprised this is his work."

She nodded, glad he had knowledge of the matter.

Valanti leveled a steely glare at her. "So what have you come to me for?"

She took a deep breath. "We wish to go to the gazettes with this. To protect the unregistered, we want their claim against Westiro Asa to be done by a third-party. So I've come to request you spearhead this case for us."

Valanti's eyes bulged. "You want me to lead these claims against Asa? You're mad! Asa is in league with high-ranking fellows in the United Setgad Party. Look at how those politicking bastards have shrugged off Corio Brandolas's accusations of cronyism and corruption all these years—with their glib tongues and fat pockets, they'll do all they can to rain hellfire upon me if I challenge them."

Lythlet leveled with him. "But you are not powerless, Valanti. You're a respectable middle merchant with long decades in your trade and friends in the right places. With your name attached to the forefront of these accusations, many would be convinced by your expertise and reputation in hive-keeping. This city is filled with sheep in desperate need of a shepherd's crook to flock under, and yours just might be the most effective one."

"Be that as it may, Asa's political compatriots are likely bankrolling numerous gazettes. You'll struggle to find one willing—or even able!—to expose this scandal."

She nodded. "That's true. But a gazette-master is ultimately a merchant of news, and surely there must be one eager to break earth-shattering word of luxurious flats aimed at the highborn being built with poisonous rot—their gazettes would be flying off the racks the moment the baltascar-blocks finish stamping the words down. I have a hunch we'll be best served by targeting the gazettes that have been charitable in their reporting of Corio Brandolas—those surely can't be in the pocket of the United Setgad Party. We can work together to find the right gazette to work with, Valanti."

"Absolutely not," he said, waving them off. "There's nothing in this for me."

She shook her head. "I came to propose a merchant's deal, did I not? The risk you undertake will be rewarded fairly."

He glowered suspiciously at her. "With what?"

"With the very things you crave most—an opportunity to grow your business and your station in life."

He wavered, curiosity coming over him.

She continued, "I've done the books for you for a long time, and I know your business as well as you do. We're both aware of one thing: you've maximized your market here in the south. Your only hope for growth is to expand to the northern or central markets. But try as you might, you haven't been able to gain a foothold there. The competition is stiff, and there are established hive-masters up there who've a stranglehold on their market. But helm this case, and you'll become a known figure to every soul in Setgad. Imagine *your* name in the headlines of every gazette for weeks upon weeks, your expertise in hive-keeping advertised. The fame you'll earn from this will grant you many new customers, and if you play your cards right, the opportunity to expand your business beyond the south."

Hope kindled in the growing silence as Master Winaro considered her proposal. But then he frowned, shaking his head, "You are asking me to take on considerable risk to help you. I may be desperate to expand my business further north, but I fail to see the necessity for me to work with you on this. I'll find another way to succeed—"

"The clock is ticking on your trade, and you know it, Valanti," she said calmly. "Solar-augmented baltascar bulbs are the way of the future, and slowly but surely, they will replace the hives up north one by one. Sit this out if you want to be a fool, and watch your craft become obsolete. This is an unbelievably timely marketing opportunity for you to take advantage of—you will be granted fame and status in this brief pocket of time when it can still be useful for you. Make your riches now, Valanti, before your viable market vanishes."

"But whether you start a northern branch or are stuck with this one, you really must treat your staff better from now on," Desil burst out. "No more beating them whenever you're in a foul mood."

"Quite right, my overly enthusiastic guardsman," said Shunvi, cheerfully clapping his back. He regarded Valanti with a stern eye. "Rest assured, hive-master, if I ever hear further word of your maltreatment of your staff, I'll be sure to let all my friends in the north know of your shameful habits. It'd be most devastating to your success and your reputation, I assure you."

Master Winaro flushed beet-red. "I never meant to—"

Shunvi waved an irreverent hand at him. "A man's dignity is revealed in his actions, not his excuses. All that matters to me is you agree to reform your ways and champion our cause."

Master Winaro stayed silent for long moments, head bowed, moments that made the anxiety in Lythlet's belly crawl to life. Had she sufficiently tempted this man with a deal he couldn't refuse?

He raised his hand—and she had a brief premonition of being slapped, that single gesture dragging to the forefront of her memory the countless times he had done so.

But then it hung in front of her, stiff, waiting for her to shake it. The hive-master lifted his head at last, eyes glinting in the bioluminescent light. "Madame Tairel, we have a deal. I will help you avenge the unregistereds."

CHAPTER TWENTY-NINE

THE TRUTH OF SAEVEM ARTHIL

"THAT HIVE-MASTER'S ON a rampage," said Ilden a week later in The Steam Dragon, thumbing through the latest edition of the *Daily Diamond*. *DEATH DUST: A ROTTEN DEAL IN INEJIO* was emblazoned proudly over the front page.

"Valanti's always been a hard worker, so I'm not surprised he's gotten so much done so quickly," said Lythlet with reluctant respect. "And he has been extremely easy to work with now." Runt snuffled by her side, gently requesting attention with her wet nose.

Ilden's eyes went wide. "Good grief, Runt just won't stop growing. I think you might've been bamboozled into taking home a bear, Lythlet."

"Wouldn't that be wonderful?" She kissed the top of her hound's head. Runt was the biggest puppy she'd ever seen in her life, now the size of a healthy, full-grown pig, and all who looked upon her would always gawk and ask Lythlet if Runt were actually a bear. Ederi as she was, Lythlet did not hold a belief in reincarnation as the Oraanus did, yet a quiet part of her wondered if this was the little bugbear cub given a second chance at life. She knew she'd never get an answer to that—but she was going to make sure it was as good a life as she could give the pup.

"Does she still not know how to bark properly?" Ilden asked, reaching over to flap Runt's jowls back and forth.

"ROO," Runt politely confirmed, tolerating his handling with the dignified manner of a highborn lady.

Chuckling, Ilden leaned back against the wall, one arm tucked behind his head. "Now that the *Daily Diamond*'s on our side, Shunvi owes me twenty white valirs. He was certain the *Diamond Edge* would be the first to side with us."

"Where is Shunvi, anyway?" Desil asked.

"Down at the Homely Home. There's much to celebrate there, what with how the case is building against Westiro Asa. That's why I've been sent here actually, to invite you two to join. Come along, won't you? And bring little Roo-Bear, too. The children would love chasing her around."

"We would love to," Desil said eagerly as Lythlet shook her head.

"I ought to stay behind to strategize," she said. "The *Daily Diamond* may be publishing our affairs, but there's much more I need to organize with Valanti. The next round of news to unleash, more information on the golden rot—"

Ilden reached forward to pinch Lythlet's nose. She wrenched out of his grip with a snarl.

"You're much too serious," he complained. "Leave tomorrow's hardships to tomorrow. Plus, I've brought along some of the finest bottles of gin Shunvi and I keep in our cellar, and you'll be missing out on that."

"Good grief," said Lythlet, rising from her seat. "You could have mentioned the free gin earlier and we'd be halfway to the Home by now."

*   *   *

ILDEN WENT AHEAD of them, saying he wanted to go greet some old friends nearby first, and he gave them the bag filled with gin bottles to carry to the Homely Home.

Shortly after Ilden stepped off the premises of The Steam Dragon, a tussle began between Lythlet and Desil.

"We're going to drink it soon enough," she complained, bottle in hand. "Why can't I open just one and have a sip or two in peace first?"

"You're developing a very serious problem," Desil scolded, snatching the bottle free from her fingers. He cradled the gin satchel protectively to his chest, trying and failing to put on his coat with his one free hand.

She made an attempt for the bottle, then paused, hand lingering midair as something caught her attention.

He narrowed his eyes, guarding the satchel in case she was tricking him. "What is it?"

She pointed at the entrance, and he hesitantly turned to look.

Saevem Arthil was peering inside The Steam Dragon, Runt and Schwala sniffing his boots. When he spotted them, he pointed questioningly at the partitioned private room at the back.

Desil nodded, scuttling off to prepare the table, and Lythlet ushered Saevem into the teahouse. Within seconds, a steaming teapot and a set of cold appetizers were waiting for them. Desil gently pulled the partition closed, shutting out the rest of the teahouse with a mother-of-pearl lacquer screen depicting the creation story of the Oraanu, droplets of moonlight spilling to the earth and emerging as sons and daughters of the Moonmachinist.

They waited for Saevem to take his seat first, poured his tea, then seated themselves.

"What brought you here today?" Lythlet asked. Something in Saevem's demeanor told her to anticipate his answer.

He leaned in, urging them to huddle closer. "The time has come for me to make my request," he said in hushed tones. "I gave you the bestiary because I thought you two were promising conquessors—promising enough to stay in the arena for a long time if you were granted some help. I'd heard before that Master Dothilos had forged strong bonds with certain conquessors he favored in the far distant past, and I needed someone in that position to help my cause."

"What does the Coalition of Hope want with Master Dothilos?"

"It's the folk he associates with that we're concerned with. He's a man with many connections, I believe."

"A fact he frequently boasts of," she said bitterly.

"There is one man we suspect he is affiliated with, however: Governor Matheranos."

Lythlet raised a brow. "Corio Brandolas has been relentlessly attacking Governor Matheranos and the United Setgad Party for ages now, accusing him of corruption, cronyism, and all that. Are you hoping to find evidence of the governor's ties to the underworld to further build your case of his corruption to present to the Court?"

"Yes," he said excitedly. "We at the Coalition believe Governor Matheranos has strong ties to the underworld—including outlawed bloodsports such as conquessing. The Eza may be the underworld's master, but his chaos has been left unchecked and unchallenged by a feckless government. We're certain Governor Matheranos receives bribes from either the Eza or his underlings like Master Dothilos to look the other way. Would the underworld trade be able to run with such ease if it were the Eza alone protecting it? No, such seamless operation requires someone with a hand in the upper reaches of the white law to connect the two worlds. You are far from the only non-party members we've entreated—we've been enlisting spies to search for evidence of anything remotely related to the underworld to submit to the Court."

"To no avail?" she asked. She was not unfamiliar with these theories, thanks to Master Winaro's political ramblings back in her hive-workshop days. A part of her remained skeptical of these rumors: to think the ever-vaunted Governor Matheranos, the very man whose duty was to broker the relationship between the city and the Einveldi Court, could have ties with the Eza was not an easy allegation to swallow.

"Unfortunately, when it comes to powerful figures who have been shaping society for decades, rumors are often the only things left in their wake. They're professionals at covering up their tracks, snuffing out dissenters before their efforts can amount to a credible case. I know this all too well: a dear friend of mine was a casualty of their menace." He turned grim, his mind casting for memories of long years past. "A long time ago, during Governor Matheranos's first term, rumors started popping up in the upper echelons of the watchmen circles of him meeting with various folk affiliated with the underworld: a supposed advisor of the Eza, a former watchman official who'd been forced to resign in disgrace after the revelation he'd participated in the trafficking of prisoners to underworld causes, a broker for an infamous brothel amongst elites that trafficked the underaged—"

Lythlet's expression sharpened. "Which brothel?"

Saevem paused, surprised by her outburst. "The madam's name is something along the lines of Kovetti, if I recall correctly."

She darkened.

He continued, "Corio and I, we had a friend working in the upper watchmen ranks—Azuran Telehir. Azuran set about his own private investigation, quietly checking if the rumors had any substance to them. Months passed, and one day, I received a note from him: he was closing in on the governor, and he was certain he'd found some damning evidence. He asked me to come over the next day to review it with him. Not four hours later did I receive more news: Azuran had been discovered dead, having jumped from the balcony of his flat. Corio and I saw his body ourselves, a mangled corpse staining the white stone with fresh blood." He palmed his face, easing the wrinkles on his grief-furrowed brow. "May the white wind guide his soul. We wept as the watchmen chased us away."

Lythlet and Desil listened in startled silence.

"A suicide, they rapidly concluded. Utter hogwash, Corio and I knew," said Saevem bitterly. "Azuran would never have killed himself. When Corio and I were finally granted access to his flat weeks later, we found everything had been scrubbed clean, not even a single scrap of parchment left behind for us to peruse. Unsubtle work, but frankly, subtlety isn't needed when you're the most powerful man in Setgad after the Einveldi Court itself. The governor must have caught whiff of Azuran's investigations and put a stop to it."

"But Corio Brandolas has been accusing Governor Matheranos of crimes for years, and he's still alive," Lythlet brought up hesitantly.

Saevem nodded. "Only because Corio is savvy enough to have made an ally in the Einveldi Court."

She raised a brow. "The Court sides with him?"

"Well, not the whole Court," he answered reluctantly, a hint of sheepishness laced in his words. "Judge Eridicea is sympathetic to Corio's claims, and she has been providing him with an independent guard force to protect him and his family. She has stated that if we ever provide her with solid evidence of the governor working with the underworld, she will entreat the other judges to our cause."

He said this with a keen sense of pride, but Lythlet struggled to return his enthusiasm.

"One judge out of twelve?" she said.

Saevem grimaced, deflating. His sure-footed passion faltered into a weariness that spoke of long years of fruitless politicking. "The odds may be against us, but we are nonetheless doggedly pursuing this case. This isn't some silly game to win the throne of Setgad, I assure you. It is so much more to me, and to Corio. We owe it to Azuran, our dear friend, to ensure his death was not in vain. That we can finish the case he had begun—and would've finished—

had he not been murdered in cold blood. Governor Matheranos robbed him of his life, just as he robs the city of justice. In his two terms, the governor has ripped apart systems his predecessors implemented for the good of the people: cutting health ward subsidies for the poorer sectors here in the south just so his balance sheet looks prettier on the page; weakening labor protections so that employers have little need to treat their workers well, allowing his rich friends to continue enjoying unfettered wealth with little responsibility; so thoroughly gutting the city's watch and ensuring the watchmen hired are not folk like Azuran had been—noble, justice-minded folk truly ready to serve their duty to the city—but pathetic weasels content with being bribed into silence."

"Why would he do this?" Desil asked tentatively. "Isn't that just destroying the city for short-term gain, when nothing good could come of it in the long run?"

"Because he only has one term left to serve, assuming the polls prove right and he does get elected for his third term in the next election. Thanks to the precedent his ancestor Hemharrow Corinthos set, he'll then have no choice but to leave office and politics as a whole—a death knell to the riches he could gain in power. But imagine this: what if he were simultaneously building his bonds with the underworld, where no such limits exist? With the Eza, who would reward him for allowing the underworld to grow without pains over the past decades? Once he's finished his governorship, Matheranos could then continue eking out a gloriously luxurious life working with the underworld. And to prepare for that, to make sure all the pieces are in place for the underworld to flourish in time for his forced retirement from politics, he enacts all of his regressive policies now, while he still has the popularity and the power to do so. The underworld thrives upon exploiting the desperately impoverished, while the highborn world does the same, albeit unwittingly. Thus, Matheranos has implemented a slow, systematic erosion of wealth equality over the years, weakening one part of the city, your southern slums, so that he can continue to eke out a prosperous living from the underworld in the future."

Lythlet remained silent, slowly growing more convinced this was no conspiracy theory.

Saevem continued, "Which is why we desperately need your help, the two of you. Leverage your connection to Master Dothilos and try to dig it out of him that he has connections to Governor Matheranos, or that the Eza and the governor travel in the same circles."

"I wish I had something to offer you, but not once has Governor Matheranos ever come up in conversation with the match-master," she said.

Saevem nodded. "We will give it time, then. Deepen your ties with him, so that you can continue your espionage for us."

She laughed bitterly. "The man is dangerous, waving threats of violence over me if I disobey him, and you want me to deepen my ties with him."

He turned somber at her words. "So your bond with him is not out of amity but obligation. Dothilos is a pitiful creature, truly, but despite his sorry past, the things he's done since are unforgivable."

"Do you know much about him?" she said, surprised.

He nodded. "Our investigations dug up Renveld Dothilos's history. He grew up in an orphanage, one whose matron was a kind soul. Then she went the way of the white wind, and in came her brother, and things took a turn for the worse."

"How so?"

Saevem looked reluctant to answer, a grave expression that aged him considerably crossing his face. "By numerous accounts, he was a violent man with an inappropriate fondness for children. His sister had done her best to keep him away from the orphans, but with her passing, there was little to stop him."

All three retreated into silence, knowledge pricking them with discomfort. Lythlet thought of Master Dothilos's impassioned vow to one day spit on Madam Kovetti's corpse. Sympathy overwhelmed her.

With a deep sigh, Saevem finally resumed, "But when they were finally old enough, both Renveld and his brother Ean left the orphanage, and somehow, they got their foothold in the conquessorial business."

"Brother?" Desil said. He looked searchingly at Lythlet, silently asking if she knew about this.

She shook her head, equally bewildered.

Saevem nodded. "They did well for themselves, in fact. Conquessing had been dying for years, but with them taking over, it started a resurgence of interest in the bloodsport. But shocking news spread one day: the orphanage had been set on fire. The orphan-keeper was found dead, charred into a blackened mess. The watchmen concluded that the fire had been started on purpose, but no culprit was apprehended. Indeed, it didn't seem there had been much effort to do so, as the investigation was quickly swept under the carpet."

"It seems you suspect something, however," she guessed from his expression. She did, too: the memory of the burn on Master Dothilos's arm emerged in her mind.

He nodded. "Not suspect—I *know* who did it. My deceased friend, Azuran Telehir, had been in charge of the case for the first couple of weeks until his superior suddenly stepped in to redirect his efforts to another case. But in just those two weeks, he had closed in on Master Dothilos as the prime suspect. He'd even brought your match-master in for questioning—and he'd admitted it. He told Azuran, without mincing words, with a great big grin like he'd just found a pot of gold, '*I did it.*'"

Madam Kovetti lurked in the fringes of her thoughts, and her heart hardened. "The Poetics may condemn murder as an unforgivable sin, yet I can't fault Master Dothilos for finding joy in getting his revenge. What the orphan-keeper did to him was heinous."

The Serpent Called Mercy

Desil nodded, looking deeply disturbed by what they'd learned.

Saevem rubbed his face, looking hesitant to continue. "I agreed with you."

"Agreed?" His choice of past tense was curious.

"I agreed that it was right for him to get revenge for his stolen childhood. How could I not? When I learned of what had happened to him, of how Renveld had been rendered mute in his early years as a result of the trauma he suffered, I'd seethed with disgust and rage. That monstrous orphan-keeper deserved death. But then Azuran shared some details with me that had never been made public. The orphan-keeper was not the only victim of the fire: oil had been deliberately dripped everywhere, all around the premises, so that not a single child inside could escape. They died trapped in the flames with their abuser and Ean."

Her mouth ran dry. "His brother?"

Saevem nodded darkly. "The investigation had discovered another charred corpse of a man in the midst of the ruins. No one came to claim him, and they could not identify him initially. But my watchman friend shared that the face had not been fully burnt, and there remained some blond hair and a large mole by his earlobe. Soon he learned Renveld's brother Ean had much the same. Indeed, as time went on, it became apparent that Ean had somehow disappeared, even as Renveld continued to succeed as match-master."

Lythlet furrowed her brow. *A traitor*, Master Dothilos had attributed his burn to. *Someone who tried to destroy me when I was on the cusp of digging myself out of poverty.* "What was he doing at the fire?"

"Unfortunately, we don't have the answer. Many things were lost in those flames, the whole truth amongst them. But I can hypothesize a few things. You see, when they took over the conquessor arenas, the bloodsport was struggling enormously. Spectatorship had been dwindling for decades. But although Renveld and Ean had taken over a long-sunken ship, they were determined to right it.

One thing they needed was participants, so Renveld arranged a deal with the orphan-keeper, that any capable orphan would find themselves funneled into the business of fighting beasts. He paid the orphan-keeper handsomely in return."

"What?" Lythlet said incredulously.

"You heard me. Believe it or not," Saevem said, "he brokered a deal, a very profitable one, with the very man who tormented them as children. However, it seemed after some time, that deal went south for reasons unknown to us. And so Renveld in a vindictive rage decided it was time to kill the orphan-keeper and erase all traces of his existence."

"So what led Ean to the fire then?"

"Here, I know little, for Azuran struggled to uncover more before he was pulled off the case—we suspect his superior had been bribed into discontinuing the investigation so Renveld would be let off the hook. But I wonder if Ean had even known of Renveld's deal with the orphan-keeper to begin with. If he had, then perhaps he grew a conscience. Or perhaps he heard of Renveld's plan to burn them all and went there to stop it and save the children but perished in his efforts. Many parts of the tale have been lost in those flames. But one thing remains clear in my mind, and it's his shameless confession. *I did it.* He did it, it was absolutely him, and he had no guilt whatsoever about killing those children and his own brother. He hadn't even killed the orphan-keeper in revenge for longstanding crimes, but only to punish him for being an obstacle in his flourishing arena. Can you believe that?"

"Somehow I can," she said quietly. "Master Dothilos is a man who values conviction, momentum, and never crossing any lines unless it benefits his coin purse. If he saw his brother as an obstacle, he'd kill him. If he saw those orphans as beneath him, he'd crush them as collateral damage without remorse."

"And he'd keep the orphan-keeper alive and unbothered as long as he was useful to him," finished Saevem. He palmed his own forehead, rubbing his skull tiredly. "The man is truly dangerous."

She nodded grimly. "I have been searching for a way to win my freedom back from Master Dothilos without jeopardizing our jackpots. My father was a victim of the riverside flats debacle, and I've been bribing the arena's physic to check on his condition and smuggle some medicine for his lungs. As you can imagine, a black-market physic isn't exactly the cheapest provider of care, and the bastard's been price-gouging me for every little thing—and I'm in no position to bargain with him. In truth, I haven't been able to save very much for myself from my jackpots lately. I need all the coin I can get to help my parents, so I can't just surrender that."

A steely determination entered Saevem's eyes. "Then the next steps are clear. Spend your three remaining matches in the match-master's good graces and learn if he has any knowledge of Governor Matheranos traversing in underworld circles. By then, you'll have won your final jackpot, and we'll hopefully gather the evidence we need to damn Governor Matheranos in the eyes of the city once and for all. If we can prove the governor's association with the underworld to the Court, chances are Master Dothilos will be dragged into the case and imprisoned for his crimes as well."

Her heart skipped at this confluence of their desires. "Deal."

"Then let me offer you a gift to celebrate your joining us," he said with a grin. He glanced between the two of them. "Both of you have pierced ears?"

They nodded.

"Excellent." He held forth two boxes and opened the lids, revealing two pairs of earrings. "These aren't purely ornamental, I must warn you."

She fumbled with the gift. "It's made of baltascar," she said, eyeing the opalescent sheen over the singular stud.

"It is indeed. Fauna-augmented baltascar, in fact."

Desil fondled one. "How so?"

"Are you familiar with the fork-tailed harvirche hawk?"

"Native to the Rengalo rainforests, this bird of prey features a humble wingspan, but a supernatural sense of hearing for its fellow kin, being able to detect the cries of other harvirche hawks even from miles away," Lythlet recited.

Saevem smiled. "You truly have made full use of the bestiary."

"So what do these earrings do? Will we be able to hear better?" said Desil.

Saevem shook his head. "Not quite. Each pair forms a one-way communication channel—I'll keep one, you keep the other. Just as one harvirche hawk can hear another, I will be able to hear you wherever you are—assuming you stay within the city limits. If you could wear these during your matches and interactions with Master Dothilos, we may be able to catch something of value. Together, we can unroot the corruption that festers in our city."

He held his teacup out to them, and they clinked theirs against his.

As sweetened jasmine tea flowed down her throat, Lythlet sent a quick prayer of gratitude spiraling up to the heavens—at long last, the cogwheels of her fate were spinning in harmony, freedom and fortune teasing at her fingertips.

CHAPTER THIRTY

THE FINAL MATCH

LYTHLET AND DESIL had been in agreement since they were young that the month of Ilvita was clearly the loveliest time of the year, when the vestiges of a gloomy winter were beginning to fade into a sweet-skied spring.

It was the Month of Rebirth and *keramila dothaya*—early promises of a prosperous new year. Melting snow gave way to the flourishing warmth of the sun, flowers bloomed fiercely through cracks in the cobblestones, and a crisp blue sky could be seen for leagues around, not a cloud in sight.

Runt had grown even bigger, dwarfing Schwala completely. Schwala, for his part, was positively smitten with his giantess companion and would refuse to let her out of his sight. The Phantom had made off with yet another successful heist, their first in months, stealing the Chalice of Brunaria-Zavigo from the private collection of a wealthy magnate in Central.

Lythlet was grateful that the Phantom had gone on a brief hiatus before this heist—had the Phantom continued their streak during the unregistereds' campaign against the Inejio riverside flats, they would have had to compete for gazette headlines. But with the riverside flats dominating every single front page for the greater part of two months, the construction had ceased entirely. Westiro Asa was now a bankrupt man under investigation by the Einveldi Court, and a number of low-tiered politicians had already been roped into his trial under claims of willful negligence, more being named as the weeks went by. Valanti Winaro was diligently spearheading the case, which had progressed to the point the Court was looking into summoning the unregistered to share their testimonies.

During the preceding months of winter, Lythlet and Desil would frequently visit the Homely Home, where the winter winds did not reach, and Lythlet would work up a much-needed sweat sparring with Shunvi. In preparation for her remaining matches, he obligingly taught her a few sleight-handed tricks of the spear that had made him popular back in his conquessing days. Most of them were entirely for show, composed of elaborate twirling and rapid-fire jerks of the wrist, but she added them to her repertoire, and used them to roaring accolades during her tenth and eleventh matches, in which their jackpots showed signs of slow healing. Both were a far cry from what they could have earned had Desil never forfeited, but they were proof nonetheless that the Rose and the Golden Thorn were slowly clambering back into the good graces of the spectators—right in time for their final match.

Yet as perfect as spring was shaping up to be, nothing could tear Lythlet away from the bestiary. She turned almost manic with her obsession in reviewing the bestiary over and over again, letting her world shrink down into nothing but the possibilities of the final match. She started forgoing anything that was unnecessary to her survival and preparation for the arena—visits to the Homely Home came to an abrupt halt, Hive-Master Winaro was left to helm the riverside flats case on his own, and thanks be to Kilinor that it seemed the rest of the world magically caught on to the fact that she had no time to care for anything but the final match. The inn she kept the books at was going through a dreadful dry spell of minimal business, the slow travel season forecasted to last until mid-spring; she could covertly study during her shifts. Ilden and Shunvi must've gotten busy with some personal matters, for they stopped popping by The Steam Dragon for chatter and food; she had Desil's absolute attention and could force him to put her memory to trial whenever he went on break. What were the two weaknesses of the hennisslei? What was the one guaranteed way to distract a yentran? What immediate effects did the venom of the ulura have?

She would journey to the arena to practice, dragging Desil along whenever he was free. Spear and sword sparred with each other, and she'd nimbly scale the yutrela poles again and again, tapping into the gifts of the divine touchstone to feel the sheer otherworldly bliss of interfacing with the cosmoscape for eight seconds. The heavenly string-driven leitmotif would thrum in her ears as she'd pluck at the meridians governing her gravitational field on the map of the cosmoscape that had unfurled within the confines of her skull. Truthfully, it wasn't a skill she needed to practice—it was just a joy she wanted to experience, a reminder that mortal she may be, there remained a way for her to transcend that for even a moment, to channel the sort of divine gifts her estranged Anvari brethren across the ocean could with their bloodrights. She would wonder at how different their lives must be, with so many of them blessed with bizarre abilities that she was only getting a brief taste of thanks to the yutrela, their civilization never being hampered by the obstacles the Ederi had faced.

She would see Master Dothilos watching her practice from the stands, smiling, pale eyes flickering. Sometimes when she rested, he would come and sit by her if she were unaccompanied by Desil.

"Always a hard worker," greeted Master Dothilos one day, crouching on the ground beside her. "Your final match next week is already all anyone can talk about. New handbills are going up all around the city as we speak. We haven't had a twelfth match in so long, half the city is talking about it, and the other half don't matter. The crowd you'll draw just might break the record set by the Poet and the Ruffian years ago. I'm hardly even certain if we can fit everyone into the stands. Be sure to give a good show, dear girl."

"You know I always do," she said, fiddling with the laces of her Sayino boots.

"I do," he said with a laugh. "Perhaps now's the time to remind you of our prior agreement. I've been lenient on you the past matches, to give you time to focus on conquessing and to regulate your emotions. But our arrangement resumes after your final match."

She turned pensive. "Another mission from the Eza?"

"Precisely. In fact, this one's a perfect fit for you."

She looked away, nodding grimly. The future was yet unmapped, but with the possibility that the Coalition of Hope might one day bring down Master Dothilos through their campaigns against Governor Matheranos, she no longer saw the match-master as the all-powerful keeper of her fate. He was as mortal as she was, and the whims of the world would reveal soon who would triumph between the two.

After a moment, the match-master cleared his throat. He spoke softly, "I really do hope you succeed. I think we'll have a much happier partnership moving forward. I know ours hasn't been an easy relationship, but I do see a spark in you, and I want only to provide the kindling so that you may burn brighter."

What stung hardest was knowing he meant those words, that there was a part of him that recognized her talents in a way few others had. He was a twisted man who'd done awful things, murdered countless innocents the moment they proved worthless to his mission, and she knew a life with him holding her chains would be utterly miserable. He deserved every bit of punishment coming his way—but at least for that one moment, she wished he weren't such a monster.

She turned to him, not meeting his eyes. "I know."

He smiled.

DAWN BROKE ON their final match, and Lythlet followed Desil to the nearest shrine for the first time in years.

The shrine was dedicated to Ashentoth, and hers was the largest of the statues there, her wild golden hair lancing about her bright stone visage, left palm extended upwards as if to cup the sun.

Behind Ashentoth, closed off to common visitors and only accessible by the tattooed monks, was the altar to the Sunsmith Pachiros, He Who Set Fire to the Sun and Navigates the Worlds, and his wife Vayatoth, the Moonmachinist and the Unbound Empress, She Who Engineered the Moon and Lights the Way, whom the Oraanu heralded as their Matron.

To Ashentoth's left stood her twin brother Kilinor, and across him was her soulbound lover Shiratoth.

It had been a long time since Lythlet last paid a visit to a shrine, but she still remembered the rites, practiced from childhood.

She dipped the fingers of her right hand into an ash bowl, then dragged it across her forehead in one long swipe. The monks burned dried labyrinth clovers overnight to supply the prayer ash; it was said to be the only plant that existed in both the realm of the divine unknown and the mortal world, Rathara, and spreading its ash over one's brow allowed the wardens to hear their prayers uninhibited.

Lythlet held forth two ash-speckled fingers as she slowly approached the likeness of Ashentoth. Standing beside Desil, she followed him, tapping her forefinger against her forehead twice and bowing. "*Umera venturi, asigo venturi,*" they recited the opening prayer. *We live according to your whims, we die according to your whims.*

They split up then, each retreating to their own patrons. Desil went toward Tazkar, whose mighty form was swathed in robes of stone, wielding a giant hammer in one hand and a long-stemmed *hista* flower in the other, representing peace amongst humanity.

Meanwhile, Lythlet stepped aside, turning to the plinth whereupon stood Kilinor, his white hair framing a face that was not unlike his twin sister's. Unlike most of the other wardens, he carried nothing, made no grand gestures—he simply wept, and stood with one hand stretched forth to an invisible supplicant below.

She bowed her head in respect, steepling her hands by her chest.

Grant me your favor today. Whatever beast I face, grant me the strength to defeat it. I have labored for a year to reach this trial, I have poured spirit and mind into these fights, I have devoted my waking hours to memorizing the bestiary back and forth scores of times. I have laid the stones in my path to happiness, and all I plead is that you grant me the chance to walk upon it.

Near the shrine gates was the ablution well, and once she'd rinsed her hands and dampened her brow, she waited for Desil.

"I've been too scared to visit a shrine for years," she confessed to him as they departed. "I thought I wasn't worthy to stand before the wardens and plead for anything, not when I had so much to ask for, yet so little to offer in return. But now, I feel myself deserving of their favor."

"I'm glad you feel that way," he said slowly. "But you can always come no matter how you feel. As it says in the third book of the Poetics, so long as your heart is true, nothing can separate you from the divine. *As a friend shares your heart in joy or suffering, so do the divine. Be it in despair or shame, come as you are, that you may one day leave differently by the grace of the heavens.*"

"*Come as you are, that you may one day leave differently,*" she echoed, smiling. "Well, let's go to the arena as we are, and return home as victors."

* * *

"Ladies and gentlemen, spectacular spectators of our city of Setgad! Welcome, welcome, *welcome* to the twelfth and final match of the Rose and the Golden Thorn!"

Master Dothilos's high baritone could be heard from leagues away. His voice echoed like a clap of thunder in the dead of night, rolling and rolling throughout the arena, bending around every corner, twisting its way through the halls to hit Lythlet's ears where she stood waiting.

"Will the conquessors honor us with their presence?"

One last time, Lythlet thought, a burst of sentimentality making her nostalgic.

The spectators were deafening as Lythlet and Desil revealed themselves from the tunnel, stepping into the wide, open arena with sanded grounds.

The gate behind them stopped groaning, and they were locked under baltascar lights that seemed brighter today, bright enough to mimic the spring sun of high noon. She winced, blocking the light with a hand as she tilted her head up to the stands.

Lythlet stared in awe of how many spectators were present. There were more people than seats, thousands forced to stand or squat in the aisles, while others had doubled up to share a seat. Never before had she seen so many people squashed together in one spot, not even during the Harvest Holiday. A far cry from their first match, when only a few hundred spectators had bothered attending.

Hoo-rah, hoo-rah, hoo-rah, a chant rose around them, cascading past her ears like a wild rush of water. This was a moment not meant for mere mortals; this was glory reserved for legends and mythic heroes. She turned giddy, adrenaline spiking, the sensation akin to drinking too deeply, too quickly, until it submerged one's mortal sensibilities and lifted them up to the divine.

Lythlet tightened her grip around her spear, an irrepressible grin growing.

Master Dothilos waited patiently with a faint smile, tapping his speaking-trumpet as the cheers continued. But the crowd would not quieten themselves, so caught up in the momentum of stomping feet and triumphant *hoo-rahs*. So he gave them the moment, letting them roar like a hurricane, until he raised his hand, and his voice cleaved them all into reluctant silence.

"They need no introduction—"

The audience whooped in agreement.

"—but take my hand and join me on a walk down the road of memories, won't you? How many of you witnessed their first match last Fethaya against the sentari, the beast of shadow?"

A surprising number of hands shot into the sky, accompanied by foot stomps. A mere fraction of the flood of spectators present, but nonetheless a heartening number of long-lasting supporters.

"And how many of you remember their second match, wrought in the name of Tazkar? Who remembers the breathtaking fight against the anzura, the beast of flame and ice? Who remembers Desil stricken by the unseen frost, his last breaths seizing in the cavern of his chest? Who remembers the Golden Thorn weeping as she tore through flesh and bone until she at last pierced the accursed heart? *Who remembers?*"

The stadium shook from the stomping feet. Lythlet could imagine the very structure of the building cracking in half from the stress.

The match-master waited until they had calmed down. He bent down to his speaking-trumpet again. "We all loved Desil Demothi from first sight, did we not? A brawler of such pedigree, a face so fair—the Maker was being unfair the day he was created! Few warrant as much love, but the Rose swiftly claimed your devotion! But let's all be honest: it took longer for the Golden Thorn to grow in our hearts, did it not?"

Hushed murmurings, furtive nods.

"We all thought the Thorn a mere burden of having the Rose in our midst—yet have we not been proven wrong? Has she not earned your love? She who conquered the yutrela, she who traversed the cosmoscape, she who pierced the heart of flame and ice, she who drowned a shark, she who is a golden, surefire bet to make! She who was BEATEN! BRUISED!"

"*BEATEN! BRUISED!*" the audience echoed.

"Condemned by fate to be no more than A THIEF, A LIAR!"

"*A THIEF, A LIAR!*"

"Yet through nothing but her own sheer wit and wiles, she now stands before you as none other than THE GOLDEN THORN!"

"*THE GOLDEN THORN!*"

His next words were drowned out by sheer riotous noise.

A well of tears overtook Lythlet, and she blinked them back. To be so loved, to be so believed in by thousands—the urge to prostrate herself before the crowd in humble gratitude rose, but she kept still, only raising a goose-pimpled hand to wipe away her tears.

But the spectators were far from done. They cheered, and cheered, and cheered. A trembling grew in her from her toes in her crisp leather Sayino boots to her lips until a violent laugh ripped from her. She wished there were somebody who could paint this moment so she could reflect on it for years to come.

She had to win today of all days.

I will, she vowed. *I swear it, I will.*

"May the Sunsmith and the Moonmachinist witness us today," Master Dothilos said, calming the crowd. "At long last, the Rose and the Golden Thorn stand ready to fight their twelfth match— their final match. Ladies and gentlemen, how many of you were present during the days of the Poet and the Ruffian, our last champion conquessors?" He laughed heartily at the ensuing cheers. "Do you remember the final match in which Shunvi Tanna and Ilden Highvind stood before us, spears raised to the heavens? And what a jackpot they went home with. No less than four and twenty pieces of gold!

"But today, today, to*day* we have a new jackpot to look forward to. We thought we may never again see the furor that circled the Poet and the Ruffian, but you've outdone yourselves today, spectators. I see your glee; I see your feverish zeal. The bids have been gathered and settled, and I am proud to announce we have a record-breaking sum. A sum that puts to shame the jackpot of the Poet and the Ruffian!"

Excited murmurs ripped through the crowd, and Lythlet's heart picked up the pace.

"Can anyone guess how much coin awaits the Rose and the Golden Thorn should they triumph? Twenty? Twenty-five? Thirty?" the match-master teased coyly.

He says these numbers as if they were paltry sums, she thought, winded. She would have been overjoyed with twenty pieces of gold, yet here was the match-master hinting at more.

The match-master raised a large white cloth bag. "To the Rose and the Golden Thorn, I am proud to announce that should we witness a victory today, you shall walk away with no less than *two and forty pieces of gold.*"

He dropped the bag onto the podium, and it landed with a thunderous clink of metal.

Lythlet's spear nearly slipped. Her heart stopped, then quickened into a pace that left her hands trembling.

Two and forty. Gold. Gold!

A single piece of gold alone would have been life changing. But forty-two, split between her and Desil—where could she not go, what could she not do with such a fortune? All fears would vanish, all promises to her parents would be upheld. Every road would unfurl before her, and she could stand proud with a fortune earned rightfully.

A hand curled on her shoulder, and she turned to see Desil give her a confident smile.

"Would you look at those faces!" the match-master bellowed. "But who wouldn't be thrilled at the thought of two and forty pieces of gold within reach? They've made quite the comeback since their river match! Now, spectators, as this is our last chance to enjoy these conquessors, we have a special event today to bid our final farewell. A special match in honor of Astos, warden of the bonds between us all."

He read aloud the Prayer of the Steadfast:

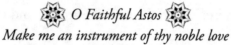

O Faithful Astos
Make me an instrument of thy noble love
To live ever-weaving the steadfast strings that binds us all to one another

Desil bowed his head and muttered a prayer, tapping the rune assigned to Astos, that of fellowship, on his rosary.

Lythlet shut her eyes, drawing fingertips to her brow. *I beg of all the Great Divine, grant me this one prayer: let us win.*

The match-master continued once the audience had finished their prayers, "Now for the oath, one last time. By the blood of your ancestors, do you proud Ederi children vow to salt the earth with the blood of the demons that once gave death upon your ancestors?"

"Witness me, upon the blood of my ancestors!" Lythlet and Desil roared, drawn to their full heights, fingers crossed as they made their oaths.

"May the Sunsmith and the Moonmachinist witness your fight! Now, allow me to announce to all you good people that today need not—I repeat! need *not*—be a death match!"

A flurry of confusion ran around the ring of spectators.

Lythlet frowned. Yet another trick the match-master had up his sleeve.

"Fear not, for you will still receive your thrills," he assured. "Today, we shall be witnesses to a once-in-a-lifetime match between strongest and strongest! Ladies and gentlemen, without further ado, let us bring out the beasts! Open the gates!"

Lythlet had barely time to parse his words as the grinding of the gates in front of them began. Instinctively, she raised her spear, clutching the haft tightly. Desil remained poised alongside, sword glinting in the harsh light.

She stepped back nervously, eyes and ears peeled for any indication of what was to tumble from the darkness. No heavy footsteps. It could not be so large a creature then. No sounds at all, in fact, which made it hard to narrow down the possibilities. No noxious smell; a relief, for dealing with a bogbear for the final match seemed rather anticlimactic.

Between strongest and strongest.

Her spear faltered, a flood of ideas running through her mind. *What had Master Dothilos meant?* She stole a brief glance at the match-master before returning her gaze to the gaping tunnel.

The baltascar lights flashed brighter, blinding her. She shut her eyes and blinked furiously, trying to force them open.

Her vision returned in garish patches.

The unblemished yellow sands. The raised black portcullis. The dark abyss beyond. Marching forth from it, two figures leaving boot prints, one by one, etching their mark on the world. Long jeweled spears with ornate hafts. Gleaming, reflecting the baltascar lights.

Advancing into the arena to a cresting wave of thrilled shrieks from the spectators were the Poet and the Ruffian, Shunvi Tanna and Ilden Highvind.

CHAPTER THIRTY-ONE

THE EZA

BLOOD DRAINED FROM Lythlet's face as the spectators exploded into a volley of deafening excitement.

Gone were Shunvi's ever-elegant silk robes, gone were Ilden's clumsily clasped cloaks—they stood before her dressed in matching leather boots, black cotton breeches, reinforced jerkins, and white shirts with the sleeves rolled up.

Her eyes met theirs, and they looked back with bitter expressions.

They're here unwillingly, she realized. *Master Dothilos must have finally made good on his old threat to them.* Harm if they did not pick up their spears again, the destruction of Shunvi's teahouses by the Eza's servants, the seizing of any of their loved ones, kidnapping them and holding them hostage in the arena— there were a multitude of ways the match-master could have forced the Poet and Ruffian back into the arena once again.

In the end, Master Dothilos was a shrewd merchant of amusement, and he could not have architected a more thrilling event for the masses.

"Spectators, witness today!" his baritone tore through the arena.

"The greatest match we've ever had, a day of legends! Witness as Ilden Highvind and Shunvi Tanna, the only two winners of all twelve matches in many a year, are pitted against our budding champions. For what greater beast could one face but their fellow man? Whether by death or incapacitation, last conquessor standing claims the gold. Shall the wise and the experienced show why they won the last time, and the Poet and the Ruffian triumph? Or shall the Rose and the Golden Thorn strike them down and steal the gold for themselves? Witness today! *Hoo-rah!*"

Lythlet breathed deeply, thinking. Death was not demanded that day. She could force the two to forfeit, and Desil and her would remain the victors. It could be a game of show, no more.

But would that appease Desil?

"Desil," she started quietly, staring at his chin, unable to meet his eyes, "this need not be fatal. We must only drive them into forfeiting. Neither Shunvi nor Ilden will fight us to the death, they wouldn't. It will be a quick fight—you are stronger than them put together. We could simply look for ways to disarm them—"

But then she met his eyes, and she silenced.

There was a quiet, anguished, desperate plea in his eyes. He would not go through with this, not again, not ever. Something had cracked in him in the brawling square, and it terrified him to fight another person again.

Lythlet knew she had been speaking a fool's hope. Even though they did not have to kill the Poet and the Ruffian, it would be naïve to think this could be a bloodless match.

The ever-bloodthirsty spectators would demand more than that.

The ever-machinating Master Dothilos would demand more than that.

This was a match Master Dothilos had orchestrated to be as devastating as possible for at least one of them. He knew Desil had left his brawling days behind to commit himself to the way of Tazkar, vowing to never raise a hand against another man again.

"Lythlet." Desil's apology was unspoken, but it scratched through the distance between them, edging closer and closer toward her like a snake.

She knew what he was asking permission for. Turmoil rose within her like a dawning sun, scorching her insides. To surrender now of all days would be the end of things, of all the effort she'd poured into the Golden Thorn for the past year. A bag of gold was waiting for them on a pedestal just a distance away, and within it was more than coins: she'd somehow tucked into that lumpy white reticule all her dreams, her hopes, and her future.

"Do as you will," she said as calmly as she could, fighting the urge to cry. She could not say much more than that, giving him one last look before turning away.

"Thank you," he murmured.

The horn was blown, igniting even more shrieks from the spectators.

"Begin, conquessors!" Master Dothilos commanded.

At once, Shunvi sprang for her, jeweled spear twirling by his side. She recognized his sleight of hand—he had taught it to her, so she knew how to parry it. Her own spear met his with a resounding clang, and his strike glanced off easily. He came again from another angle, and she knocked his blade away with the haft of her spear.

He's not putting any weight behind his strikes, she realized. Shunvi was entirely ready to throw the fight for them, to stage a bloody fight that would end in victory for her.

Off to her side, Ilden was circling Desil, whose blade remained pointed to the ground.

"Raise your sword, Demothi," he hissed, spear tip out.

Please change your mind, she begged Desil in that split second. *They're going to let us win—they'll forgive anything we do to them. We could bruise them and make them bleed, and they'd understand.*

But she had already given Desil her permission. She watched

grimly as Desil snatched the small white shard around his neck, breaking the string. He flung the baltascar pendant onto the ground and slammed the heel of his boot against it.

"Forfeit!" he roared into the deafening stands. Green smoke poured from the broken glass, and there he stood, wreathed in it.

At last, a wind of silence swept through the spectators, knocked back from their cheers.

Shunvi froze, his attack staggered midair. Ilden simply stared in horror.

All eyes fell upon Lythlet, waiting for her response.

Avarice pressed heavily on her chest. She could force Desil's hand—she could withhold her forfeit as she had done in the goblin-shark match and force him into fighting alongside her.

Desil remained turned away, his eyes drawn to the stunned crowd. A few stray boos were unleashed, but rapidly hushed up by others, wanting to hear her response.

They hate him, she realized. As much as they had loved him, their affection had just as quickly unraveled. They hated him for his forfeit in the river match but had forgiven him since. They would not forgive him a second time. They would despise her, too, if she threw in her lot with him, if she denied them the fight they'd come for. Even bearish spectators would hate them—they would be forfeiting before the ten-minute mark.

Her eyes swept through the spectators, coming to rest on the match-master, waiting by his pedestal with a calm smile. His arm, slender as a birch, arced elegantly into the air, and *snap!* he called his crossbowmen to hold Desil in contempt.

Master Dothilos had to have known Desil would never fight this match. He would have known bringing out Shunvi and Ilden would eke only another forfeit out of him. And for what reason?

To make me choose between Desil and the jackpot. To test me and my conviction to win, the momentum of my greed—to see what lines I am willing to cross. He sees Desil as beneath me in the hierarchy of potential, so he wants me to show that I'm ready to force him to betray his vow to Tazkar and recant his forfeit for all that gold.

It would be a quiet decision to make. A small one. She could press on, and the threat of the crossbowmen would have Desil pick up his sword once more. Perhaps Desil would forgive her one day. He knew deeply how much she needed this, how much this final victory would weigh in her soul.

But the scorching burn of that dream-star nestled deep within her paled into a winter's mist as she looked once more at Desil. He kept his gaze to the ground, wavering in shame under the burden of the spectators' judgment.

I won't do this to him, not again.

She snatched at her baltascar pendant and flung it on the ground.

The sole of her boot rose and fell, crushing it into shards, and she held her breath as crimson smoke poured out all around her. The fumes funneled up into the air, following the trail its green brethren had left behind.

Smoke swallowed the sky above her in a menacing streak of red: blood that would be unspilled that morning.

She mouthed *forfeit*, feeling faint. The word left her without sound, shattering her and all her hopes even in its silence. Then she stood straight, tightened her hand on her spear, and looked up at Master Dothilos.

"Forfeit," she shouted, voice echoing throughout the area. Her future slipped as a rug beneath her feet. Desil wrapped his fingers around her wrist, and she found fortitude in that.

"Forfeit," she cried again, louder, braver.

At their joint agreement, the crossbowmen lowered their weapons—no unconsecrated vows of fellowship were being violated, no contempt could they hold Desil in.

All at once, the breathless audience erupted into a frenzy, flying out of their seats. Vulgarities spilled from their throats, their fury at their bids going to waste turning incendiary.

But all Lythlet allowed herself to hear was Desil whispering, "Thank you."

Lythlet nodded briskly, not meeting his eyes. She did not want him to see her on the verge of tears. She kept herself as still as stone as the audience jeered at them. Master Dothilos looked flustered, calling one of his attendants over.

He never expected me to forfeit, she realized with surprise. *He was certain I'd force Desil into fighting with me.*

None of the spectators had expected her to forfeit either, enraged all the more at her having the gall to do so.

Something hard smashed against her cheek, tearing her skin. She yelped, stumbling backward in shock. A silver pendant watch landed in the sand, its clasp stained with her fresh blood.

She stared back at the crowd, wondering which spectator had flung it at her. It was too wild to make out the culprit, the dense forest of infuriated patrons growing thicker by the second.

Desil wrapped his arms around her protectively. "Let's go," he whispered into her ear, "before things get worse."

They stepped backward, but a voice made them still at once.

"Ladies and gentlemen, please return to your seats!" Master Dothilos roared, baritone leonine with might. "*Do not throw things at our conquessors!* There is no need to resort to such uncivilized behavior."

It was a miracle to behold, how the spectators scuttled backward like timid little rats, the more stubborn ones relinquishing their positions after more merciless orders from the match-master.

"Now, we must be fair," he said sternly into his speaking-trumpet. If he were at all desperate, he hid it beneath a placid mask. "We must understand that it is very different to be up here in the stands and down there in the arena. The Rose and the Golden Thorn came today with the heart to fight a sun-cursed beast, and instead we've surprised them with another pair of conquessors. Perhaps they are disappointed! You see, they are young, and they've not had the privilege of seeing the Poet and the Ruffian in their glory days. They know not what an honor it is to face them, what a challenge it will be. This is, of course, highly unprecedented. So let us offer them a chance to recant their forfeit."

The spectators *hoo-rah*ed in approval. In that moment, it did not matter whether they were bullish or bearish: they all sat in silent agreement that they had come for a fight amongst slumdogs, and they deserved one.

"First, the Rose," Master Dothilos said. "Desil Demothi. I offer you a chance to revoke your forfe—"

"Your offer is unneeded," shouted Desil.

A rumble started in the audience once more, but the match-master simply nodded and gestured for them to keep quiet. "Yet it is not your choice alone. To the Golden Thorn, Lythlet Tairel, I offer you your last chance to earn this bag of gold. I remind you that no less than two and forty pieces lie waiting in here, desperate for a good home. What say you, Golden Thorn? Will you revoke your forfeit?"

Lythlet met his eyes. "No."

It ached to answer him. To turn away from so much coin, to bury all her efforts with a single word. But she refused to succumb to her greed and pay for it with Desil's conscience.

Another rumble threatened to break through the spectators.

The match-master waved at them impatiently, façade finally cracking. "Think carefully, children! Why do you turn your backs so easily on a fortune most will never attain in their lives? On a fortune you will most certainly never be offered ever again? Why do you seek to disappoint your loyal supporters? Tens of thousands have come today to witness your skill. Will you deny them each their right?"

What right have any of you sitting here to force my hand? she thought in growing wrath. *We're no more than animals to you, slumdogs whose singular purpose is to suffer for your joy. You care only to see us sweat in vain and bleed for your entertainment. We'll be discarded just as quickly for whatever catches your fancy next.*

But all this would fall on deaf ears. These were not people who cared for her thoughts, for her humanity. These were warmongers who had never fought a battle in their lives, a mindless horde who would scoff at the idea of sacrificing their entertainment so that another might live in dignity.

"We have the right to forfeit, and we have taken it," she said determinedly.

Master Dothilos slammed a hand against the pedestal, the sound ringing through the trumpet, making everyone jump in their seats. "Do you think you have a choice?" His voice crackled with rage. "I have brought you this far, lifted you up with my words, and now you think you are beyond gold—you think you are beyond me? Have you no care for your obligations to me? Have you no care for what I could do to you?"

She stared sadly up at him. The threat of the Eza once terrified her, but with the backing of the Coalition of Hope behind her, it now seemed empty, vacuous, a toddler's whine. The match-master desperately needed her to revoke her forfeit—it was what he had counted on. He must have known Desil would forfeit, refuse to engage in a brawl, but he must have also assumed Lythlet would repeat her choice from the river match—the choice to prove herself over a dear friend. It was beyond him to imagine she would refuse.

It was beyond him to imagine she was not like him.

This will not end well. But I must do what is right, what I should have done a long time ago. It is time for him to know I refuse to accept his third lesson.

She aimed the tip of her spear downwards, and with one swift stroke, she sheared through the strings of her Sayino boots, first the left, then the right. She stepped out of them, feet coming to rest on the gritty sands. It felt cool, a relief to sink her toes into the foundations of the world. She stared up once more and met his furious gaze.

"I have served my obligations to you, match-master, longer than I should have. What favors you have shown me, you have forced me to repay twicefold. I now exercise my right to decline. Farewell, Master Dothilos." She bowed.

For once, he was lost for words. He spluttered, finger arched out accusingly at her, but he made no coherent argument.

She took Desil's hand and turned away with him, heading toward the armory. She took a step forward, barefooted, sand glued to the soles of her feet. Noise erupted at once, but she paid no mind. It was the match-master throwing a tantrum, it was the raucous chaos of an unreasonably entitled warmongering horde.

The cacophony swelled upon their backs as they made for the corridor, then shrank into echoes as they disappeared into the darkness.

"I'm sorry, Lythlet," Desil murmured, clutching her wrist.

"It's fine," she said, stomach ill. "We'll be fine."

But the moment they entered the armory, they were slammed face first into the stone wall by unseen assailants. Their arms were bound, their eyes blindfolded, gags forced into their mouths. Then they were hoisted up and pushed forward into unknown paths. Paralyzed by fear, Lythlet took mild comfort in hearing Desil's muffled shouts beside her—at least they were still together.

Forth they were marched, the tip of something sharp pressed into their backs, Lythlet's mind racing nonstop. Were these the match-master's servants? Were they about to be punished for forfeiting? Where were they going?

With her bare feet, Lythlet tried to note what she could, her other senses stifled. They had left the stone flooring of the armory, and she could feel smooth concrete—they were in the transitory hallways Master Dothilos had led them through to meet the upper circle of elites. Then the wooden grain of elaborate parquetry—this was not a room they had ever been in before. A heavy door slammed shut, a clatter of metal bolts locking them in. Hands as rough as mallets shoved them backward, until she fell to her bottom on a spindle-backed chair, the knobs carved into the wood digging into her back.

Where are we?

"Well! I was led to believe I'd be meeting a pair of champion conquessors—not last-minute forfeit-keeners. What a fascinating turn of events!" a jovial voice spoke, posh in the way he rolled his syllables.

The gag loosened and fell from her mouth.

"Who are you?" she said, fear coursing through her veins.

"Did your Master Dothilos not inform you of our meeting?" spoke the voice, sounding amused.

She halted, skin rising in goose pimples. "Are you the Eza?"

"I am indeed."

The air went still.

"Should we bow to you?" she stammered.

He laughed. "Please, Golden Thorn, none of that."

She bowed anyway, folding herself in half on the chair, knowing better than to trust such generosity.

There was something oddly familiar in the way he spoke—she couldn't quite put her finger on it, but somehow this was not the first time she'd heard this chic, refined curl of vowels.

"You came highly recommended by Renveld—Master Dothilos to you, of course. I believe you assisted him before on a prior request of mine, on that business with Khavi Monul, that cheeky bugger. Which was settled very neatly, thanks to you."

She kept her body bent forward, deep in thought. *Have I met him before?* She tried to recall every single highborn Master Dothilos had ever introduced her to beneath the arena.

The Eza continued, unbothered, "I must commend Renveld on his ability to spot talent. He's brought many prior conquessors into my service, and to this day, not a single one of them has failed me. First time I met him, I thought he was just another one of those bloviating popinjays our city is littered with, but he's certainly proved me wrong."

Lythlet's mouth ran dry, and she sat up.

A childhood pastime of running her fingers along unusual vocabulary had developed into a lifelong love of words, and that meant one thing: she paid attention when one used words she rarely encountered beyond the written page. The words *bloviating*

popinjay had spilled so effortlessly from only one other man in
her life—

"Governor Matheranos."

A hush fell on the room.

"What?" said the Eza.

She quivered. "I know your voice. I heard it once before when you
came to visit my former workplace. You're Governor Matheranos."

Desil hitched his breath beside her. There was a rustle of
confusion, perhaps from the Eza's guardsmen. She felt a gentle
brush of wind before her, as if the Eza were lifting a hand to
gesture at them.

Her blindfold fell loose, her vision restored.

"Clever girl," praised the governor, leaning back in his chair and
smiling at her.

CHAPTER THIRTY-TWO

THE LIES OF DESIL DEMoTHI

GOVERNOR MATHERANOS SAT in a grand high back chair, his prominent widow's peak highlighting the symmetry of his leonine mane of white hair.

Vision returned, Lythlet turned her head in all directions, trying to gain her bearings. The room was round, small, but with tall, vaulted ceilings that made Lythlet feel minuscule. Two doors—one behind, one in front, both outfitted with heavy door bolts. Not a room she recognized—she had no idea where within the massive arena they were located. Ever so faintly, she could still hear the audience's uproarious rage through the ceiling. No less than three huge men were posted around the room, the Eza's guards awaiting their command. Two held their crossbows forth, aimed at Lythlet and Desil.

"Master Dothilos told me you were cunning," the Eza laughed, wagging a finger at her. "I suppose I shouldn't have bothered with the blindfolds and all that nonsense with you."

Lythlet caught Desil's eye, and they stared bewildered at one another. Certainly, they had been convinced by Saevem's appeal that the governor was working with the Eza—but the idea that the governor *was* the Eza had never crossed their minds.

She thought immediately of their earrings, praying desperately a member of the Coalition of Hope had been listening all the while. If that were the case and they had any common sense, they'd send someone in now to seize Governor Matheranos at the scene—tangibly finding him at the arena would be key evidence.

"An honor to be here with you, Governor," she said, settling into her seat and deciding to buy time.

The Eza took a moment to soak in her sycophancy with a smile. "Wise enough to know when to grovel, aren't you? But let's get on with it. I have a special request perfectly suited to your particular skills. You came with special recommendation from Renveld, who assured me you have an expertise in fraudulent accounting. I do have my own trusted accountants, but Renveld was adamant that I consider enlisting you in this as a trial for your capabilities."

Lythlet grimaced, intuiting the reason. She could not say no to the Eza, to the most powerful man in Setgad—and thus Master Dothilos was restarting their poisonous relationship with no chance for her to decline.

"What is it you wish me to do?" she asked.

"Fabricate the financial records of Corio Brandolas. Create an incontrovertible case for his corruption I can present to the Court."

Her eyes widened.

"That man has been a pest for years, and I want to squash him once and for all." A glimmer of genuine frustration broke through the Eza's jovial demeanor. "Forge a set of accounts that I can use against him and vilify him in the eyes of the city. The whole works, if you please. Unlawful misuse of allowances and expenses, mysterious 'donations' from unsavory folk and foreign entities, entertainment expenses being spent at the most debauched brothels, illicit siphoning of party funds into his own private accounts—anything. Make me believe the Coalition of Hope is a party teethed on graft, patronage, and immoderation."

He went into further detail, outlining the sheer range of parties she could implicate in these forged records, the timeline the transactions ought to cover, and certain key members of the Coalition who he especially wanted to tear down together with their party leader.

By the end of it all, Lythlet needed a moment to let everything soak into her frazzled mind. "So, you want me to destroy Corio Brandolas's reputation," she said slowly, winded.

"Oh, I do like how you phrased that. Corio Brandolas— destroyed! Yes, indeed, I want the man shamed by the whole damn city, until he can't even crawl out of his house without being pelted with tomatoes. We'll have the whole city speculating that Corio spends his nights snorting euphoriants off whores with colluders from the Ora Islands before long. Maybe his wife and her damn family will finally cut that pathetic parvenu off from suckling at their teat any longer. You exercise your creativity, and I'll have my people move the funds around to make reality match your imagination. We have a disgruntled former aide of his who's defected to our party, and he's more than willing to publicly support whatever allegations of corruption and moral profligacy you forge by claiming the accounts were recorded by him secretly over the tenure of his service to the Coalition."

Lythlet breathed in deeply, contemplating the task he'd so gleefully laid out. "Very well. A question, if I may."

"Certainly."

"Why have you brought my friend here?" She tilted her head toward Desil.

Governor Matheranos smiled. "Renveld told me I may need something to remind you of what you'd lose if you failed me. I thought your darling childhood friend would be the most convenient option. Disobey me, and the Rose shall have his petals plucked by these men."

Desil shifted uncomfortably.

"Have you always been the Eza?" she continued, wondering how long she could stall for.

"There has always been an Eza, and there will always be one. Just as there has always been a governor of Setgad, and there will always be one. It just so happens I decided to have my time as both coincide with one another." He let out a genteel laugh. "I doubt Hemharrow Corinthos would be glad to know his bloodline's been abusing his good reputation to leverage a foothold in the world of politics, but I thank him for the leg up he granted me when I decided to broaden my scope beyond the underworld decades ago."

"Aren't you worried?" Desil blurted out. "That we now know who you are?"

Governor Matheranos stared at him incredulously. "Dear boy, you really are as daft as Renveld says. What could you possibly do to me? I am in control of both upperworld and underworld laws. I could have these men gut you on the floor before me right now. If I wanted to play by the tedious rules of Court law, I could simply have you arrested for participating in an outlawed bloodsport. Even if you made the poor decision of betraying my identity to the world, what difference could you make? Good luck finding folk willing to believe two penniless slumdogs running around the city, shouting that Governor Matheranos is the Eza. Better men than you have attempted to drag me down for more credible crimes and failed. Why would I fear you?"

They had no answer, sitting in silent petrification.

"I believe I've made my point sufficiently clear," the governor said. "Now, Miss Tairel, if you could have your work ready by the end of the week for my people to collect." He arced his gaze to one of his guards. "Inform the match-master I'll be taking my leave."

The guard departed the room, and the remaining two stood at attention, awaiting orders.

"Blindfold our guests once more and take them to—good grief, are those spectators *still* making such a ruckus?" He turned his head upward, glaring disdainfully at the ceiling, through which came a rising swell of noise.

Indeed, the audience shouts had gotten louder, crescendoing throughout their discussion. Bull and bear were united in fury, screaming and shouting like children having their favorite toys snatched away from them, Master Dothilos suffering the task of pacifying them. The muffled baritone of Master Dothilos bled through periodically, the words lost to the layers of stone between them.

Louder, the shouts grew, louder. Foot stamps could be heard, coordinated at first, then scattered like the thunderclaps of a stormy night, voices dissolving into shrieks. Lythlet strained her ears—there was one particular sound pattern she kept detecting. A single word, two syllables, altered beyond comprehension.

Ch-ma? Hitch-an?

Her eyes widened.

Watchmen?

She cast a quick glance at Desil, wordlessly telling him to get ready. A golden opportunity was lurking around the corner.

"Sunsmith, these incorrigible animals," the Eza said, shaking his head. He rose, ready to complete his order to the remaining two guards.

At that moment, the guard who'd left minutes ago came racing back, red in the face. He shut the heavy wooden door behind him, slotting in the bolts to lock it. "Watchmen!" he panted. "Watchmen raiding the arena!"

"What in the Sunsmith's name are you on about? I haven't called for a raid."

"Not your watchmen, Eza. The ones given to Corio."

Governor Matheranos froze. "How would that bastard get the Court to sanction an independent arena raid? On today of all days?"

"I don't know, Eza, but they're hunting for you."

Governor Matheranos glanced sharply at Lythlet. His eyes narrowed. "What's that on your ear, Golden Thorn?" He reached up and snatched her earring, ripping her earlobe. She shrieked at the pain, raising her bound hands to comfort her bleeding ear.

"Were you spying on me?" he shouted.

He struck her, and she spat out a mouthful of blood. He was about to strike her again, but she stared up at him. "You better run if you don't want to get caught, Eza."

He sucked in his breath, irritated. Then he spun on his heels. "You, follow me," he shouted at one guard. "The rest of you—kill them."

The Eza and his chosen guardsman forged on ahead, unbolting the door in front and departing the room. The remaining two stepped forward, their crossbows aimed at Lythlet and Desil.

The one targeting Desil fired first, the click of his crossbow and the whistle of its quarrel shrieking through the air.

But Desil had leaped off his seat in a split second, the bolt piercing the back of his chair instead. Its shaft gleamed with a pearlescent aura, telling of a baltascar core. The bolt ballooned up then, spikes ramming out from the shaft. Lythlet's eyes bulged, imagining how painful that would've been had it pierced either one of them. Fauna-augmented, she guessed, tempered to take after a pufferfish in distress.

Desil thrust his bound wrists down on the spike-bloated quarrel protruding from the chair, holes perforating the cloth. Those slight rents in the cloth were all he needed to rip the rest apart with his raw strength, the tatters falling around him.

"Chair!" he shouted, kicking his own toward her so she could free herself.

But she knew what he actually meant—she stood and kicked

hers toward him. He snatched it up and smashed it against both crossbowmen in one blow. A chair leg snapped off; Desil caught it and rammed its end into the nearest crossbowman's face like a spoke into a wheel. As the crossbowman groaned in pain, clutching his jaw, Desil twisted his wrist sideways, trying to force him into releasing his weapon.

Meanwhile she sawed her hands back and forth on the bolt, snapping thread after thread. A brawler's strength was not hers, and she needed more time than Desil had to snap the cloth loose. Her hands came free just in time to catch the crossbow Desil threw at her.

"Go after the governor!" he shouted, wrestling with the last armed guardsman to destroy his crossbow. The splintered edge of the chair leg he wielded smashed into the weapon, snapping its string in half.

She grunted in agreement—under no circumstances could they let Governor Matheranos escape the arena. But she worried for Desil. He would be fighting bare-fisted against two men hired by the Eza for their prowess in brutal skirmishes. She thought of Lorent Bicarda, the bellicose savagery he'd been all too happy to unleash, and imagined these men to be kindred spirits. Could Desil hold his own against them?

I must have faith in him, she decided, sprinting for the door Governor Matheranos had escaped through. Desil Demothi was a twenty-six-time bare-knuckle brawling champion, after all—that had to be good for something.

There was something in the last words she heard before she left the room that surprised her, though.

"Gentlemen," Desil said, an unflinching, almost coy, color to his voice, one Lythlet had never heard before in her life, "I've never once lost a brawl. I don't intend today to be the first exception."

The sound of a fist meeting its target followed, and the sickening echoes of cracking wood and crunching bone chased after Lythlet as she hunted the governor down the halls. Running, she glanced down briefly at the weapon Desil had tossed her—it was a repeating crossbow, three bolts loaded and waiting to be deployed.

Poetry in the hunt, she told herself, steeling herself. She noted the crystalline gleam of baltascar on the weapon's risers, deducing that passing through that zone would trigger the baltascar-augmented abilities of the quarrels.

Her shadow shrank and lengthened on the stone walls as she raced down the halls, chasing the silhouettes of Governor Matheranos and his guardsman. Statues of the Twelve Wardens dotted her journey, heralding every grandiose doorway she passed. Then a stroke of luck—the governor had been halted by a door shut with bolts and a complicated series of morticed locks. It was locked on their end, and they'd eventually open it—but it stalled them long enough for her to catch up with them.

Governor Matheranos turned back with a glare as she approached. He pushed his swordsman toward her. "Kill her," he barked, turning back to deal with the locks.

The guard, a huge barrel-chested man, trudged toward her. He pulled his sword from its scabbard, and she took aim with her crossbow.

The first bolt missed him by inches, penetrating a pillar behind him. A few seconds later, the pufferfish spikes must have been activated, extra cracks fissuring on the pillar and threatening its structure. She cursed at herself—it was harder to control than she had expected.

He laughed. "Those things aren't easy to aim for first-timers, Golden Thorn." He closed in on her, faster than she could pull the crossbow's lever to reload. She dodged his sword's tip in the nick of time, the screech of metal on stone jarring her ears. She pushed the lever up, felt a quarrel slip into place, and slammed the lever down as quickly as she could.

The guard howled as a bolt pierced straight through his knee. He fell to the floor, and Lythlet kicked the sword far from his grasp. But he grabbed Lythlet's leg, pulling her down with him, and within breathless moments, he had his muscle-corded arm around her neck, squeezing tight.

She choked, grappling his arm in vain.

He cursed at her as he used his free hand to box her ears, getting his revenge.

Pain lanced her senses, blinding her momentarily. The way they were positioned, if she were to try to arc her crossbow to fire back at him, he'd easily duck or snatch it from her.

She slipped her fingers into the crossbow's magazine, fishing out the last quarrel. Clutching it in her fist, she rammed the bolt tip straight into the groin of her assailant.

He bellowed in her ears with an agony that made her feel sorry for him. His arm loosened around her, and she pushed him off, letting him crumple into a ball, screeching in pain. Stray beads of blood dotted the stone floor beneath him.

She scrambled away from him, panting for air like a dog, her mind spinning as she regained her balance. She returned the last quarrel back into the crossbow. Lever shifting, she took aim at the governor. He was hunched over the lower third of the door, an effigy of Ezrinara towering over his side. There was one last mortice lock on the door he hadn't opened.

"Surrender, Governor," she shouted.

The governor did not even look at her, focused on unlocking the door.

"I'll shoot you," she warned. She did not want to. The divine were watching, and she dared not let the theft of a soul mar her divine record, but she had to deter him.

To her surprise, he spun around, clenching his teeth at her. "Do it. Shoot me." He stepped away from the door, marching toward her with a wide smile. No more than an arm's span away from her, he held his hands up in the air. "You can't miss with me right in front of you, can you?"

His brazenness unnerved her.

I can't kill him, she realized, another reason becoming transparent.

His death would let his identity as the Eza remain buried—and my name would be splashed across the gazettes as the slumdog who killed the governor in cold blood.

Governor Matheranos smiled, knowing she'd arrived at the same conclusion as him. He wheeled around, making for the door and the last lock to disentangle.

Her mind leaped helter-skelter through her options. *I can't kill him, but I have to stop him.*

She fired her final quarrel.

It whistled through the air, crashing straight through the feet of the statue of Ezrinara.

"You missed." Governor Matheranos laughed at her, nearly drowned out by the sound of stone cracking and tumbling. A heartbeat later, more cracks sounded, the pufferfish spikes growing.

She shook her head. "I did not."

Perturbed, he turned to follow where she pointed.

The bloated baltascar quarrel had worked precisely as she'd hoped, shattering Ezrinara's enormous ankles and rocking the statue off its base. The majestic form of the flame-wielding warden tumbled forward, crashing against the door the governor had worked so hard to unlock, covering it entirely. He had nowhere to run but back—into the arms of the Coalition force.

He turned back to her with murder in his eyes. Then he sprang forth to where his guardsman's sword had been kicked to.

She held up her crossbow, the empty magazine weighing heavily on her. "Be still or I'll shoot!"

But he did not care for her bluff. He raced for the sword, and she abandoned her ploy, racing forward at the same time.

They collided into each other, and his fist connected with her skull, reducing her vision to a dizzying mosaic. He wasted no time, rising to his feet and slamming the heel of his boot on her nose, on her chest, on her gut. She had no time to rise, no time to breathe, no time for anything but to bring her hands up to shield herself in vain. Pain pierced her like bolts of lightning. The boot ceased, and she feared the worst as she vaguely made out his hand reaching for the sword.

Then the hand vanished, retracted backward, the sword remaining untouched on the ground.

A harried scream escaped the governor as something unseen ravaged him.

Her eyesight took a minute to settle. They came to focus on the governor, pinned to the ground by the knee of a tall, bloodied figure.

It was Desil, she realized, stunned at the bizarre sight of him. He was drenched in blood—his own, or others', she could not tell. His hair was matted with sweat and blood, his clothes ripped, yet he tirelessly rained blow after blow into Governor Matheranos, looking like a man possessed.

Governor Matheranos retaliated, jamming his finger into Desil's eye, making him scream. But Desil yanked that finger to his mouth and bit into it, hard enough to force a pitiful howl from the governor's throat, and he held it between his teeth as he resumed pummeling the governor. Blow after blow, Governor Matheranos cried out, louder and louder, trying to shield his face to no avail. His mane of white hair was starting to seep red.

It was an ugly sight, and Lythlet understood for the first time why Desil loathed his brawling days as much as he did—because he was frighteningly good at it. Good at the thing he despised the most.

As much as she loathed the governor, as much as he deserved to suffer, a strange fear grew in her then that Desil would not know how to stop before it was too late. If he crossed the line and brought a man to death, she knew he would never forgive himself.

She staggered to her feet and stumbled forward, weak and dizzy, but desperate to reach him as he battered the governor mercilessly. Governor Matheranos was barely conscious now, lying beneath Desil limply; he had no more in him to fight with.

"Desil," she called.

He did not respond, too lost in his rage.

She shrank back momentarily, alarmed at what she saw in his face.

She had seen it before, many times—too many times. In Valanti Winaro, when he despaired that his expertise had yet to be rewarded by him moving upwards in society, and thus felt it was only fair he took out a little rage on a timid bookkeeper. In Master Dothilos, when he'd received four penalizing whiplashes from the Eza instead of the unfettered praise he'd hoped for, and thus felt it was only fair he passed on a little wrath to a naïve slumdog.

It was the reckless, unyielding anger of a man tired of feeling small in a world yet to recognize his self-perceived greatness—a rage incandescent Lythlet knew full well to be the hardest for a man to free himself from because if she dug down deep enough, she'd find an identical one within herself.

Shaken, but wanting more than anything to doubt her instinct, she called again, keeping herself in his clear sight. She did not want to approach him from behind. The fear of not knowing whether he'd recognize her as a friend sat heavily on her shoulders.

"Desil, that's enough. You need not hurt him anymore. You've already won the battle."

Desil didn't seem to hear her. He went on with bloody, balled-up fists descending over and over again into the governor. She reached out and pressed a shaking hand gently to his head, where brow met unruly hair. He tensed beneath her, and she trembled, wondering if he would listen. Somehow, he seemed inhuman then, more like a wolf set upon feasting on its prey than someone who could comprehend her words.

But he slowed, his hands coming to rest in a tight, blood-stained grip together. He breathed, in and out, entire body shaking from the effort.

She drew a silent breath of relief. He was still here. She could still reach him.

"We need to tie him up just in case," she said in a shaky voice. It was hard to keep her thoughts straight when her skull throbbed so much. "There's rope back in the room where they tied us."

Desil nodded and hoisted the governor over his shoulder. He made no eye contact with her, and Lythlet watched him concernedly as they lurched down the halls, returning to the room.

The barely conscious governor was soon tossed on the floor, mouth gagged, hands and feet bound.

At last, with a moment to rest, Desil collapsed on the grand throne the Eza had been seated upon. Lythlet went to him, clutching his face worriedly, even as the crushing pain in her head overwhelmed her.

But he cradled her to his chest, hands stroking her head gently. "They hurt you." His voice shook. He brushed her forehead, sweeping her fringe from her sweaty, flushed face, and kissed it with pity.

She shut her eyes, mind fading to white as he rocked her back and forth. His touch comforted her, a faint light lingering beyond her eyelids. Seconds passed and she opened them once more.

"You look much worse off than me," she murmured after a moment, pulling back to worriedly wipe the blood smeared all over his face. One of his eyes was alarmingly red where Governor Matheranos had jabbed. They were both bruised and battered, in dire need of a physic.

"I don't feel good," he murmured, head drooping down.

Alarmed, she held his hands, wincing at his swelling knuckles. Dried blood was sprawled over his bloated joints. His rosaries were missing. She glanced around, wondering where they'd gone. Stray beads were scattered across the floor, some crushed into a fine powder, and they led to the back of the room where the two barrel-chested crossbowmen Desil had fought were heaped.

Lythlet blanched at the sight, bile rising in her.

One lay on his back, blood smeared over his face, slack lips revealing missing teeth, a freakish dent in the dome of his head.

His chest heaved minutely with a struggle for air. Not too far away was the second, unmoving on the ground. She turned ill at the sight of his mangled face, bloodied and already starting to swell. His front teeth were broken, their jagged ends like rocky crags. But it wasn't his teeth alone contributing to the image—the skin of his mouth had been punctured by a broken jawbone at a painful angle.

She stared, horrified. These were not wounds they could possibly recover from.

She turned back to Desil, uncertain what to say.

"I've damned myself, Lythlet," he murmured.

"No," she comforted, holding his face in her hands. "You haven't. You did this in self-defense. Surely the divine will have mercy on you."

"Perhaps they will spare mercy for the death of these two," he said quietly, "but will they for the first man I killed?"

Her blood turned cold. "What?"

He did not answer for long moments, his consciousness seeming to slip temporarily. She shook him, afraid of losing him.

After a moment, he raised his head, looking wearily at her.

"I haven't been truthful with you, Lythlet," he said. "I didn't quit brawling because I couldn't stomach the violence. I quit because I realized too late I was enjoying the blood-spill. In the brawling square, I had finally found something I was outrageously good at—and I let it overcome me. I sent man after man to the health ward, week after week, always to a cheering crowd. I never knew how to hold back in the square, and I never bothered to learn how."

She stared at him, wide-eyed as her consciousness struggled to stay intact. "But you were only doing it for the coin."

"I only told you that because I couldn't bear the shame of the truth: I loved the fights, and only regretted it when it was too late. I went beyond what was necessary every time. The spectators praised me for it. They reveled in the beast I became. For the first time after years of going nowhere and being worthless, I finally felt powerful, competent, strong. That's why I never wanted you to spectate. The last thing I wanted was for you to find out I was anything but the boy you grew up with."

"But you quit," she said. "You quit because you knew better."

"I quit," he said quietly, "because at my last brawl, I sent a man to his grave."

She paled.

His words grew rushed, panicked, and his throat visibly tightened above her, veins cording a violent cobalt on pale skin. "His name was Joshir Vethina. I pinned him down, and I beat him, blow after blow. I felt like I was possessed by a spirit. The crowd cheered and cheered. I turned him black and blue and red. Even after he surrendered, I didn't stop, not until I was dragged off him, declared the champion, and sent on my way with my bag of coins. I was leaving the square, coming home to you, when I saw a few of the attendants lugging out a body through the back. He'd bled out. I'd done that to him."

Memories of that night reeled through her failing mind, bright flashes of what had seemed like a mundane night. He had come home, thrown the bag of coins on the floor. She'd congratulated him, he'd turned away. She thought he was simply tired, worn out and detached as he often was after a brawl, and he left for the communal well for a drink and to splash his face with water. But when he came back up to the kataka flat, he had caught her in the spare moments before she turned over to sleep. He cried in front of her, tears flowing freely, and all she had gotten out of his incoherent rush of words was that he wanted to end his brawls.

All she had imagined was that at last his soul had been worn out by fighting.

She had never imagined what he'd been keeping from her.

"You've killed a man," she said, stunned, "and you pretended nothing had happened." Her mind was being torn into too many pieces for her to say more than that.

He bent to touch his forehead against her hand. "I've broken one of the high commandments, to take not what cannot be returned by mine own hand. And I did it for pleasure, for vanity. There's something wrong with me."

He stopped talking for some time, or perhaps his consciousness slipped. But she heard him resume.

"And yet," he whispered, "even knowing what I was, what I had done, and vowing to myself to never take on violence once again, I could not resist. When you brought home that handbill, I thought I had an opportunity to once again partake in something greater than myself."

She felt ill. "The conquessor handbill?"

He wept over her, his tears falling hot upon her cheek. "I acted like I was joining only because I wanted to keep you out of trouble, but in truth I couldn't have been happier to have the chance to fight again. I thought of being loved once more, of winning the praise and love of spectators by my own might, and the temptation was too much. You have always thought me honorable, Lythlet. Do you think I've never taken advantage of your faith in me? Do you think I don't know you see me ever-honest, ever-pure, and that only made it easier for me to lie to you?"

Her voice sank into a trembling whisper, overrun by emotions. "I just forfeited a fortune for you. A fortune that would've ensured the comfort and care of my family, one I'll never see again in my life. All because I believed you would never be able to handle a brawl. When all this time, you've been lying to me." A singular notion then pricked her, and the possibility of it enraged her. "Does Master Dothilos know?"

Her question surprised him. "I suspect he does. There's a glint in his eyes whenever he talks about my brawling days. I wouldn't be surprised if he sent his servants digging around the square and learned that."

"So," she said, fury tinging her words, "when we were holding that funeral for the bugbear cub and you told me to stay away from the match-master, was that because you were worried for my safety, or were you simply worried he'd tell me the truth one day?"

The guilt on Desil's face told her all she needed to know.

She stared at his face, her vision splitting him into two, into four, into a million smashed fragments. Her mouth was dry; no reply sprang from her lips. Every thought seemed vapid, worthless. She looked at him and felt the keen horror of seeing someone she loved unveiled as someone she did not know at all.

He slumped forward then, flesh failing him at last, and she caught him, panicking. She shouted his name, and he made no response.

The door behind them banged hard, someone throwing their weight against it.

Her heart lifted. The Coalition—they'd found this network of hallways; they'd come to rescue them.

"We're in here!" She raced to the door. She lifted the bolts and pulled the metal handle with both hands, heaving it open.

"You're behind this, aren't you?" Master Dothilos spat in her face, barging into the room. "Did you think you could defy me and ruin me in one day? Is that why you had the gall to say no to me?"

She paled.

Without a second to think, he had gripped her by the collar, yanking her into the air and shaking her by the neck. She slung a blow into his cheekbone, but he continued unfettered, rage blinding him to pain.

"All I ever wanted was to grant you the chance to become all you've ever wanted in your pathetic little life—and what have you done? You stupid, stupid girl! I've given you more coin than you've ever had, I've given you a story to be proud of. I've given you all this and only asked for a few favors in return. And yet here I behold a serpent coiled in the grass, quick to betray me."

He came in with both hands, tightening them around her neck. She gagged, reddening. She turned lightheaded, her mind being torn in four directions at once as a grayish-green darkness descended upon her, the sensation making her stomach swirl nauseously.

Footsteps were coming, heavy footsteps, a jangle of metal rattling with their approach. Perhaps the match-master's servants were coming to assist him. Her conjecture faded into the recesses of reality as all at once, the pain in her skull blossomed into red sparks, and she passed out, hand falling limp by her side.

The Golden Thorn knew no more.

CHAPTER THIRTY-THREE

THE TROUBLE OF VIRTUE

WHEN LYTHLET CAME to, she was resting atop plush, lavish upholstery with gold thread inlaid. A thin white blanket covered her from neck to toe.

The ceiling was stark white, brightened by sunlight coming through a large bay window. A massive chandelier dangled, throwing reflections around spitter-spatter.

Have I been guided by the white wind to the halls of healing? she thought, stunned at the simple majesty of her surroundings. Relief flooded her, knowing that the divine had witnessed her record and found her worthy of a peaceful afterlife.

She creased her brow, and something shifted on her forehead. Her fingers brushed against linen wrapped tightly around her skull. *How odd. Do wounds not heal immediately here?*

"You're finally awake."

Lythlet jumped at the voice, blanket falling to the crimson carpet, a hysteria of pain stampeding through her head. She hissed in agony, clenching her eyes shut, now certain she had been thoroughly mistaken, and was, in fact, in the halls of damnation.

"Don't strain yourself," said the voice, and when she finally opened her eyes, she saw Saevem Arthil sitting not too far away, half-hidden behind a grand study desk.

Her mouth ran dry. Where was she? Where was Desil? She looked around, trying to gain her bearings. It was a posh private office and, judging from the massive wedding portrait of Saevem hanging on a wall, it belonged to him.

"Is this your home?"

He nodded. "I brought you here after the health ward discharged you last night."

"Health ward? Where's Desil?"

"When we finally caught up with the match-master, he had inadvertently led us to you and Desil. You had just passed out from strangulation, Desil from his wounds. I had the both of you sent to a health ward here in Central immediately. The mercy-workers looked after Desil for a week, then transferred him to Southeast— Chuol Ward, where he's registered. Your injuries, on the other hand, required you to remain under their care for nigh a fortnight. But you're a surprisingly quick healer, all things considered. Mind your head in the coming weeks and rest as much as you can. I also noticed you had nothing on your feet—I'm not sure if someone stole your boots—but I bought you a new pair in case. They're by the door. But first, you must be hungry. I had my house staff prepare a feast for you."

Lythlet rested against her seat apprehensively as he rang a bell on his desk.

A reedy fellow soon wheeled in a tray stacked with dishes. A bowl of thick, creamy pumpkin soup filled with generous chunks of beef and seasoned with curry leaves entered her view. Her stomach growled pathetically. She nearly drained the bowl in one swallow, then set upon a nearby plate of honeyed roasted chicken, and once her belly began feeling full, she set down her fork. Her mind reeled with a slaughter of questions. She finally settled for asking, "What happened to Governor Matheranos?"

Saevem grinned and tossed her way a rolled-up edition of the *Daily Diamond*. She unfurled it to read the massive headline

blazoned across the front page: GOVERNOR CONVICTED OF
CORRUPTION!

Numerous subheadings competed for Lythlet's attention: COURT
BLASTS GOVERNOR: "NATIONAL DISGRACE"; THE EZA'S
REIGN OF CARNAGE AND CHAOS; COURT CONFIRMS
EARLY ELECTION TO BE CALLED; BRANDOLAS A SHOO-
IN, EARLY POLLING SHOWS; CORIO SAYS NEXT ELECTION
"LAST CHANCE TO REFORM SETGAD."

"Absolutely brilliant," Saevem crowed. "This is but a taste of
the excitement of the press these days. Every single day, a brand-
new revelation comes out, exposing each and every one of the
Eza's monstrous crimes over the decades. Graft, murder, child
sex trafficking—it's all over the news, and the whole city has been
stirred into demanding justice. Matheranos has been dethroned,
shamed, and the city—nay, the whole world west of the Palisades—
knows of his deeds. The public has turned against him, to say the
least, and the Einveldi Court has never had to work harder to keep
things calm. His execution is to be scheduled soon."

She raised her head from the gazette to meet his eyes. "Was
Madam Kovetti and her brothel implicated in his crimes?"

"Her monstrous den has been shut down," Saevem assured with
utmost solemnity. "Kovetti herself is being prosecuted for a great
many things, and the Einveldi Court has judged her crimes heinous
to the degree she will be granted no leniency even for her testimony
against the governor."

"And what of the children?"

He softened. "They're being cared for by good folk now, thankfully.
Whether they will ever know peace in their hearts remains to be
seen, but at the very least, they will be kept safe from now on."

Lythlet heaved a deep breath, drawing the rites of mercy and
divine intervention in the air, praying for those little souls.

He smiled at her. "And it's all thanks to you. The moment you
encountered the Eza, Corio and I ran to Judge Eridicea and
convinced her we had to raid the arena then. She graciously granted

us her personal guardsmen and the swiftest destriers of her stable. We charged down here like our lives depended on it, and caught the governor neatly tied up like a package for us to retrieve. The Coalition owes its gratitude to you and Desil."

He bowed to her.

She had piled a generous heap of sauté potatoes onto her fork, but she set it down silently. "You're welcome," she said awkwardly.

"Having said that, I must inform you that your names have been kept off the record," Saevem said. "No one will know what you and Desil have done. The Eza may be destroyed, but the underworld has not been completely dismantled. We decided for the sake of your safety from any parties seeking revenge, a complete expungement of your involvement would be wise. Judge Eridicea agreed with us. You may find yourself blessed with silent protection henceforth, at least until the dust has settled."

She nodded quietly.

"Is something bothering you?" he said tentatively as she remained silent.

"I was forced into forfeiting the match," she said quietly. It had only been a fortnight ago, yet memories of her final match flitted through her weary mind like dragonflies in autumn, hard to catch and pin down. Ripping the pendant off her neck, smashing it on the ground, smoke wreathing her as she announced her decision to the arena—a decision she'd made to spare Desil the agony of confronting his brawling past. A past she now knew he had actually relished. Her heart sank, weighed down by an alloy of misery and anger.

She raised her head, hope piercing through the fog in her mind. "Could I have the jackpot?"

"It's been confiscated by the investigation," Saevem said uncomfortably.

"Oh," she said, tiredly. What could she ask for? She hadn't made a financial bargain with the Coalition. They owed her nothing but gratitude.

"The Coalition doesn't have much in party funds," Saevem

continued, not quite meeting her eyes. "And we spent what little we had for your health ward fees."

She stared back at him, this highborn fellow sitting in his grand chair in this grand room outfitted with a crystalline chandelier and elaborate woven tapestries she'd never afford in her life.

"I see," she said flatly.

He coughed.

She looked away, not wanting to belabor this miserable moment. She pointed at the massive portrait she'd noticed earlier. "Your wedding day?"

"The happiest day of my life," Saevem replied, relaxing. He stood and went to the portrait, a huge oil painting that spanned nearly the entire wall. Saevem and his wife were in the center, looking joyous with their hands clasped together. Matching wedding pendants laced their necks, thin silver chains bearing ornate ring-pendants from which sparkled a violent burst of red gems. Behind them were members of their wedding party, and Lythlet startled at those standing behind Saevem.

"Corio Brandolas," she murmured, recognizing that startlingly handsome, flaxen-haired fellow who was now guaranteed governorship. "He was in your wedding party."

"We go back a long time, as I mentioned before."

"He must be very busy now."

"Indeed! Between dealing with Matheranos's trial and preparing for the upcoming election, he's barely had any time to meet even me."

"I wonder what his first act as governor will be." *Will the city really improve under his governorship?*

"To unban his book, maybe." Saevem's laughter faltered as Lythlet stared at him. He cleared his throat. "Of course, the Coalition has many plans to reform the unfair policies Matheranos implemented during his terms."

"Good," Lythlet answered hollowly.

He turned back to the portrait and waved a hand over the man besides Corio, a dark-haired man with a strong brow and a gentle smile. "That's Azuran Telehir, rest his soul." He sighed wistfully up at the portrait. "How things have changed. He'd be proud to see us as we are now. We've done justice to his name, at long last."

"I suppose I won't ever see you again after this," said Lythlet thoughtfully, pushing away the tray of now-empty dishes. "You'll be busy helping Corio Brandolas with his governorship."

"Perhaps. But the world has strange ways of making paths cross." He smiled at her. "If you wish to rest a little longer, you may."

"I think it's time I left." She gently eased herself off the settee.

He nodded, guiding her to the front door and swinging it wide open to reveal a posh neighborhood. "Take care of yourself while you're on the mend. I trust you know how to make your way home from here. Desil must be waiting for you."

A pang in her heart, a conflicted twist of emotions rising at the thought of him. She could not bear the thought of returning to Southeast then, of facing Desil once more. Not after what he'd told her, not with what she now knew.

Nor did she want to linger in Central, surrounded by architectural markers of absurd wealth she no longer had any hope of attaining. White mansions, tall fences, treehouses for children—they taunted her as she stared out at the neighborhood, looming over her like giants.

Without thinking, she shook her head.

He raised a brow. "Have you another destination in mind?"

She paused, eyebrows knitting together. "What of the match-master? Is he to be executed, too?"

Saevem shook his head. "He's been spared the death penalty for his testimony against the governor. He provided some key evidence to corroborate with Matheranos being the Eza, but his own crimes will keep him in gaol for a long time. He'll be serving a life sentence in Haginuvo Penitentiary instead."

"Could I go see him?"

He looked at her, surprised. "You wish to visit the man who tried to strangle you to death?"

"I have some unfinished business with him."

"He's not actually allowed visitors in the interim. But wait a moment." He dashed back down the corridor, disappearing into his office. Moments later, he re-emerged, holding something out to her. "My name paired with this will make the turnkeys amenable to your cause."

It was the Coalition's calling card, the diamond-encased *hista* flower vibrant as ever.

"Thank you, Master Arthil," she said, bowing her head.

Her pointed politeness made his smile falter. "Lythlet," he tried nervously, "I know this pales in comparison to the jackpot you'd hoped for, but perhaps this will help." He presented a loosely tied bag to her.

Not daring to hope, she tugged at the neck of the bag until it was wide enough to peek into it. Bone-colored disks met her sight.

White valirs.

A considerable amount of coin—not nearly enough to match even a fraction of the bag of gold she had forfeited, nothing that would impact Saevem's reticule deeply. But most certainly not an amount she could afford to reject out of pride.

"Thank you, Master Arthil," she said once more, pocketing the gift. She appreciated his generosity, she truly did. She did not appreciate the symbolism behind it, however: she was returning to a life of having to rely on the charity of others.

"You're welcome, Lythlet," he said, looking relieved she'd accepted it.

She left the mansion, stepping out onto cobblestone pavements lined with baltascar lamps. The westering sun limned the residential street in golden rays. The cold, fresh air stung her lungs bitterly. She wandered toward Haginuvo Penitentiary, her thoughts her only companions. A fog of melancholy embraced her, wordless fears gnawing at her insides as her footsteps stumbled over the cobblestones. The boots Saevem had bought her didn't fit well, not the way Master Dothilos's had, but they did the job, protecting her swollen soles from the streets.

Her stint as a conquessor had come to an end, one she had never expected. No gold, no longer. Her dreams of leaving behind the southern slums had been crushed, not for the first time, likely not for the last. She wondered then what hand she could ever wield over her fate. The world was a labyrinth, and she was a traveler without a map, and that frightened her beyond belief.

A sign swinging over a cast-iron gate welcomed her to HAGINUVO PENITENTIARY FOR WAYWARD SOULS. A guardswoman with an enviable musculature gestured her down a pebbled path to a huge building looming before them, like a mountain threatening to blot out the sun.

Inside, another guard greeted her, jotting down her details. The moment Lythlet said she wished to visit Renveld Dothilos, the guard shook his head.

"None are permitted to—"

Lythlet flashed the calling card, ensuring the embossed *hista* flower glinted in the light. "Master Saevem Arthil sent me here."

It worked like a charm, the guard clasping his hand to his heart and bowing. He requested she wait in the courtyard for another guardsman to escort her to Dothilos's cell.

The courtyard housed an ill-maintained shrine, a forlorn, time-vanquished structure of semi-crumbled pillars and dusty spires. She squinted at the primary statue at the head of the twin rows of wardens—it was Kilinor, his ashy and chipped face just barely recognizable by the single carved tear sliding down his stone cheek. Lichen with a blooming crust covered half his head, and tall flowering weeds sprang up around his feet.

"Why was I born under you, O warden of grief and mourning?" she asked in a shaking voice. "Is this what you've condemned my life to? That I shall struggle uphill until I die, and remain unrewarded for any effort I make, always trying, always failing? Was I asking for too much when I asked to be happier, to have the joy I've always read about, the joy I've seen others have?"

He had no answer for her, but remained weeping, hand outstretched to an invisible supplicant below.

She reached upwards for that hand, tears blurring her vision. Tightening her grip over it, she wished she could break it off, wished she could maim her warden. "Is this how you want me, clinging to you from below, begging for scraps of joy from you like a dog? Must I beg for mercy just so I can live a life half as good as others?"

She released a shuddering breath, hand falling slack, tears splashing her boots. She turned away from Kilinor, crushing flowering weeds beneath her, coming to a stone bench beyond the shrine and waiting for the guard to fetch her.

IN A SMALL corner cell outfitted with a humble cot, a man leaned against the bars, arms folded across his chest, head turned to the small window. He was mourning the sun, his angled jaw set in a bitter clench.

Master Dothilos.

There was a voice inside Lythlet telling her to turn back. Leave this man behind and abandon the poison he'd been feeding her.

But I will never have this chance again, she thought, grimly taking step after step forward, boots clunking against the cool concrete.

He turned as she approached the bars, pale eyes widening. "You," he said, quietly.

She knelt to his level, staring at him. With the iron bars framing his face, he seemed different. He was not the malevolent tyrant, master of the arena she knew. He was not a man with his underworld connections in place, their strings tightly holding him poised and immaculate.

He was now but a shrunken figure hunched over in the corner of a gaol cell, alone at last with his thoughts.

He glared at her. "I didn't think I was allowed visitors. Have you come to laugh at me?"

"I have not."

"Surely you must feel joy at the sight of me now, ruined and locked behind bars."

She stayed quiet. She felt many things then, things she needed time to articulate. Joy entwined with relief. Anger, of course, at someone who had threatened her at every turn and beaten her once he believed her a traitor. But she could muster neither triumphant smile nor vindictive sneer then. She merely looked at him, and weariness flooded her.

He stared back. "You're fortunate these bars are here. I didn't get to finish the job earlier thanks to the Coalition, but I would have killed you if I could. You wretched cur, you fork-tongued serpent—how long have you been working with them?"

"Not very long," she said quietly. "Just long enough to make a difference."

"Fool," he spat through the bars. "If this is about the governor, why must I be torn down for his crimes?"

"Do you think you've committed none of your own?"

"Mine are trifles compared to his! If one must burn, let it be him alone."

"You chose to serve a man who has allowed corruption to infest our city for decades," she said calmly. "You may pretend you're better than him, but the fact remains you chose to be a cogwheel in the cycle of injustice."

"And what have you received for all your noble efforts?" he sneered. "Working for the penniless Opposition would never make you rich, and you were foolish enough to turn down a mountain of gold back in the arena. Do you truly think your precious Coalition will reform this city?"

She fell silent, doubt clouding her mind. The grim reflection of how politicians will happily appeal to the oppressed with bromides and lip service that fail to manifest actual change crept up on her. At last, she muttered weakly, "I will wait and see the deeds of Governor Corio Brandolas before I judge him."

He laughed, seeing through her pretense. "You should never count on others to uphold their duties to serve justice or mercy. A bitter lesson I was forced to learn a long time ago. I have grown up seeing things you could never stomach, I have suffered in ways you cannot count—"

"I know what you suffered as a child," she said softly, "and I am sorry."

He stopped, spluttering as if the wind had been knocked out of him.

"A member of the Coalition of Hope told me about the orphanage," she explained. "He told me what you suffered as a child. And I know these are just words, but I truly am sorry you ever had to go through that."

He stared at her, blue eyes wide and alarmed. But then he hardened, sheer rage lighting his eyes up like a spark. "Keep your mock platitudes to yourself."

She felt very sorry for him then. He reminded her of the hound in Khavi Monul's cramped kennels, the one she had hoped to free at first but couldn't for its violent reaction—a beast so damaged by its own life, it could not understand she wanted to help it. As she looked at Master Dothilos, she saw a man so damaged by his life, he could not recognize unmanufactured sympathy not meant to manipulate him.

He went on, "If you were truly sorry for me, why would you fault me for making something of myself, for rising above my past?"

"Master Dothilos," she said, grimly. "You allowed your abuser to spread his wickedness, and you gave him coin for it. You suffered, but you chose to pass that suffering on to people you deemed beneath you. Now, at long last, your crimes have caught up with you—the trading of nameless children from abuse into abuse, the fire, the deaths of countless innocents and your own brother."

His eyes flickered in nervous agitation as she listed these things, dipping down to the burn on his arm. After a moment of contemplation, he said in a low voice, "If you had gone through what I had, would you have done anything different? Would you truly be able to live a life free of rage, unburdened by your past and unwilling to make necessary sacrifices to ensure you'd never go through the same things again?"

She stayed quiet. "Perhaps not," she admitted. She did not see the point in lying to him. "I am as you are, in many ways. Mine is a moral compass readily pulled astray by fear, greed, and anger. I share the same fondness for petty revenge as you, the same vindictive hopes for the future. In the end, I am torn between condemning you and pitying you."

He glowered at her. "If you did not come to mock me, then what did you come here for?"

She breathed in and out, the one question that had been bothering her itching to spring free from her throat. "Did you know?"

"What?"

"Desil," she said reluctantly. "What he did at his final brawl."

A look of grim realization settled on his face. "So you've finally found out."

She buried her face into her knees, feeling like a fool.

"I've known for a long time," he said. "Ever since I had my servants investigate you. I had them look into Desil as well, and the brawling square of Chuol Ward wasn't shy to reveal the truth. At first, I thought you knew, too—that you were keeping it secret for him. But as time went on, I realized you genuinely hadn't a clue what he was keeping from you."

"Why didn't you tell me?"

Master Dothilos did not speak for long moments. But at last, he turned to her and said quietly, "Because I knew that knowledge would break you. Your darling childhood hero being unmasked as a lying brute. How could you possibly cope with that? Yours is an honor that blinds you from conceiving of dishonor in anyone you love." He smiled at her then—but not out of spite. It was fondness, genuine as gold. "It seems that though mine may be meager compared to yours, I am not without my own supply of mercy."

She stared at him, stunned.

"Thank you," she said after a moment.

He hesitated, then scoffed dismissively. "Don't thank me. I've done nothing for you."

"But you have, Master Dothilos. You've taught me many things," she said sadly, wishing the two of them had chosen many different forks in the road, "and I'm grateful for them. Conviction, momentum—knowing to trust myself, knowing to run forth bravely. I will go far if I can truly hold on to these things. Even your third lesson has its merits in the right moments."

"Would that you hadn't betrayed me, Golden Thorn, so that I could've taught you even more. Perhaps I could have saved you the heartbreak of thinking your ideals could amount to anything in this world. If there's one thing I mourn, it's that I didn't teach you the foolishness of faith and hope before it was too late. You will face much worse than me in your life, and you won't know how to save yourself the trouble of virtue."

"I think you have taught me something new, Dothilos," she said in slow realization. "A lesson you did not quite intend on teaching. You once said that satisfaction lies in succeeding with spite at others, that it'd be wise to have rage and vengeance at the center of my convictions. But I think I've found a better way to live. For all you speak of conviction, I wonder if you truly hold no regret for the decisions you've made in your life." She retraced the memory of the fleeting, unbridled sadness that had crossed his face when he first revealed his burn to her.

The Serpent Called Mercy

He stared up at her witheringly. "If you're about to announce some asinine creed you'll calibrate your moral compass by, I'll curse you and your unborn descendants to an early grave. Live your life as you will, and we shall see what the whims of the world do to you."

"Then let us part, Dothilos. I wish you as well as you deserve," she said, sticking her hand through the bars.

His eyes followed her fingers, and for a second, she could have sworn his hand twitched toward hers, ready to take it. Then he snarled and spat a thick glob of saliva over her palm.

"And I you, Little Candle Flame."

She withdrew her hand slowly, contemplating the futility of reaching out to a man whose heart would accept neither kindness nor sympathy. She wiped her hand dry on the ground and rose to her feet.

"Farewell," she said, looking down at him and meeting his glowering eyes.

Two souls stared at one another with nothing but genuine pity for the other.

On the way out, she passed by the courtyard shrine once more. She crouched before Kilinor, one knee pressed into the earth, tightening her grip over his offered hand.

"My parents named me Lythlet, and that means 'candle-flame'," she spoke to her warden. "A dismal name, I've always thought, like I could be blown out by a puff of air. But if that is to be my destiny, then I shall ask for one thing only: before I die, let my little candle-flame light another wick, and then another, that my life will leave an inferno in my wake. I won't ask for riches; I won't ask for joy. I'll only ask for the chance to carve out a path I alone can in this cosmic sphere, to be a piece that adds to the puzzle of this universe."

She drew the rite of supplication in the air—a two-fingered flick from right to left that looped around and then drew a line down to her chest.

Kilinor stared down at her, and it seemed to her that his everlasting tear glimmered for a second.

Thank you, she thought with a smile.

She rose to her feet. She clapped her hands thrice, steepled them by her chest, and bowed. "*Umera venturi, asigo venturi,*" she said in farewell to the shrine.

We live according to your whims, we die according to your whims.

CHAPTER THIRTY-FOUR

THE FOURTH LESSON

THE IVY-CLAD HOMELY Home was flushed with warm yellow light leaking from its windows and doorways as always, and muted chatter welcomed Lythlet as she knocked on the door. "It's me, Lythlet!"

The door flung open within seconds, Shunvi looking like he'd raced to be the one to greet her, Ilden peering nervously from behind him.

"Lythlet," Shunvi said, her name a sigh on his lips, one of both joy and regret. He embraced her without hesitation, his emerald-and-ivory silk robe rubbing pleasantly over her arms.

"So glad to see you again," Ilden said, dark brows knitted with worry. "You look awful—I mean, you look like you got into a fight or two."

"Come on, come in," said Shunvi, leading her through the hall to the dining table. Naya was sitting there, a pillow cradled underneath her head, a cup of iced tea in her hand, condensation dripping onto the table.

"Oh, you poor dear—your poor face!" she cried, beckoning

Lythlet to sit next to her. "Ilden, be a peach and pour some of the opalten tea for her."

"I'm a peach," Ilden chirped, eagerly grabbing a teacup from a cupboard and pouring out a drink from an iced jug. After he slid it to Lythlet, a grim silence fell, the men exchanging uncomfortable stares.

At last, Shunvi spoke, "I want to apologize about the final match."

"We both do," said Ilden.

"You don't have to," she said quietly.

"No, we must," said Shunvi. "We did not want to fight you, but the match-master came to us not long before the match, demanding we reprise our roles as the Poet and the Ruffian."

"We laughed in his face, of course," said Ilden. "But then his demand turned into a threat, and he told us we could either repay him for all the success we've managed for ourselves, or he'd get the Eza to hound our backs."

"We didn't agree then either," said Shunvi bluntly, gaze turning hard with anger. "It'd take more than petty threats of violence to bring us back to the arena—to bring us to fight you. We know how to take care of ourselves, after all. But then he spoke of getting certain charges stacked against us and my teahouses—charges that would not only have us thrown into gaol, but most certainly ruin the livelihoods of everyone I employ, if not have them join us in a cell, too. I hope you'll forgive us, Lythlet, but I could not bear the thought of jeopardizing their lives. He set his spies upon us for the month leading up to the match, so we couldn't visit you and tell you what was transpiring without fear of reprisal."

"I understand," she said gently. "You were doing what was best."

"In any case, we may have capitulated to the match-master's demands, but we weren't seeking victory that day, I promise you," Shunvi said.

"We would have fought just enough to put on a good show for the spectators—you know, exchange a few blows, cut each other up at the non-vitals, spill a non-threatening amount of blood," said Ilden. "You and Shunvi could do those showy spear maneuvers you've practiced together. The crowd would go wild for it—and then we'd ease into us giving it up to you in a way that wouldn't draw suspicion. We weren't expecting you to forfeit at the very beginning."

A quiet laugh leaked from her. "You've known Desil for an entire year, and you thought he'd fight you?"

"We expected a forfeit from him, but not you. We thought you'd read between the lines and force him back into the game."

"I knew the two of you were willing to throw the battle, but I couldn't force Desil to fight, especially not those he considers friends," she grieved. Would she have chosen differently had she known the truth then, that Desil had done much worse and kept it secret? Thinking about it only stung fresh wounds. "What happened to you two once the Coalition's watchmen arrived? Were you caught in the chaos?"

"Luckily, no. We ran home like our feet were on fire," Ilden answered.

"It took a while for news of everything that had gone down to reach us," Shunvi said. "The whole hubbub with Matheranos being the Eza blew us away. We went looking for you and Desil, but we couldn't find you—what have you been up to?"

She hummed quietly, rubbing her cold teacup. "Perhaps I'll tell you another time."

He glanced at her curiously. "You're not leaving already, are you? You haven't even finished your tea. Stay longer, won't you?"

She smiled in appreciation of his kindness. "Thank you, but I really must go. I have some business to settle with my family. But before I do, there's something I'd like to say—I would like to run together with all of you again."

Ilden blinked in confusion. "What, now? I'd really rather not work up a sweat."

"And my brain's a fine mush at the moment," Naya added, not lifting her head from the pillow.

"Shunvi, you go run with her," Ilden said, jabbing his friend in the ribs.

"Gladly," said Shunvi with a laugh, "but I believe she's speaking metaphorically."

Lythlet nodded, relieved she made sense to at least one person. "One of the happiest moments of recent times for me was working with all of you to help the unregistered take down the riverside flats. Because of you, I was able to help my father get the justice he deserved. I even got an apology from a man who'd terrorized me for months in the process. I doubt we've seen the last case of an unregistered or slumdog being taken advantage of in this city, so when it happens again, I would like it if we could all run together."

Shunvi smiled brightly. "Of course, Lythlet. And I'm glad we could've helped your parents."

"Me, too," added Ilden.

"Send our regards to Uncle and Aunty when you see them again," Naya finished, beaming.

"Honestly, I'm relieved," Shunvi admitted. "Ilden and I were worried you wouldn't even want to speak to us again after that final match, let alone continue our friendship."

Lythlet froze, the teacup slipping from her fingers to land on the table with a heavy *thunk*. She stared at him, then Ilden, then Naya.

"What?" Shunvi said, alarmed.

"Are we all—" she hesitated, a tentative lilt entering her voice "— friends?"

Silence met her question, the other three exchanging puzzled looks.

"I mean," she continued nervously, "I knew you were all friends with Desil, but I didn't know I was included in that equation."

"What did you think we were?" said Ilden, baffled.

"Acquaintances," she said. "Co-workers, of a sort. Co-conspirators."

"As fond as I am of 'co-conspirator,' we are friends, and we have been since the first time we met," Shunvi said with a gentle laugh.

"Honestly, if it's taken you a whole year to cotton on to this, I don't think I want to be friends with you anymore," Ilden added.

"I'm sorry," she said, winded from this brand-new information. "It just never occurred to me that I'd ever have another friend besides Desil. This is a very novel concept for me."

"Oh, you poor, poor emotionally undeveloped woman," Naya said, pulling her in for a hug.

"I'm feeling very rich at the moment, actually," said Lythlet, lips turning upwards. "I really must go now—but thank you for, well, I suppose everything, including your friendship."

At the sight of her enormous smile, they laughed, waving goodbye to her. Shunvi escorted her to the door, and as he waved her off, he shouted, "Take care, Lythlet! I'll come visit you one of these days. We still have a Phantom to unmask!"

"That we do! Bring your journal next we meet," she answered, waving back. Her smile did not fade as she made for Hemharrow Corinthos's estate.

"Today?" Lythlet whispered, knocking on the open attic door.

Father looked up from the little locked-box puzzle he played with, about to answer, but his jaw fell slack at the sight of her. She self-consciously touched her cheek, remembering the bruises and bandages covering her swollen face.

"I'm fine," she said quickly.

It took him a moment to gather his words. "What happened?"

"I wound up in a... fight, of sorts. But I am fine. Today?"

The door swung open wider, revealing Mother standing by it. "Today," she said. She said nothing further, turning aghast at the sight of Lythlet.

"Please ignore my face for now," Lythlet said hurriedly, already feeling the premonition of a barrage of questions raining down upon her. She edged toward them, hands clasped behind her back, posture becoming unnaturally rigid as she stood before them. "I have something more important to tell you. Would you sit down?"

Father and Mother waited on the mattress with bated breath.

"I've come to inform you that I will be unable to fulfill my promise," she said, ashamed.

"What promise?"

"I swore to save you from here. To return you to a life aboveground with a proper house. But my purse strings have been cut, and I can no longer keep my word. You were right to tell me not to make a promise I couldn't keep, Father." She did not mean to, but she ended on a bitter note, the sting of her own failure like the bite of winter's frost. There was little elegance to her words to begin with, but the way she rushed through her sentences and hunched her shoulders made them even feebler.

They gave no response, in neither twitch nor words, silently ruminating. She sat there, petrified as they receded into their thoughts without her.

Lythlet's eyes fell upon the slight bulge beneath Father's sock, that she knew was the silver chain with the *neira* charm, the birthday gift she'd given him. The first generous gift she had ever given him, the last she could foresee for a long time.

She lowered her head, ashamed. She despised having them see her like this, bruised, battered, defeated by life. She had taken pride in being relied on, in having them smile quietly at her presence, and now their disappointment would be a heavy shroud over her shoulders on the long walk home.

After a moment of prolonged silence, she wondered if they had heard her at all. She parted her lips, thinking of repeating herself.

Then Father pushed down his sock and ripped the silver chain off his ankle.

For a brief moment, she flinched, thinking he was about to fling it in her face, as the spectator had done with the pendant watch during the final match, but he clutched it with trembling fingers and lifted his linen shirt. A pouch was tied about his waist, and he clawed at it frantically until it came undone.

He held both the chain and the pouch toward her.

She looked at him, slack-jawed. "What are you doing?"

"These are all the coins I have left. We can pawn this chain. If there are people chasing you for money, then take this and send them away. Or is it not enough to get you out of trouble?"

It was difficult to make out his rambling, but realization dawned upon her, and she pushed his hands back to his chest. "No, Father. I am fine."

"You're not," he cried, clearly frustrated. "You cannot stand before me looking like that and tell me you're fine. I am not clever, but I am not stupid. If you don't want to tell me what troubles you, I understand. But you mustn't lie. If you're in danger, I'll help you. I can try. I can think of something."

"No, Father." She choked on her words. She had been a fool to not remember her state, to not think of how frightened he would be at the lumps of black and blue deforming her. "I'm fine. No one is after me, not anymore. I'm safe, I swear it. My wounds are only temporary—I've been told I'm a quick healer. I came only to apologize to you."

She took the chain from him and returned it to its rightful owner, tying the clasp firmly around his skeletal wrist. Then she pressed his pouch onto his palm, curling his fingers over it. She folded her own fingers over his, holding him tight.

He halted, unused to the affection. He heaved a deep breath. "Will you keep coming to see us anyway?"

She blinked. "Pardon?"

Father looked too sad to continue, so Mother spoke in his

stead. "We'd like it if you kept coming to see us anyway. It's been nice having you around and seeing how you've grown. But we understand if you don't want to. I'm sorry we keep causing you so much trouble."

Lythlet stared wide-eyed at them. It occurred to her then the story she had unwittingly told them in the intervening years since she'd left home—the message left behind in the negative space of her absence. "Is that why you think I never came to visit?"

"Isn't it?" said Father, rubbing his face tiredly. "I was never a good father to you. I'm a halfwit and I always have been. Never knew how to give you better things to do with your time than stealing books or whittling away at blocks of wood at the smithy."

"And I..." Mother began and ended in a single breath, instead pressing her head into Father's shoulder. He stroked her hair. After a moment, she finished her sentence in a whisper, "I'm not much pleasant company on most days."

"We figured you didn't like us much. We've only caused you trouble after trouble," Father said softly. He held up his wrist, eyeing his birthday gift. "If you could somehow find a way to afford this, you could've done even more had you been born to a better family."

"I have never once been sorry to be born to you," Lythlet interrupted. She went on her knees before them, tears brimming in her eyes. "I never came visiting for years because I was ashamed of myself. The thought of confessing that I hadn't been doing well for myself kept me away from you. I feared my existence would continue adding to your burdens. Taking care of me as a child was difficult on the both of you, and the last thing I wanted was to repeat that. I know you did your best for me. I do not grudge you, at all, for anything you lack. You are my father and mother, and you always will be, and I hold no regret against you."

Father began to weep, futilely hiding his sobbing behind a hand. She—awkwardly, nervously—extended her fingers to wipe away his tears, feeling his wrinkled eyebags and hard cheekbones for the first time beneath her fingertips.

"I," he said, struggling hard to get the words out, "hold nothing against you either. I don't know why you keep talking about being a burden, but I'm sorry if we ever made you feel that way. We were happy when you started coming around. It was good to see you again. Good to know you were doing so well. We were proud of you."

Her heart pricked in regret, but she forced herself to smile. But what he said next softened the sting.

"We still are, I mean. Proud of you. You did well for yourself for a long time. And even though you're in a rough patch now, I've seen what you could do since you were a child. You knew how to read so much so quickly. My smithmates used to say they admired how you never gave up no matter how hard they sparred with you. You never let them knocking you off your feet stop you from dusting yourself off and picking up your spear again. The forge-master once said you had the willingness to learn bone-deep the value in rising over and over again. I've always known you'd do better than me, and I don't think I've been proven wrong yet."

"So will you keep coming to see us?" asked Mother, shyly.

Eager bashfulness filled her words, and Lythlet stared incredulously. Somehow, they appeared younger then, as if someone had smoothed out their wrinkles and darkened their hair.

She nodded, a genuine smile stretching across her bruised face. She blinked away tears.

"Yes," she said at last, a little shyly. "I would like to."

Lythlet left with a lightened heart, leaving Father and Mother behind with the promise of visiting again soon.

But a tinge of apprehension rose as she stepped over the threshold of The Steam Dragon, thinking of the remaining things she had to attend to.

Runt's oversized head bobbed up, large obsidian eyes scrutinizing

Lythlet. The giant mongrel lay still, black brows shifting in belabored thought.

Lythlet smiled wanly. *Poor thing can't recognize me with all my wounds.*

Then Runt bounced to all fours and nearly bowled Lythlet over with one tremendous leap. Writhing in unbridled joy, Runt left black fur all over her cloak. Lythlet laughed at the happy, snuffling noises reverberating from Runt's throat.

"You sweet girl. You still know me, don't you? But I'm sorry to say I have some bad news: I don't think I'm in a position to get a house on the ground any time soon. I won't be able to take you in, not now, and perhaps not for a long time."

In response, Runt licked her chin and tried to climb her as if she were a tree.

Lythlet burst out laughing, wrapping her arms around Runt's neck. "Kilinor bless you. If you aren't a manifestation of divine love, I don't know what is. I have nothing to offer you, but I can come to you as I am, and you will love me still." She pressed her face into Runt's fur, smiling. "Day by day, I am learning there are many who will do the same."

With a wave of her hand, Runt obediently sat on the floor, tail thumping, hind legs twitching in anticipation, and Lythlet indulged in some hearty belly rubs. Schwala joined after a moment, scuttling out from the kitchens.

"About time you showed up!" cried Madame Millidin, appearing behind Schwala. "I can't believe you left your dog alone for so long. Desil was bad enough, but at least he showed up days ago to beg off. And I thought you were the responsible one—goodness gracious, what happened to your face?"

Madame Millidin froze in her spot, recoiling at the sight of her.

Lythlet hesitated. "I was beaten up by some bad folk."

Madame Millidin sucked in her breath. "Is that what happened to Desil, too? He didn't want to talk about it. Only popped in to apologize and say he needed time to rest, and then he disappeared until just an hour ago, when he came to fetch some food and tea for himself. He didn't seem much in the mood for talking, so I didn't ask. But looking at you now—goodness. What mess did the two of you get yourselves into?"

Lythlet said nothing, letting Runt snuggle on her lap. Schwala tried to squeeze his way on, too, but to no avail.

Madame Millidin stared at her with a growing frown. Then she called over her shoulder, "*Adan! Adan! Inimeyi kalou batarang!*"

A commotion could be heard from the kitchens, and Mister Millidin soon emerged, holding two long wooden rods pierced through all over with thick rusted spikes. He tossed one to his wife. "*Evaya?*"

Madame Millidin nodded at Lythlet's direction, hefting the spiked pole easily. "Quickly, Lythlet. Who needs a good beating, and where do we find them?"

Lythlet stared in bewilderment.

"Oh, don't look so shocked. You think The Steam Dragon could survive this long without us knowing how to chase off lowlifes? Come, hurry, we have a few hours before the dinnertime rush starts. Bring Runt along; she'd tear apart a man or five for you. Schwala's useless in a fight, but he can cheer us on from a distance."

"Thank you," she spluttered, "but they're in gaol now."

"Oh," said Madame Millidin, lowering her bat dejectedly. "Well, let me know if that changes."

Absolutely not, thought Lythlet, thoroughly alarmed by the teahouse-master's unexpected proposal.

"We could make one for you if there's ever need," Mister Millidin offered shyly, gesturing at the spiked weapon.

Or perhaps I will, thought Lythlet, struggling to hide her excitement as she eyed the bat.

"Thank you," she said. "But I suppose that can wait. For now, I would like to take Runt for a walk."

"Take Schwala, too," was all Madame Millidin said, walking away with her spiked bat and disappointment.

LYTHLET LED THE two dogs to the nearest shrine, and there she spent one of the coins Saevem had given her, buying two sets of rosaries. After returning a satisfied Runt and a sleepy Schwala to The Steam Dragon, she turned homewards, facing the giant kataka trees growing in the distance. A conflicted mix of emotions rose at the sight.

Home, and what a bittersweet thought that was.

It was a home of poverty and failure, a wooden cage lifted high into the sky, juxtaposing her suffering against a good view of the Tower of the White Sun. Now with the final jackpot lost, she'd most certainly never leave it.

Before long, the rope ladder dangled within reach. Up her hand rose, fingers curling around the lowest rung, and she hoisted herself up. She took her time, letting her thoughts percolate, ascending through the branches and up the sky, the setting sun on her back.

The name of the Golden Thorn had failed her. Her dream of consuming starfire had failed her. Even her lifelong trust in Desil had failed her—but something in her demanded she pressed on. Her hands rose again and again, conquering the sky rung by rung, never flagging in her efforts until her fingers met the overhanging ledge of the kataka flat. She swung herself up.

Desil was seated by the entrance, knees folded to his chest. A pot of tea sat by his side, one steaming cup in his hand, an empty one waiting upside-down on the tea tray. A look of surprise took him. "You're back," he breathed out in relief, but then he fell silent, nervous.

They looked upon one another. She had prepared no script for this moment—she'd hoped the words would come to her when she saw him, but they didn't. How does one address the fact that their dearest, beloved friend has killed a man?

She sat on the ledge, back pressed against their wooden flat, the doorway separating her from Desil. Stretched before them was the vast expanse of the white city. On any other day, the orange-soaked sky would have comforted her, the weight of the warm rays resting on her shoulders like a blanket on a winter's night. But now, there was nothing but awkward silence between her and Desil.

Desil fumbled with the teapot, pouring into the empty cup. He pushed the tea tray toward her, timidly, as if uncertain whether she were friend or foe. She accepted it with a nod—eniseya tisane, sweet on the tongue, cooling in the aftertaste, with more than the usual tiny chunks of bitter ginseng root floating around, enough for Lythlet to guess that Madame Millidin had quietly thrown in extra to quicken Desil's healing.

She set the teacup down and heaved a deep breath. "Desil," she said, withdrawing her hand from her pocket. Dangling from her fingers was a rosary she'd just bought at the shrine.

He stared at her, lost, making no move to accept it.

"Will you not wear it?" she asked. "Yours broke."

"Do I have the right to wear it?" he asked in return, eyes flooded with doubt.

She fingered the white bone runes thoughtfully. "Must we be faultless to wear these rosaries? If so, no mortal can wear them. You taught me that verse from the Poetics: *come as you are.* So come to me now as you are and tell me the truth. When you learned you had killed Joshir Vethina, what did you do?"

He puzzled at her question. "I quit brawling."

"And then what? I remember in the weeks—no, months—that followed, you went out often. Where did you go?"

"I went all over the city looking for Joshir's family," said Desil quietly. "I wanted to make amends—I didn't know how, of course. But it didn't feel right to end a man's life, and then leave his family stranded without hope. But I couldn't find anyone. It seems he was alone in life, and brawling had been his last resort to make some coin." He buried his face in his hands. "Isn't that just awful? If the chronoscape were my bloodright, I'd ride the threads of time back to the day and stop myself from killing him."

"It may be too late to strike this sin from your divine record. But it's never too late to learn from your mistakes and choose a better path for yourself. So, what do you want to do instead? You know what you've done wrong. You know the gravity of your sin."

"What am I allowed to ask for?" he said softly.

"I am not asking what you think you deserve. I'm asking what you *want*. If you want to live a life worth living, you must first find your conviction. You have the answer in you."

Desil sat there, thinking. In a small voice, he said, "I want to make things right. I want to earn forgiveness. But what could possibly redeem the killing of an innocent man? The reason why taking that which cannot be returned by thine own hand is considered the greatest sin is because there's no true equitable justice to be given. I cannot bring a man back to life."

"No, but you can show others the mercy Joshir was not shown in life." She stood and went before him, reaching forth a hand toward him.

He hesitated, then raised his hand to her. She wondered briefly if this was what Kilinor saw every time a supplicant grasped his offered hand.

She took his wrist and tied the rosary on for him. "The man you killed had no family for you to beg forgiveness from. But let the city he once called home become the family he did not have in life. Live your life in honor of Joshir Vethina and ensure no one like him ever falls through the cracks forgotten and abandoned again. Find your conviction now and hold fast to it, and perhaps the divine will show you the way to your absolution, that you may someday earn your forgiveness. I will be there for you; I will go with you until the end."

He teared up and crushed his eyes behind his palms. "Why are you being so gracious to me?"

"Because once upon a time, you saw a girl crying outside your schoolhouse, and you chose to be kind and patient with her even when you couldn't understand a damn thing she was saying," she answered with a smile. "I'm not here to pardon your sins, Desil. That's not upon me to do so. But I will hold you accountable as you find your road to redemption. As long as you hold onto your conviction, I will help you maintain your momentum." She withdrew another rosary from her pocket and deftly tied it over her wrist, turning it until the fellowship rune faced upwards.

Desil raised an eyebrow.

Rosaries were a tradition in which she'd never partaken. Some wore them out of superstition or performative morality, but she was not one of them; this was not an act done lightly by her.

She knelt and took his hand, tightening her grasp until he reflexively returned the grip. She raised their hands and brought the back of his against her brow. "I am not as learned in the vows as you are, so you'll have to correct me," she murmured softly.

His eyes were wide and wet, glistening in the light of the setting sun. "You wish to make the sacred vow of fellowship?"

"If you will let me. We were bound under the unconsecrated vow of the arena for a year—I wish to bind myself to you with the real one, instead."

The gravity of her offering struck him dumb—it meant she knew him for who he was, virtues and vices, and held nothing against him, willing to make a vow under heaven to support him as he strove to do better, asking him only to return the favor. He leaned in, brow brushing against the back of Lythlet's hand. There they sat, joined in fellowship, flesh to flesh, spirit to spirit.

"By the blood of my ancestors and the blood of my unborn," she began nervously, but hearing him echo the words fortified her voice, "I vow to uphold your soul ever in pursuit of the divine, that I will stand by you until the white wind rises in your wake. For your glory and honor alone would I forfeit my soul. For the edification of your mind, the purification of your heart, and the ascension of your soul unto the Sunsmith and the Unbound Empress. By wind and water, I bind myself to you, brother by Tazkar—"

"—sister by Kilinor—"

"—until the end of my days."

They raised their heads and pressed their lips to each other's hands, eyes shut.

When they opened them, there was something flickering anew in his olive-flecked eyes, a little flame. He sat back, staring at her fondly. "I don't understand you, Lytha. We've lost everything. We forfeited the final match, we lost the jackpot, we're sitting here at the end of everything as a bruised and battered duo. You saved the city and jammed the spokes of its corruption, but you'll get no reward or credit for it. And yet you're so—you're so hopeful. Have you figured out what we're going to do next? You know, I was cleaning out my things, and I found this." He dug into his pocket and retrieved a folded piece of parchment.

She unfolded it: it was the handbill Master Dothilos had commissioned. **THE ROSE AND THE GOLDEN THORN — A GOLDEN BET TO MAKE!**

Quiet laughter spilled from her. To think she had once been so proud of something so worthless now.

"The Golden Thorn will fight no more," she muttered, rising to her feet. "The Golden Thorn will be loved no more."

She gave the handbill a final glance. With a small smile, she ripped it into tiny little shreds and held them forth in her palm as an offering to the whims of the world. The blustering spring winds accepted it, whisking it far away to scatter across all four corners of the city.

With a surprised look on his face, Desil rose and joined her side. Together, they glanced out at the vast world around them. The city of Setgad was starting to light their fires for the night. Soon, the setting sun would vanish into the thin line of the yellow-cast horizon and give way to a night of a thousand stars. It was a city they could yet make their mark on, a city brimming with good yet to grow.

"I harbored so much hope for myself this past year: my escape from the slums seemed certain, my ascent into highborn society guaranteed, my path to riches paved by my own lauded wit and wiles. But what was that you once said? That hope in times of happiness isn't hope—it's expectation. And now I've lost everything, all my expectations crumbling into ash. But there's a little fire inside me that's pushing me forward, and it's hope true and proper, at last. I truly don't know what lies ahead of me, Desil, I have no machinations or plans or schemes any longer. Our lives will return to what they were: we are slumdogs, as ever, and high society will never care for us as we cobble together a livelihood from our humdrum vocations. But perhaps my life still has value as it is. Perhaps I needn't shrink my shoulders or hide away just because I haven't made something of myself yet. Change is afoot in our city, Desil, and by fair means or foul, I will not let it be for the worse. I may no longer be the Golden Thorn, but I am not without the means to protect those in even worse positions than me. I'll make my mark on the canvas of revolution one way or another, and I intend to do so with a fourth lesson Master Dothilos never wanted me to learn."

"What's that now?"

"Perhaps the most important thing one needs to know: what they wish to set as the needle of their moral compass. Mine shall be mercy at all costs—to extend the hand of mercy to those in need and show them a kindness they never knew before. I don't think Master Dothilos ever got an ounce of mercy in his childhood, and for that, he never learned the value of it. But you showed me kindness when no one else did, and because of that, I want to pass it on."

"An unintended fourth lesson," Desil murmured with a soft smile. A slightly concerned expression came over him. "Oh, that's not a good number to end on."

"No," Lythlet said, laughing as the first star appeared in the darkening sky, "but some things are worth crossing the line for."

ACKNOWLEDGMENTS

For most of my life, writing was a lonely pastime, an intentionally solitary journey I carved out for myself to find some peace and joy. Publishing, on the other hand, has been by necessity a collaborative effort to transform what was once a humble, badly formatted document trapped on my hard disk into the creation you're now reading, a milestone that has been marked by much joy and pride. This would not have been possible without the efforts of everyone who so kindly believed in this book and fought for it every step of the way.

My agent Keir Alekseii deserves all my gratitude, praise, and awe for her tremendous work in getting *The Serpent Called Mercy* from my hands into the publishing world. From our first call, I knew there was something electrifying about the way you were ready to champion my book, how you connected so deeply with the themes, picking up the minor worldbuilding and cultural details I thought only I would appreciate. I can't quite put into words just how much it means to me, a BIPOC writer based in the Global South, to have a BIPOC agent based in the Global South, someone who understood on a fundamental level the type of geopolitical and socioeconomic setting I wanted to write about. Thank you for making my publication journey not only possible, but a thousand times easier than it would have been otherwise.

My absolute and utmost adoration for my editor Amanda Raybould cannot be adequately put into words. Once upon a time, you promised to make my publication dreams come true, and though the journey took a few detours neither of us expected, you delivered on that. My thanks to the rest of the brilliant team at Solaris who drew upon their skills and talents to get this book on shelves in the United Kingdom and the Commonwealth: Chiara Mestieri for editorial support, Jess Gofton for marketing, Natalie Charlesworth for PR, Dagna Dlubak for production, Sam Gretton for final design, Gemma Sheldrake for ARC design, and Owen Johnson for sales. Additional thanks to Laurel Sills for copy edits, and Donna Scott for proofreads.

Thanks to the powerhouse team at DAW for their ceaseless hard work on launching this book in North America. Katie Hoffman, who grokked the heart of this book; Aranya Jain, who enthusiastically grabbed the baton for the second lap; Madeline Goldberg, who did a stellar job as editorial assistant; Laura Fitzgerald as marketing and publicity manager and provider of cute horse photos; Betsy Wollheim as DAW's publisher; Joshua Starr as executive managing editor; and Elizabeth Koehler as production supervisor.

The gorgeous illustrations you see on the cover were done by the astoundingly talented Rowynn Ellis under Katie Anderson's art direction. Thank you both for your remarkable ability to understand my semi-coherent ideas and translate them into a cover I'm proud to debut with.

Special thanks to Saara El-Arifi, who saw the potential in this book earlier than most and taught me to trust my instincts as a writer. You remain a gem—a friend and a mentor.

My sincere thanks to the various beta readers who commented on bits and pieces of old versions of this manuscript over the years. Poor record-keeping skills and lost account passwords prevent me from naming specific people, and I apologize for that—but know that each and every one of you left an indelible mark on this book, whether it be through insightful critique or providently timed encouragement.

Thank you to the various friends who made this journey a little easier, a little more joyful: fellow writers who adopted this severely introverted soul into your communities (much love to my precious

Pitch Wars survivors, Keir Bears, Inklings, SFF BIPOC writers, and 2025 Debuts); Sophira for gifting me a much-needed photoshoot for my author photos; Sarah for crying tears of happiness when I shared news of my book deal (what the heck! so cute!); all my other wonderful friends for their heartfelt enthusiasm over my achievements; and all the talented and generous writers and publishing professionals who reached out to congratulate me and provide vital advice along this occasionally bumpy and frequently overwhelming journey. The sense of community you've all allowed me to experience over the past year has been delightful.

Thank you to my parents and the libraries of Melbourne for ensuring I didn't have to resort to thievery to feed my book addiction growing up. A well-stocked bookcase and quiet, but steadfast support were the formative contributions of Mom and Dad to my love of writing. To my sister Rachel for lovingly reading to me when I was young, and not getting offended when I got big enough to yoink the book out of your hands, insisting I could read faster than you. Sorry for being such an impatient baby. (But damn were you slow!) Thank you to Malaysia for always being the refuge my spirit can re-root itself in no matter what happens to me.

And last of all, my thanks to you, dear reader, for letting this book find its way into your hands. It took a long time for the seed of this story to sprout, the characters and the world taking root in my brain a very, very long time ago, then wending an unexpected journey through the years. But thanks to the brilliant people listed above, it has borne fruit at long last. For it to be finally read by you is my personal honor. Thank you, truly.